Our Common Dwelling

Our Common Dwelling: Henry Thoreau, Transcendentalism, and the Class Politics of Nature

Lance Newman

Portions of this book have appeared in different form in the following journals: *New England Quarterly, American Literature, ISLE, The Concord Saunterer,* and *Nineteenth Century Prose.*

First published in 2005 by
PALGRAVE MACMILLAN™
175 Fifth Avenue, New York, N.Y. 10010 and
Houndmills, Basingstoke, Hampshire, England RG21 6XS
Companies and representatives throughout the world.

PALGRAVE MACMILLAN is the global academic imprint of the Palgrave Macmillan division of St. Martin's Press, LLC and of Palgrave Macmillan Ltd. Macmillan® is a registered trademark in the United States, United Kingdom and other countries. Palgrave is a registered trademark in the European Union and other countries.

Library of Congress Cataloging-in-Publication Data

Newman, Lance.
    Our common dwelling : Henry Thoreau, transcendentalism, and the class politics of nature / Lance Newman.
        p. cm.
    Includes bibliographical references and index.
    ISBN 1–4039–6779–2 (alk. paper)
        1. Thoreau, Henry David, 1817–1862—Political and social views. 2. Politics and literature—New England—History—19th century. 3. Literature and society—New England—History— 19th century. 4. Wordsworth, William, 1770–1850—Appreciation— New England. 5. Social classes—New England—History—19th century. 6. Wordsworth, William, 1770–1850—Influence. 7. New England— Social conditions. 8. Transcendentalism (New England). 9. Social classes in literature. 10. Nature in literature. I. Title.

PS3057.P64N48 2005
818'.309—dc22   2004059985

A catalogue record for this book is available from the British Library.

Design by Newgen Imaging Systems (P) Ltd., Chennai, India.

First edition: April 2005

10 9 8 7 6 5 4 3 2 1

Printed in the United States of America.

How can we apply the energy, the creativity, the knowledge, the vision we know to be in literature to the human-made problems ecology tells us are destroying the biosphere which is our home?

—William Rueckert

People have often said "the city" when they meant capitalism or bureaucracy or centralized power, while "the country" has at times meant everything from independence to deprivation, and from the powers of an active imagination to a form of release from consciousness. . . . Most obviously since the industrial revolution, but in my view also since the beginning of the capitalist agrarian mode of production, our powerful images of country and city have been ways of responding to a whole social development. That is why, in the end, we must not limit ourselves to their contrast but go on to see their interrelations, and through these the real shape of the underlying crisis.

—Raymond Williams

CONTENTS

FOREWORD

During the summer of 2004, a blockbuster Hollywood disaster film, *The Day After Tomorrow*, ignited new interest in global warming and its potential effects on human life on earth. The film's events seem fantastic: tornadoes destroy Los Angeles, the ocean floods New York City, and a new Ice Age starts overnight, but the Statue of Liberty still stands. Speculative though it may be, the plot is extrapolated from predictions made by reputable scientists. It includes rising sea levels, shifts in ocean currents that result in rapid climate change, and even large storms that pull intensely cold air down from the troposphere. The film's director, Roland Emmerich, simply speeds up the likely pace of climate change to make a point: "It says to be a little more concerned about what we're doing to our environment, to think about tomorrow, and the day after."[1]

After all, the 1990s were the warmest decade of the millennium. According to the Union of Concerned Scientists, the earth's average annual temperature rose almost a full degree Celsius during the twentieth century, faster than at any time in the last 600 years. Glaciers around the planet are receding. The Arctic ice pack has lost about 40 percent of its thickness in the last 40 years. In February of 2002, at the other end of the globe, the 3250-square-kilometer Larsen B ice shelf separated from Antarctica. Partly as a result of melting like this, sea level has risen about three times faster during the twentieth century than at any time in the previous three millennia. Human-produced greenhouse gasses, especially carbon dioxide, account for about 55 percent of this global warming. The burning of fossil fuels adds 6 billion tons of carbon dioxide to the atmosphere every year. The United States and the European Union, the two richest nations on the planet, with a little over 10 percent of the world's population, are responsible for just under half of worldwide carbon dioxide release.[2]

The UN Intergovernmental Panel on Climate Change (IPCC) predicts that if currents patterns continue there will be an additional increase in average global temperature of 3.0° Celsius (5.4 F) over the next century. This is the same difference as between the last Ice Age and the present. Warming at this pace is likely to cause increasingly unpredictable weather patterns as the water cycle absorbs more energy. Increased overall evaporation will mean increased precipitation in some areas, but it is also likely that there will be more drought and desertification in others. Changing weather will produce serious disruption of agriculture, especially in poor countries where subsistence farming is common. Plant and animal species will also shift their range and behavior as ecosystems change. Already forests on the West Coast of the United States from Baja California to British Columbia are suffering multiyear droughts that have weakened their resistance to pine bark beetles. In many forests, one in four trees has been killed by the beetles and is standing dead, waiting to fuel another big fire season. The most devastating effect of climate change may well be what it will do to exacerbate an already developing global water crisis. According to Vandana Shiva, "In 1998, 28 countries experienced water stress or scarcity. This number is expected to rise to 56 by 2025. Between 1990 and 2025 the number of people living in countries without adequate water is projected to rise from 131 million to 817 million."[3]

As our picture of the causes and consequences of climate change becomes increasingly clear, the administration currently occupying the White House is under fire for suppressing a recent Pentagon report on global warming. This is the administration that withdrew the United States from the Kyoto accords that were designed to limit the release of carbon dioxide by the major industrial nations. This is also the administration that invited industry executives to help draft a national energy policy that cut funding for research into sustainable fuel sources and laid the groundwork for construction of up to 1,500 new coal- and nuclear-powered electricity generation stations. The suppressed Pentagon report argues that global warming "should be elevated beyond a scientific debate to a US national security concern" far more significant than terrorism. It predicts that abrupt climate change could provoke global anarchy as countries struggle over dwindling food, water, and energy resources, and it states that by 2020, "disruption and conflict will be endemic features of life. Once again, warfare would define human life."[4]

Of course, warfare already does define human life in the new millennium—in large part because of the way that the U.S. government, working for the interests of energy corporations, uses its massive military to control the major oil-producing regions of the planet. In fact, the current wars for oil will define all life for some time to come. Depleted uranium, a by-product of the process of enriching uranium fuel rods for reactors, is almost twice as dense as lead, and is therefore used by the U.S. military in everything from bullets to huge bunker-buster bombs. After penetrating a target, each of these shells disintegrates into a cloud of burning dust that contaminates the area and is often inhaled by survivors. During the 1991 invasion of Iraq, about 350 tons of depleted uranium munitions were fired. During the 2003 invasion, as many as 2,000 tons of these weapons were used, with as many as 200 tons being fired on Baghdad alone. The rate of leukemia in Iraq has increased 600 percent since 1990, especially in children under 15. Women as young as 35 are developing breast cancer. Sterility amongst men has increased ten-fold. Birth defects and miscarriages have skyrocketed. In 1991, after the first invasion, Jawad Al-Ali, an oncologist and member England's Royal Society of Physicians, wrote: "The desert dust carries death. Our studies indicate that more than forty percent of the population around Basra will get cancer. We are living through another Hiroshima." Depleted uranium has a half-life of 4.7 billion years.[5]

As bleak as the prognosis is, these trends can be reversed, the social order that produced them can be overturned, and how we think about nature can play a part in that process if it inspires us to engage in collective action for change. When I started working in Grand Canyon, I made 600 dollars a month guiding wealthy tourists from the coasts. We lugged their bags, cooked their meals, rigged their tents, rowed their boats, and packed out their waste. But all the while I was getting to know the bighorn sheep, coyotes, pink rattlers, side-blotched lizards, ravens, herons, arrow weed, Mormon tea, and willows. I felt dwarfed by Cape Solitude, then welcomed by a mirage of whispers in Surprise Valley. I learned how to read the turbulent surface of the big river and how to relax into the darkness of moonless nights. But the more I learned, the more I came to see that this was second nature, an artificial paradise. Invasive tamarisk provided new habitat for yellow-breasted chats, indigo buntings, and cedar waxwings that had not bothered with the riparian zone when it had been stripped to bare rock by every spring run-off. The bighorn sheep I admired had wandered into the river corridor from Paria Canyon where they had been reintroduced, and an albino variant was far more common than it ought to be in a healthy population. Mornings, before the dudes got moving, obese stocker trout cruised in the unnaturally cold, green eddies, hunting introduced freshwater shrimp. Always, there was the silent weight of the flooded canyon upstream of the dam— Glen Canyon, a place known only to old timers who steer their nighttime stories clear of it for fear of insomnia—Glen Canyon, now no more than a huge silt trap. The dam stands over 600 feet tall and two-thirds of a mile wide. It contains almost ten million tons of concrete, which took three years, day and night, to pour. The reservoir took 17 years to fill and drowned almost 200 miles of pristine canyon on the main stem of the river system that drains all but a corner of the continent west of the divide. This massive plug seemed to me then to be an error, a bad mistake made by a bureaucrat somewhere who did not know what would die. But when I read the pro-dam propaganda, with its braying about making the desert blossom as a rose and the recreational opportunities that would be opened to the common man, it became clear that something was wrong with the way these people thought. They could see the canyons and the desert, but somehow they had learned to see them wrong.

So I decided to investigate the history of ways of seeing the land, the history of American cultures of nature. The long process of capitalist conquest, beginning with John Smith inventorying the continent's store of profitable commodities—that was clear enough. But what about subordinate or emergent ways of thinking? When and where did the conscious appreciation of nature, and conscious defense of it against the encroachments of modernity, begin in earnest and how did it develop? According to most, environmentalism sprouted on the shore Walden Pond. But as I reconstructed the historical context of Thoreau's experiment in simple living, I came to see that he was far from alone, that he was, in fact, plowing the main field of New England's counterculture, as he transformed nature into a refuge from what he called the "spirit of commerce." As he wrote the book that would inaugurate the tradition of American environmental writing, *Walden*, he was participating in a widespread movement of revulsion at the sudden explosion of class conflict in the industrializing northeast. And this movement had been triggered in turn by a wave that had traveled the Atlantic from the English Lake District where Wordsworth had gone to look for an answer to the filth and misery of London and Paris.

This book sets out to examine the pattern of coincidence between Romanticism's turn to nature and its apparent turn away from the city, more specifically, away from the bitter class divisions of the city under capitalism, arguing that what most American Romantics hoped to find in nature was the means to redeem their fractured republic. It offers a new contextual interpretation of some texts that are familiar (Thoreau's *Walden* and Emerson's *Nature*) and of others that are less so (Fuller's *Summer on the Lakes, in 1843* and Thoreau's poems and late natural history essays). My argument is historicist, and proceeds mainly by relating internal, textual evidence to large-scale historical trends as they manifested themselves in and around Boston. It differs from most other work on the period in this: its argument is that the ghost in the machine of American Romanticism is class. The reality to which our most canonical authors were responding most directly was class division. More specifically, the romanticization of nature, the central trope of American Transcendentalism, was a direct response to changes in the balance of class forces in New England in the 1830s and 1840s.

I believe that the perspective on New England Transcendentalism that is developed here, with its emphasis on the class politics of the period, offers a significant corrective to the broad tradition of Americanist literary and cultural history, which has too often accepted the Romantic claim that America is a classless republic of loners. Nevertheless, I have framed my argument in such a way as to engage most directly with the critical subdiscipline ecocriticism, specifically because I admire its tradition of activist engagement and its attempt to make cultural history relevant to one of the most important social and political questions of our time. Rather than making a case for the immediate transhistorical relevance of the Transcendentalist texts to our situation today, I make an attempt to recover as accurately as possible their historical social function, since I believe that process of recovery is the most reliable way to put them to use in the present. Rather than idealize a past cultural moment, I hope that understanding both the rich creativity and political utopianism of Romantic nature-love can help us understand analogous patterns within the developing ecocritical effort to incorporate nature writing into the ideological foundation of contemporary environmentalism. Tom Athanasiou argues that in the face of an environmental crisis that is sharply disproportionate in its effects on the global South, we can no longer afford the "political innocence" of the claim that we are "neither left nor right." In a world that is being radically reshaped as habitat for multinational corporations, "it is past time for environmentalists to face their own history, in which they have too often stood not for justice and freedom, or even for realism, but merely for the comforts and aesthetics of affluent nature lovers." Sentimental liberal environmentalism took shape in the aftermath of Romanticism, as a resolution of the conflicts and contradictions that structured that movement's response to the rise of capitalism. Reexamining that cultural moment may help us think more clearly as we face a truth that Athanasiou states in refreshingly decisive terms: "History will judge greens by whether they stand with the world's poor."[6]

I hope that this project also sheds light on the cultural geography of Grand Canyon. Since World War II, the number of hours worked annually by the average U.S. family has increased steadily, reaching almost 4,000, the equivalent of two full-time jobs. During this same period, wilderness recreation has exploded in popularity. In 1946, the national wilderness preservation system saw a total of just over 400,000 user days of recreational use. By 1996, half a century later, this number had risen above 17 million user days. I believe that there is a direct relationship between the rise in the intensity of exploitation of labor under capitalism and the increasing demand for recreation. Throughout the United States, but especially in the West, millions of working people use their increasingly sparse time away from the factory, the office, or the store, to camp, hike, climb, bike, kayak, raft, and pursue a range of other wilderness-based leisure activities that are deliberately nonproductive and categorically opposed to work. The areas where these activities occur have been legislatively marked off from the surrounding cadastral grid and carefully cleansed of all visible reminders of the modern society that prevails beyond their borders. In the words of the 1964 federal Wilderness Act, "a wilderness, in contrast with those areas where man and his own works dominate the landscape, is hereby recognized as an area where the earth and its community of life are untrammeled by man, where man himself is a visitor who does not remain." Moreover, according to the law, a wilderness "has outstanding opportunities for solitude or a primitive and unconfined type of recreation." The recreation that occurs in these natural cathedrals is a cultural ritual, a secular religious practice that both compensates for the alienation from nature that results from industrial capitalism's concentration of workers in hyper-artificial cities, and maintains a living vision of a different kind of social life on the land. In other words, I believe that wildernesses and wilderness recreation are natural features, so to speak, of capitalism. They are parts of a cultural tradition that has evolved within and in response to capitalism over the course of the last two and a half centuries. And they depend on an imaginary geography in which a degraded and oppressive society is opposed to a pure and free wilderness. When we inhabit that geography, we are sometimes renewed, sometimes transformed, and sometimes we are even inspired to participate in the heroic narratives it implies. But in the end we are living at an angle, sometimes even an obtuse one, to reality.

My debts are far more extensive than I can map, but here is a sketch. The Graduate School and the English Department of Brown University provided fellowship support during the research and writing of the first draft of this book. Jim Egan, Philip Gould, Bill Keach, and Barton St. Armand offered critically important guidance during the project's early stages. Daryl Ogden provided a year of most welcome postdoctoral support at Georgia Tech. David Newton and the rest of my colleagues at the

State University of West Georgia gave me a warm and supportive home during two productive years. Over the years, too many people to name shaped my thinking about the politics of nature. Ron Briley, Robert Knox, John McDiarmid, Mac Miller, and Sandra Jordan mentored me along the way. My comrades in the International Socialist Organization provide a clear perspective on the past and present. My crewmates at CRATE and Moki Mac keep me honest and keep me up too many nights trying to figure why nature's nation built Glen Canyon Dam. The Stinson and Newman families have always been there. And Willow always will be.

Abbreviations

CE   Henry David Thoreau, *Collected Essays and Poems*, ed. Elizabeth Hall Witherell (New York: Library of America, 2001).

CW   *The Collected Works of Ralph Waldo Emerson*, ed. Alfred R. Ferguson (Cambridge: Harvard University Press, 1971).

M   Nathaniel Hawthorne, *The Snow-Image and Uncollected Tales*, ed. J. Donald Crowley (Columbus: Ohio State University Press, 1974).

S   Margaret Fuller, *Summer on the Lakes, in 1843*, ed. Susan Belasco Smith (Urbana: University of Illinois Press, 1991).

W   Henry David Thoreau, *Walden, or Life in the Woods*, ed. J. Lyndon Shanley (Princeton: Princeton University Press, 1971).

WF   Henry David Thoreau, *Wild Fruits*, ed. Bradley P. Dean (New York: Norton, 2000).

Y   William Wordsworth, *Yarrow Revisited and Other Poems* (Boston: James Munroe, 1835).

CHAPTER 1

THE COMMITMENTS OF
ECOCRITICISM

The Romantic approach to nature was fundamentally ecological; that is, it was concerned with relation, interdependence, and holism. Nowhere is this . . . outlook more clearly revealed than in the writings of Henry David Thoreau. . . . Thoreau was both an active field ecologist and a philosopher of nature whose ideas anticipated much in the mood of our own time. In his life and work we find a . . . complex and sophisticated ecological philosophy. We find in Thoreau, too, a remarkable source of inspiration and guidance for the subversive activism of the recent ecology movement.

—Donald Worster

During the last decades of the twentieth century, it became a matter of scientific consensus that human society, as it currently functions, poses a potentially lethal threat to what Henry David Thoreau once called "our common dwelling" (W 124). At first a nuclear winter seemed the clearest threat to the global environment, but this was gradually replaced by the prospect of climate change induced by greenhouse gases produced during the burning of fossil fuels. In 1977, the National Academy of Sciences issued an uncertain report called *Energy and Climate*, and two years later, the World Meteorological Organization held its first World Climate Conference, but the evidence was still unclear. By the end of the 1980s, there was no longer any uncertainty. In 1988, the United Nations Environmental Program established the Intergovernmental Panel on Climate Change, which, two years later, released its first report, finding half a degree Celsius of net global warming during the twentieth century. These two decades also saw the development of a broad awareness of the need for a new collective relationship with the planet. The first Earth Day in the United States was held in April 1970; from then on, as the scope and seriousness of the problem became clearer, a truly impressive and diverse movement for change grew at the grassroots of society.[1]

A literary critical current coevolved with this environmental movement, its members unified by a commitment to enlist their scholarship in the struggle to contain or even reverse the global crisis. Cheryll Glotfelty explains the connection quite bluntly: "Many of us in colleges and universities worldwide find ourselves in a dilemma. Our temperaments and talents have deposited us in literature departments, but, as environmental problems compound, work as usual seems unconscionably frivolous. If we're not part of the solution, we're part of the problem." The critical current inspired by this impulse takes its name from a ground-breaking 1978 essay, "Literature and Ecology: An Experiment in Ecocriticism," in which William Rueckert, after describing a dizzying proliferation of literary critical methods, maintains that "there must be a shift in our locus of motivation from newness, or theoretical elegance, or even coherence, to a principle of relevance." Three decades later, this is still sound advice.[2]

Rueckert proposes a particular combination of method and commitment, arguing that ecocriticism should "experiment with the application of ecology and ecological concepts to the study of literature, because ecology (as a science, as a discipline, as the basis for a human vision) has the greatest relevance to the present and future of the world we all live in." Such an experiment is inherently "radical" since "ecological visions . . . attempt to subvert the continued-growth economy which dominates all emerging and most developed industrial states." In other words, applying ecology to literature implies political commitment. Rueckert offers this commitment as his proposal's central strength, as the guarantee of its relevance, arguing that teachers and readers of environmental literature should dedicate themselves to "the discovery, training, and development of creative biospheric apperceptions, attitudes, and actions."[3]

Over the next 15 years, ecocriticism gradually coalesced, then burst into the open in 1992 with the founding of the Association for the Study of Literature and the Environment. Ecocritics united around a clear vision of what it meant to be an environmentalist literary scholar. William Howarth offers this definition: an ecocritic is "a person who judges the merits and faults of writings that depict the effects of culture upon nature, with a view toward celebrating nature, berating its despoilers, and reversing their harm through political action." Lawrence Buell is equally emphatic, defining ecocriticism as the "study of the relation between literature and the environment conducted in a spirit of environmentalist praxis." Buell even describes ecocriticism as a critical "insurgency" that, like contemporary cultural studies of identity and the body, is "more issue-driven than methodology-driven." And because "the twenty-first century's most pressing problem will be the sustainability of earth's environment," he argues that "environmentally valenced critical inquiry . . . will increasingly be seen as the responsibility of *all* the human sciences. . . ."[4]

One of the clearest markers of ecocriticism's pressing concern to maintain its radical credentials is the appearance of real anxiety about the potential for institutionalization. Michael Branch, for instance, argues that ecocriticism "has the potential to alter the mission of higher education in this country in a radical way" but worries that after being incorporated into existing institutions, "we may simply reproduce the habits of mind that precipitated the environmental crisis." This anxiety motivates ecocritics to try to break out of the confines of the academy in order to make contact with broader audiences and movements for change. Jonathan Bate, for instance, argues that if ecocriticism is going "to lead to a serious rethinking of the relations between humankind and the environment, it has got to operate within the language of intellectual enquiry as well as the practical getting your green welly boots on. . . . All revolutions need an intellectual arm as well as the people out there on the ground, taking the risks." Ecocriticism, then, is a movement based in university literature departments that reaches beyond them in pursuit of a truly ambitious goal: the radical transformation of human relations with nature.[5]

This ecocritical project is strongly shaped by a particular analysis of the environmental crisis. Most ecocritics feel that the problem we face is one of destructive habits of thought. Cheryll Glotfelty asks, "How can we contribute to environmental restoration, not just in our spare time, but from within our capacity as professors of literature? The answer lies in recognizing that current environmental problems are largely of our own making, are, in other words, a by-product of culture." Or, as Lawrence Buell writes, "the success of all environmentalist efforts finally hinges . . . on attitudes, feelings, images, narratives." Buell believes that the "environmental crisis involves a crisis of the imagination the amelioration of which depends on finding better ways of imaging nature and humanity's relation to it" because "how we image a thing, true or false, affects our conduct toward it, the conduct of nations as well as persons." The dominant ecocritical way of thinking emphasizes the power of ideas to determine how society is structured and how it evolves over time, both internally and in its relations with the rest of the world. Given this way of analyzing the problem, Glen Love argues that "the most important function of literature today is to redirect human consciousness to a full consideration of its place in a threatened natural environment." Most ecocritics see themselves as agitators for an ideological revolution and rest their hopes on what Scott Slovic calls the "power of awareness." Most, in other words, set themselves the task of changing our minds, of convincing us to think in ways that will, in turn, change how we behave.[6]

To this end, ecocritics set out "to look searchingly at the most searching works of environmental reflection," recognizing that "artistic representations of the natural environment have served as agents both of provocation and of compartmentalization, calling us to think ecocentrically but often conspiring with the readerly temptation to cordon off scenery into pretty ghettos." Thus, a first priority has been to mount a negative critique of "anthropocentric" ways of thinking about nature, such as the idea that people were meant to maintain dominion over nature, or that nature is a passive receptacle of the fertilizing human mind, or that limitless growth is the essence of social destiny. Most ecocritics take to heart Lynn White's observation that: "What people do about their ecology depends on what they think about themselves in relation to things around them. Human ecology is deeply conditioned by beliefs about our nature and destiny—that is, by religion." For White, the "victory of Christianity over paganism was the greatest psychic revolution in the history of our culture" and produced an "exploitative attitude" based on "an implicit faith in perpetual progress." In another version of this argument, Glen Love points to the legacy of "humanism," arguing that modern society is deformed by the idea that human well-being is the highest good. Humanism has produced an ecocidal obsession with merely "internal" conflicts over resources, at a time when "human domination—never mind the subdivisions of human—of the biosphere is the overriding problem."[7]

Most ecocritics, though, move quickly from negative to positive critique, working to direct public attention to texts that embody the green values they wish to promote. Jonathan Bate argues that much English Romantic poetry can engender environmental awareness since it is informed by an "ecopoetic," that is, "a *poiesis* (Greek 'making') of the *oikos* (Greek 'home' or 'dwelling place')." Ecopoetry affirms "not only the existence, but also the sacredness, of the-things-of-nature-in-themselves." And James McKusick shows how the "ecological understanding" that emerged "among the English Romantic poets": crossed the Atlantic to become "a conceptual and ideological basis for American environmentalism" as it germinated among the New England Transcendentalists. McKusick concludes that by "envisioning alternatives to the unsustainable industrial exploitation of natural resources," Romantic nature writers "offer pathways to a better future than we might otherwise be able to imagine." Daniel Philippon narrates the history of the materialization of nature writers' ideas in the organized environmental movement from Mabel Osgood Wright and the National Audubon Society, to John Muir and the Sierra Club, to Edward Abbey and Earth First! Although poems and nonfiction nature writing have been the main focus of scholarship, ecocritics have also interrogated environmental texts of almost every imaginable kind and from every moment in history, from foundational epics and sacred texts, to novels and stories, to drama and film, to park and garden designs, to patterns of outdoor travel and recreation.[8]

Ecocritics hope to find far more in such texts than the history of our understanding that the environment is threatened and requires protection. Many admire the philosophical ideas of deep ecology, especially as formulated by Bill Devall and George Sessions, who call for "cultivating ecological consciousness," which they describe as "a process of learning to appreciate silence and solitude and rediscovering how to listen. It is learning how to be more receptive, trusting, holistic in perception, and is grounded in a vision of non-exploitative science and technology." Thus, Charles Brown calls for a "quest for a new worldview" based on the principle of "ecocentrism," which Robyn Eckersley defines as an ethical philosophy that sees "the question of our proper place in nature as logically prior to the question of what are the most appropriate social and political arrangements for human communities."[9]

Environmental literature has struck scholars as a likely place to find such a worldview. An early and influential statement of this position comes in John Elder's study of the descent of nature poetry from Wordsworth to Robinson Jeffers, Gary Snyder, Denise Levertov, A.R. Ammons, and others:

> Poets' vivid and informed response to the earth can also foster . . . a vision of human culture in harmony with the rest of the natural order. . . . A solitary voice from the mountains calls upon the community to renew itself; a socially eccentric impulse makes possible a more balanced culture, concentric with the planet.

Although environmental poetry has been the focus of a good deal of attention, many have felt that nonfiction nature writing was the most directly relevant genre. Peter Fritzell locates a special rhetorical effectiveness in nonfiction nature writing's tensions, arguing that the genre is characterized by "a rather unusual combination of intense personal 'narrative,' a dialectic amalgam of self-analysis and self-reflection (if not self-celebration), on the one hand, and extensive, impersonal scientific description and explication, on the other." This tense combination of elements allows such texts to inquire with a rare intensity and clarity into relationships between the self and nature. Thomas Lyon argues that "the fundamental goal of the genre is to turn our attention outward to the activity of nature. . . . The literary record time and again displays the claim that there is a lifting and clarifying of perception inherent in this refocusing, which opens up something like a new world."[10] Similarly, Lawrence Buell notes the genre's characteristic closeness of observation and concern for accuracy, and argues that these are evidence of a definitive humility before complex and delicate natural processes, even a passionate dedication to the health of the land. For Scott Slovic, nonfiction "nature writing is a 'literature of hope' in its assumption that the elevation of consciousness may lead to wholesome political change, but this literature is also concerned, and perhaps primarily so, with interior landscapes, with the mind itself." The vibrant states of awareness described by nature writers, he hopes, will inspire their readers to cultivate similar "habits of attention." Ecocritics, in other words, interpret the individual epiphanies recorded in nature writing as political events of the first importance since they may inspire real change in the way humanity lives on the earth.[11]

The environmental text to which ecocriticism returns most often in its search for new ways of seeing is Henry David Thoreau. Thoreau is American culture's eye. Looking into him, we measure the depth of our own commitments. For the patriotic canon-makers who elevated him to the pantheon, his was the first truly American voice, speaking the national creed of vigorous self-creation. But his descriptions of the land around Concord were significant only as proof of his will to talk about his self. Walden Pond was a metaphorical frontier where he made the virgin land say Yankee. For less jingoistic early readers, he was valued most as a polemicist, just as uncompromising in his verbal assaults on northern hypocrisy as in those on the slavocracy. Either way, he was swept up long ago into the main current of American liberalism. But such readers usually regarded his lyrical praise of the woods as little more than a quaint, even embarrassing, preoccupation of his times. Perry Miller, for instance, remarks that some "students—scientists with literary curiosity—occasionally argue that he was perceptive about ecology or some branch of botany, but if he was, the praise should go to the general Transcendental sense of 'discipline,' not to Thoreau's primary intent." Miller goes on to claim, with defensive exaggeration, that

Thoreau "was not a lover of nature itself: as he said, he ever sought the 'raw materials of tropes and figures.' For him these metaphors . . . were the rewards of an exploitation of natural resources, as self-centered, as profit-seeking, as that of any railroad-builder or lumber-baron. . . ." Miller's brassy tone and his mannish similes mark the anxiety that many of his mid-century contemporaries felt about Thoreau's nature-writing, a subject they preferred to ignore.[12]

Roderick Nash was among the first to argue, in *Wilderness and the American Mind*, that Thoreau's primary cultural importance is as a proto-ecologist. Nash's purpose in reading Thoreau as he did was to codify a usable past for the broad preservation movement that was, as he wrote, pushing through Congress the historic Wilderness Act of 1964. Since then it has become increasingly common to see Thoreau as an innovator, one who moved beyond purely instrumental ways of thinking about nature, valuing it instead as a site for intellectual and spiritual transformation. But variations on the idea of nature as the instructive mirror, or even crucible, of human nature were basic to the writings of innumerable figures of international Romanticism. And in colonial North America, Anne Bradstreet and Jonathon Edwards recorded transformative experiences of grace in nature. A list of alternative points of origin could go on forever. The problem is not so much with the answer as with the question, which was formed according to the methods of study that prevailed in American Studies when Nash was writing. The standard was a kind of intellectual history based on isolating definitive American myths and symbols and then tracing their internal development. R.W.B. Lewis states the concerns of the movement succinctly:

> I am not concerned with matters of anthropology and sociology, or with folklore and legend; nor am I primarily concerned with the psychology of myth, any more than with the facts of economic geography and political history. I am interested rather in the history of ideas and especially in the representative imagery and anecdote that crystallize whole clusters of ideas; my interest therefore is limited to articulate thinkers and conscious artists.

This method produced fascinating, but inevitably skewed, histories, since the myth or symbol under analysis always bore the unmistakable traces of the analyst's political preoccupations. Thus, Nash's project—sifting the past for the figure who originated American environmentalism by first seeing nature as "attractive" rather than "repulsive"—tells us more about the sifter than it does about nature or the past.[13]

Nevertheless, most ecocritics acknowledge a debt to the myth and symbol tradition, since it offers the most sustained previous analysis of the interaction between American culture and the continent. But, writing at a time when a univocal "American Mind" is unmistakably a fiction, they have shifted the emphasis in their description of Thoreau. Rather than portraying him as the inaugurator of a characteristically American way of appreciating the beauty of nature, they praise him as the first defender of wilderness, as one whose work records the achievement of a radically alternative kind of consciousness. They position him as the founder of a countercultural tradition of environmental writing that looks at the land in and for itself, rather than at the land as America. William Rueckert asks, "Does he not tell us that this planet, and the creatures who inhabit it, including men and women, were, have been, are now, and are in the process of becoming?" For Rueckert, the "beautiful and true concept of the biosphere" that Thoreau developed is "so radical even in the mid-nineteenth century, that we have still not been able to absorb and act upon it more than a hundred years later." Similarly, in an article that shows how Thoreau's Journal demonstrates his commitment to the ethical "inhabitation and exploration of a wild place" and to "the necessity of wildness at home," Don Scheese describes Thoreau and later writers in the tradition he established as "secular prophets in the modern religion of environmentalism." Scott Slovic maintains that "the Thoreauvian process of awakening is not merely a timeless private quest, but a timely—even urgent—requirement if we are to prevent or at least retard the further destruction of our planet." And Lawrence Buell argues that Thoreau's Walden project provides "a record and model of a western sensibility working with and through the constraints of Eurocentric, androcentric, homocentric culture to arrive at an environmentally responsive vision." Buell maintains that we "know much more than Thoreau did about how humans mispossess the environment but do less with what we know. If everyone lived like him, there would be no environmental problem." For most ecocritics, then, Thoreau's writings record an achieved ecocentric consciousness, a model of ideal relations between a properly respectful human consciousness and an endangered natural environment.[14]

If Thoreau is the central figure in the ecocritical canon, the central axiom in its critical theory is that nature is irreducibly actual. This is in direct contradiction to the dominant tendency in most recent theories of culture, which has been to emphasize the power of language (or discourse or culture) to structure human being in the world. At times, this post-structuralist claim has even become absolute: language has seemed to be the only "world" to which we have access. Ecocriticism responds by insisting on the independent reality of the nonlinguistic material world.

As Jay Parini puts it, ecocriticism "marks a return to activism and social responsibility; it also signals a dismissal of theory's more solipsistic tendencies. From a literary aspect, it marks a re-engagement with realism, with the actual universe of rocks, trees and rivers that lies behind the wilderness of signs." Not only does this universe seem somehow "real" in a way that precedes language, but more, it must in some sense determine or structure language and culture. Cheryll Glotfelty observes: "Literary theory, in general, examines the relations between writers, texts, and the world. In most literary theory 'the world' is synonymous with society— the social sphere. Ecocriticism expands the notion of 'the world' to include the entire ecosphere." Karl Kroeber takes this a step further: "Realizing that anything cultural must be understood as part of a natural ecosystem should radically reorient *all* critical theorizing of the past 50 years." This has been ecocriticism's most distinctive axiom: nature is real and culture, self-consciously or not, is rooted in it.[15]

Ecocritics practice an eclectic critical method that begins from this commitment to the fundamental reality of nature, and is informed by principles borrowed from an ecology approached, in Rueckert's words, as a "human vision" rather than as "science." Thus, Barry Commoner's famous first law of ecology, "Everything is connected to everything else," has inspired an interest in textual structures and figurative language that reflect or embody holistic systems, complex organisms, and self-regulating networks. Moreover, Glen Love demonstrates, in an article inspired by E.O. Wilson's call for "consilience," or a rapprochement between the sciences and humanities, that ecology has also inspired a vibrant tradition of interdisciplinarity. Detailed knowledge of the natural world has come to seem a necessary tool for evaluating textual representations of that world. Thus, there has been a sharp stress not only on acquiring field experience, but also on understanding the natural history of the places depicted by individual writers. This emphasis has allowed for refreshingly specific accounts of the give and take between writer, language, and physical world that produces good nature writing, that produces in fact any good writing at all. It has also allowed for important kinds of particularization as we have moved from talk of the abstraction "nature" to more concrete discussions of how wetlands, rivers, prairies, mountains, canyons, farms, and even city parks and abandoned lots are represented in our culture.[16]

Another kind of particularity has begun to develop as well. On one hand, ecocriticism has extended the long-standing critique of gendered and racialized representations of nature in the dominant culture. For instance, Kevin DeLuca and Anne Demo show how in the early twentieth century an imaginative erasure of social difference defined wilderness as a space empty of people of color and the poor. And Michael Bennett argues that this continuing problem is part of the legacy of slavery since for African Americans in the South the countryside was a place of violence and oppression, whereas the landscape of freedom and renewal was the city. Similarly, a substantial body of ecofeminist work develops the argument that there are, as Vera Norwood remarks, significant ideological "connections between the oppression of nature and the oppression of women in Western culture" and that the destruction of the environment is another effect of androcentrism.[17]

On the other hand, ecocriticism has also begun to show just how diversified representations of nature have been across North America's many cultures. The ecocritical canon as initially constituted, with its focus on nonfiction nature writing, was heavily Euro-American, but ecofeminism and Native American studies, especially, have developed powerful accounts of the alternative ways of seeing nature generated within the experience of subaltern groups. Vera Norwood, for instance, provides a rich history of the "collective work of nurturing [and] preserving" nature carried on by American women over the past two centuries, concluding that the strength of ecofeminism is its vision of "how women's culture can offer a better future." Similarly, Donelle Dreese shows that "American multicultural writers who have experienced a colonizing form of displacement" can practice a kind of literary "reterritorialization" in which "recovery of lost stories and cultural practices" allows reconnection with the land. Finally, Lawrence Buell has taken a large step in the direction of expanding the field both geographically and culturally in his *Writing for an Endangered World*, which sets out "to put 'green' and 'brown' landscapes, the landscapes of exurbia and industrialization, in conversation with one another." Buell shows, for instance, that the literary and activist work undertaken by Jane Addams at Hull House to transform the urban environment of Chicago's poorest neighborhoods meshes smoothly with John Muir's literary and activist work in defense of California Sierra Nevada.[18]

Ecocritics, then, take Commoner's third law of ecology, "Nature know best," as a political and critical imperative. They articulate the clear belief that environmental literature can help us understand what is happening to the environment, as well as change how we think about and relate to the natural world. And they engage in ecological reading practices in order to help us understand our culture and its ways of seeing nature. Jhan Hochman articulates ecocriticism's goals especially clearly: "the project of green cultural studies is the examination of words, image, and model for the purpose of foregrounding potential effects representation might have on cultural attitudes and social practices, which, in turn, affect nature itself." This is to say, ecocriticism recognizes that ecological destruction, like racial and sexual oppression, is a diagnostic feature of modernity. And it expands the vibrant tradition of radical literary scholarship in order to address this important truth.[19]

CHAPTER 2

THE NATURE OF CULTURAL
HISTORY

They feel that they are never so fit for friendship, as when they have quit
mankind, and taken themselves to friend. A picture, a book, a favorite
spot in the hills or the woods, which they can people with the fair and
worthy creations of the fancy, can give them often forms so vivid, that
these for the time shall seem real, and society the illusion.

—Ralph Waldo Emerson (CW 210)

In order for the potential radicalism of the ecocritical project to be fully
realized, the contradictions at its heart must be faced and worked out. As
ecocritics have wrestled with the implications of their distinctive critical
project, they have been made to confront quite fundamental theoretical
questions. The most central of these is raised by the dissonance between,
on one hand, the culturalist epistemological theories that have dominated literary studies for some years now, and, on the other, the common
ecocritical claim that there is something unambiguously real about
nature. How, we ask, can it be meaningful to say that nature, the
irreducibly material world, is a cultural construct? Many have been
attracted to the sharpness of Samuel Johnson's no-nonsense refutation of
Bishop Berkeley. We rap our knuckles on the nearest desk and move on.
But the question requires closer thought than that, for how we answer it
will do much to shape the future of ecocriticism. Also, our answer will
go far toward determining whether ecocriticism and the environmental
movement it informs succeed in reversing the historical trends that
called them into existence. There is a particular history behind the
culturalist position. Understanding it can help ecocritics produce a
genuinely new form of critical practice rather than merely reproduce in
reverse the ideology of their predecessors.

America represents itself as gathering its cultural vitality from a
feminized nature. It then proceeds immediately to the task of transforming
the source of its uniqueness. This definitive cultural contradiction was
recognized and "nature" was adopted as a key term of analysis at the

moment when American literature was constituted as a subject of study. D.H. Lawrence, for instance, argues that characteristically American literature was produced by the rejuvenation of European culture through contact with uncivilized landscapes. Similarly, Norman Foerster maintains that the mark of the nineteenth century was "a fresh enthusiasm for nature—for man's natural impulses, for 'natural rights,' for natural science. With only two or three exceptions, all of our major writers have displayed both a striking curiosity as to the facts of the external world . . . and an ardent emotional devotion to nature because of her beauty or divinity." Lucy Lockwood Hazard makes Foerster's claim more concrete, arguing that the nation's first cultural flowering, Transcendentalism, was an expression of the individualism inherent in democracy that itself was an inevitable result of the availability of cheap land.[1]

Americanists writing out of the political landscape of the mid-twentieth century made their careers out of triumphal assessments of this exceptional American relationship to nature. Perry Miller's "Nature's Nation" thesis became dogma. In the story of the English settlers and their errand into the wilderness, "*the* American theme" was the battle for supremacy "of Nature vs. civilization." The leading intellectuals of Miller's generation accepted the political fiction of America's struggle to protect freedom and democracy from the twin threats of fascism and communism. Thus, they assumed attitudes of hard-nosed political realism toward what they liked to call the dark side of U.S. expansion. While they were sure to gesture briefly at what they felt was history's unfortunate harshness, they professed awe at the sublime transformation of the wild continent. Nature was a fallow field into which the idea of America struck its fertilizing root, impregnating it with modernity. The virgin land was usually pliable and productive, but was given to occasional bursts of destructive rage. The best literature, the most tough-minded, was that which integrated recognition of Nature's capacity for evil with reverence for human creativity and progress.[2]

The complacent liberalism of Cold-War criticism was overset by radical scholars who took inspiration from the liberation struggles of the 1960s. Most of these revisionists deployed theories of the cultural construction of knowledge, focusing on the power of dominant social formations to control this process. After all, invocations of a naturally selfish human nature demanded the rejoinder that there is no such thing as nature, that social hierarchies do not reflect natural facts, but are built in history. The revisionist attack was carried out on two main fronts. First, there were many who documented rich structures of feeling in alternative cultural traditions, challenging fables of a homogeneous American Mind.

These countercultures were created and sustained especially by nonwhites and women who had been symbolically exiled into nature, whose subordination in society had been justified in part by the claim that they were uncultured, and thus were no more than symbolic resources for, or obstacles to, progress. A second revisionist strategy was to reread the existing Americanist canon in solidarity with the oppressed. Those who followed this course showed how texts structured by liberal ideology had underwritten a brutal history of imperial conquest, domestic oppression, and the destructive exploitation of an entire continent. Sherry Ortner, for instance, influentially refuted biological determinist explanations of women's inequality by showing that women are "identified or symbolically associated with nature, as opposed to men, who are identified with culture" and that since "it is always part of culture's project to subsume and transcend nature, if women were considered part of nature, then culture would find it 'natural' to subordinate, not to say oppress, them."[3] Here too nature was reduced to a neutral canvas made meaningful only by thought. And despite the radical intent behind much early culturalist scholarship, its central strategy tended to overemphasize the power of ideology as false consciousness, its apparently limitless ability to contain dissent. In order to argue that ideology was seamlessly self-referential, that there was no outside of discourse, it became necessary to conceal the messy dialectical process of knowledge by placing nature under erasure.

In the past two or three decades, culturalists in the academy have become increasingly detached from the vital debates within which such absolute positions were once rhetorically necessary, and so they have fallen into the habit of wooden repetition of theoretical formulas. Alan Liu remarks cynically that culturalist scholarship "is our latest post-May 1970, post-May 1968, post-1917 . . . post-1789 (and so forth) imagination of a role for intellect in the renascence of society."[4] In other words, the movement's retreat into the world of pure thought was a direct response to the demobilization of just those liberation struggles that had first inspired critical reassessment of American literature. Currently, the charge of quietism that radical culturalists once lodged against their liberal elders too often describes their own practice. For culturalism all too often becomes a blank spectatorship, a mere ogling of the postmodern perpetual textual motion machine and the prostrate subjects it mass produces. In such cases, orthodox culturalism becomes a scholarship of prophesied defeat. The critical tools that once opened up room for maneuver between representation and reality are no longer sharp. And the slough of ideology has become the sole subject of a deflected polemic that seeks no longer to change the world, but simply to bemoan it.

Some of the most trenchant attacks on the contemplative abstractness of orthodox culturalism have come from ecocritics, who make the counterclaim that nature is an irreducible reality beneath a comparatively insignificant overlay of cultural mediation. James McKusick maintains that "our continued existence is radically contingent upon the ecological cycles of energy and matter that sustain and nourish us. In this material sense, nature is a ground of existence." Jonathon Bate argues that contemporary criticism ignores this "economy of nature." And Lawrence Buell insists that "embeddedness in spatio-physical context is even more intractably constitutive of personal and social identity, and of the way that texts get constructed, than ideology is. . . ." When culturalists insist that physical bodies and natural worlds are cultural and political artifacts, many ecocritics scoff. And some have even allowed themselves to complain that the postmodernist focus on the cultural politics of race, gender, and class seems misguided when the environmental crisis threatens the earth in its entirety.[5]

Given ecocriticism's premise that anthropocentric habits of thought have detached humanity from nature, this naturalist position has seemed a necessary way to reground ideas of nature in reality. Karl Kroeber, therefore, calls for an ecological literary criticism based on the insight that thought is produced by a physical organ, since if we wish to "criticize and improve social constructs, even of 'nature,' we must understand how society arises out of humankind's place in the natural world." He argues that the English Romantics were prototypical ecocritics who even anticipated ecological science by seeing nature in holistic terms, focusing on "the fantastically complicated interrelations that make up even the smallest ecosystem according to an evolutionary understanding of the multiplicity of evanescent processes within a totality continuously reconstituting itself in response to a unique play of internal and external pressures—to no transcendental purpose." Thus, the Romantics "would not wish to contradict the current critical banality that 'nature' is a social construct. . . . They would regard the assertion as question-begging, however, because they believed that human consciousness (and the social constructs made possible by it) is a result of natural processes." The problem, though, is that when we say nature is a social category, what we say depends on why we say it. It is one thing to say that nature is a cultural construct while crowing about the spectacular productivity of human discourse. It is quite another to say so while analyzing how our way of thinking about nature as virgin land or primitive wilderness obscures and sometimes even ratifies the dominance of the current ruling class and its behavior on the land.[6]

Not surprisingly, from the moment that it was first articulated, ecocritical naturalism has come under sustained pressure by critics who see their work as sharing the same political motivations, but who are unwilling to down the tools of culturalist theory. Terry Gifford for instance, replies to the naturalists that "there can be no 'innocent' reference to nature in a poem. Any reference will implicitly or explicitly express a notion of nature that relates to culturally developed assumptions about metaphysics, aesthetics, politics, status—that is, in many cases, ideologies. In other words, in literature, nature is culture." Verena Andermatt Conley, on the other hand, does not directly refute the naturalist position; instead she attempts to engage ecocritics with postmodernism in a survey of what she sees as elements of "ecological consciousness" in the writings of postmodernist figures like Claude Lévi-Strauss, Michel Serres, Ilya Prigigone, Paul Virilio, Felix Guattari, Michel de Certeau, and Luce Irigaray. Conley argues that "relational" thinking promises to counter "the current ideology of growth and development" and push forward "the struggle for an ecological democracy" by decentering the Cartesian subject, collapsing the culture/nature dyad, and repicturing the world as a chaotic system. Unfortunately, the ecocritical practice proposed here suffers from the weaknesses of the postmodernist tradition it extends. Thus Conley argues that "ecological problems are . . . the result . . . of dominant modes of valorization of human activity" and argues that a cure lies in avant-gardist ideological agitation, in which intellectuals lead a revolution in "the ways in which the world [is] being *thought*." Conley, in other words, inhabits a now familiar position in which what Homi Bhabha calls "liberationist aesthetics" operates as a self-contained and self-reinforcing politics in its own right. As Bhabha argues: "Forms of popular rebellion and mobilization are often most subversive and transgressive when they are created through oppositional *cultural* practices." The most serious weakness of this brand of postmodern cultural politics is that it is so willing to see performing radicalism, thinking difference, or renarrating history, not just as necessary but also as *sufficient* forms of political action. Thus, Chantal Mouffe argues that all "positions that have been constructed as relations of domination/subordination [can] be deconstructed because of the subversive character of democratic discourse." This is certainly true, in theory, but no matter how many cultures of resistance develop, if we satisfy ourselves with deconstructing our subordination, we will remain subordinate. Overcoming domination finally will require overturning the material structures of power that have allowed those responsible for the ecosocial crisis to ignore or simply co-opt radical democratic discourse for so long.[7]

A more grounded culturalist rejoinder is David Mazel's *American Literary Environmentalism*, which deploys Foucauldian discourse theory to show that not only "the environment *itself* is a myth, a 'grand fable,' a complex fiction, a widely shared, occasionally contested, and literally ubiquitous narrative" but also that "conservative and often exclusionary assumptions have infiltrated its basic conceptual vocabulary." Mazel reads everything from colonial settler narratives, to local color writing, to Park Service interpretive documents in order to argue that the environment is "a discursive construction, something whose 'reality' derives from the ways we write, speak, and think about it."[8] With help from Judith Butler's postmodernist critique of essentialist feminism, Mazel demonstrates powerfully that the environment has become "a canon of Great Texts" that "discipline an entire society." Nature is "a powerful site for naturalizing constructs of race, class, nationality, and gender," especially insofar as it "reveals itself as an 'exclusionary matrix' producing the (implicitly white and male) national subject and the 'natural' body of the environment." This culturalist analysis undergirds Mazel's claim that "traditional environmentalism's focus on 'nature' " has often led it "to undermine its most progressive aims by obscuring and enabling the economic, political, and historical relationships at the root of both environmental destruction and human oppression." This is absolutely accurate.[9]

Nevertheless, the most serious gap in Mazel's argument is a characteristic postmodernist way of thinking of oppressive discourses as self-identical with the institutions that are said to produce them. In other words, the concrete social institutions within which discourses function are themselves dematerialized by this form of critique. Rather than analyzing racist and sexist ideas, including some forms of environmentalism, as tools deployed in history by particular ruling classes in order to justify the material processes of exploitation and imperial expansion, postmodernism sees these ideas as the final "reality" within which it is possible to operate. White supremacy and patriarchy become the main targets of critical action, rather than the material social order that uses them to prop itself up. While Mazel admits that this "may seem a rarefied opportunity for political action, wholly peculiar to postmodern thought," he believes that agency and "resistance in this formulation reside most fundamentally in the way people revise and retell the nation's environmental narratives." Oppressive discourses, in other words, are allowed to seem freely self-generating, and in the face of such an abstract process, the cultural critic can adopt a quite romantic but sharply limited self-representation, as an individual conscientious resister of the shadowy ideological formations that threaten the careless and uncritical. Terry Eagleton makes a sharp assessment of the broad culturalist position that Mazel localizes to ecocriticism, arguing that "the postmodern cult of the socially constructed body, for all its resourceful critique of naturalism, has been closely linked with the abandonment of the very idea of a politics of global resistance— and this in an age when the politics of global domination are more importunate than ever."[10]

In the ten or so years since ecocriticism became a public phenomenon in 1992, the movement has matured and solidified in many ways. Nevertheless, that decade is framed by two pairs of texts that together demonstrate that the debate between naturalism and culturalism remains unresolved. The year 1995 saw the now famous debate between what Kate Soper called "nature-skeptics" and "nature-endorsers." Environmental historian, William Cronon, edited a collection of essays, *Uncommon Ground: Toward Reinventing Nature*, that made a direct and uncompromising attack on the naturalist position. This met with an immediate and passionate naturalist rejoinder in the form of a second collection of essays, edited by environmental scientist, Michael Soule and cultural historian, Gary Lease, titled *Reinventing Nature? Responses to Postmodern Deconstruction*. Ten years later, there has been no resolution of this polarized argument. Two books appeared in 2003 in which naturalist and culturalist positions are argued at new levels of complexity and sophistication.[11]

First, Glen Love, who was actively practicing ecocriticism before the discipline had become aware of itself, has published *Practical Ecocriticism*, a book whose allusive title announces an ironic antitheoretical bent. Love argues that in "a real world of increasing ecological crisis and political decision making, to exclude nature except for its cultural determination or linguistic construction is also to accept the continuing degradation of a natural world that is most in need of active human recognition and engagement." Love draws on his experience of the last 30 years during which criticism has become intensely politicized, and extends his moralizing beyond the epistemology of the culturist position, to the political motivations shaping the tradition in which it is rooted: "Curiously enough while literary attention fastened upon the admittedly important social conflicts associated with race, class, and gender, there seemed little or no concern for literature that addressed the overarching and increasingly stressed natural systems within which these cultural conflicts were playing themselves out." While Love claims that his cultural politics are neither Left nor Right, *Practical Ecocriticism* sets out to recuperate sociobiological notions about how humans are wired, differentially according to gender of course, to appreciate particular kinds of interaction with nature. More, it does so in order to ground a quite conservative Arnoldian way of talking about literature as a record of universal human experiences to which we should appeal in order to cure a sick culture.[12]

As if in direct response to Glen Love, in *The Truth of Ecology*, Dana Phillips sets out "to philosophize with a hammer." Phillips rightly observes that "as dogma the proposition that nature is socially constructed seems to me either nonsensical . . . or trivial. . . ." Nevertheless, he insists that it is rhetorically necessary. There "are brands of social construction that, if draughts of them are taken in the right measure and somewhat watered down, can help prevent and may even cure certain kinds of naiveté: some versions of realism, for example. . . ."[13] Thus, he often uses quite caustic humor to deflate Lawrence Buell's naturalist claim that nature writing can represent or "register actual physical environments as against idealized abstractions of those." Phillips complains that trees in a book, no matter how much we may wish them to be somehow real or even accurate, are "textual functions, in the form of words or phrases postulating an imaginary object, describing an imaginary setting, or suggesting a vaguely personified imaginary entity (such as the woods that we encounter in fairy tales). . . . It seems not so much naive as occult to suggest otherwise." Phillips shows that many ecocritics want to rediscover "a literature of presence" based on a theory of mimesis that he regards as hopelessly anachronistic. And he concludes that "we need to cure ecocriticism of its fundamentalist fixation on literal representation, and shift its focus away from the epistemological to the pragmatic." The best way to do this, he demonstrates, is to engage with ecology not as a source of grand metaphors, but as an actual empirical science, one that will show us a world much more disjunctive, patchy, and stochastic than we like to imagine.[14]

Despite the intensity of the disagreement between naturalists and culturalists, there are some very central ways in which the two are mirror images of one another. Philosopher of science, I.G. Simmons, maintains that both are totalizing statements that make nonsense out of sensible propositions that are not contradictory. For instance, Christopher Manes, whose argument is postmodernist insofar as it deploys a Foucauldian vocabulary of "epistemes" and "discourses," argues that we are suffering an environmental crisis because "the language we speak today, the idiom of Renaissance and Enlightenment humanism, veils the processes of nature with its own cultural obsessions, directionalities, and motifs that have no analogues in the natural world. . . ." The power of such humanist habits of thought is so great that "it is as if we had compressed the entire buzzing, howling, gurgling biosphere into the narrow vocabulary of epistemology, to the point that someone like Georg Lukacs could say, 'nature is a societal category'—and actually be understood." The difficulty here is that the analyst has become immersed in the fantasy under examination and is using its language to make the diagnosis. The disorder, we are told, is that modern society thinks of itself as separate from nature when, in fact, it is not. But the dominance of this way of thinking is explained without reference to the society's actual, rather than fantasized, relationship to the material world. Similarly, ecocritical naturalist, Harold Fromm, writes that "man's Faustian posturing takes place against a background of arrogant, shocking, and suicidal disregard of his roots in the earth." According to the naturalist position, anthropocentric ideas cause society to see and therefore to treat nature as no more than a fund of resources to be exploited. But the way that these habits of thought developed and spread in response to and as part of specific ecosocial orders is left unexamined. In other words, both naturalist and culturalist positions are varieties of historical idealism. Culturalists set out, according to one characteristic vocabulary, to map the genealogy of various discourses and the subjects they produce. The result is a deracinated history of successive epistemes, a sequence of worldviews reactive only to one another. Naturalists retell this tale, making it cautionary and diagnostic.[15]

The similarities between culturalism and naturalism do not stop with their fundamental agreement that the dominant ideas in society develop according to an internal process. The two also agree on the question of how the history of ideas might be interrupted. SueEllen Campbell notes, "theory and ecology" share a "critical stance . . . in relation to tradition and to authority," as well as a determination "to question the concepts on which the old hierarchies are built," revealing that they are "artificial, biased, and oversimple. . . ." They also both hope "to overturn old hierarchies, to take value from the once dominant and give it to the weak." Andrew McMurry somewhat self-mockingly describes a pessimistic version of the narrative of social transformation implied by this shared emphasis on criticism and questioning: "dialogue can serve to raise consciousness, and thereby transform the person and by extension the culture she inhabits." Because of dialogue of this kind, "the discipline [is] fully open to its larger social environment, quite capable of stimulating and changing it, if only at a snail's pace." But change is envisioned as a truly mysterious process. McMurry looks to Emerson and Thoreau, focusing on what he sees as habits of thought and patterns of figurative language that anticipate modern systems theory and cybernetics. With their help, he paints a picture of "self-organizing, self-referential, complex social systems" within which individual acts of consciousness-raising may, by a kind of evolutionary magic, produce sudden qualitative change: "Ethical evolution—punctuated, fitful, and transitory as it often is—can continue only if we assure the many and varied ways of seeing the world are never occluded, the ways of voicing it never silenced." McMurry himself derogates this position as a kind of "flaccid moral/ethical pluralism." Many culturalists are not just pluralist, but flaccidly defeatist, contenting themselves with the feeling that in the face of the juggernaut of discourse, the most we can hope for is an occasional moment of individual liberation attained through the exercise of critical awareness. True, there is a more sanguine thread. Consider just the titles of these two recent books: *Contesting Earth's Future: Radical Ecology and Postmodernity* and *Ecocritique: Contesting the Politics of Nature, Economy, and Culture*. Nevertheless, such optimism represents a minority culturalist position.[16]

Naturalists, meanwhile, assert that human creativity, especially in response to immediate encounters with real nature, can break the chains of discourse, allowing the reconstruction of our relations with the planet. As Lawrence Buell argues, "most seasoned ecocritics are likely to take more or less in stride" the culturalist critique of "the illusion of an essential 'ecological self.' " They would agree that notions of ecocentricity and nature's holism are "culture-produced myths, although they would probably [want] to envisage these myths as potentially more enabling than disabling." Buell also claims that the nature–culture distinction forms the potential basis for an enabling "myth of mutual constructionism: of physical environment (both natural and human-built) shaping the cultures that in some measure continually refashion it." Such a myth would allow us to move beyond abstract arguments about anthropocentricity and ecocentricity, in order to recognize that "a stronger ethic of care for the nonhuman environment would make the world a better place, for humans as well as for nonhumans."[17]

Ecocritics of both kinds, then, hope to open up space for cultural work to engage meaningfully with the history of ideas. If they disagree on anything, it is on the prospect for this kind of work to have real effects. In order to settle this disagreement, we not only need to explain why ecologically maladaptive ideas remain dominant and why the ways of thinking we admire remain subordinate, but also to imagine the material conditions in which alternative ways of thinking can become possible and even make a bid for actual dominance. But, like much nature writing, at the same time that ecocriticism urgently condemns the ongoing destruction of our world, it also obscures the historical specificity of that process. It conceals the truth that wholesale environmental destruction is not a transhistorical characteristic of human societies, but a specific feature of class societies, and one that has dangerously accelerated under capitalism. Human ideas of nature developed within a particular collective history in which material conflicts between particular social classes have driven a process of modernization, a process that has finally made it possible to think of nature and society as different orders of being. But by telling an abstract tale of how humanity has lost touch with nature, ecocriticism disables its critique in the act of making it.

In his *Philosophical Notebooks*, the Marxist revolutionary, V.I. Lenin remarks: "Intelligent idealism is closer to intelligent materialism than is unintelligent materialism." And as the debate between naturalism and culturalism has continued, there have been many gestures in the direction of an intelligent resolution. William Howarth observes that "writers and their critics are stuck with language, and although we cast *nature* and *culture* as opposites, in fact they constantly mingle, like water and soil in a flowing stream." And Cheryll Glotfelty maintains that literature "does not float above the material world in some aesthetic ether, but, rather, plays a part in an immensely complex global system, in which energy, matter, *and ideas* interact." Both statements exemplify Buell's observation that ecocriticism's initial "resistance to theory" has given way to "an anxiety to achieve a constructive engagement with poststructuralist thinking and ensuing strands of literary and cultural theory." Buell begins to make that engagement himself by observing that the nature–culture debate takes place between two reductive positions: there is "reductionism at the level of formal representation, such as to compel us to believe either that the text replicates the object-world or that it creates an entirely distinct linguistic world; and reductionism at the ideational level, such as to require us to believe that the environment ought to be considered either the major subject of concern or merely a mystification of some other interest." In order to resolve these dilemmas, he proposes a "post–post structuralist . . . critical practice that operates from a premise of bidirectionality."[18]

There is a valuable alternative to idealist methods, one based on a "premise of bidirectionality," that has been available for some time in the heterogeneous Marxist practice of cultural materialist historiography, which examines the role culture plays in the material relations between people, ideas, and the world as they develop over time. This tradition's founding proposition is that people are part of nature. As Fredric Jameson puts it: "Marxism may be seen as the 'end' of philosophy, in that in its very structure it refuses system, or what amounts to the same thing, metaphysical content." By metaphysics, Jameson means ideas considered in artificial isolation from the material world and subjected to a kind of analysis made possible by "a hypostasis of the mental processes, an attempt to hold something aside from the concrete operation of the mind upon its determinate object, something which can then be treated in absolute fashion as the universally valid."[19] In other words, we live in the material world and we should explain how we think on the basis of this truth. Cultural materialism explores how our ideas, including that of nature, simultaneously develop out of and react on specific modes of collectively organizing the ecological and social, or ecosocial, process of subsisting within nature.

The materialist tradition has been passed over by most ecocritics, who have tended to misunderstand it as simply one more form of anthropocentric culturalism. This rejection reflects a long history of mutual hostility between Marxism and political ecology. Kate Soper describes how the poor ecological record of the Soviet Union led to political ecology's hostility to Marxism's alleged "productivism." To be brief, the state-capitalist regimes of the East physically defeated the socialist revolutionary movements that preceded them, instating bureaucratic rule in order to oversee the intense exploitation of land and labor required by military–industrial competition with the West. In that context, they developed pseudo-Marxist rhetoric as a stabilizing ideology whose primary function, rather like the ideology of the democratic free market in the United States, was to obscure class divisions within a deeply oppressive and destructive society. Genuine materialist social and cultural theory, on the other hand, is a set of analytical procedures that has developed as a tool of revolutionary movements in both East and West. Its goal is not to authorize the infinite expansion of production for its own sake, but to bring under truly democratic control decisions not only about how much we produce, but also what we produce and how. It bears the same relation to the sorry discourse of Stalinism as it does to the current ruling-class orthodoxy, neoliberalism. The tragic history of the twentieth century only continues when ecocriticism rejects, by association, what remain a powerful and adaptive set of tools for liberation.[20]

Before discussing more systematically how cultural materialism differs from current denatured idealisms, I will apply what I believe are its most valuable procedures and emphases to the most central text in the ecocritical canon, the inaugural moment in the tradition of American environmental literature. It will take some time, though, to get there, since, as Jameson observes, the "peculiar difficulty of dialectical writing lies indeed in its holistic, 'totalizing' character: as though you could not say any one thing until you had first said everything. . . ."[21]

CHAPTER 3

CLASS STRUGGLE IN
NEW ENGLAND

The stockholder has stepped into the place of the warlike baron. The nobles shall not any longer, as feudal lords, have the power of life and death over the churls, but now in another shape, as capitalists, shall in all love and peace eat them up as before.

—Ralph Waldo Emerson

During the period between the Revolution and the Civil War, New England underwent a complete ecosocial revolution. Over the course of about 80 years, the colonial agricultural and mercantile order evolved into the first stage of industrial capitalism. Local and regional economies dominated by barter were replaced by a national market that was integrated by roads, canals, and railroads. Farmers planted their fields with saleable commodities rather than subsistence crops. Factory and shop production of goods for market replaced home production for family use. Economic and political power that had been relatively dispersed among the merchants, clerics, and farmers of colonial New England was consolidated into the hands of the increasingly wealthy owners of commercial and industrial capital. By 1860, the wealthiest five percent of the population owned 53 percent of total capital, whereas the bottom half controlled about one percent. Concentration of capital and power produced a society increasingly organized around one goal: the pursuit of profit. It was a deeply contradictory society in which spectacular technological innovation and wealth coexisted with new forms of grinding poverty and exploitation.[1]

These economic changes produced a radical transformation of human relations with the land in New England. Market integration and national expansion in the West released a flood of cheap farm goods from the richer soils of the Ohio Valley. In order to keep their farms, many thousands of New England farmers were forced to send their children to work in factories and towns for cash. In many cases, competition drove whole families off the land. This was the first intensive period of urbanization in U.S. history. In 1790, 90 percent of New England's population lived on farms averaging 128 acres, or in small towns of no more than 2,500. Most people interacted directly with the land as a part of their daily routine of farm chores: plowing with teams of oxen, planting, harvesting, and processing crops, cutting timber for fuel and construction, and so on. By 1860 though, one-third of the population lived in towns and cities with more than 2,500 residents, where the varied cadences of rural life had been replaced by the more insistent rhythm of wage labor. Boston had about 18,000 residents in 1790. By 1860, there were over 175,000—an increase of almost 1000 percent. More significantly though, from 1800 to 1860, the overall percentage of the population who worked for wages rose from 10 to 40 percent.[2]

The most visible innovation in labor relations was the invention of the large factory. In Massachusetts, the sons of the old merchant princes built mills and factories at falls on the major rivers. The core of this capitalist elite was Francis Cabot Lowell's Boston Manufacturing Company, which developed the first integrated mill for the production of cotton cloth at Waltham in 1815. Soon members of the wealthiest Boston dynasties had built mills at Lawrence, Lowell, Lynn, Chicopee, Dover, Manchester, Holyoke, and other towns near water power around New England. The demand for labor at the mills was so great that recruiters were sent in wagons to scour the countryside for women and children to tend the spinning frames. As many as half of factory operatives were children 12 and under, earning less than one dollar per week. Adult women were paid between two and three dollars a week. Former Lowell worker, Harriet Jane Hanson Robinson, remembered these conditions in an 1883 essay, "Early Factory Labor in New England":

> The early mill girls were of different ages. Some were not over ten years old; a few were in middle life, but the majority were between the ages of sixteen and twenty-five. The very young girls were called "doffers." They "doffed," or took off, the full bobbins from the spinning-frames, and replaced them with empty ones. These mites worked about fifteen minutes every hour and the rest of the time was their own. When the overseer was kind they were allowed to read, knit, or go outside the mill yard to play. They were paid two dollars a week. The working hours of all the girls extended from five o'clock in the morning until seven in the evening with one half-hour each for breakfast and dinner. Even the doffers were forced to be on duty nearly fourteen hours a day. This was the greatest hardship in the lives of these children.

An atmosphere of benevolent paternalism was maintained in the mill villages in order to ease public anxieties about children and single women working and living away from home. Shop-floor overseers and dormitory matrons enforced strict punctuality and punished what they defined as immoral conduct, including insubordination.[3]

Although the women of the textile mills have come to stand for the experience of the working class as a whole in many histories of the period, their experience was not typical. Even in Lowell, factory operatives made up only about one-third of the work force. Under the putting-out system, a great deal of manufacturing occurred in much smaller and more informal workshops, and even in sweatshops, often located in private homes. And mechanics working in traditional crafts and trades still made up the largest section of the working class in the large cities. They cut meat, baked bread, drove carriages, and made hats, shoes, and other articles of clothing. They built homes, shops, and ships. They set, printed, and bound books, magazines and newspapers, and performed all the other necessary work of life. In the trades and crafts, a well-paid skilled worker earned one dollar for a workday that ran from sunrise to sunset with little time off for meals.

This growing working class had been central to the Revolution and in the early national period its members hoped to make their urban environment into what one reformer called a "miniature likeness of a well-regulated republic."[4] Workers built a semiautonomous culture based on class-conscious congregations, militias, cooperative savings banks, as well as temperance, athletic, and self-education societies. They also published newspapers, journals, addresses, and manifestos that together make up one of the least studied bodies of American literature. In New York, Robert Dale Owen and Frances Wright edited the *Free Enquirer*, while George Henry Evans edited *The Working Man's Advocate*, in which he distinguished himself by passionately defending the Nat Turner rebellion. In Massachusetts, Charles Douglas published *The New England Artisan*, mouthpiece of the New England Association of Farmers, Mechanics, and Other Working Men. A decade later, *The Voice of Industry*, edited by William Field Young, served as the official organ of the New England Workingmen's Association. In Boston, there were *The Man*, *The Bee*, and *The Laborer*; in Lynn, there were *The New England Operative* and *The Awl*. These periodicals maintained a class tradition of fierce independence and they clearly identified working-class interests in opposition to those of the people presiding over the period's wrenching social and economic changes. Frederick Robinson captured this mood in "An Oration delivered before the Trades' Union of Boston and Vicinity, July 4, 1834": "Our destiny, fellow citizens, is in our own hands, and we must rely upon ourselves alone for the improvement of our republican institutions, the reform of our laws, and the bettering of our social and political condition."[5]

Although there was substantial ideological variation within the movement, the dominant strain was Paineite natural-rights radicalism strengthened by a class analysis of U.S. society. Working-class radicals represented themselves as defending the republican principles of equality and freedom against the growing power of an elite cabal. Stephen Simpson, for instance, in *The Working Man's Manual: A New Theory of Political Economy, on the Principle of Production the Source of Wealth*, called for a campaign to defeat "the party of the stockholders and capitalists" by a "*party of the producers*, which is a real party of *general interest*, whose ascendancy could not fail to shed a genial and prosperous beam upon the whole society." One of the hardest-hitting orators of the period was Theophilus Fisk, author of *Labor the Only True Source of Wealth* (1837), and editor of the journals, *Gospel Herald and Universalist Review* and *Priestcraft Unmasked*. In "Capital against Labor, An Address delivered at Julien Hall before the mechanics of Boston on Wednesday evening, May 20, 1835," he states that the "history of the producers of wealth, of the industrious classes, is that of a continued warfare of honesty against fraud, weakness against power, justice against oppression. The purchasers of labor have in all ages had the advantage of the sellers and they have rarely failed to use their power to the furtherance of their own interest. . . ." The labor theory of value and the idea that profits represent expropriated labor, as they are deployed here by Fisk, were widely shared across the movement: parasitic capitalists fattened by consuming wealth produced by workers whose natural right to the whole produce of their labor had been denied by the device of wages.[6]

Fisk's economic analysis of the sources of social power led him to predict violent class conflict. He warns the elite that before they "determined to treat the unmanacled workingman as they would a convict in the state prison, they would do well to pause. Beneath their feet an earthquake slumbers." Like many of his contemporaries, he believed that the situation was rapidly worsening and that a final confrontation between the classes was quickly approaching: "There is a period in the affairs of men when forbearance ceases to be a virtue, when patient endurance becomes criminal. Let the interested beware how they accelerate the sands in Time's hourglass and thereby hasten a season when resistance and not resignation and passive obedience will be the rallying watchword." Despite the pitch of his rhetoric, Fisk does not call for organized direct action. He appeals finally to workers to vote capital down by electing Democrats.[7]

Another speaker, and one who was more solidly rooted in the radical wing of the movement, was Seth Luther, the main organizer of the New England Association of Farmers, Mechanics, and other Working Men. Luther first earned wide public exposure with his *Address to the Working Men of New England*, which quickly sold through three editions after it was printed in 1832. The title page of the second edition boasts that before the address was printed it was delivered before audiences in "Boston, Charlestown, Cambridgeport, Waltham, Dorchester, Mass., Portland, Saco, ME., and Dover, N.H." Luther's main goal is to advocate shorter working hours and better conditions in the textile mills, but he builds his argument on a foundation of republican political theory. The United States is only "a *nominally* free country; for we cannot admit that any country *is*, or any people *can* be free, where distinctions in society exist, in opposition to that 'self evident truth,—ALL MEN ARE CREATED EQUAL.' " Like Fisk, Luther explains inequality by invoking the labor theory of value, maintaining that wealth is stolen labor since "those who labor—those who produce *all* the wealth . . . enjoy so *small* a portion of it themselves." The system of wage labor, "which prevents the producing classes from a participation in the fountains of knowledge," has been created and sustained by the "avarice" of the factory owners. In order to satisfy their "*lust* of possession," they conspire to destroy "the happiness of the MANY, that the FEW may roll and riot in splendid luxury." Luther reviles the hypocritical patriotism of "statesmen, capitalists, and monopolists" who "cry out about *national* glory, *national* wealth, march of improvement, march of intellect" under "the *American System*." Under this system, he insists, "the *wives* and *daughters* of the *rich* manufacturers would no more associate with a '*factory girl*,' than they would with a *Negro slave*. So much for equality in a *republican* country." Luther details the long hours, low wages, harsh working conditions, and brutal oversight faced by mill workers whose lives are ruined by "*Republican* TYRANTS." And he concludes that the "whole system of labor in New England, *more especially in cotton mills*, is a cruel system of exaction on the bodies and minds of the producing classes, destroying the energies of both, and for no other object than to enable the 'rich' to 'take care of themselves,' whereas 'the poor must work or starve.' " Under these circumstances, he declares, the "unfinished monument" at Bunker Hill "is a most excellent emblem of our unfinished independence." And he calls on his audience "to form a *front*, which will show all *monopolists*, and all TYRANTS, that we are not only determined to have the name of freemen, but that we will LIVE FREEMEN and DIE FREEMEN."[8]

Luther's insistence that the struggle between "Money and Labor" represented the next stage of the American Revolution became stronger and clearer as time went on. In 1835, he was elected to head a committee charged with drafting a "Ten-Hour Circular" that would be printed in working-class newspapers around the Northeast. The circular begins by aggressively appropriating the rhetoric of republicanism: "We are contending for the recognition of the Natural Right to dispose of our own time in such quantities as we deem and believe to be most conducive to our own happiness, and the welfare of all those engaged in Manual Labor." The sunup-to-sundown workday was an "odious, cruel, unjust, and tyrannical system which compels the operative Mechanic to exhaust his physical and mental powers by excessive toil, until he has no desire but to eat and sleep." The mill owners and the bosses in the trades and crafts were traitors to the Republic: "No man or body of men who requires such excessive labor can be friends to the country or the Rights of Man." Under these circumstances, the logic of republicanism leads directly to radical conclusions: "We claim by the blood of our fathers, shed on our battle-fields in the War of the Revolution, the rights of American Freemen, and no earthly power shall resist our righteous claims with impunity." Luther and the committee call on the "Mechanics of Boston" to "stand firm" for the time had come "to enroll your names on the scroll of history as the undaunted enemies of oppression, as the enemies of mental, moral and physical degradation, as the friends of the human race."[9]

During the first half of the 1830s, radical working-class activity based on these ideas reached a crescendo. First, there was a broad movement toward the ballot box. The first Workingmen's Party had been launched in Philadelphia in 1828, and the idea had quickly spread across the Northeast, attracting a large and diverse following. The next year in New York, the Workingmen succeeded in electing Ebenezer Ford, president of the Carpenters' Union, to the state assembly where he was threatened with expulsion. The New England Association of Farmers, Mechanics, and Other Working Men was founded in February 1831. Among the reforms the Workies demanded were the breaking up of monopolies, a ten-hour workday, universal suffrage and direct popular elections, free schools, an end to Indian removal, and the abolition of slavery, child labor, convict labor, imprisonment for debt, and the death penalty. Another key demand was free distribution of federal land in tracts of no more than 160 acres. The rapid growth of the Workingmen's Party inspired Andrew Jackson's Democrats to aggressively borrow planks from its platform, sand off their rougher edges, and reuse them as their own. This process culminated in 1832, with Jackson's veto of the charter for the Bank of the United States, an institution seen by many as the organizing center of the aristocracy of money. This act alone convinced many urban workers that the Democratic Party was genuinely what it claimed to be, the party of the poor in their class war against the rich. Before long, their Workingmen's Party entered a steep decline from which it would never recover.[10]

Through this same period, workers across the Northeast launched a large-scale unionization campaign. Strikes and turn-outs at individual workplaces had been regular, if not common, occurrences as early as the beginning of the century, bringing together sailors, carpenters, caulkers, rope makers, shoemakers, hat makers, coopers, and more to fight for shorter hours, increased wages, and better working conditions. These were mainly small-scale events, and many were crushed by blacklisting and conspiracy trials. Nevertheless, they produced a tradition of collective struggle that now exploded into a period of militancy as workers banded together into larger and larger organizations in order to apply collective strength to the improvement of their situations. Women shoe binders working from their homes in Reading, Massachusetts and surrounding towns including Lynn, attempted to form a union in the summer of 1831, taking out an ad with as many as 300 signatories calling on others to join them in fixing the piecework rate. In the spring of 1832, Boston's ship carpenters combined to adopt the ten-hour day and announced, "We were all born free and equal, and we do not ask to have our grievances redressed as a favor, but we demand it as a right."[11]

From 1833 to 1836, there were more than 150 strikes across the Northeast. Workers built more than 200 trade and craft unions, with membership estimated as high as 300,000. In December 1833, as many as 1,000 women, mostly shoe binders, attended a convention in Lynn to form the "Female Society of Lynn and Vicinity for the protection and promotion of Female Industry." They demanded higher wages, an end to payment in store goods, and equal rights for women in the workplace. Their constitution protested the "want of justice, and reasonable compensation to the females" at a time when "the business of their *employers* has appeared to be improving, and prosperous, enabling them to increase in wealth. These *things ought not so to be!*" In 1834, the women of Lowell's mills struck against a 15 percent wage reduction. And Boston's Trades Union formed by far the largest contingent in the Independence Day parade, gathering 1,000-strong for a dinner in Faneuil Hall. In the same year in New York, a movement was launched to build a National Trades Union that would take in all skilled workers on a national basis.

This was the next logical step following the founding of the New York General Trades Union in 1833 "to defend itself against the infringements of the aristocracy, to assert its natural and political rights, to raise its moral and intellectual level, to narrow the differences between workers and employers. . . ." A celebratory march stretched a mile and a half along Broadway, strengthened by sailors, shipwrights, riggers, and stevedores who were mounting a combined strike just at that time. In Pennsylvania, bloody battles broke out between organized Irish workers on the Chesapeake and Ohio Canal and a group of scabs, prompting Andrew Jackson to use federal troops to police a labor struggle for the first time in American history. And a dockworkers strike on the Schuykill River in the summer of 1835 turned into a general strike that shut down Philadelphia, winning the ten-hour day.[12]

The victory in Philadelphia inspired a wave of militant strikes across the Northeast throughout 1836 and early 1837, but the rising momentum and militancy were crushed when a speculative bubble in Western land burst, producing the financial panic of 1837. Tens of thousands were thrown out of work as the economy ground to a halt. Ninety percent of the Northeast's factories simply closed their doors. Hard-won unions collapsed as they lost the majority of the jobs they had organized either to closures or to scabs. Average wages fell by a third. The effects on the poor were shattering. In New York, broadsides circulated that read: "Bread, meat, rent, fuel! Their prices must come down!" During the winter of 1836–1837, anger boiled over into bread riots, including the famous assault on Hart's Flour Store. Sections of the unemployed succumbed to racist scapegoating, beating and killing black workers and burning free black neighborhoods. The depression that followed the panic lasted well into the 1840s, and by all accounts, the levels of dislocation and misery exceeded those of the Great Depression a century later.[13]

Nevertheless, after a period of retreat, workers returned to organized activity in the mid-1840s. Over the next two decades, until the beginning of the Civil War, the class gradually regained momentum on three fronts. First, workers began to focus new energy on building cooperatives, both producers cooperatives, which would allow individuals to combine their forces in order to launch large-scale manufacturing concerns, and consumers unions that allowed for bulk purchasing and distribution of goods and services. Second, the campaign for a ten-hour day became a renewed focus of agitation. In June 1844, a group of workers in Fall River issued a call for a "Convention of Mechanics" to address the problem that the length of the workday prevented "deep thoughts, systematic study, and real mental culture." They called on their fellow workers to arise "to crush, annihilate, forever destroy the system which is fast carrying us forward to the disagreeable, servile and degraded condition of the English laborer." Mill workers across the state formed the Ten-Hour Republican Association and collected tens of thousands of signatures on petitions calling on the state legislature to limit the workday.[14]

At the same time, fresh attempts at building unions and other class-based organizations revived as the economy picked up steam again. Mechanics' and Laborers' Associations sprouted everywhere from the ashes of the old organizations. Boston hosted the first convention of the New England Workingmen's Association in October 1844. The Association brought together veterans of the radical working-class movements of the 1830s with a new layer of elite radicals. The hundreds of delegates to the first meeting included George Ripley, Parke Godwin, and others from the utopian socialist community at Brook Farm. However, "the most numerous delegations were those from Fall River, Lynn, and Lowell, who came into the Hall in procession, bearing banners with appropriate mottoes which were arranged near the President's seat under the full length portraits of Washington, Hancock, and other revolutionary worthies." The text of these parade standards gives a sense of the confident anger of the movement: "One of the Lowell Banners was inscribed on one side with the words 'We know and claim our Rights'; on the other side, in beautiful gold letters, 'Union is Strength'. . . ." The assembled delegates resolved that under "the present system of labor the interests of capital and labor are opposed, the former now securing the reward that should only belong to the latter" and recommended "the formation of practical associations, in which workingmen can use their own capital, work their own stock, establish their own hours, and have their own price." The New England Workingmen's Association convened again in 1845, this time at Lowell, and called for a National Industrial Congress that would "propose and adopt such measures as shall be found necessary to secure the rights and interests of honest industry and to hasten the accomplishment of the grand industrial revolution which is alike demanded by the nature of man, the mission of free America, the hopes of humanity and the law of eternal truth and justice."[15]

In sum, the antebellum period in New England was marked by relentless and widespread working-class organization and militancy. There were ebbs and flows in the movement to be sure, but self-conscious, aggressive, collective struggle along class lines was a consistent feature of modernization in New England. More, this dynamic movement, with its uncompromising demand for working-class self-determination and its powerful traditions of collective class struggle, was the historical bedrock of the antebellum period. It was the most fundamental reality of the material social world and it powerfully shaped the lives and ideas of the period's elite, especially its elite radicals.

Chapter 4

Transcendentalism as a Social Movement

It is unquestionably true that the need for art is not created by economic conditions. But neither is the need for food created by economics. On the contrary, the need for food and warmth creates economics. It is very true that one cannot always go by the principles of Marxism in deciding whether to accept or reject a work of art. A work of art should, in the first place, be judged by its own law, that is, by the law of art. But Marxism alone can explain why and how a given tendency in art has originated in a given period in history, in other words, who made a demand for such an artistic form and not for another, and why.

—Leon Trotsky

There is way of talking about the New England Transcendentalists that takes solitary departure as their most representative trajectory, focusing especially on Emerson's retirement from his Boston congregation to his sage's retreat in Concord. Emerson, it is said, lead a circle of intellectual revolutionaries who rooted out the last vestiges of Puritan conformity and birthed the long-awaited self-creating Individual, the high-toned older brother of the self-made man, the American Adam. This last phrase is borrowed, of course, from the great Americanist R.W.B. Lewis, who described the Transcendentalists as leading the creation of national mythology based on the figure of "an individual emancipated from history, happily bereft of ancestry, untouched and undefiled by the usual inheritances of family and race; an individual standing alone, self-reliant and self-propelling, ready to confront whatever awaited him with the aid of his own unique and inherent resources." The idea that the Transcendentalist movement was unified by a commitment to individualism rests on a tenacious set of mutually reinforcing assumptions about the movement. Emerson is the major Transcendentalist. Transcendentalism is a philosophy of individualism. Individualism is the ground of American thought. American thought begins with Emerson. Emerson is the major Transcendentalist.[1]

An early historian of the movement, Octavius Brooks Frothingham, was among the first to give scholarly credentials to this circle of reasoning. Speaking of Emerson without naming him, Frothingham argued in 1876 that if the Transcendentalist "was a reformer of society, it was as a vitalizer, not as a machinist. . . . [He] would not be committed to experiments that did not assume his first principle—the supreme dignity of the individual man. The systems of French socialism he distrusted from the first; for they proceeded on the ground that man is not a self-determined being, but a creature of circumstance." Frothingham is performing here the familiar trick of retrospectively redefining the criteria for membership in a group so as to exclude one's opponent in a sectarian debate. The fact is that systems of French socialism, among other radical collectivist ways of thinking, were deeply influential within the Transcendentalist movement. Emerson was among a minority who engaged thoughtfully with these collectivist ideas, and then wrote in defense of individual self-culture as a means of spontaneous, organic, social change.[2]

Like Frothingham before them, R.W.B. Lewis and most of the prominent Americanists of his generation had a way of briefly acknowledging the manifold radicalism of Transcendentalism before moving on to analyses that smoothly incorporated it into a spruced-up version of the liberal tradition—what Vernon Louis Parrington called the main currents of American thought. F.O. Matthiessen, for instance, in the preface to *American Renaissance: Art and Expression in the Age of Emerson and Whitman*, envisions an alternative book to be called *The Age of Fourier* that would examine the period's "voicing of fresh aspirations for the rise of the common man." He then goes on to say that he will not write that book, but will instead focus on evaluating works by Emerson, Thoreau, Hawthorne, Melville, and Whitman "in accordance with the enduring requirements for great art." Perry Miller offers a common justification for this tendency toward erasure: "That the revolutionary threat to the established order contained in the Transcendental premises has been forgotten is to be accounted for mainly on the ground that little or nothing ever came of it. . . ." Miller acknowledges that in "the early 1840s the critique of Unitarian Boston had become also a critique of State Street and investment banking." But he dismisses that critique as a kind of juvenile fantasy:

> As studies of our society, as formulations of the meaning of democracy and of freedom in what had suddenly become (and remains) a "business" culture, these documents are as alive as the day they were written, even

though in historical fact they produced no more earth-shaking actions than Brook Farm or Brownson's opposition to President Harrison.

There is a kind of doublethink at work here that is closely related to the anticommunist crusades of the 1950s. The political sanitization of Transcendentalism for inclusion in the liberal tradition is carried out by dismissing the radical wing of the movement as insufficiently serious to merit attention in a real world where Stalinism and New Deal Liberalism contended for global dominion. The introduction to Miller's anthology, *The American Transcendentalists*, provides another example of trivializing rhetoric: he argues that the movement is "the first outcry of the heart against the materialistic pressures of a business civilization." Its members "turn their protest against what is customarily called the 'Protestant ethic': they refuse to labor in a proper calling, conscientiously cultivate the arts of leisure, and strive to avoid making money." Outcries of the heart may be stirring, but they are by no means sober.[3]

The idea that Transcendentalism's historical importance rests on its having first articulated the fundamentals of a uniquely American individualism remains deeply ingrained in the critical tradition. Even so oppositional a figure as Frank Lentricchia can write, in the context of a call for activist intellectual production, that "an American ('self-reliant') Marxism is fundamentally an absurd proposition. The 'active' critical soul in America, from Emerson to Burke, joins parties of one, because it is there, in America, that critical power flourishes." Myra Jehlen agrees, arguing that individualism has become incarnate in the land itself:

> the coincidence of America's discovery and settlement by Europeans with the decisive political rise of a new class identified the very land with the ascendants: beyond any political or economic superiority, the material fact of the North American continent itself enabled insurgent merchants, artisans, and adventurers to declare themselves *incomparable* and the universal representatives of mankind. Their personal and political ways thus became, indistinguishably, the ways in and, more important, *of* America.

For Jehlen, the radical energies of the American bourgeois self are directed fluidly into the spiritualized processes of national expansion and economic development. Perhaps the most influential variation on this theme is Sacvan Bercovitch's theory of cohesion and dissent, with its heavy emphasis on the process of incorporation in American ideology. For Bercovitch, antebellum elite radicalism is always already co-opted: "the defiant act that might have posed alternatives to the system becomes instead a force for change within established patterns of life and belief."[4]

Investigating the tradition of Puritan jeremiads led Bercovitch to develop this now famous model of dissensus, and it provides a truly powerful way of reading much liberal humbug, but it too easily passes over moments of authentic rebellion by remarking, in effect, that they have not changed anything. Carol Colatrella writes, "Bercovitch's explanation of how dissensus is incorporated as an affirmation of culture itself becomes an ideology privileging consensus and negating the possibility that dissenters are truly able to effect change in society." Moreover, the dissensus model too uncritically accepts maps of the cultural landscape bequeathed to it by surveyors who were working to very different ends. Its arguments rest on the evidence of a narrowly limited range of writers and kinds of texts. Thus, when reading Transcendentalism, Bercovitch does engage with some of the more radical figures of the period, but only to provide a background for an account Emerson's exemplary slide from early uncertainty to a later confidence in individualism as the soul of the American Way. For Bercovitch, "Emersonian dissent reminds us that ideology in America works not by repressing radical energies but by redirecting them into a constant conflict between self and society: the self in itself, a separate, single, non-conformist individuality versus society en masse, individual-ism systematized." Although there is a measure of truth to this as an assessment of Emerson's thought *per se*, the truth is that his trajectory was only one among many.[5]

Just as important were Orestes Brownson's journey from a poor farm family to a mission as a Unitarian preacher among workers in the slums of Boston, Margaret Fuller's voyage to the front lines of revolutionary struggle in Rome, George Ripley's withdrawal to the socialist utopia at Brook Farm, and Bronson Alcott's to Fruitlands. Transcendentalism was much more heterogeneous than we have been taught to think, for this full range of activity, at the least, must be included as part of the movement. In "Communal Romanticism," Jeffrey Cox asks, "Might we not discover a scene of writing somewhere in the middle between the imperial author and the national psyche?" Transcendentalism existed in this middle space. It was less a coherent flowering of particular ideas than a move-ment of particular people, a social movement unified not by any strict ideological conformity, but by the common social and geographic ori-gins of its members and by their sense of participation in a widespread rebellion against an unacceptable status quo. One especially clear index of its diversity is the table of contents of Elizabeth Palmer Peabody's single issue of *Aesthetic Papers*, published in May 1849. The magazine includes an article by socialist and prominent music critic, John Sullivan

Dwight. This is followed by an Emerson essay on "War." Next comes an article on "Organization" by leading socialist propagandist and Brook Farm resident, Parke Godwin. Peabody herself contributes a piece on "The Dorian Measure," which is followed by a long political sketch, "Main-Street," in which Nathaniel Hawthorne derides the values of the commercial elite. Then, of course, there is the volume's most famous selection, Thoreau's essay, "Resistance to Civil Government."[6]

Transcendentalism was, then, a movement of elite radicals of many kinds taking place within a period of broad ideological turmoil. Under the pressure of rapid and often brutal national expansion, industrialization, urbanization, and above all, class stratification and conflict, many among the elite had lost faith in once-reliable truisms about their identity as a class. In the face of working-class radicalism and its appropriation of the rhetoric of republicanism, their social authority and their right to govern no longer seemed so solidly founded in the old presumptions of superior reason, virtue, and access to God's will. One outcome was that the staunch authoritarianism of Orthodoxy disintegrated in the face of Unitarian liberalization. That story has been the focus of much critical attention. Another arena where ruling-class confusion and anxiety registered immediately was the electoral system. In the first party system that had developed after the Revolution, federalism had represented the interests of urban-based mercantile, shipping, and financial interests, while republicanism had loosely united a landed agricultural constituency by claiming to oppose the aristocracy of money. After the collapse of federalism in 1823, National Republicans and Democratic Republicans contended for power and for the support of the various radical movements that surfaced through the period. By 1834, this struggle had produced the Whig and Democratic Parties, the first mass parties in which professional politicians electioneered for the support of a broad electorate. These parties differentiated themselves along the lines of the old Federalist–Republican split. The Whigs united around the patrician John Quincy Adams, and came increasingly to represent the interests of an urban elite who favored tight fiscal policy and aggressive moral legislation by a strong central government. Andrew Jackson's Democrats drew their support from the agricultural entrepreneurs of the rural periphery, supporting an expansive monetary policy that would reduce the debt-load on farms and demanding minimal governmental interference in the operations of the markets for goods and labor.

Both Whig and Democratic organizations remained under the effective control of the upper strata of the social order, and the two parties increasingly competed to capture the support of working-class voters. E. Malcolm Carroll has shown that "Jacksonian Democracy not only controlled the federal government from 1828 to 1840 but it was also perhaps the most important influence in shaping the character of the opposition." Frederick Robinson, addressing a trade-union audience in 1834, was somewhat more direct about the political shenanigans of the Whig elite: "in order to prevent the true appellation of aristocracy from being attached to them, they continually contrive to change their party name. It was first Tory, then Federalist, then no party, then amalgamation, then National Republican, now Whig, and the next name they assume perhaps will be republican or democrat." The Whigs tried to appeal to voters by posing as defenders of the republic against the arbitrary power of King Jackson, and especially by developing two central doctrines: the importance of self-reform and the harmony of interests between classes. Arthur Schlesinger, Jr. maintains that these ideas "satisfied the feeling of the business community in all shades of ambivalence, from the compulsions toward power to the lurking intuitions of guilt [and] represented a vigorous and versatile strategy, finding enormous support in the hopes of American life and a certain support in its realities." The power of these ideas was not sufficient, though, to prevent the Democrats from harnessing working-class anger. They borrowed the radical rhetoric of the class struggle although they rejected its substance (such as the demand for a ten-hour day). And they represented themselves as an agrarian yeomanry at war with a usurping "money power."[7]

Jackson's election to a second term in 1832 confirmed the absoluteness of the Democratic victory. Whig observers read the event typologically according to their notions of the French Revolution's decline into radicalism and violence. It was not that liberty had led to license, rather, centuries of monarchic despotism had degraded the people. Weakened citizens were easily swayed by ambitious demagogues who might well lead them to destroy the hard-won republic. As the city came to seem infested with mobs demanding higher wages and free land, the nature of rural and wild landscapes seemed far preferable, and became a central reference point in the evolving self-definition of the New England's Whig elite. Many adopted the paradoxical role of benevolent, country patriarchs in relation to the turbulent working class. They occupied the Democratic enemy's high ground by purchasing and settling large agricultural estates to which they repaired on weekends and holidays. On these model farms, they not only won ribbons for innovative farming techniques, but more importantly, they harvested a rich crop of positive associations with rural life. They made cultural and political hay from the Puritan doctrine of a productive calling, the physiocratic idea that agriculture formed the true foundation of national prosperity, and the agrarian notion of virtuous producers defending the nation against luxury and vice. These country-seat Whigs fashioned themselves a benevolent leadership, whose rationality and impartiality were most centrally symbolized by their adopted role as wealthy farmers.[8]

In the context of this broad ideological realignment within the ruling class, a layer of radicals emerged who devoted themselves to the conquest of cultural authority. As the mainstream of the Whig elite attempted to regain their hold on political power by mimicking the language and sentiments of Jacksonian democracy, this layer of elite intellectuals adopted the position of cultural advisors to their embattled class. Emerson saw imminent class conflict as a moral crisis, the natural comeuppance of spiritual degeneration:

> A selfish commerce and government have caught the eye and usurped the hand of the masses. It is not to be contested that selfishness and the senses write the laws under which we live, and that the street seems to be built, and the men and women in it moving not in reference to pure and grand ends, but rather to very short and sordid ones.

What seemed sordid was both open profiteering by capitalists and the loud demands of organized workers. So he and many like him pieced together careers as preachers, lyceum speakers, writers, editors, and other kinds of cultural workers. Together they mounted a critique of the deepening class divisions in the cities and offered themselves as cultural leaders who could guide the nation out of crisis. They built a broad spectrum of single-issue reform movements, pushing for temperance, prison reform, educational reform, changes in debtor laws, and the abolition of slavery. And, as during all such periods of tumultuous dissent, some began to see that the multitude of abuses they deplored were connected. Orestes Brownson, for instance, writing in his influential *Boston Quarterly Review*, argued that, "The greatest evil of all modern society, in relation to the material order, is the separation of the capitalist from the laborer,—the division of the community into two classes, one of which owns the funds, and the other of which performs the labor, of production." Brownson spoke for a large section of the movement in claiming that social problems of all kinds had a common root in capitalism's sharply unequal distribution of economic, and therefore political, power. He spoke for an even broader section when he remarked that "No one can observe the signs of the times with much care, without perceiving that a crisis as to the relation of wealth and labor is approaching."[9]

New England Transcendentalism, then, was a social movement, a movement of elite radicals who shared common social origins and positions as cultural producers, and who faced a common problem. In an article on Brook Farm, Brownson asks the question that the Transcendentalists all felt compelled to answer:

> The spread of Christian principles, the great doctrines of the unity of the race, human brotherhood, and democratic equality, has enlarged men's hopes, and made quite apparent the glaring disproportion there is everywhere between the actual and the possible condition of mankind . . . . How shall be introduced that equality of moral and physical well-being which is the expression of the equality of all men before God and the State?

Although there were a great diversity of Transcendentalist answers to Brownson's question, all had one feature in common, a conviction that the way to redeem society was to get back in touch with the divinely ordained laws of nature. In Concord, Emerson called on American scholars to prepare themselves for leadership by educating themselves not only through books, but also through action and nature. Thoreau moved to the woods, planted his beans, surveyed the pond, and sat down to write. George Ripley proselytized energetically for the Brook Farm community, where manual labor in nature would rejuvenate those who had been deformed by society's unnatural division of labor. In Boston, Brownson warned that only drastic measures could prevent a bloody working-class rebellion, but he hoped that direct intuition of natural law would provide the basis for unity between the classes. In cooperation with Emerson and Thoreau, Margaret Fuller shaped Transcendentalism's collective voice at the *Dial*. Her own most famous contribution to the journal asks that woman be given room "as a nature to grow" for if this were accomplished "the Divine would ascend into nature to a height unknown in the history of past ages, and nature, thus instructed, would regulate the spheres not only so as to avoid collision, but to bring forth ravishing harmony."[10]

This catalog can only begin to suggest the range of ways in which the term "nature" was deployed within the movement in response to a sharply negative assessment of the contemporary social order with its spirit of commerce, competitive institutions, and moral and spiritual dullness. The dissonance between visions of a just, natural society on one hand, and the stark contradictions of life in New England's growing cities on the other, united elite radicals into a broad movement in which they participated in a wide range of social and ideological experiments. However, just as the black abolitionists of the North, led by Frederick Douglass, must finally be seen as the first cause of the movement that culminated in the Civil War, so the region's radical working-class movement must be seen as the motive force behind Transcendentalism. Once they had been moved, the Transcendentalists' first instinct was to look beyond the often brutal realities of class society into a realm of moralistic abstractions. But they consistently returned to this world, bearing programs—often ill conceived, always heroic—for redemption. Always, these programs were based on a belief in the restorative discipline of nature.

CHAPTER 5

NATHANIEL HAWTHORNE, DEMOCRACY, AND THE MOB

> I agree with you that there is a natural aristocracy among men. The grounds of this are virtue and talents. . . . There is also an artificial aristocracy founded on wealth and birth, without either virtue or talents; for with these it would belong to the first class. The natural aristocracy I consider as the most precious gift of nature for the instruction, the trusts, and government of society.
>
> —Thomas Jefferson

Nathaniel Hawthorne's story "My Kinsman, Major Molineux" records especially clearly ruling-class anxieties about democracy in an urbanizing republic and about the potential importance of the experience of nature.[1] The tale describes the progress of Robin, a rural innocent who travels to Boston for the first time and learns a series of hard lessons about the brutality, selfishness, and cynicism of the modern city. He discovers that the wealthy are more concerned with enforcing the deference of the lower orders than with ensuring their well-being, that poverty is tantamount to criminality, that drunkenness, prostitution, and other crimes are beneath the notice even of the police, and that religion is a cold, empty form. But above all, he learns that democracy amounts to mob violence instigated by demagogues. At the story's end, the country bumpkin sits exhausted on a stoop, lost and baffled by the hostile and sinful world of the city. Down the street comes a mysterious man on horseback leading a huge mob. They have tarred and feathered the boy's missing Tory uncle, Major Molineux, and are now parading him through the streets in shame. Robin stands and stares, and a gale of laughter works its way through the crowd when they witness his surprise.

The story would be an uncomplicated agrarian parable—a kind of *Rasselas* for early national America—were it not for what happens next:

> Robin seemed to hear the voices of the barbers, of the guests of the inn, and of all who had made sport of him that night. The contagion was

spreading among the multitude, when all at once, it seized upon Robin, and he sent forth a shout of laughter that echoed through the street,— every man shook his sides, every man emptied his lungs, but Robin's shout was the loudest there. The cloud-spirits peeped from their silvery islands, as the congregated mirth went roaring up the sky! The Man in the Moon heard the far bellow. "Oho," quoth he, "the old earth is frolicsome to-night!" (M 270)

When this storm of cynicism subsides, the mob moves on, "in counterfeited pomp, in senseless uproar, in frenzied merriment, trampling all on an old man's heart" (M 230). But Robin has changed. He has shed his innocence and the tale ends on a note of resignation. He turns to a kind gentleman who has befriended him and says "rather drily,"

"Thanks to you, and to my other friends, I have at last met my kinsman, and he will scarce desire to see my face again. I begin to grow weary of a town life, sir. Will you show me the way to the ferry?"

"No, my good friend Robin,—not to-night, at least," said the gentleman. "Some few days hence, if you wish it, I will speed you on your journey. Or, if you prefer to remain with us, perhaps, as you are a shrewd youth, you may rise in the world without the help of your kinsman, Major Molineux." (M 231)

The echo of Benjamin Franklin's *Autobiography* in the final sentence drives home the point that only those who remain shrewd and flexible stand a chance of succeeding in a world of such absolute moral corruption and political opportunism.

"Molineux" is often read as a conservative political parable, the kind that might be told by the crassest kind of Hamiltonian. But there are problems with this interpretation. Hawthorne's politics have always been a critical puzzle. As Douglas Anderson remarks, "Concentrated attention upon the political implications of [his work have] produced no consensus on the author's purposes and sympathies. The subversive mingles with the apologist in our accounts of Hawthorne's character, the artist with the place-seeker, the critic with the defender of the status quo." The problem is that there is a sharp disjunction between the patrician attitudes expressed in some of his stories and the democratic convictions seemingly implied by his biography. After all, he wrote a glowing campaign biography of Franklin Pierce, and for much of his working life he occupied positions secured for him by his allies in the Massachusetts Democracy. A central challenge for readers of "Molineux," then, has been to square these facts with the bitterly ironic tone of the story's closing pages.[2]

Hawthorne wrote "Molineux" in late 1828 or early 1829, during and just after the election season in which Andrew Jackson finally defeated John Quincy Adams unequivocally. The tale glosses this watershed event. Jackson's inauguration, on March 4, 1829, has become one of the most frequently cited markers of the transition from the early Republic to the new realities of brawling democratic America. Margaret Bayard Smith, a Washington socialite, described the day this way:

> Thousands and thousands of people, without distinction of rank, collected in an immense mass around the Capitol, silent, orderly, and tranquil, with their eyes fixed on the front of the Capitol, waiting the appearance of the president. . . . After reading his speech, the oath was administered to him by the chief justice. The marshal presented the Bible. The president took it from his hand, pressed his lips to it, laid it reverently down, then bowed again to the people. Yes, to the people in all their majesty. . . .

Smith makes the scene emblematize the basic pieties of early national republicanism, however the utopian tableau does not remain undisturbed for long:

> [At the White House] what a scene did we witness!! The majesty of the people had disappeared, and [we saw] a rabble, a mob scrambling, fighting, romping. . . . The president, after having literally been nearly pressed to death . . . escaped to his lodgings at Gadsby's. Cut glass and bone china to the amount of several thousand dollars had been broken in the struggle to get refreshments. . . . Ladies fainted, men were seen with bloody noses. . . . Ladies and gentlemen only had been expected at this [reception], not the people en masse. But it was the people's day, and the people's president.

So far this is little more than a slapstick episode, with the plantation owner, Jackson, who campaigned as a military hero and man of the people, scurrying to escape their suffocating affection. But Smith then makes an associative leap that would have felt inevitable to many readers:

> God grant the people do not put down all rule and rulers. I fear [for] they have been found in all ages and countries where they get power in their hands, that of all tyrants, they are the most ferocious, cruel, and despotic. The . . . rabble in the president's house brought to my mind descriptions I had read of the mobs in the Tuileries and at Versailles.[3]

Smith embodies an attitude that had become common among the ruling class of the period: support for the abstract political idea of democratic participation combined with a visceral fear of mobocracy. They sincerely approved of leaders who won the respect of common people, but they worried about the danger of demagoguery and were horrified at the prospect of those same people exercising power independently. "Molineux" captures a similarly complex mixture of progressive and conservative positions, though Hawthorne was by no means so serene in his self-contradictions as Smith.

The narrator of "Molineux" establishes the story's theme in the first few sentences while setting the historical stage. The incident occurs in the years after the Massachusetts Bay Colony was reconstituted under a new charter according to which the "the kings of Great Britain had assumed the right of appointing the colonial governors" (M 208). Similarly, in 1824, Congress had assumed the right of appointing John Quincy Adams president, following an election in which Jackson won a plurality of the popular vote, but lost the electoral vote in an episode of transparently corrupt partisan deal making. And throughout the ensuing Adams administration, just as in Hawthorne's colonial Boston, "the people looked with most jealous scrutiny to the exercise of power which did not emanate from themselves . . ." (M 208). The election of 1828 was widely interpreted as a revolt in which the American electorate reasserted its power vis-à-vis Congressional usurpers. Two factual details further cement the analogical connection between the story's imagined political crisis and the national one contemporary with its composition. The narrator notes that there have been six governors in the 40 years prior to the events described in the story. Precisely the same number of years intervened between the signing of the Constitution and the defeat of Adams, the sixth president, by Jackson, who was the seventh. This first paragraph, then, announces that Boston here stands for the United States and that the story will explore the relationship between ruling-class acts of arbitrary power and popular rebellion.

"Molineux" glosses this subject through a series of overdrawn character sketches, lampoonish figures in what amounts to a verbal political cartoon. First, the story centrally features the threatening horseman, whom Robin sees for the first time in a tavern:

> His features were separately striking almost to grotesqueness, and the whole face left a deep impression on the memory. The forehead bulged out into a double prominence, with a vale between; the nose came boldly forth in an irregular curve, and its bridge was of more than a finger's breadth; the eyebrows were deep and shaggy, and the eyes glowed beneath them like fire in a cave. (M 213)

This figure is the famously sharp-featured Jackson. When we first see him, he is represented as a conspirator, "holding whispered conversation with a group of ill-dressed associates" (M 213). We encounter him again on the street when he tells Robin where to wait to see his kinsman pass by. The narrator gives us another description of his face:

> The forehead with its double prominence, the broad hooked nose, the shaggy eyebrows, and fiery eyes were those which [Robin] had noticed at the inn, but the man's complexion had undergone a singular, or, more properly, a twofold change. One side of the face blazed an intense red, while the other was black as midnight, the division line being in the broad bridge of the nose; and a mouth which seemed to extend from ear to ear was black or red, in contrast to the color of the cheek. The effect was as if two individual devils, a fiend of fire and a fiend of darkness, had united themselves to form this infernal visage. (M 220)

Like the participants in another popular rising against arbitrary power, the Boston Tea Party, the man has painted his face to disguise his identity, but the pattern Hawthorne chooses marks him as a diabolical jester, a simultaneously comical and terrifying lord of misrule. We see him one more time, at the head of the mob: "The single horseman, clad in a military dress, and bearing a drawn sword, rode onward as the leader, and, by his fierce and variegated countenance, appeared like war personified; the red of one cheek was an emblem of fire and sword; the blackness of the other betokened the mourning that attends them" (M 227). Jackson's popularity as a candidate had much to do with his reputation, emphasized in campaign portraits of him astride a rampant charger, as a relentless warrior at the Battle of New Orleans and in the Creek and Seminole Wars. From this moment in the story on, the sharp-featured horseman is referred to as "the leader." In context, this epithet amounts to an imputation of demagoguery. And the mob he leads is nothing if not dangerously passionate: "In his train were wild figures in the Indian dress, and many fantastic shapes without a model, giving the whole march a visionary air, as if a dream had broken forth from some feverish brain, and were sweeping visibly through the midnight streets" (M 227–228).

Robin finally sees his kinsman, Major Molineux, who until now has functioned as an absent marker of titled authority. The Major appears "in tar-and-feathery dignity" at the center of the mob: "He was an elderly man, of large and majestic person, and strong, square features, betokening a steady soul; but steady as it was, his enemies had found means to shake it" (M 228). Molineux is Adams, the aristocratic Whig who was infamously cold and reserved in his bearing. Adams was bred for the office by his father, as though it were hereditary, and he staunchly advocated a strong, centralized national executive. Hawthorne forces the reader to commiserate with Adams/Molineux, describing him in language heavily laden with pathos: "His face was pale as death, and far more ghastly; the broad forehead was contracted in his agony, so that his eyebrows formed one grizzled line; his eyes were red and wild, and the foam hung white upon his quivering lip" (M 228). This climactic scene concludes with a middle-distance view in which almost all the characters take their places as in a *tableau vivant*:

> When there was a momentary calm in that tempestuous sea of sound, the leader gave the sign, the procession resumed its march. On they went, like fiends that throng in mockery around some dead potentate, mighty no more, but majestic still in his agony. On they went, in counterfeited pomp, in senseless uproar, in frenzied merriment, trampling all on an old man's heart. (M 230)

The political implications of this scene could not be clearer. The aristocratic remoteness of Adams/Molineux, his absence throughout the story, has opened the town gate to anarchy, to a violent and criminal mob that is the mindless tool of a demagogic agitator.

There is one character who is missing though, Robin, the consciousness who observes all this riot and ruin. He is described elsewhere in strongly positive language, tinged with an ironic awareness of his innocence:

> a youth of barely eighteen years, evidently country-bred, and now, as it should seem, upon his first visit to town. He was clad in a coarse gray coat, well worn, but in excellent repair. . . . Under his left arm was a heavy cudgel formed of an oak sapling, and retaining a part of the hardened root. . . . Brown, curly hair, well-shaped features, and bright, cheerful eyes were nature's gifts, and worth all that art could have done for his adornment. (M 209)

Robin is an agrarian yeoman. And he is an Everyman figure, even an Every-voter—something of which he himself is dimly conscious: " 'The double-faced fellow has his eye upon me,' muttered Robin, with an indefinite but an uncomfortable idea that he was himself to bear a part in the pageantry" (M 228). Robin embodies the basic virtues of the republican citizen: physical strength, alertness, resourcefulness, and self-reliance. But he is also fundamentally naive. Throughout the story, he repeatedly misunderstands urban situations because of his rural innocence and the narrator describes him with a kind of avuncular and satiric tone. For instance, when he admits to having no money at the tavern, the owner accuses him of being a criminal runaway. After escaping, he reflects on the experience:

> "Now, is it not strange," thought Robin, with his usual shrewdness, "is it not strange that the confession of an empty pocket should outweigh the name of my kinsman, Major Molineux? Oh, if I had one of those grinning rascals in the woods, where I and my oak sapling grew up together, I would teach him that my arm is heavy though my purse be light!" (M 215)

This "youth," as he is repeatedly called, is comically naive and, at the same time, he is morally superior to everyone else in Boston. In the story's closing paragraphs, a future of cool-headed leadership is forecast for him.

Robin's characterization, along with those of the devilish horseman, the rampant mob, and the sorrowful Major, records a way of thinking about class relations that had become dominant during the 1830s in the New England ruling class, but especially among its Whiggish upper echelons. The story records a mixture of disillusionment and urgent determination about the realities of electoral democracy. The Democrats had appealed successfully to urban workers by striking populist poses and cynically recycling the logic of Jeffersonian agrarianism. Henry Nash Smith summarizes that logic with a clarity that has not been superseded, showing that it consists of a set of self-reinforcing propositions:

> that agriculture is the only source of real wealth; that every man has a natural right to land; that labor expended in cultivating the earth confers a valid title to it; that the ownership of land, by making the farmer independent, gives him social status and dignity, while constant contact with nature in the course of his labors makes him virtuous and happy; that America offers a unique example of a society embodying these traits; and, as a general inference from all the propositions, that government should be dedicated to the interests of the freehold farmer.

Agrarianism is a way of establishing an ideal form of valuable labor from which other forms may be invidiously distinguished: the office-bound labor of the new bourgeoisie produces wealth indirectly and is morally damaging, whereas manual labor in nature directly produces usable goods and ethical experiences free of the degenerative influence of the market.[4] New England's Whigs struggled throughout the period to catch up. They painted the leaders of Democratic and Worky organizations as unprincipled demagogues preying on the passions of the mob. And they too appropriated Jefferson's idea of a "natural aristocracy," imaginatively casting themselves as country-bred Robins who were morally grounded in the pure soil of the countryside. The selves they grew on their model farms were claims about the naturalness of their own eminence. By the late 1840s, this way of thinking had taken such deep root in New England culture that Thoreau was able to allude to it without explanation in *Walden*. He calls the authors of great books "a natural and irresistible aristocracy" who "more than kings or emperors, exert an influence on mankind," and who admit the "scornful trader" to "circles of intellect and genius" only after he has realized "the vanity and insufficiency of all his riches" (W 103).

Thomas Jefferson's notion of a "natural aristocracy" was certainly already in circulation when Hawthorne was student at Bowdoin. And this may help explain why, together with the rest of the members of his elite radical fraternity, the Athenean Society, Hawthorne supported the agrarian hero, Jackson, against the Adams dynasty in the election of 1824. It may also explain why he evidently repudiated Jackson six years later in "Molineux." In any case, the grounds of those decisions will remain matter for conjecture, since Hawthorne left no programmatic statement of political ideology during the Jackson years. He burned his notebooks and letters from the 1820s, and those from the 1830s are silent on the subject. What we do find in the later notebooks is that he did not think in terms of what we would recognize as political assessments of real people or fictional characters—progressive versus reactionary, Whig versus Democrat. Instead, when he categorizes, he does so according to class: the rotten old aristocrat, on one hand, and the crude plebian, on the other, both opposed to intelligent solitary gentlemen like Molineux and the fatherly old man who befriends Robin. Moreover, his notebooks reveal that he identified himself as a sturdy, country-bred youth. His entries alternate between two types: pastoralizing accounts of leisurely walks in the countryside, and hundreds of plans for stories about the sinfulness of the fallen social world. He captures this Manichean opposition in one short entry: "Man's finest workmanship, the closer you observe it, the more imperfections it shows:—as, in a piece of polished steel, a microscope will discover a rough surface.—Whereas, what may look coarse and rough in nature's workmanship, will show an infinitely minute perfection, the closer you look at it."

Hawthorne was a Democrat, but he came to his democracy as an elite radical, not a working-class republican. In other words, he was not the sort of Democrat who based his political affiliation on a desire for political and social equality that was grounded in the experience of class struggle. In fact, what the dystopian emblem "Molineux" demonstrates is that he was immersed in the main currents of ruling-class thought about the relationships between country-bred redeemers and the working-class denizens of degenerate cities. He believed, not in popular democracy, but in virtuous leaders, gentlemen bred in nature, who he hoped could galvanize the common people and direct their dangerous power in progressive directions. Perhaps the disjunction between the political calculus of "Molineux" and the formal egalitarianism of the Democratic Party accounts for the story's fate. Hawthorne seems have been uncertain about allowing it to circulate. It was published in an annual gift book in 1832, before his public career began. But once he had staked his family's financial well-being on offices bestowed on him by Democratic politicians, he chose not to reprint the tale until 20 years had passed and its immediate context had faded from view.[5]

CHAPTER 6

MARGARET FULLER, ROCK RIVER, AND THE CONDITION OF AMERICA

Those who labor in the earth are the chosen people of God, if ever He had a chosen people, whose breasts He has made his peculiar deposit for substantial and genuine virtue. It is the focus in which he keeps alive that sacred fire which otherwise might escape from the face of the earth. Corruption of morals in the mass of cultivators is a phenomenon of which no age nor nation has furnished an example. It is the mark set on those, who not looking up to heaven, to their own soil and industry, as does the husbandman, for their subsistence, depend for it on the casualties and caprice of customers.

—Thomas Jefferson

If Hawthorne's "Molineux" registers the ideas of the New England ruling class about natural aristocrats and class conflict, Margaret Fuller's *Summer on the Lakes, in 1843* records the desire to imagine another kind of solution to class war. In the spring of 1842, Fuller had turned over the editorship of the *Dial* to Emerson in order to write her ground-breaking manifesto, "The Great Lawsuit, or Man vs. Men, Woman vs. Women." Then, in May 1843, she left for a summer-long tour of the country around the Great Lakes with her friends Sarah Ann and James Freeman Clarke. There, she wrote to Emerson, telling him that her "time was chiefly passed in the neighborhood of a chain of lakes, fine pieces of water, with the wide sloping park-like banks, so common in this country." But while the West generally fulfilled her expectations of conventional picturesque beauty, she was not satisfied, for she also hoped "to see some emigrant with worthy aims, using all his gifts and knowledge to some purpose honorable to the land, instead of lowering themselves to the requisitions of the moment, as so many of them do." If Fuller's letter associates higher motives with an idealized nature that is threatened by low utilitarianism, her narrative of her trip, *Summer on the Lakes, in 1843*, is structured by the tension between a vision of a just society rooted in nature and the bleak reality of America's westward expansion, between an abiding faith in the human potential to live up to the beauty of picturesque landscapes and a clear understanding of the cold social calculus of immediate profit.[1]

Thus, *Summer on the Lakes* presents a strangely contradictory picture of the physical setting of the Western settlements, a picture by turns disparaging and idealizing. Through much of the narrative, the frontier is a ravaged landscape, a place "where the clash of material interests is so noisy" that religion and spirituality are almost forgotten (S 12). The conventional elements of the picturesque have been destroyed by the advance guard of capitalist expansion: "the old landmarks are broken down, and the land, for a season, bears none, except of the rudeness of conquest and the needs of the day, whose bivouac fires blacken the sweetest forest glades" (S 18). Alongside this ecological damage, *Summer on the Lakes* details the social destruction the settlers left in their wake, displacing and impoverishing whole native tribes. More, the text focuses closely on the isolation and alienation, especially of women, bred by the societies the emigrants built. As Annette Kolodny argues, *Summer on the Lakes* offered a corrective to a flood of contemporary promotional tracts that peddled a deceptive "domestic fantasy," depicting the West as a place where "a societal Eden and the individualized home at last became one on a landscape that had always been christened Paradise." Unlike the authors of these tracts, Fuller reported that women were confined to an "exclusively domestic role" even on the frontier, and that their "new home constituted not any flowering garden but only a rude cabin, sometimes without even windows from which to gaze out on the surrounding beauty."[2]

In sharp contrast to such realistic reportage, there are also substantial passages of rhapsodic landscape description, especially those concentrated in Fuller's account of the Rock River country, west of Chicago. This Illinois material is a gauzy vignette inserted into what is elsewhere sharply focused on the harshness of the capitalist frontier. Fuller describes the Rock River country as a restorative retreat the equal of which she feels she may never see:

> Farewell, ye soft and sumptuous solitudes!
> Ye fairy distances, ye lordly woods . . .
> I go,—and if never more may steep
> An eager heart in your enchantments deep,
> Yet ever to itself that heart may say,
> Be not exacting; thou hast lived one day;
> Hast looked on that which matches thy mood . . .
> A tender blessing lingers o'er the scene,

Like some young mother's thought, fond, yet serene,
And through its life new-born our lives have been. (S 42–43)

Given her intense literary activity during the preceding few years, it may seem unsurprising that Fuller experienced a sense of renovation on the prairies and forests of the West. But the Rock River country is more than this. It is a classless society described in the idiom of the picturesque:

> [It] bears the character of a country which has been inhabited by a nation skilled like the English in all the ornamental arts of life, especially in landscape gardening. That the villas and castles seem to have been burnt, the enclosures taken down, but the velvet lawns, the flower gardens, the stately parks, scattered at graceful intervals by the decorous hand of art, the frequent deer, and the peaceful herd of cattle that make the picture of the plain, all suggest more of the masterly mind of man, than the prodigal, but careless, motherly love of nature. (S 27)

This enchanted landscape is markedly empty of both architectural monuments to the Old World ruling class and the hedges that were the main mechanism of early capitalist agricultural rationalization in England. What remains are the stylized pastoral settings of the country estate, settings that were dedicated to leisure activities. In this idealized countryside where both social hierarchies and labor are invisible, Fuller finds what she told Emerson she was looking for: "There was a peculiar charm in coming here, where the choice of location, and the unobtrusive good taste of all the arrangements, showed such intelligent appreciation of the scene, after seeing so many dwellings of the new settlers, which showed plainly that they had no thought beyond satisfying the grossest material wants" (S 29). Here in the Rock River country, Fuller and her friends felt "free to imagine themselves in Elysium [and] the three days passed here were days of unalloyed, spotless happiness" (S 29).

Again, Fuller's concentrated utopian vision contrasts quite sharply with what is otherwise a self-consciously skeptical travel narrative, one in which she promises to avoid the hyperbole of so many of her contemporaries, promises not to "confound ugliness with beauty, discord with harmony, and laud and be contented with all I meet, when it conflicts with my best desires and tastes" (S 18). One influential explanation of this anomaly is Annette Kolodny's assertion that the Illinois chapter represents an "adult reversion to childhood raptures." It offers "less an impression of physical topography than an immersion in the fantasies that topography seemed to invite." Kolodny points to Fuller's relationship with her father and argues that the chapter records her unwitting resolution of childhood emotional trauma. Timothy Fuller was a prominent Massachusetts lawyer and politician, who gave his daughter a famously rigorous education, delivered with perhaps too stern discipline; he had her reciting Latin to him nightly at the age of six. According to an autobiographical fragment, she considered the best hours of her childhood those in which she retreated to her mother's garden, where it was possible to relax and play at will, if only for a time. Kolodny concludes that, in Illinois, Fuller was able to relive her childhood dream of rural retreat: "what Fuller was able to repossess on the parklike and flowered prairies of the middle west was her unmediated pleasure in 'the dear little garden' remembered from childhood." In other words, despite her professions of balance and fairness, Fuller "*wanted* to see settlement without despoliation." The Rock River country came close and "because she was so eager to recapture the garden of her childhood . . . the habitually tough-minded Fuller allowed herself to overlook contradictions and inconsistencies" that would have destroyed her fantasy.[3]

Such an interpretation requires us to believe that although she was writing her book in the Harvard College library, constantly reminded by cold stares that she was the first woman allowed the privilege to enter there, the "habitually tough-minded" Fuller suffered a lapse of writerly self-consciousness. Also, that lapse lasted just long enough for her to produce an internally consistent chapter that contrasts unmistakably with the rest of her book. Such a reading surrenders to the kind of logic that drove Perry Miller to dismiss *Summer on the Lakes* as an "intolerable monstrosity" and Orestes Brownson to the deliver the exaggerated condemnation of his 1844 review: "Her writings . . . are sent out in a slipshod style, and have a certain toss of the head about them which offends us. Miss Fuller seems to us to be wholly deficient in a pure, correct taste, and especially in that tidiness we always look for in woman." In the end, to interpret Fuller's apparent incongruities as lapses of intellectual self-control is to recycle the kind of thinking that had kept women out of libraries like the one she homesteaded, that motivated Emerson and his co-conspirators to bowdlerize her memoirs, and that kept *Summer on the Lakes* unavailable except in expurgated versions for more than a century.[4]

Now if we assume that there was nothing slipshod at all about Fuller's work, why did she single out the Rock River country for description as a scene of such beauty and promise? James Freeman Clarke suggests in an 1844 review that Fuller "has done wisely in not making a guide book, which . . . would have become useless in another year; she has not given us a volume of maps, but a portfolio of sketches, some in outline, some filled out and carefully finished." More recently, Stephen Adams argues that *Summer on the Lakes* mobilizes the Romantic convention of the fragment in which the protagonist narrates a "dramatic, explorative literature of process." *Summer on the Lakes*, he maintains, is a narrative of disappointed hopes, of "great potential that will never be fulfilled" in which "occasional glimpses of an ideal emerge—hints of harmonious junction in the national, social, and personal spheres." But throughout "the potential union of human and divine is frustrated, just as the western settlers fail to realize their heaven on earth because of their materialism and failure to fulfill the potential of women."[5] Fuller herself writes that "the poet must describe, as the painter sketches Irish peasant girls and Danish fishwives, adding the beauty and leaving out the dirt" (S 18). She believes that it is her duty, at least once during the course of her narrative, to see the pure, ideal world behind the grubby, material one.

The idea that Fuller's portrait of the Rock River country offers an heuristic glimpse of an ideal can be combined with Kolodny's observation that Fuller "recognized in the fertile and well-watered grasslands a potential economic refuge from the hard scrabble farms of her native New England, where sons fled to the cities or the frontier to seek a livelihood and daughters left home for fourteen-hour days and slave wages in the proliferating textile mills and shoe factories."[6] As we have seen, the rapid development of capitalism in New England in the decades of Fuller's youth had changed the region from an agrarian colony into a thriving center of industrial production, sharply intensifying both the rural poverty and the urban exploitation that Kolodny suggests were in the back of Fuller's mind. This total transformation of her home is the key to understanding *Summer's* apparent contradictions. Fuller weighs the West as a potential alternative to Boston. In so doing, she both faces up to the disappointing reality of the frontier and systematically employs the vocabulary of the picturesque to envision a society that transcends the utilitarianism of America as a whole.

Now, as she contemplated New England's probable future from the perspective of the West, Fuller had clearly in mind the bad example of England. On the first of June, she was at Niagara Falls, and she wrote to Emerson about the book she had been reading there, Thomas Carlyle's *Past and Present*. Carlyle was by now famous for asking the "Condition-of-England Question" in *Chartism*, his 1840 assessment of social progress under capitalism. In this book Carlyle had suggested that the fantastically productive textile mills of England's industrial cities were as sublime as the most famous of American natural scenes:

Hast thou heard, with sound ears, the awakening of a Manchester, on Monday morning, at half-past five by the clock; the rushing off of its thousand mills, like the boom of an Atlantic tide, ten-thousand times ten-thousand spools and spindles all set humming there,—it is perhaps if thou knew it well, sublime as a Niagara, or more so.

There was more to justify the energy of this rhetoric than the awful infinitude of interchangeable parts and workers, for "cotton-spinning is the clothing of the naked in its result [and] the triumph of man over matter in its means." However, Carlyle also recognized a threat to his vision of the technological sublime, a threat that was the real subject of *Chartism*. The vast increases in productivity made possible by capitalist industrialization had been matched by shocking concentrations of pollution and poverty. Nevertheless, he insists, this is not necessarily so: "Soot and despair are not the essence of [Manchester]; they are divisible from it,—at this hour, are they not crying fiercely to be divided?" The book Fuller was reading, *Past and Present*, which Emerson had just arranged to have published in the United States, extends *Chartism's* diagnosis of "the bitter discontent of the Working Classes" and prescribes an authoritarian cure for the condition of England.[7] Carlyle begins by maintaining that:

> England is full of wealth, of multifarious produce, supply for human want in every kind; yet England is dying of inanition. With unabated bounty the land of England blooms and grows; waving with yellow harvests; thick-studded with workshops, industrial implements, with fifteen millions of workers . . . and behold, some baleful fiat as of Enchantment has gone forth, saying, "Touch it not, ye workers . . . no man of you shall be the better for it; this is enchanted fruit!"[8]

In other words, England is suffering one of the inevitable crises of capitalism, a crisis of overproduction brought on by the competition between individual capitals. Driving down wages in order to maintain profit margins, capitalism has impoverished the vast majority of workers and thus has created both economic stagnation and political unrest. As a solution to this crisis, Carlyle holds up a twelfth-century cleric, Abbot Samson of St. Edmundsbury: a model leader who overcomes social instability through hard-nosed practicality and determination.

Fuller, like many others in New England, valued Carlyle's sharp analysis of the class tensions in Old England's capitalist social order, but she was not so enthusiastic about the solutions he offered. In her letter to Emerson, she writes:

> There is no valuable doctrine in [Carlyle's] book. . . . His proposed measures say nothing. Educate the people. That cannot be done by books, or

voluntary effort, under these paralyzing circumstances. Emigration! According to his own estimate of the increases of population, relief that way can have very slight effect. He ends as he began; as he did in Chartism. Everything is very bad. You are fools and hypocrites, or you would make it better.

Beneath her sarcastic dismissal there is nevertheless a silent and grave recognition of the developmental parallel between England and America. For New Englanders, there was an inevitable extension of "the Condition-of-England question." Phyllis Cole identifies it especially clearly with special reference to Emerson:

> Witnessing the mechanized landscape of industrial England, the limited mental scope of the people who dwelt within it, and their largely unsuccessful attempts to alleviate the suffering that the social machinery had produced, Emerson realized how delimiting and in the end blighting modern society could be. . . . "Birminghamization" became universalized as "Fate" [and] was not finally limited to England; it became a part of Emerson's vision of America as well.

By 1843, then, Fuller and many others had begun to wonder whether the northern United States was traveling England's path into the industrial future. Orestes Brownson, for instance, in his review of *Chartism*, had already asked this question: "Our economical systems are virtually those of England; our passions, our views, and feelings are similar; and what is to prevent the reproduction of the same state of things in relation to our laboring population which gangrenes English society?" If industrialization necessarily produced urban misery, what was the future of America? Could the young republic modernize without generating the same kind of class war that was shaking England so deeply? *Summer on the Lakes*, then, with its contrast between real and ideal frontiers, is Fuller's response to the Condition-of-America question.[9]

By way of prologue, the book's first chapter describes Fuller's eight-day visit to Niagara Falls. The chapter operates as a parable about real and ideal, or utilitarian and aestheticist, ways of seeing nature. Upon arriving at the Falls, she finds that her appreciation of the scene is blocked by the mediation of reproduced images and the touristic conventions that governed such encounters: "When I first came here I felt nothing but a quiet satisfaction. I found that the drawings, the panorama, &c. had given me a clear notion of the position and proportions of all objects here; I knew where to look for everything, and everything looked as I thought it would" (S 4). She captures the flatness of this moment by comparing herself to "a little cowboy" she once saw looking at "one of the finest sunsets that ever enriched this world" and saying gruffly "that sun looks well enough." In order to uncover a satisfying meaning in the prospect of the Falls, Fuller experiments with various customary modes of perception:

> All great expression which, on a superficial survey, seems so easy as well as so simple, furnishes after a while, to the faithful observer its own standard by which to appreciate it. Daily these proportions widened and towered more and more upon my sight, and I got at last a proper foreground for these sublime distances. Before coming away I think I really saw the full wonder of the scene. After awhile it so drew me into itself as to inspire an undefined dread, such as I never knew before, such as may be felt when death is about to usher us into a new existence. (S 4)

After abandoning the picturesque, with its painterly conventions of "position and proportions," Fuller, here, tries the alternative tradition of the Burkean sublime, in which natural scenes trigger intense emotional responses (S 4). Finally, on "Table Rock, close to the great fall" she experiences a fulfilling moment of sublime immediacy: there "all power of observing details, all separate consciousness, was quite lost" (S 5). In order to come to grips with the scene, then, she must experiment with alternative modes of interpreting it. She must take her time and get to know it intimately before she is rewarded with an experience of compressed, intense aesthesis.

Just when she has at last discovered a satisfying perspective on the falls, she is interrupted in the rudest way possible. A "man came to take his first look. He walked close up to the fall, and, after looking at it a moment, with an air as if thinking how he could best appropriate it to his own use, he spat into it" (S 5). This interruption, she writes, "seemed worthy of an age whose love of *utility* is such that [it would be no surprise to see] men coming to put the bodies of their dead parents in the fields to fertilize them . . ." (S 5). The spitter's rushed, homogenizing way of seeing is directly linked to what he sees: a nature whose sole purpose is appropriation for personal profit; his crude realism and his utilitarianism are two sides of the same coin. Disgusted, Fuller tries to drown out the image of this utilitarian by losing herself again in an awe-inspiring whirlpool at the base of the falls. There, the "river cannot look more imperturbable [and seems] to whisper mysteries the thundering voice above could not proclaim . . ." (5). She even goes so far as to imagine an appropriate death for the spitter, noting that "whatever has been swallowed by the cataract, is likely to rise to sudden light here, whether an uprooted tree, or body of man or bird" (S 5). Her reaction is so strong because she has come to Niagara Falls precisely to escape a New England ruled by utility, by the spirit of commerce. Now, that spirit has followed her, confronting her at a long-awaited moment of self-transcendence in the face of the premier icon of the American sublime. Her disappointment is so sharp that, in the end, she can do no more than voice a forlorn hope that such events may not "be seen on the historic page to be truly the age or truly the America" (S 5).

The remainder of Fuller's journey is a search for an alternative to the country for which the spitter stands. Throughout, the process of learning to see nature on its own terms remains central to her imagination of that alternative. As she travels west from Niagara, she sees reminders of the spitter everywhere she looks. On the boat to Chicago, she hears "immigrants who were to be the fathers of a new race, all, from the old man down to the little girl, talking not of what they should do, but of what they should get in the new scene" (S 12). Buffalo and Chicago seem to be mere shipping depots full of "business people" (S 19). She complains of the "mushroom growth" of the West, observing that "where 'go ahead' is the only motto, the village cannot grow into the gentle proportions that successive lives, and the gradations of experience involuntarily give . . ." (S 18). The settlers are given over entirely to "habits of calculation"—habits that make emigration seem to offer "a prospect, not of the unfolding of nobler energies, but of more ease, and larger accumulation" (S 12).

In reaction to this utilitarianism, Fuller attempts to see the beauty in the prairie near Chicago as she did at Niagara. But this requires a more complex act of perceptual manipulation than locating her body close to noise and mist. "At first, the prairie seemed to speak of the very desolation of dullness. . . . It is always thus with the new form of life; we must learn to look at it by its own standard" (S 22). She finally engages successfully with the prairies by traveling through them in a fashion that was at the limits of permissible exposure for a single woman of the Boston elite. She goes camping with a male guide, deliberately courting the feeling of being lost in the wilderness:

> We set forth in a strong wagon, almost as large, and with the look of those used elsewhere for transporting caravans of wild beasts, loaded with every thing we might want, in case nobody would give it to us—for buying and selling were no longer to be counted on—with a pair of strong horses, able and willing to force their way through mud holes and amid stumps, and a guide equally admirable as marshal and companion, who knew by heart the country and its history, both natural and artificial, and whose

clear hunter's eye needed neither road nor goal to guide it to all the spots where beauty best loves to dwell. (S 23)

Fuller represents this land where "buying and selling were no longer to be counted on" as Eden before the fall, as a place where nature "did not say, Fight or starve; nor even, work or cease to exist; but merely showing that the apple was a finer fruit than the wild crab, gave both room to grow in the garden" (S 38). In this land of natural plenty, there is neither commerce nor property: "there was neither wall nor road in Eden [and] those who walked there lost and found their way just as we did" (S 40). Though she is traveling through the American imperial frontier at the moment of its most breakneck settlement and development, she sees the land as a poet, adding the beauty and leaving out the dirt. She makes believe she is lost in order to experience nature's sublimity and blind herself to ever-present reminders of the degraded world she has left behind.

This pattern of initial disappointment and poetizing response is repeated during Fuller's approach to Rock River through another stretch of prairie. Again she attempts "to woo the mighty meaning of the scene" by using perspectival experiments to clear the foundation for a more optimistic response (S 18). She begins by attempting to see the immense prairies as sublime in their monotony, but in the end finds that they are no more than infinitely dull. After a time, though she begins "to love because I began to know the scene, and shrank no longer from 'the encircling vastness' " (S 21). Then, at the town of Geneva on the Fox River, she takes further encouragement from a group of "generous, intelligent, discreet" settlers, who seem to be "seeking to win from life its true values." They seem "like points of light among the swarms of settlers, whose aims are sordid, whose habits thoughtless and slovenly" (S 23). Next, she comes upon an English gentleman's home in the forest: "This habitation of man seemed like a nest in the grass, so thoroughly were the buildings and all the objects of human care harmonized with what was natural. The tall trees bent and whispered all around, as if to hail with sheltering love the men who had come to dwell among them" (S 24). At this gentleman's home, high thinking combines with careful attention to the specific character of a given spot in the material world to produce a harmonious mutualism between humans and nature. A few paragraphs later, Fuller follows through on the hint that this relationship can be both admonitory and sustaining: at "Ross's grove . . . the trees . . . were large enough to form with their clear stems pillars for grand cathedral aisles. There was space enough for crimson light to stream through upon the floor of water which the shower had left. As we slowly plashed through, I thought I was never in a better place for vespers" (S 25). Nature in Illinois is immanently divine.

When she finally arrives at Rock River, Fuller gives an idealized picture of the kind of community that might be built by people working together in harmony with a divine nature. She begins with a visit to the "large and commodious dwelling" of an "Irish gentleman," where she establishes a series of complex distinctions between those who can and cannot make such adjustments. This Old World aristocrat is sensitive enough to fit his dwelling into "the natural architecture of the country," whereas the vast majority of settlers build slovenly "little brown houses" (S 29). However, both aristocrats and commoners occupy land that once belonged to others: "Seeing the traces of the Indians, who chose the most beautiful sites for their dwellings, and whose habits do not break in on that aspect of nature under which they were born, we feel as if they were the rightful lords of a beauty they forbore to deform" (S 29). The rights of these natural aristocrats have been forcibly extinguished by the democratic mass of philistinish settlers whose "progress is Gothic, not Roman, and [whose] mode of cultivation will, in the course of twenty, perhaps ten, years, obliterate the natural expression of the country. . . . This is inevitable, fatal; we must not complain, but look forward to a good result" (S 29). Just as inevitable, by implication, is the disappearance of such antiquated gentlemen as the builder of this estate on the frontier. This passage could be read as a no more than a formulaic Whiggish eulogy—a lament for history's erasure of both natural and cultivated nobility. But the distinction between Gothic and Roman modes complicates the initial class interpretation of imperial conquest, layering it with a new distinction between the violence of invading barbaric hordes and the orderly settlement of republican citizens. In other words, Fuller imaginatively reassigns the ability to see nature properly, formerly the province of natives and aristocrats to the citizens of a potentially ideal republic.

After doing so, Fuller sketches a portrait of the seedbed of this imagined alternative republic, beginning with a paean to the area's auspicious natural beauty:

Here swelled the river in its boldest course, interspersed by halcyon isles on which nature had lavished all her prodigality in tree, vine, and flower, banked by noble bluffs, three hundred feet high, their sharp ridges as exquisitely definite as the edge of a shell; their summits adorned with those same beautiful trees, and with buttresses of rich rock. . . . Lofty natural mounds rose amidst the rest, with the same lovely and sweeping outline, showing everywhere the plastic power of water,—water, mother of beauty, which by its sweet and eager flow, had left such lineaments as human genius never dreamt of. . . . (S 32)

In this natural cathedral, there are still many traces of a native village whose location had been "chosen with the finest taste." Surveying the site, Fuller grieves for the vanished natives as noble predecessors to whose "Greek splendor" their Roman conquerors should turn for guidance. With the help of this implied claim about cultural continuity through imitation, she concludes that she has "never felt so happy" that she "was born in America" (S 33). At first this seems to be a jarring kind of patriotism, but it quickly becomes clear that she is alluding wryly to the stale profundities of Americanism in order to point out the disparity between the ideal and the real. Thus, she maintains a serious tone describing her uncle,—a model citizen who has built "a double log cabin," that is, "the model of a Western villa" (S 36). But when she at last joins "the free and independent citizens" of the town of Oregon for a celebration of Independence Day, Fuller becomes sardonic, even arch. The evening begins with speeches, composed mainly of "the usual puffs of Ameriky." These are followed "by a plentiful dinner, provided by and for the Sovereign People, to which Hail Columbia served as grace" (S 37). This musty celebration marks the distance between the actual West and the possible utopian republic she envisions germinating there.[10]

Nevertheless, the republic of Rock River is still germinal, so Fuller returns to cataloguing harbingers of its future. Just as important as nature's beauty is its material productivity. First, harmonious inhabitation itself is made possible by the land's fertility and abundance; here one "need not painfully economise and manage how he may use [all his land]; he can afford to leave some of it wild, and to carry out his plans without obliterating those of nature" (S 37–38). But also, the fertility of this region promises to close the class divide by allowing all settlers access to the independence and leisure that make true citizenship possible. Here, "with a very little money, a ducal estate may be purchased, and by a very little more, and moderate labor, a family be maintained upon it with raiment, food and shelter" (S 37). More, fertility pacifies the domestic quarrels that lead to divisive and destructive factions; here "a man need not take a small slice from the landscape, and fence it in from the obtrusions of an uncongenial neighbor" (S 37). Finally, individual happiness based on material plenty makes possible a redeemed social order: "A pleasant society is formed of the families who live along the banks of this stream upon farms. They are from various parts of the world, and have much to communicate to one another. Many have cultivated minds and refined manners, all a varied experience, while they have in common the interests of a new country and a new life" (S 38). If Carlyle's Manchester was an alleyway of soot and despair where the vast majority of workers went hungry in sight of the palaces of the rich, then Fuller's future America is a picturesque garden inhabited by an organic community of equals supporting themselves by their own labor on the fertile floodplains of the Rock River country.

Despite its speculative optimism, Fuller's Rock River is no mere agrarian idyll. She remains acutely aware that things will likely not go the way she hopes and she brings her account of Illinois to a close by restating the book's central tension between envisioned and actual worlds: "Illinois is, at present, a by-word of reproach among the nations, for the careless, prodigal course, by which, in early youth, she has endangered her honor. But you cannot look about you there without seeing that there are resources abundant to retrieve, and soon to retrieve, far greater errors, if they are only directed with wisdom" (S 65). Abundant land provides the material conditions for the growth of a new kind of society. But that is all. Although there "was a large proportion of intelligence, activity, and kind feeling" among the people of Illinois, there was not "much serious laying to heart of the true purposes of life" (S 65). Reading *Summer on the Lakes*, then, as a speculative answer to the Future-of-America question resolves the apparent contradiction of Fuller's enthusiastic response to the Rock River country. Rather than a lapse into nostalgic reverie, this episode uses the idiom of the picturesque to envision an organic utopia, an alternative to the steady expansion of capitalism.

Fuller's journey through the West forced her to confront the oppressive reality of America's developing social order and it started a process of rapid and decisive radicalization. Over the next few years she would evolve, in Margaret Allen's words, from a "political innocent to dedicated activist." She would revise "The Great Lawsuit" into *Woman in the Nineteenth Century*, America's first book-length public argument in favor of equal rights for women. Then she would produce the acute political analysis of the *Tribune* letters. Finally, she would become a revolutionary, operating a field hospital during the Siege of Rome. We can only speculate about who she would have become had she survived her journey home to America, but it seems more than likely that she would have ended up playing an important role in the abolition movement and the second American Revolution that began in 1861.[11]

CHAPTER 7

WILLIAM WORDSWORTH IN NEW ENGLAND AND THE DISCIPLINE OF NATURE

Owing to their historical position, it became the vocation of the aristocracies of France and England to write pamphlets against modern bourgeois society. . . . In this way arose Feudal Socialism: half lamentation, half lampoon; half an echo of the past, half menace of the future; at times, by its bitter, witty and incisive criticism, striking the bourgeoisie to the very heart's core, but always ludicrous in its effect, through total incapacity to comprehend the march of modern history.

—Karl Marx and Frederick Engels

One writer above all taught Margaret Fuller and other elite radicals about the ways of feeling about nature and class most suited to a natural aristocracy, William Wordsworth. During the first three decades of the nineteenth century, his books had sold slowly in the United States. An 1824 reviewer, F.W.P. Greenwood, of the first American edition of the poems had been able to write:

If we have unworthily neglected this original and admirable poet, we have but followed the example of our countrymen. . . . With the exception of the Lyrical Ballads, which were printed many years ago, if we remember rightly at Philadelphia . . . not a single work of Wordsworth has been republished in this country. We have republished . . . Byron to his last scrap. Hogg, Rogers, Brown, Milman, Montgomery, Bernard Barton, Barry Cornwall, Leigh Hunt, and a host of more minors, have . . . been spread abroad throughout our land; but he, who has done more than any living writer to restore to poetry the language of feeling, nature, and truth, remains unread, unsought for, and almost unknown.

The small edition under review sold somewhat more steadily than its predecessors had. More importantly though, Joel Pace has shown that the modest distribution of Wordsworth's books was supplemented by "the hundreds of times that passages from *The Excursion* were reprinted in Unitarian anthologies and the thousands of times Wordsworth's verse appeared in magazines, journals, papers, and miscellanies." His poems also consistently found their way into classrooms: "American reprints of one school reader containing Wordsworth, Lindley Murray's The English Reader, sold through thousands and thousands of copies." Also, an anthology, *The American First Class Book*, edited by the Unitarian John Pierpont was, according to law, issued to every schoolchild in Massachusetts. . . ." Perhaps the clearest indicator of his influence is that, as Karen Karbiener is discovering, the magazines of the period were full of unabashed imitations produced by dozens of genteel versifiers, including "American Lakers" such as Nathaniel Parker Willis, Richard Henry Dana, William Henry Channing, and James Percival.[1]

Wordsworth received an especially warm welcome at Harvard, where young intellectuals studying for the ministry had begun looking for an alternative to "corpse-cold" Unitarianism. Charles Mayo Ellis, in an 1842 manifesto titled *Transcendentalism*, captures the spirit of this rebellion against rational religion:

> The results of the two systems may show their comparative merits. The old deriving all ideas from sensation, leads to atheism, to a religion which is but self-interest—an ethical code which makes right synonymous with indulgence of appetite, justice one with expediency, and reduces our love of what is good, beautiful, true and divine, to habit, association or interest. The new asserts the continual presence of God in all his works, spirit as well as matter; makes religion the natural impulse of every breast; the moral law, God's voice in every heart, independent on interest, expediency, or appetite, which enables us to resist these; an universal, eternal, standard of truth, beauty, goodness, holiness, to which every man can turn and follow, if he will.

Despite the emphasis here on intuitive apprehension of spiritual truth, intellectual experimentation in this insecure provincial college town still centered on consumption of a carefully selected range of British literary texts. Thoreau speaks of how Harvard students worked through two curricula: official course work and the "more valuable education" to be had by "associating with the most cultivated of his contemporaries" (W 50). James Freeman Clarke describes the period this way: "While our English professors were teaching us out of Blair's 'Rhetoric,' we were forming our taste by making copious extracts from Sir Thomas Browne, or Ben Jonson. Our real professors of rhetoric were Charles Lamb and Coleridge, Walter Scott and Wordsworth." Elizabeth Palmer Peabody, who later ran the

Transcendentalist library and bookstore on West Street in Boston, wrote to Wordsworth in 1829: "You can never know what a deep and even wide enthusiasm your poetry has awakened here."[2]

In 1835, after a decade of growing interest in Wordsworth, James Munroe, the Boston publisher who would bring out Emerson's *Nature* the following year, published *Yarrow Revisited and Other Poems.* The book met with a small storm of praise from reviewers for American magazines. Two years later, James Kay of Philadelphia published *The Complete Poetical Works of William Wordsworth, together with a Description of the Country of the Lakes in the North of England,* which was widely reprinted throughout the century and was among the first American critical editions of any poet. It was edited by Henry Reed, Professor of English at the University of Pennsylvania, who argued that the Poet of Nature's genius was to "spiritualize humanity." Reviewers greeted the book as a national triumph: "It is, what it professes to be, a complete edition of his poetical works, such as might be sought for in vain in his own country. . . . The publishers may challenge for themselves a full portion of praise, for having sent forth a book which confers credit on the American press."[3]

By 1840, Emerson was able to declare in "Thoughts on Modern Literature," that "the fame of Wordsworth is a leading fact in modern literature." He went on, though, to say that, "more than any other poet his success has not been his own, but that of the idea which he shared with his coevals, and which he has rarely succeeded in adequately expressing." The "idea" in question is a complex of attitudes that Emerson glosses in his next few sentences: "The Excursion awakened in every lover of nature the right feeling. We saw the stars shine, we felt the awe of the mountains, we heard the rustle of the wind in the grass, and knew again the ineffable secret of solitude. It was a great joy. It was nearer to nature than anything we had before." For the New England Transcendentalists, Wordsworth was above all the Prophet of Nature. Christopher Pearse Cranch, a young member of the Transcendentalist Club, assessed the poet's importance in a retrospective piece on his career:

> One of his deepest beliefs was in the beneficent ministry of nature to the soul of man. . . . Nature is for him never dully and densely material, but radiant and glowing with spiritual meanings. . . . What an antidote was his sanative poetry to the morbid Byronism and Werterism that enervated the youths and maidens of the early years of this nineteenth century! Honor to the seer . . . whose laborious hands gave such help in draining off the stagnant scum of the malarial waters which infected those days!

That Cranch's rhetoric should remain so elevated half a century later gives some indication of the fervor with which the Transcendentalists consumed Wordsworth's works in the 1830s.[4]

Now since Percy Bysshe Shelley so forcefully claimed that when Wordsworth became the "Poet of Nature," he abandoned his duties as the Prophet of Democracy, it has been difficult to see that many of his readers felt that these two roles were cognate.[5] In fact, many of New England's elite radicals in the 1830s felt that the turn to nature was a turn *toward* the people. For these readers, Wordsworth's rustic persona—the Bard of Rydal Mount—embodied an especially "sanative" version of the democratic impulse. With his help, they transformed early national America's fields of enlightened political experimentation into meadows of Romantic self-discovery.

Emerson's Journal provides a sketch of this history. His library included a copy of the 1824 Boston *Poetical Works*. And it was not long after this book's appearance that he began to quote and allude to its contents from time to time. He also began to mention Wordsworth in his obsessive lists of important contemporaries. But his comments on Wordsworth remain relatively sparse and hesitant, until after the appearance of Munroe's 1835 edition of *Yarrow Revisited and Other Poems*, which he also owned, and probably bought and read on its publication. Following his encounter with this text, his tone shifts. In July of that year, he wrote that "some divine savage like Webster, Wordsworth, & Reed whom neither the town nor the college ever made shall say that [which] we shall all believe. How we thirst for a natural thinker." This passage is diagnostic, focusing as it does on the persona rather than the poetry, and emphasizing Wordsworth's rootedness in a nature sacralized as an alternative to both the crass amorality of the urban elite and the dry scholasticism of college-bred clergy. Emerson records his first extended appreciation of the poet in May 1836: "It is strange how simple a thing it is to be a great man, so simple that almost all fail by overdoing. There is nothing vulgar in Wordsworth's idea of Man." Again, the focus is on the persona, on Wordsworth the great man, the genius, whose greatness inheres in the plainness, the naturalness, and by implication, the apparent democracy of his sentiments. In response to the intense antielitism of the working-class movement, Wordsworth provided a perfect model of the ways of thinking appropriate to elite radicals. As Emerson put it in August 1837, "Wordsworth now act[s] out of England on us. . . ."[6]

Yarrow Revisited was issued as a supplement, meant to satisfy a hungry public between complete editions of the poems. A note in the front matter explains that "the purchasers of his former works, who might wish for these pieces also, would have reason to complain if they could not procure them without being obliged to re-purchase what they already possessed" (Y vii). The contents are a diverse mix of "evening voluntaries," romances like "The Egyptian Maid" and "The Russian Fugitive," and occasional poems. The most unified sections are two sequences of sonnets bound together by implied travel narratives. The first of these sequences, "Poems Composed during a Tour in Scotland, and on the English Border, in the Autumn of 1831," opens with the ballad, "Yarrow Revisited." Wordsworth remarks that the ballad's title "will stand in no need of explanation, for Readers acquainted with the Author's previous poems suggested by that celebrated stream" (Y 3). This is the third of three separately published poems commemorating visits to the river of that name. The other two are "Yarrow Unvisited," composed in 1803, and "Yarrow Visited, September, 1814." Read together, the three form a parable of maturation: "the Morn of youth / with freaks of graceful folly" gives way to "Life's temperate Noon," and "her sober Eve" (Y 4). This intertextual parable announces that the Yarrow travel sequence as a whole, will embody the experience and wisdom of achieved eminence. Making sure no one misses this point, Wordsworth explains that "the following stanzas are a memorial of a day passed with Sir Walter Scott, and other Friends visiting the Banks of the Yarrow under his guidance, immediately before his departure from Abbotsford, for Naples" (Y 3). We soon find that

> Grave thoughts ruled wide on that sweet day
> Their dignity installing
> In gentle bosoms, while sere leaves
> Were on the bough, or falling. (Y 4)

Given such portentous beginnings, what follows seems oddly slight. "Yarrow Revisited" is a gracious leave-taking, making Scott's immanent departure for the Mediterranean to restore his failing health into an occasion for conventional sentiments on the redeeming eternity of Nature and the Muse. The poem makes a virtue of the claim that

> No public and no private care
> The freeborn mind enthralling,
> We made a day of happy hours,
> Our happy days recalling. (Y 4)

The rest of the sequence is similarly bare of the gravid public pronouncements for which Wordsworth was so esteemed and hated during his career as laureate. Instead, we read a loosely connected series of solemn effusions on rural scenes, ruined mansions, highland huts, ancient trees, Roman antiquities, worn monuments, and brownies. The poems seem to aspire no higher than the placid assurance that Christopher Pearse Cranch felt was the most central claim of Wordsworth's poetry: "all is somehow and somewhere for the best."[7]

One way to give context to the Yarrow sequence is to point out that while Wordsworth was pacing Yarrow's banks with Scott in "the autumn of 1831," the House of Lords was rejecting the Reform Law. Widespread unrest surrounding this decision culminated in the Bristol Riots on October 29–31. Supporters of wider franchise wrecked Mansion House and set Bishop's Palace on fire. Troops and cavalry attacked demonstrators, killing many, and in the following weeks four dissidents were executed and 22 deported. A familiar way of interpreting the poetry in light of these facts would note Wordsworth's incongruous observation, in the concluding "Apology":

> Every day brought with it tidings new
> Of rash change, ominous for the public weal. (Y 32)

On this basis it would be possible to argue that this sequence of poems represents another example of the Wordsworthian strategy of displacement, that characteristic way of evading deeply significant political events and social realities, taking refuge instead in the cheap comforts of the romantic ideology of natural supernaturalism. But, as Nicholas Roe has demonstrated, "Romantic Nature could never serve as an escape from 'the ruins of history' precisely because of its implication in the ruinous processes of revolutionary change and betrayal." Wordsworth would not have alluded to these events unless he felt that there was something to be gained from meditating on the coincidence. And he would not have earned reviews as deeply respectful as those published by Cranch, Emerson, and Greenwood unless they felt that he offered valuable answers to deeply important questions. There are clues in the poems to a definite politics based on a theory of the poet's social and political function in a natural republic.[8]

The Yarrow sequence might seem to be an insubstantial foundation on which to build a new social estate. But the sequence both asks for, and received, serious consideration as political argument. Does Wordsworth, then, offer an alternative to the leveling of Mansion House and to the Tory thuggery that followed? A hint comes in the concluding "Apology":

> No more: the end is sudden and abrupt,
> Abrupt—as without preconceived design
> Was the beginning. . . . (Y 31)

These poems are not, then, a sequence structured around a narrative or argument:

> The several Lays,
> Have moved in order, to each other bound
> By a continuous and acknowledged tie,
> Though unapparent, like those shapes distinct
> That yet survive ensculptured on the walls
> Of Palace, or of Temple, 'mid the wreck
> Of famed Persepolis; each following each,
> As might beseem a stately embassy,
> In set array; these bearing in their hands
> Ensign of civil power, weapon of war,
> Or gift, to be presented to the Throne
> Of the Great King; and others as they go
> In priestly vest, with holy offerings charged,
> Or leading victims drest for sacrifice. (Y 31)

These lines guide our experience of a heterogeneous cast of characters. In "At Tyndrum," we meet Scotland's "hardy Mountaineer," who unlike the garlanded shepherds of polite Arcadian pastoral,

> will cross a brook
> Swoln with chill rains, nor ever cast a look
> This way or that, or give it even a thought. (Y 18)

Similarly, "The Brownie" tells of an old clansman whose independence was so fierce and proud that he retired to a hut to live out his last years "with no one near save the omnipresent God" (Y 22). And in "On the Sight of a Manse in the South of Scotland," a good gardening priest

> Who faithful through all hours
> To his high charge, and truly serving God,
> Has yet a heart and hand for flowers,
> Enjoys the walks his Predecessors trod,
> Nor covets lineal rights in lands and towers. (Y 11)

Finally, "Countess's Pillar," memorializes Anne Countess Dowager of Pembroke, who in 1656, erected a monument to her mother and left an annuity of four pounds "to be distributed to the poor of the parish of Brougham, every 2d day of April for ever":

> While the poor gather round, till the end of time
> May this bright flower of Charity display
> Its bloom, unfolding at the appointed day. (Y 29)

Like the figures of the ancient Persian officers, functionaries, priests, and sacrificial victims on the wall at Persepolis, these figures are defined not by their individuality, but by their representativeness, by their exemplary performance of the functions that define the positions they hold in a definite social hierarchy. The Yarrow sequence, then, does not spin a tale nor does it expound an explicit argument; rather, it displays emblematic portraits of the various stations in life that together form a coherent social order. These figures compose an "embassy" of subjects to a "King," carrying out the rituals of mutual indebtedness and obeisance that maintain peace and stability. This romanticized feudal order, the residuum of which Wordsworth claims to have found in the border country, is the proper subject of the Yarrow sequence.

Wordsworth goes further to make nature itself embody the character of this idealized social estate. The reader is invited to see the border country through the eyes of its inhabitants, who learn *from it* the simple virtues on which they pride themselves, and who memorialize their simultaneously economic and pedagogical relationship with the land by naming "yon towering peaks, 'The Shepherds of Glen Etive' " (Y 17). Likewise, "The Avon," emblematizes modesty, "contented, though unknown to Fame" (Y 26). The planet Venus is a sign of aristocratic benevolence:

> Holy as princely, who that looks on thee
> Touching, as now, in thy humility
> The mountain borders of this seat of care,
> Can question that thy countenance is bright,
> Celestial Power, as much with love as light? (Y 23)

A rest station for weary travelers "at the Head of Glencroe" allegorizes the "absolute stillness" that "faith bestows," allowing the soul to "win rest, and ease, and peace" (Y 20). The just peace of this republic depends on the piety and humanity that the mountainous country breeds in the people, bidding them, even, to "love, as Nature loves, the lonely Poor" who are

> Meek, patient, kind, and, were [their] trials fewer,
> Belike less happy.—Stand no more aloof! (Y 21)

In Wordsworth's organic utopia, the concrete oppressions and privations of class society have been erased by an abstract parallelism of duties, trials, and rewards, and by an emphasis on the moral and spiritual richness of the exchanges that occur within its complex networks of social power.

The poems, though, are distinctly elegiac, for the reader is being asked, like a tourist at Persepolis, to contemplate the beauties of a decidedly past order. This pastness is marked by such monuments as "The Earl of Breadalbane's Ruined Mansion and Family Burial-Place, Near Killin" (Y 19). And by "The forest huge of ancient Caledon" where

> The feudal warrior-chief, a ghost unlaid,
> Haunts still his Castle, though a Skeleton,
> That he may watch by night, and lessons con
> Of Power that perishes, and Rights that fade. (Y 27)

Paradoxically, this spectacle of impermanence, and the knowledge that "life is but a tale of morning grass, / Withered at eve" (Y 13), serve simultaneously to "chasten fancies that presume / Too high," *and* to deliver a lesson on the potential contemporary value of lost virtues. Contemplating "Roman Antiquities," the rural poet realizes that if

> of the world's flatteries the brain be full,
> To have no seat for thought were better doom. (Y 30)

In other words, overly ambitious dreams of personal triumph or social perfection can lead only to disappointment or disaster. A more just and humane social estate will come not through conscious striving, but when people, rich and poor, learn from nature, when the nation reads the rural landscape of the border country and cultivates the modesty, decency, and fairness recorded there. The poet's duty, then, is to rediscover the virtues of the rural utopia that once graced these mountains and then model them for the modern nation.

This was Wordsworth's answer to both the working-class radicalism and the Tory repression that industrialization had brought to England— and that had appeared on the horizon of modernizing New England. He sent forth an embassy of sonnets, appealing to his readers to learn from the example of a rural society whose fairness and stability depended on its people's hardiness, independence, modesty, generosity, devoutness, and, above all, on their pious dedication to the duties of their station. *Yarrow Revisited* maps that idealized past, offering it as a schematic diagram of the benign social order that will result should the discipline of nature take wide hold.[9]

Now if demagoguery seemed an immanent threat to New England's elite radicals, the Wordsworth of *Yarrow Revisited* offered a possible line of defense. Early nineteenth-century readers were steeped in the notion, formed in the Protestant practice of Bible-study, that reading was a deeply uncertain process of self-education, of citizen building. The potential for misconstruction was great, as were the dangers of exposure to vicious texts, especially for women who were increasingly responsible for spiritual and moral education. Poetry, with its mysterious power of sound, threatened to overcome the reason and judgment of vulnerable readers. Adding to these fears was the complex Romantic redefinition, against the more temperate ideas of the eighteenth century, of the poet as a genius, as an inspired figure who spoke for and to an essential national consciousness. Literary texts were read, then, not as isolated aesthetic objects, but as the civic utterances of figures whose public histories were well known and much debated, and whose private lives were matters of fervid curiosity.

For instance, "D.L." published a defense of Shelley in Cincinnati's *The Western Messenger* for March 1837, arguing that his "Spirit of Nature" bears a far closer resemblance to the God of the New Testament than does the thundering Jehovah of Calvinist religious verse. The review opens, not with interpretation or evaluation of a poem, but by stating that

> Among Shelley's moral characteristics, may be numbered an intense sensibility, that seems wonderful, when considered in connection with his great power of intellect. His face, with its singular expression of sensitiveness and thought, shews this characteristic. . . . Shelley was an unbeliever. For this, we mourn, and must condemn him for not making better use of his power and intellect. . . .

The bulk of this article consists of two opposed long quotations, one from Shelley, the other from Robert Pollok, a pious Scotch Calvinist poet. There is no textual analysis; the reader is simply asked which is "most Christian." D.L. ends by saying "we had rather be damned with Percy Bysshe Shelley, than go to Heaven with John Calvin and Robert Pollok. Their Heaven must indeed be a hell to one, who feels a single thrill of love for universal man, or feels a single spark of the divinity stirring within." Shelley is being evaluated here, not as a creator of verses, but as a public intellectual. His habits of religious and political thought are being weighed as model civic acts, as a potentially representative way of life. The embodiment of these habits in poetry implied the possibility of their widespread adoption by impressionable readers, and this, in turn, bore on the health of the republics made up of those readers. [10]

Likewise, the story of Wordsworth's retirement to the Lake Country, and of his subsequent devotion to the pursuits of country life—this was the central focus of contemporary assessments of the poet and his works. But most American reviewers in the 1830s and early 1840s told that tale differently than has been usual recently. For instance, Henry Theodore Tuckerman argued that:

> In an intellectual history of our age, the bard of Rydal Mount must occupy a prominent place. . . . The mere facts of his life will preserve his memory. It will not be forgotten that one among the men of acknowledged genius in England, during a period of great political excitement should voluntarily remain secluded amid the mountains . . . from time to time sending forth his effusions, as uncolored by the poetic taste of the time, as statues from a quarry.

This is not the now familiar story of malfeasance, of neglecting the duties of revolutionary struggle. Rather, Wordsworth was represented as working for the same end by different means. First, his choice of subjects was regarded as a kind of democratic radicalism in its own right. Tuckerman asks, "A waggoner, a beggar, a potter, a pedlar, are the characters of whose feelings and experience he sings. . . . Who shall say that through such portraits . . . a more vivid sense of human brotherhood . . . has not been extensively awakened?"[11]

But Wordsworth's way of directing his readers' attention to the plight of the poor was only a small part of the political errand he was seen as pursuing. Above all, reviewers admired him for helping to form the minds and hearts of a model republican citizenry by means of the example of his life, of which the poems were a distillation. According to an anonymous reviewer, during the long years of his neglect

> the poet was silently working a revolution in the taste and literature of the age. . . . The poetry of passion and of sense was gradually giving way before that of thought and sentiment. Piety, benevolence, love, patriotism; all the purer and nobler sentiments of the heart . . . were silently triumphing over the cravings of unholy passions. . . . This happy revolution, in letters and in taste, was chiefly effected, we repeat, by the simple, solitary, soul-trusting Wordsworth, who, from his shrine among the mountains, sent forth strains of aerial music, which, long-neglected, have at length found an echo in the hearts of thousands.

Although the word "revolution" can strike today's reader as exaggerated, it makes sense in context. The survival of the experimental republic seemed to depend on whether the (white, male, propertied) citizenry could resist unholy passions—both their own tendencies to luxury and vice *and* the anger of the mob. This anxiety was rooted in a reading of the French

Revolution as a decline into destructive radicalism and violence: in France, the "philosophers and philanthropists, who had given the first impulse to the movement, were soon rudely pushed aside by unprincipled dema-gogues and sanguinary fanatics, who turned their fair land into a vast slaughter-house; one revolting scene of hideous saturnalia." It was not that liberty had led to license, rather, centuries of monarchic despotism had degraded the people, rendering them "emancipated slaves unfit for those blessings to which man is as much entitled as to the air he breathes."[12]

For the postrevolutionary ruling class, the main line of defense had been the "reason" they enshrined in their neoclassical estates. But for their radical offspring, Wordsworth modeled a new principle of civic peace, democratic sympathy:

> A hermit among the mountains, attaching himself to no party, and asking no favors from power . . . he has never deserted the cause of freedom and of man. On the contrary, everything that he has written . . . expresses that high and enduring sense of the innate and essential dignity of man, which must ever be the chief foundation and support of republican institutions. . . .

It was precisely his lifelong association with nature that guaranteed Wordsworth's ability to feel "the purer and nobler sentiments of the heart" together with the common people. Because of this ability, he "is emphatically a poet of liberty, not by passionate invocations to popular enthusiasm, but by calm and beautiful appeals to those manly qualities, those chastening virtues and noble sentiments, which are perhaps more often found in the cottage than in the halls of opulence." This Wordsworth, the poet of natural democracy, demonstrated how to lead without resorting to demagoguery, how to control the lawless passions of the mob with republican feelings.[13]

Finally, what is most remarkable about this ideological constellation is the firmness of the association between nature and healthy political sen-timents: "All which is worthy man's attainment can be and is realized in far higher perfection amid the genial influences of rural life, than in the hot and unquiet atmosphere of the crowded city. . . ." The Wordsworth who had grown up under these influences was revered by "the young" of New England as a "guide and teacher" because he embraced "his appro-priate duties as a poet" with high seriousness. What were these duties? First among them was the responsibility to use nature to teach sympathy:

> Man has been clothed with sympathies such as were fitted to bind him to his fellow-man in bonds of love. . . . But the tendency of man is to

degrade himself by sensuality and cunning; to harden himself against all gentleness by a false and foolish pride, or the lying and hollow vanities of social life. . . . In all ages, the true poet awakens man from his brutishness, and excites his kindlier and nobler feelings.[14]

The poet's most reliable method for redeeming people who have become lost in material pursuits is to direct "our eye and our heart to all that is lovely upon earth." He teaches the hardened rationalist "to draw forth from his bosom his most cherished feelings, and to associate them with those objects in nature with which they seem to correspond, thus making those feelings more distinct and permanent." This role is critically important, for people have been imbruted by modernization to such a degree that learning to see correspondences between feelings and nature requires a kind of cultivation only the poet can now provide:

> From his own mind he will spread over all nature associations more various and exciting than any which we could originate; and he will teach us to look on her with feelings like his own. The lofty mountain-top, which awakens in him grander and more elevating emotions than it excites in the minds of the great mass of mankind, he should cause, by the magic of his verse, to become to us all that it is to himself.

Directed observation of nature becomes, then, "a course of self-inspection," even self-adjustment, wherein the subject recovers "those feelings, those unchanging realities, which the given object is fitted to awaken in the bosom of every one who calls himself a man." This restorative contact with the eternities reflected in nature makes possible "a noble and a true generosity" toward "humanity," teaches us to sympathize, and therefore to be democratic.[15]

Wordsworth, who opposed parliamentary reform and poor laws in the 1830s, may seem a strange hero for New England's elite radicals. But many sincerely felt that he offered a viable road to social redemption. Emerson provides an answer to this puzzle in his "Man the Reformer":

> Let our affection flow out to our fellows; it would operate in a day the greatest of all revolutions. It is better to work on institutions by the sun than by the wind. The state must consider the poor man, and all voices must speak for him. Every child that is born must have a just chance for bread. Let the amelioration of our laws of property proceed from the concession of the rich, not from the grasping of the poor. (CW 1.158–1.159)

In the manner of an idealized country gentleman, Wordsworth was felt to combine sincere concern for the poor (what was once called, approvingly, condescension) with properly stern opposition to their self-organized attempts to improve their lot. New England's ruling class had seen their Enlightenment habits of thought come under withering attack: the idea that rational pursuit of the social good prepared one for political eminence had begun to seem unreliable, even dangerous. Now, the Wordsworthian idea that the discipline of nature could form properly republican sentiments allowed the elite radicals of a new generation to begin to reconstruct the grounds of their social and political legitimacy. Emulating his democratic sentimentality allowed them to represent themselves as wearing the mantle of nonviolent evolutionary progress during a period of intensifying class conflict.

CHAPTER 8

WILLIAM WORDSWORTH, HENRY DAVID THOREAU, AND THE POETRY OF NATURE

And one there was, a dreamer born,
Who, with a mission to fulfill,
Had left the Muses' haunts to turn
The crank of an opinion mill,
Making his rustic reed of song
A weapon in the war with wrong,
Yoking his fancy to the breaking-plough,
That beam-deep turned the soil for truth to spring and grow.
—John Greenleaf Whittier

One young New Englander who enthusiastically emulated Wordsworth's persona and poetics was Henry David Thoreau. The central focus of scholarship on the relation between Wordsworth and Thoreau has always been on their habits of thought about the relationship between humans and nature. For decades, debate centered on whether Wordsworth saw Imagination (or Mind or Man) as shaping Nature or vice versa, and on whether Thoreau maintained the same position. But the terms of the debate have shifted with the rise of ecocriticism. Ecocritics give an environmentalist edge to the question by asking whether Wordsworth and Thoreau were anthropocentric or ecocentric. James McKusick provides the culminating statement of this position, arguing that the British Romantics founded a tradition of organicist, localist, ecocentric writing that the New England Transcendentalists cultivated and extended in order to found the American environmental tradition. In any case, it has never been seriously questioned that there are extensive ideological parallels between Wordsworth and Thoreau, and sequence has been taken rightly to imply a strong vector of influence.[1]

The next question then has been this: what was the tone of their relationship: grudging, indifferent, unconscious, reverential? Especially in the context of recent interest in Romanticism as a transatlantic phenomenon, the connection between Wordsworth and Thoreau has come to operate as a central case study, bearing the weight of generalizations about the overall relation between British and American national literatures. Robert Weisbuch argues that Wordsworth's influence was not only strong, but also strongly resented, and that Thoreau had to reject it in order to claim his own voice. This psychologistic reading individualizes what had long been understood as the necessary anxiety of Boston's provincial literary society with respect to London, the English-speaking world's cultural center. More recently, Richard Gravil argues compellingly that retrospective cultural nationalism has led to exaggeration of nineteenth-century intellectuals' desire for literary independence. Gravil shows that Thoreau's writing manifests an "astonishing openness to the living Wordsworth" and that Thoreau's attitude toward the elder poet was one of "profound identification."[2]

Thoreau began to train himself seriously as a poet during the year before his 1837 graduation from Harvard. His most ambitious and compelling project was an intensive study of the history of poetry in English. He consumed two massive anthologies, including Alexander Chalmers's 21-volume collection of the British poets, which he claims in *Walden* to have read through "without skipping" (W 259). Thoreau's zeal was no doubt redoubled by Emerson's address, "The American Scholar," which called on recent graduates to lead a cultural revolution. During the next ten years, Thoreau wrote hundreds of poems and he filled several commonplace books with extracts of poetry. Indeed, it is not too much to say that for first decade of his life as a writer, he thought of himself mainly as a poet. It was likely that he had quite compelling encouragement to think so. Emerson wrote to Thomas Carlyle, telling him, "I have a young poet in this village named Thoreau, who writes the truest verses." In his Journal, Emerson effused that Thoreau's poetry was "the purest strain, the loftiest . . . that has yet pealed from this unpoetic American forest." Years later, in his disappointed eulogy, he went on to claim that Thoreau "wanted a lyric facility and technical skill," but still insist that he "had the source of poetry in his spiritual perception . . ."[3]

During this time, Thoreau's primary model was Wordsworth. His personal library included a copy of the 1837 edition of the *Complete Works*. Wordsworth appears consistently in Thoreau's early essays in literary criticism as a benchmark of poetic excellence. The "Poet of Nature" is always described, either explicitly or implicitly, as one of the most important English writers, though Thoreau's praise is always mixed. For instance, in a passage from the early essay, "Aulus Persius Flaccus," he simultaneously pays homage to Wordsworth and dismisses him in a gesture of youthful bravado: "Homer, and Shakspeare, and Milton, and Marvell, and Wordsworth, are but the rustling of leaves and crackling of twigs in the forest, and not yet the sound of any bird." Of course, the implication is that Thoreau himself will burst into bird-like song at any moment, silencing his rustling, but necessary, forebears.[4]

Like Emerson and the rest of his contemporaries, Thoreau read Wordsworth's poems through the lens of a deep interest in the poet's life and public persona:

> To live to a good old age such as the ancients reached—serene and contented—dignifying the life of man—in these days of confusion and turmoil—That is what Wordsworth has done—Retaining the tastes and the innocence of his youth—There is more wonderful talent—but nothing so cheering and world famous as this.

The center of interest here is the poet's role as a public intellectual, as what Shelley called one of "the unacknowledged legislators of the World."[5] Thoreau often complains, again like Emerson, that Wordsworth's poetry does not match the stature of the public man:

> Wordsworth with very feeble talent has not so great and admirable as persevering genius
> heroism—heroism—is his word—his thing.
> He would realize a brave & adequate human life. & die hopefully at last.

Wordsworth operated on Thoreau, then, not just through the medium of printed matter but above all through the cultural text of his life. His poetic achievement was inseparable from, only one part of, the complete picture of his historical and cultural importance. In the early essay, "Homer Ossian Chaucer," Thoreau specifies the terms of his admiration: Wordsworth embodies "a simple pathos and feminine gentleness." This is not, though, a genteel or trivial emotionalism. Thoreau goes on to stress the radicalism of Wordsworth's preference for "his homely but vigorous Saxon tongue, when it was neglected by the court, and had not yet attained to the dignity of a literature. . . ." In other words, Thoreau valued Wordsworth on the poet's own terms, as expressed in the preface to the *Lyrical Ballads*: he appreciated the democratic implications of the decision to write in "a selection of language really used by men," a decision that reflected a poet's "rational sympathy" for "the great and universal passions of men."[6]

Moreover, Thoreau saw such democratic sentiments as a necessary corollary of a close relationship with nature. This habit of thought is repeated in the early essay, "Thomas Carlyle and His Works," he describes the Scotch intellectual's early moral education. From Carlyle's home in "Annan, on the shore of Selway Frith," Thoreau reports, "you can see Wordsworth's country. Here first [Carlyle] may have become acquainted with Nature, with woods, such as are there, and rivers and brooks . . . and the last lapses of Atlantic billows." After taking the impress of this decidedly natural place, Carlyle produced books that Thoreau describes this way:

> When we remember how these volumes came over to us . . . and what commotion they created in many private breasts, we wonder that the country did not ring from shore to shore . . . with its greeting; and the Boones and Crocketts of the West make haste to hail him, whose wide humanity embraces them too.

Carlyle, like Wordsworth, learned his "wide humanity," his ability to embrace the experience and win the sympathy of proud commoners, from the rugged border country in which he was raised. Moreover, such democratic sympathies are a key measure of natural vigor, as opposed to degeneracy. While making a final comparative assessment, Thoreau states that "Carlyle has not the simple Homeric health of Wordsworth." Carlyle may not measure up entirely, nevertheless, he and Wordsworth occupy one end of a spectrum whose implied other is occupied by the decidedly unnatural figures of Byron the Rake, Shelley the Atheist, DeQuincey the Addict, and so on. During "days of confusion and turmoil," when the health of the body politic was an object of great concern, Wordsworth's "sanative poetry," as Christopher Pearse Cranch put it in a retrospective assessment of the poet's career, offered an "antidote" to "the morbid Byronism and Werterism . . . the stagnant scum of the malarial waters which infected those days!"[7]

Thoreau generalized from this understanding of Wordsworth's cultural significance to develop his initial sense of the social and political functions of poetry and the poet. First, poetry is a vehicle for the weightiest and most urgent human truths: "There is no doubt that the loftiest written wisdom is either rhymed, or in some way musically measured,— is, in form as well as substance, poetry." The ability to create such music is not the reward of study, not the produce of culture: "Yet poetry, though the last and finest result, is a natural fruit. As naturally as the oak bears an acorn, and the vine a gourd, man bears a poem, either spoken or done." It is not just that poetry is the natural language of humanity, but more, that when people produce poetry, nature is working directly and immediately through them: "The poet sings how the blood flows in his veins. He performs the functions, and is so well that he needs such stimulus to sing only as plants to put forth leaves and blossoms. . . . It is as if nature spoke." Just as poetry is the language of nature, it is also definitively wholesome, even hygienic: "Good poetry seems so simple and natural a thing that when we meet it we wonder that all men are not always poets. Poetry is nothing but healthy speech."[8] Not surprisingly, during diseased times the poet must protect himself by maintaining a safe distance: "We are often prompted to speak our thoughts to our neighbors or the single travelers we meet, but poetry is a communication addressed to all mankind, and may therefore as well be written at home and in solitude, as uttered abroad in society." The poet's solitude should not be mistaken for aloofness though. Detachment from particulars allows a more general engagement, a clear focus on matters that the rest of humanity has lost sight of: "Though the speech of the poet goes to the heart of things, yet he is that one especially who speaks civilly to Nature as a second person, and in some sense is the patron of the world." This last phrase, "patron of the world," renders with exquisite accuracy Thoreau's developed sense of the cultural role of the poet in degenerate times. The poet serves as a beacon of natural health and wholesome sentiments in a world diseased by the rising tide of urbanization, industrialization, and class conflict under capitalism.[9]

Thoreau shared his way of thinking about the cultural role of the poet with many in his milieu. In her *Dial* essay, "The Great Lawsuit," Margaret Fuller includes a brief sketch of the figure of Orpheus, a sketch suggested in part by Bronson Alcott's decision to title his famously opaque meditative verses, "Orphic Sayings": Orpheus "understood nature, and made all her forms move to his music. He told her secrets in the form of hymns. . . . Orpheus was, in a high sense, a lover. His soul went forth towards all beings, yet could remain sternly faithful to a chosen type of excellence."[10] Likewise, in his essay, "The Poet," Emerson emphasizes stern idealism: "The poet is the sayer, the namer, and represents beauty. He is a sovereign, and stands on the center. . . . the poet is not any permissive potentate, but is emperor in his own right" (CW 3.5). The aristocratic metaphors here are appropriate since the poet is not just "a music-box of delicate tunes and rhythms" but a cultural authority appropriate to a secular republic, one who would lead the young nation into its millennial political future (CW 3.6). His ability to lead had centrally to do with the use of natural language, for at a time rife with harbingers of mobocracy, the poet could remind the nation that "the world is a temple, whose walls are covered with emblems, pictures, and commandments of the Deity" (CW 3.10). And he could compel obedience by his command of the authentic language of nature: "Nature offers all her creatures to him as a picture-language. . . . Things admit of being used as symbols, because nature is a symbol, in the whole, and in every part" (CW 3.8). The "universality of the symbolic language" (CW 3.10) meant it was especially powerful: "every man is so far a poet as to be susceptible of these enchantments of nature; for all men have the thoughts whereof the universe is the celebration" (CW 3.9).[11] The organic form of the poet's utterances would attest to their authenticity, "for it is not metres, but a metre-making argument, that makes a poem,—a thought so passionate and alive, that, like the spirit of a plant or an animal, it has an architecture of its own, and adorns nature with a new thing" (CW 3.6). Crucially, the poet's formative retreat to nature is described in class terms: "O poet! a new nobility is conferred in groves and pastures, and not in castles, or by the sword-blade any longer" (CW 3.23). This is not just a matter of gentlemanly bearing: "Thou shalt have the whole land for thy park and manor, the sea for thy bath and navigation, without tax and without envy; the woods and the rivers thou shalt own; and thou shalt possess that wherein others are only tenants and boarders. Thou true land-lord! sea-lord! air-lord!" (CW 3.24). The poet—a figure of secular authority, empowered by his command of natural language, which in turn was guaranteed by his spectatorial ownership of the landscape— had the potential to lead the nation out of its interminable crisis, had the potential to provide the kind of leadership that could forestall the degeneration of the young republic into a wilderness of mechanics.

The understanding of poetry and the role of the poet that Thoreau appropriated from Wordsworth provided a base of operations, but it was one from which he increasingly departed as time went on. He produced a remarkably various body of poetry, at first writing reverential imitations, and later experimenting, searching for ways to embody in verse ideas and stances that extended and developed the tradition he had entered. Perhaps his clearest attempts to emulate his predecessor come in poems that, like Wordsworth's great odes, take "a fact out of nature into spirit," mounting extravagant sallies of speculative thought in response to common events or conventional scenes. For instance, the deceptively simple poem, "The Bluebirds," begins with the building of a nest box "in the midst of the poplar that stands by our door." Thoreau lovingly and particularly narrates the arrival of a breeding pair, their mating rituals, nesting, and eventual migration. Only once this preparatory work is complete does he go on to describe a moment of self-transcendence triggered by contemplation of this example of the spectacular perfection of the natural world:

> I dreamed that I was an waking thought—
> A something I hardly knew—
> Not a solid piece, nor an empty nought,
> But a drop of morning dew. (CE 514)

In this kind of romantic lyricism, the premium is on the immaterial, the spiritual revelation or emotional response stimulated by encounters with physical phenomena that are only indistinctly particular. In many poems the stimulus is even left unstated so that we read only the revelation, stripped of its triggering context, as in the following quatrain that Thoreau composed for *A Week on the Concord and Merrimack*:

> True kindness is a pure divine affinity,
> Not founded on human consanguinity.
> It is a spirit, not a blood relation,
> Superior to family and station. (CE 577)

This is a kind of abstract poetry that we are no longer trained to appreciate. However, it has a recoverable coherence, based on the idea that the poet's special ability was to distill the universal from the particular, to harvest the truth from experience, refine it, and deliver it pure. Thoreau explains in *A Week*:

> There are two kinds of writing, both great and rare; one that of genius, or the inspired, the other of intellect and taste, in the intervals of inspiration. The former is above criticism, always correct, giving the law to criticism. It vibrates and pulsates with life forever. It is sacred, and to be read with reverence, as the works of nature are studied.

Thoreau approached the discipline of poetry with the kind of high seriousness reflected here, striving in his early work to achieve just such inspiration, to breathe directly the atmosphere of the ideal.[12]

However, as his poetic decade progressed, his practice began to shift. He moved increasingly in the direction of particularity, isolating and focusing on the moment of generative stimulus. By doing so, he began to develop his own distinctive practice, informed by the idea that the poet should speak directly about his immediate experience to an audience of his actual peers:

> I seek the Present Time,
> No other clime,
> Life in to-day. . . .
> What are deeds done
> Away from home?
> What the best essay
> On the Ruins of Rome? (CE 608)

His initial response to this imperative was to compose loco-descriptive poems. At first, his efforts in this mode were only weakly local: "On Ponkawtasset" and "Assabet" use Eastern Massachusetts place names but operate in the generic space of highly conventional pastoral. On the other hand, poems like "The Old Marlborough Road" sustain a high level of detailed engagement with quite particular places:

> Where they once dug for money,
> But never found any;
> Where sometimes Martial Miles
> Singly files,
> And Elijah Wood,
> I fear for no good;
> No other man
> Save Elisha Dugan,—
> O man of wild habits,
> Partridges and rabbits,
> Who hast no cares
> Only to set snares,
> Who liv'st all alone,
> Close to the bone,
> And where life is sweetest
> Constantly eatest. (CE 626)

Thoreau's emphasis on the specifics of a place and its peculiar inhabitants was at least partially validated by Wordsworth's practice in the many pieces of occasional and travel verse titled simply with dates or place names. Moreover, the choice of subject matter here constituted an extension of Wordsworth's theoretical focus on "incidents and situations from common life," for Thoreau particularized the common: Elisha Dugan is an actual local, not an idealized commoner like "Simon Lee."

Similarly, one of Thoreau's most successful poetic innovations was his attempt to complete Wordsworth's decision to write in the "real language of men"—in this case, real Yankees. Many of the published poems are marked by the kind of elevated diction that was felt to reflect the universality of the ideal:

> Thou dusky spirit of the wood,
> Bird of an ancient brood,
> Flitting thy lonely way,
> A meteor in the summer's day. (CE 579)

But at the same time that he was writing in this vein, he was also experimenting with pithy and local language, attempting to go Wordsworth's language of vagrancy one better, and invent a poetry of extravagancy:

> Conscience is instinct bred in the house,
> Feeling and thinking propagate the sin
> By an unnatural breeding in and in.
> I say, Turn it out doors,
> Into the moors.
> I love a life whose plot is simple,
> And does not thicken with every pimple,
> A soul so sound no sickly conscience binds it,
> That makes the universe no worse than't finds it. (CE 615)

Colloquialisms like "bred in the house" and "turn it out doors" give a familiarity to the diction that is new in Thoreau's writing, and in Romantic poetry generally, as is the decision to abandon iambs for a more spontaneous, unmetered verse. Moreover, Thoreau rounds out the localism of the voice with his comical and deflationary rhyme on "simple," giving real weight and authenticity to the homely philosophy of the final couplet. This decision to recreate New England vernacular speech reaches its peak in verse that never saw print in Thoreau's lifetime, much of which has only quite recently become available. At its best, Thoreau's poetry in this mode is vibrantly alive:

> I have seen some frozenfaced Connecticut
> Or Down east man in his crack coaster
> With tort sail, with folded arms standing
> Beside his galley with his dog & man
> While his cock crowed aboard, scud thro the surf
> By some fast anchored Staten island farm,
> But just outside the vast and stirring line
> Where the astonished Dutchman digs his clams
> Or but half ploughs his cabbage garden plot

> With unbroken steeds & ropy harness—
> And some squat bantam whom the shore wind drownd
> Feebly responded there for all reply,
> While the triumphant Yankee's farm swept by. (CE 614)

Not only is this resolutely anchored in the physical specifics of New England, but also the clotted, spondaic rhythms combine with the insistent alliteration and the arresting vernacular to produce a poetry that is quite new and powerful. Had Thoreau produced a large and consistent body of work in this mode, he might well be ranked with Walt Whitman and Emily Dickinson as one of the inaugurators of modern American poetry.

Part of what drove Thoreau to innovate was the pressure of historical events on his working model of poetry: there was an inherent conflict between the urgency of the period's social and political debates and the genteel lyricism apparently required by the genre. Early on, Thoreau had attempted to address political questions, but was unable to break free of a kind of contemplative abstraction:

> In the busy streets, domains of trade,
> Man is a surly porter, or a vain and hectoring bully,
> Who can claim no nearer kindredship with me
> Than brotherhood by law. (CE 517)

The depression of 1837–1844, the movement to abolish slavery, Polk's invasion of Mexico—all these demanded passionate and particular response. And Thoreau responded, writing several poems that directly addressed the most urgent questions of the mid-1840s. His earlier efforts are often quite conventional, as in this address to the people of the North, which draws a parallel between southern chattel slavery and the slavery to convention and money of the North:

> Wait not till slaves pronounce the word
>   To set the captive free,
> Be free yourselves, be not deferred,
>   And farewell slavery. (CE 577)

At a time when the abolition movement had become an immovable fact of daily life, this poem is so uniformly abstract that it is quite possible to forget that it makes an argument against slavery. It is almost as though Romantic metaphoricity caricatures itself here: Thoreau deliteralizes, dematerializes the brutal oppression of millions, using it to figure the rather less urgent bondage of his fellow townspeople. More successful is

Thoreau's meditation on the woman question, a poem that enacts the kind of essentialist beliefs that were typical even of the feminists within his milieu:

> Ive seen ye, sisters, on the mountain side
> When your green mantles fluttered in the wind
> Ive seen your foot-prints on the lake's smooth shore
> Lesser than man's, a more ethereal trace,
> Ive heard of ye as some far-famed race—
> Daughters of god whom I should one day meet—
> Or mothers I might say of all our race. (CE 604)

Still, this remains cast in elevated and artificial language that almost lampoons the spirituality it ascribes to its implied female audience. It was not until Thoreau deployed the vernacular, that his political verse became truly compelling. For instance, in his Journal for November 28, 1850, he transcribed the following Blakean monologue:

> I am the little Irish boy
> That lives in the shanty
> I am four years old today
> And shall soon be one and twenty
> I shall grow up and be a great man
> And shovel all day
> As hard as I can[,]
>
> Down in the deep cut
> Where the men lived
> Who made the Rail road. (CE 631)

The absolute simplicity of Thoreau's language gives real power to this sketch of the stark poverty afflicting hundreds of thousands of Irish immigrants. Overall, then, Thoreau's poems became increasingly forceful as he followed through on the implications of his mentor's ideas about how to write poetry. He did so in fact more consistently than Wordsworth himself, abandoning accentual-syllabic meter and closed verse forms for more flexible, organic structures, and focusing his work directly on the vocabulary and experience of Concord's common inhabitants, rather than limiting that material to the subordinate function of stimulating conventional idealisms.

There is no shortage of speculation about why Thoreau shifted his attention from poetry to prose in the mid-1840s. The most practical reason is that once the *Dial* folded in 1844, he was left without a venue for his poems. But it has been usual, even among the most dedicated admirers of his verse, to intuit a narrative of failure. Emerson started this tale in motion with his assessment that Thoreau's "verses are often rude and defective. The gold does not yet run pure, is drossy and crude. The thyme and marjoram are not yet honey. But if he want lyric fineness and technical merits, if he have not the poetic temperament, he never lacks the causal thought, showing that his genius was better than his talent." Arthur L. Ford follows suit, maintaining that Thoreau failed to "become Emerson's poet [because] he lacked the courage to throw off all conventions and create a new expression." And Elizabeth Hall Witherell makes this final assessment: "In aspiring to write poetry Thoreau set higher standards than he could reach in that medium: his efforts survive as relics of the apprenticeship of a master of poetic prose."[13] As Witherell suggests, it is an open question whether Thoreau did in fact abandon the medium. Certainly the rhythms and melodies of the prose bear witness to his lifelong dedication to the music of language. One widely quoted quatrain suggests an alternative reading of this speculative tale:

> Each more melodious note I hear
> Brings this reproach to me,
> That I alone afford the ear,
> Who would the music be. (CE 530)

In other words, it is not that Thoreau was unable to compose regular verse and so dropped the genre, but rather he recognized that the essence of poetry was not accentual-syllabic meter and regular form. As he puts it in *A Week*: "My life has been the poem I would have writ, / But I could not both live and utter it."[14] Does Thoreau mean here that he was unable to maintain simultaneously the poet's heightened receptivity to experience and the discipline of poetic composition? Probably not. After all he never quit writing intensively composed material; he just quit writing formal verse. Instead, Thoreau may have meant to record his recognition that the poet's stance of speaking in an inspired voice is more culturally important than meter or rhyme. Indeed, the narrative persona he adopts throughout *Walden* corresponds closely to his exalted notion of the poet as a great man. He establishes himself as one whose total immersion in nature authorizes an admonitory relationship, based on democratic sympathies, to a degenerate society badly in need of liberation from debilitating conventions. Moreover, these changes in his writerly practice mirrored the overall direction of his intellectual development during the 1840s: he moved away from Emersonian idealism, toward increasingly particular engagement with the material world. So the larger truth must certainly be that he turned to prose because to do so was the culmination of the trends that had developed in his poetic experimentation, to do so allowed him to directly engage the particular natural and social landscape before him, in language wrought into organic structures rich in local music.

In fact, Thoreau refreshed his connection to his old mentor at a critical time during the composition of his most unmistakably poetic piece of prose. He acquired a copy of the *Prelude* not long after it was published in 1850. And although we cannot fix the date that he read it absolutely, his Journal suggests that he did so sometime in late 1851: the volume for August 1851 through April 1852 is littered with references to Wordsworth, poets, and poetry. Then, energized by this new encounter, Thoreau began the most intensive period of rewriting *Walden*. From early 1852 to 1854, he amplified the manuscript's account of his retreat into nature, with its central critique of alienation under capitalism and added a much more particular account of his life at the pond.[15] Finally, he added the "Conclusion," in which he speaks in the voice of a "patron of the world," a poet rooted in nature who can see "the character of that morrow which mere lapse of time can never make to dawn" (W 333). The rewritten book recapitulates the structure of a Wordsworthian lyric poem, building from a recollected experience to a crescendo of wisdom. Above all, that wisdom and the voice that speaks it remain deeply rooted in the particulars of an actual place. In other words, were it not for Thoreau's apprenticeship to Wordsworth, rather than becoming one of the nineteenth century's most powerful long poems, *Walden* might well have remained the story of a field of beans.

CHAPTER 9

RALPH WALDO EMERSON, ORESTES BROWNSON, AND TRANSCENDENTALISM

A young man, named Ralph Waldo Emerson, a son of my once loved friend William Emerson, and a classmate of my lamented son George, after failing in the every-day avocations of a Unitarian preacher and schoolmaster, starts a new doctrine of transcendentalism, declares all the old revelations superannuated and worn-out, and announces the approach of new revelations and prophecies. Garrison and the non-resistant abolitionists, Brownson and the Marat Democrats, phrenology and animal magnetism, all come in, furnishing each some plausible rascality as an ingredient for the bubbling cauldron of religion and politics.

—John Quincy Adams

Enthusiasm for Wordsworth was not universal. More than one reviewer used the appearance of *Yarrow* as an opportunity to wonder whether there was anything authentically democratic about the poet at all:

> At the time when [Wordsworth] came forward . . . to offer his productions, the world was storming with passion. Political strife was consuming and overwhelming everything. . . . Our poet, as if from another state of being, and like a bird, singing above a field of battle, published verses with such unpropitious titles as "Goody Blake and Harry Gill," "The Female Vagrant," [and] "The Thorn." . . . How could the world regard, but with disgust, a man who, while war was raging abroad, and revolutionary excitement at home, could nestle in the chimney corner and listen to the singing of a tea-kettle.

There was more to this counter-narrative than the familiar complaint about lost leaders. Perhaps the most ideologically explicit critique of Wordsworth's politics of natural democracy came from Orestes Brownson.[1]

Brownson watched silently the outpouring of praise that followed Munroe's publication of *Yarrow* and the *Works*. When it had begun to subside, in April 1839, he decided "to offer some considerations on the merits of William Wordsworth as a poet," noting that "our brethren of the reviewing tribe seem to have conspired to elevate [him] to the throne of English Poesy, and we are in danger of suffering decapitation if we do not go with them, and pretty sure of being hung as traitors to the legitimate sovereign if we do." After mock-defiantly declaring his allegiance to "the old dynasty," Brownson turns this ironic political metaphorizing inside out with a long disquisition on the question "who is a true poet."[2] He argues that the "many approve only that which is common to human nature, which is general, adapted to the race. To say of a poet that he is unpopular, is about the same as to say that he is no poet at all." Poetry is "that branch of Art, which seeks to express in words the revelations of God made to the soul by the spontaneous reason." The bedrock of such revelation was conviction in the inherent dignity of all people—a conviction that, for him, led directly to radically democratic political conclusions. Thus, the established line of succession in poetry that Brownson sets out to defend against the usurper, Wordsworth, is that which runs from Milton the revolutionary to Byron the republican martyr. The true poet "kindles the souls of all who listen to his inspired chant, and makes them burn as he burns." For Brownson, such poets burned to push forward the divinely ordained triumph of democracy over all forms of aristocratic privilege and oppression. "Genius is essentially democratic; his voice is always music to the democracy, and only they who love not the democracy, or have a private end to gain, ever dream of stifling his voice."[3]

From these premises, Brownson argues that it "is evident from their great want of popularity" that Wordsworth's "works do not deserve the highest poetical rank." The enthusiasm for Wordsworth, he implies, has been limited to a small circle of counterrevolutionists who have attempted to overthrow legitimately democratic poetic tastes. The problem is that Wordsworth has disengaged himself from truly natural relations with the ordinary people and places he writes about: "His selection of subjects from humble life always appeared to us a sort of condescension on his part, for which no democrat need thank him." In attempting to speak the "life-imparting" word of the divine in all people, he must stoop, and "the voice he utters is the voice of William Wordsworth, not the voice of God."[4] Thus, when he "aims to be simple and natural . . . he becomes silly." And his "nature is bald and naked. Notwithstanding his spiritual philosophy, he does not spiritualize nature. He leaves it cold and material, uninviting and uninspiring." His pretensions to the legitimacy of democratic sentiments will never be more than pretensions, for he "has begun by framing a system, by constructing a philosophy—such as it is—and then he has sought to poetize it. This is an inversion of the order of nature, and it renders Wordsworth the most unnatural of poets."[5]

Having elaborated this highly politicized theory of poetic evaluation and applied it to Wordsworth, Brownson now turns to explaining why, given recent political history, Wordsworth's admirers should have made such a mistake:

> With the present century commenced a reaction against the stirring and revolutionary spirit of the last. . . . Disappointed in its hopes for social progress, saddened and disheartened by the failure of so many projects for advancing man's earthly weal, the soul at the commencement of the present century turned away from active pursuits, came to the conclusion that the only cure for the ills of life is to bear them, and therefore that the passive virtues are most Godlike. To the soul in this state Wordsworth is doubtless an acceptable poet.

Brownson interpreted the political events of the 1830s, to which much of his elite audience reacted with such unease, as manifestations of divine plans for human emancipation on earth. Working-class radicalism was a continuation of the human struggle for liberty and equality: "Life is a warfare, and demands perpetual battle,—a warfare in which there is much undoubtedly to be borne, but in which there is still more to be done." For Brownson, the eventual triumph of democracy was inevitable and the Whig elite's defensive attempt to learn, with nature's help, to sympathize with the people was a gesture, at best, of half-hearted support. At worst it was cynical posturing. Above all, to remain disconnected, at such a time, from full immersion in the people's divinely ordained forward movement, was an act of small-minded complacency, even of historical treason.[6]

Brownson continues, announcing that he has "little faith in Wordsworth's democracy," and describing the poet in terms that echo his assessment of the political tendencies of many of his readers:

> He is a kind-hearted man, that would hurt no living thing, and who shudders to see a single human being suffer. So far, so good. But he has no faith in anything like social equality. He compassionates the poor, and would give the beggar an "awmous"; but measures . . . which would place the means of comfortable subsistence in the hands of all men, so that there should be no poor, he apparently contemplates not without horror. . . . He would lead us to love all men, but always in the condition in which we find them.

For Brownson, Wordsworth and his admirers in New England had developed not democratic sentiments, but aristocratic sentimentality—a sentimentality that allowed them to play at a complacent and self-aggrandizing philanthropy, without seriously confronting the implications of the republican rhetoric they mouthed:

> They, who have outgrown the material, the soulless philosophy of the last century, and turned their minds inward to find a more spiritual and living philosophy, seem to themselves to find in Wordsworth a congenial soul. . . . Wearied with the pomp of kings and artificial strut of kinglets, too often and for too long a time the theme of the poet's chant, they have joyed to meet a brother who has an eye for the unpretending objects of nature, and a heart to sympathize with the humble and unobtrusive emotions of ordinary and every-day life.

Among the symptoms of this frivolity was the anti-Jacobinism that remained an article of unquestioned orthodoxy. Brownson uses the concluding paragraph of his article to lay down a challenge that simultaneously sums up his feelings about the weakness of the politics of the Wordsworthian natural republic:

> We are aware that the French Revolution is a bugbear to many; but we dare be known among those who see in it a great, though terrible, effort of Humanity to gain possession of those rights which Christianity had taught her to regard as her inalienable patrimony . . . and we can own no man as a friend . . . who sided [as did Wordsworth] with those who took up arms against it. . . . That Revolution needs no apology. . . . Its excesses will be forgotten much sooner than . . . the murders, the soul-destroying tyrannies, of kings and aristocracies.

This was not an argument Brownson was destined to win, at least with those to whom he addressed it. Within a year, he had been abandoned to his radicalism by the Boston elite, including its radicals. In the end, their rejection amounted to a bitter confirmation that he was right in his assessment of their politics of natural democracy.[7]

Brownson has been written out of the history of the period. But he was a founding member of the philosophical club that has since come to be seen as a starting point for the movement. Emerson called it "The Symposium" when it met for the first time in Boston just after the 1836 appearance of his little book, *Nature*. As we have seen Transcendentalism tends to be defined as a movement united by the Kantian epistemological ideas expressed there. But such a definition excludes figures who very definitely thought of themselves as sharing what were widely called the

"New Views." This phrase comes from the title of another little book published in 1836, Brownson's *New Views of Christianity, Society, and the Church*. The truth is that throughout the 1830s, Brownson was one of the elite's most acute internal critics and rivaled Emerson for leadership of the movement overall. After all, many New England ministers had come to hope that their liberal faith, Unitarianism, could be made to dampen the growing fires of class antagonism, and Brownson's Society for Christian Union and Progress, a congregation built on the principles outlined in his book, was the spotlight experiment of their theory.[8]

Part of Unitarianism's initial appeal had been its unabashed faith in the virtuousness of worldly success. However, many began to argue that this spirit of commerce had gotten out of hand. They directed their critique of utilitarianism both against those among the ruling class who had abandoned a sense of social duty, and against workers who they saw as motivated increasingly by envy and pride. The elder William Ellery Channing was the "bishop" of this forward-looking "new school" of Unitarians. He universalized the faith's emphasis on human perfectibility, arguing that "true religion consists in proposing as our greatest end, a growing likeness to the Supreme Being." This "likeness to God . . . has its foundation in the original and essential capacities of the mind." Moreover, "as we approach and resemble the mind of God, we are brought into harmony with the creation [which] is a birth and shining forth of the Divine Mind, a work through which his spirit breathes."[9] Channing won a wide following among urban sections of the ruling class with his confident and optimistic refutation of orthodox Congregationalism's emphasis on the inherent depravity of human nature in a fallen world. This was especially true as he developed the idea of likeness to God into the foundation of his doctrine of self-culture. Channing observed that there "is a spreading conviction that man was made for a higher purpose than to be a beast of burden, or a creature of sense. The divinity is stirring within the human breast, and demanding a culture and a liberty worthy of the child of God." He regarded this awakening spirit of aspiration as the best hope for the future, since he saw poverty as evidence of spiritual torpor. And he offered religious and intellectual self-improvement as a program of action for the working class, arguing that the truly valuable things in life were available to all: "Thought, intelligence, is the dignity of a man, and no man is rising but in proportion as he is learning to think clearly and forcibly, or directing the energy of his mind to the acquisition of truth. Every man, in whatsoever condition, is to be a student."[10]

Channing's ideas were enthusiastically taken up by a broad spectrum of the elite, by ministers, writers, editors, teachers, and others who organized ministries to the poor, and from this base, built campaigns for free education, prison reform, peace, and temperance, and instituted a range of benevolent societies and charities. After all, his sermons were quite progressive compared to Orthodox calls for bloody repression of strikes and demonstrations. But it is also true that his emphasis on self-culture was quite specifically meant to outflank the threat of independent working class action. He maintained that "there is nothing cruel in the necessity which sentences the multitude of men to eat, dress, and lodge plainly, especially where the sentence is executed so mildly as in this country." And he was quick to reassure his audiences that what he called "the elevation of the labouring portion of the community" was specifically "not an outward change of condition. It is not release from labour. It is not struggling for another rank. It is not political power. I understand something deeper. I know but one elevation of a human being, and that is elevation of soul."[11]

A section of Channing's disciples, generalizing from their experience with skeptical and intelligent working-class congregations, rejected his patrician notions of purely spiritual elevation, while extending his ideas about the rhetorical power of plain-style preaching and the importance of "personal religion." George Ripley, Theodore Parker, William Henry Channing, and Orestes Brownson, all urban-based ministers who were subsequently to form the radical wing of Transcendentalism, transformed Channing's liberal doctrine into an egalitarian theology that sought to realize heaven on earth. They started from fundamental agreement on a set of interlocked concepts: (1) the laws of nature were ordained by God; (2) the laws of nature were likewise the laws of human nature; (3) religious institutions needed to be rebuilt in accordance with these laws; and (4) these revitalized religious institutions could redeem a degenerate modern society.

The most radical of these ministers, Brownson, had been convinced for some years of the need to address the deepening class divide in society, but his ideas about how to do so were in constant flux. He had spent the late 1820s in New York building the first Workingmen's Party with Robert Dale Owen and Fanny Wright. But disenchantment with electoral politics finally convinced him that the amelioration of the condition of the working class could be best pursued by transforming religious institutions. In 1835, after several years preaching from various New England pulpits, Brownson proposed a "Church of the Future" to a committee of Unitarian ministers who had convened to determine how best to spread the faith. The next year, the elder William Ellery Channing and George Ripley called him to Boston and charged him with founding a congregation that would enchurch the city's dangerously free-thinking tradesmen and mechanics. He established the Society for Christian Union and Progress, which he was to lead until 1844 when he converted to Catholicism. The Society drew congregations 500-strong of day laborers, journeymen, and curious reformers.[12]

At first, Brownson energetically preached Channing's doctrine of self-culture, but he was quickly radicalized by his congregation. After the onset of the depression in 1837, he began attacking the idea of individual reform directly:

> Reformers . . . would have all men wise, good, and happy; but in order to make them so, they tell us that we want not external changes, but internal; and therefore instead of declaiming against society and seeking to disturb existing social arrangements, we should confine ourselves to the individual reason and conscience. . . .

Brownson's sarcastic assessment of Channing's ideas focuses on how they function in a class society: "This is a capital theory, and has the advantage that kings, hierarchies, nobilities,—in a word all who fatten on the toil and blood of their fellows, will feel no difficulty in supporting it." He goes on to accuse ministers who preach self-reliance of hypocrisy. Ventriloquizing an imagined capitalist, he addresses a representative New England minister: "If you will only allow me to keep thousands toiling for my pleasure or my profit, I will even aid you in your pious efforts to convert their souls. . . . if a few thousand dollars will aid you, Mr. Priest, in reconciling him to God, and making fair weather for him hereafter, they are at you service." Brownson may also have had Channing in mind when writing his farcical "Conversation with a Radical":

> The lamb is necessary to the wolf; for without the lamb the wolf might want a dinner; and the wolf is necessary to the lamb, for without the wolf the lamb might fail to be eaten. "Therefore," says the benevolent wolf to the lamb, "do not be hostile nor excite your brother lambs against us; for you see we wolves and you lambs are mutually necessary to each other. We are dependent on you for something to eat, as you are on us to be eaten." "But I don't want to be eaten," exclaims the lamb in great trepidation. "Not want to be eaten!" replies the wolf. "Now that's odd. You and I are very far from thinking alike, and I must needs consider you very unreasonable, and radical in your mode of thinking."

Brownson moves well beyond this kind of satire in his many essays for his *Boston Quarterly Review*. He describes in detail how the wage system exploits workers by paying them far less than the exchange value of the produce of their labor; how competition among companies forces them to keep wages at the bare minimum necessary to allow workers to subsist; how division of labor in factories empties work of meaning, ruining it as a source of pride; how the labor market sets workers into competition with each other and thus produces ethnic and racial tensions; and, especially, how endemic poverty forces good people to take desperate measures to survive. Working from this clear recognition of the systemic nature of the oppression of the working class, Brownson felt the solution must be wholesale social revolution led by his Society for Christian Union and Progress.[13]

New Views of Christianity, Society, and the Church (1836) is Brownson's most sustained manifesto. It is a classic in a long tradition of liberation theologies that express working-class demands by calling for the restoration of primitive Christian ideals of equality and community in a heaven on earth. The book's concluding paragraphs are a resounding call to build what Emerson snidely dubbed the "church militant." Brownson's radicalism consists in his reversal of emphasis of the Unitarian critique of the "spirit of commerce." Where Channing had focused on convincing the lower orders to satisfy their hunger with spiritual bread, Brownson exhorted the elite to share the wealth. His final goal was to build an institution that would reconcile labor and capital, which would unify them in Christian brotherhood, and usher in peace on earth:

> I do not misread the age. . . . It craves union. . . . And for progress too the whole world is struggling. Old Institutions are examined, old opinions criticized, even the old Church is laid bare to its very foundations, and its holy vestments and sacred symbols are exposed to the gaze of the multitude; new systems are proclaimed, new institutions are elaborated . . . and the whole world seems intent on the means by which it may accomplish its destiny. . . . Every where there are men laboring to perfect government and laws. The poor man is admitted to be human, and millions of voices are demanding that he be treated as a brother. . . . He, who takes his position on the "high table land" of Humanity . . . beholds with a prophet's gaze his brothers, so long separated, coming together, and arm in arm marching onwards towards the Perfect, towards God. . . .

This utopian and millenarian Christianity was based on an uncompromising interpretation of the Kantian notion of the universality of higher reason, the faculty of immediate perception of divine law. Brownson was quite explicit about the political conclusions that followed from this emphasis:

> The democrat is not he who only believes in the people's capacity of being taught, and therefore graciously condescends to be their instructor; but he who believes that Reason, the light which shines out from God's throne, shines into the heart of every man, and that truth lights her torch in the inner temple of every man's soul, whether patrician or plebeian, a shepherd or a philosopher, a Croesus or a beggar. It is only on the reality of this inner light, and on the fact, that it is universal, in all men, and in every man, that you can found a democracy, which shall have a firm basis, and which shall be able to survive the storms of human passions.

Brownson inverts the association of republic-threatening passion with "the mob," implying that a true democracy has far other enemies within. And while Channing's "essential capacities of the mind" were a matter of mostly unrealized potential, Brownson insists on the far more radical claims that all people enjoy direct access to divine truth, that individual regeneration is a paltry goal, and that the church should set social reform as its primary task. This unabashed epistemological leveling directly underwrote the conviction that people's anger about the social order was divinely ordained, and that burgeoning working-class demands for material equality required not merely a hearing, but active institutional embodiment in the "Church of the Future."[14]

James Munroe printed Brownson's *New Views* in 1836, the same year that he published Emerson's *Nature*, which has come to be seen as *the* Transcendentalist manifesto. The two texts take up quite distinct positions on several of the central arguments among the members of the Symposium. Most centrally, Emerson and Brownson are sharply different when it comes to epistemology. *Nature* is, of course, a systematic defense of philosophical idealism:

> Intellectual science . . . fastens the attention upon immortal necessary uncreated natures, that is, upon Ideas; and in their beautiful and majestic presence, we feel our outward being is a dream and a shade. Whilst we wait in this Olympus of gods, we think of nature as an appendix to the soul. (CW 1.34)

From this perspective, human history is an unimportant flux behind which eternal truths remain stable, for idealism "beholds the whole circle of persons and things, of actions and events, of country and religion, not as painfully accumulated, atom after atom, act after act, in an aged creeping Past, but as one cast picture, which God paints on the instant eternity, for the contemplation of the soul" (CW 1.38). In a review of *Nature* in the *Boston Reformer*, Brownson protests: "He who denies the testimony of his senses, seems to have no ground for believing the apperceptions of consciousness; and to deny those is to set oneself afloat upon the ocean of universal skepticism."[15]

In contrast to Emerson's unilateral and ahistorical idealism, Brownson, in *New Views*, espouses a dialectical interpretation of world history as driven by the antithesis between what he calls "Spiritualism and Materialism." These terms "designate two orders, which, from time out of mind, have been called spiritual and temporal or carnal, holy and profane, heavenly and worldly, &c." "Spiritualism regards purity or holiness as predicable of Spirit alone, and Matter as essentially impure. . . . Materialism takes the other extreme, does not recognise the claims of Spirit, disregards the soul, counts the body everything, earth all, heaven nothing. . . ." He deplores what he sees as a fundamental and mistaken habit of thinking of "Spirit and Matter in opposition," which in turn requires an "antithesis between God and Man, the Priesthood and the State, Faith and Reason, Heaven and Earth, and Time and Eternity." For Brownson, this "antithesis generates perpetual and universal war. It is necessary then to remove it and harmonize, or unite the two terms." Through much of history, spiritualism or idealism had remained dominant because people had no "faith in the practicability of improving their earthly condition." Protestantism represented the "rebellion of Materialism" and culminated in the French Revolution. But Napoleon's imperial conquest caused a sharp reaction. People "despaired of the earth" and took "refuge in heaven." In the 1830s in New England, the time had at last been reached when a synthesis was possible. Brownson argues that the New England churches have placed too much emphasis on the spirit and should recognize and care for the material needs of the body. They should begin by supporting the demands of Boston's organized workers for better pay and working conditions, just as Jesus Christ, who was a mediator between spirit and matter, would have done. Brownson's "Church of the Future" would collapse the opposition between materialism and spiritualism, feed both body and soul, and usher in a new era of peace and prosperity on Earth.[16]

In the end, Brownson's response to the class divide was to imagine that society could be reunited in the crucible of a giant congregation of both rich and poor, who would read together the divine laws that decree their equal rights to life, liberty, and happiness. Compared with the directness of such a vision, it is easy to imagine that Emerson's *Nature* is pure philosophy. But Emerson too was reacting to the increasingly unavoidable presence of the working class. He briefly lifts the curtain that usually shrouds this fact in *Nature*: "Is not the landscape, every glimpse of which hath a grandeur, a face of [God]? Yet this may show us what discord is between man and nature, for you cannot freely admire a noble landscape, if laborers are digging in the field hard by" (CW 1.39). For Emerson, the most worrisome sign of social degeneration was the increasing deep divide between "laborers" and people who could not look at them without feeling a certain discomfort.

Five years after the simultaneous appearance of *Nature* and *New Views*, Emerson would take an opportunity to simultaneously differentiate himself from his old friend and pay him the compliment of incorporating the spirit of his ideas. In the lecture, "The Transcendentalist," Emerson announces that the "first thing we have to say respecting what are called *new views* here in New England, at the present time, is that they are not new, but the very oldest of thoughts cast into the mould of these new times" (CW 1.201, emphasis in original). Having alluded unmistakably to Brownson, Emerson next retrospectively defines him out of the movement: "What is popularly called Transcendentalism among us, is Idealism" Just in case his audience has missed the point, he now paraphrases Brownson quite directly: "As thinkers, mankind have ever been divided into two sects, Materialists and Idealists. . . . The materialist insists on facts, on history, on the force of circumstances and the animal wants of man; the idealist on the power of Thought and of Will, on inspiration, on miracle, and on individual culture" (CW 1.201). Finally, to conclude his opening paragraph, Emerson serenely proclaims that every "materialist will be an idealist; but an idealist can never go backward to be a materialist" (CW 1.202). The first half of the lecture then elaborates a long series of variations on this theme by way of explaining what drives the "many intelligent and religious persons [who] withdraw themselves from the common labors and competitions of the market and the caucus, and betake themselves to a certain solitary and critical way of living . . ." (CW 1.207). Emerson praises the reformist intentions of "these seething brains, these admirable radicals, these unsocial worshippers, these talkers who talk the sun and moon away" (CW 1.207–1.208). But in the end he offers them some stern advice borrowed directly from Brownson:

> The good, the illuminated, sit apart from the rest, censuring their dulness and vices, as if they thought that, by sitting very grand in their chairs, the very brokers, attorneys, and congressmen would see the error of their ways, and flock to them. But the good and wise must learn to act, and

carry salvation to the combatants and demagogues in the dusty arena below. (CW 1.211)

Eventually, Emerson followed his own advice and succeeded in making himself relevant to the most material social question of the antebellum period, slavery. Lawrence Buell argues that, like the period's radicals and socialists, Emerson "hated all systems of human oppression; but his central project, and the basis of his legacy, was to unchain individual minds." Buell rightly acknowledges the limits of this radical individualism, and maintains that "the Emerson most worth preserving" is one for whom "mental emancipation at the individual level" was important because "individual freedom . . . is what makes equality possible." This conviction, to which we turn now, underwrote Emerson's initially reluctant, but finally uncompromising abolitionism, *and* his role as an apologist for American capitalism.[17]

Chapter 10

Transcendentalist Reformers, Scholars, and Nature

Mr. Emerson is the most American of our writers. The Idea of America . . . appears in him with great prominence. We mean the idea of personal freedom, of the dignity and value of human nature, the superiority of a man to the accidents of a man. Emerson is the most republican of republicans, the most protestant of dissenters. . . . The most democratic of democrats, no disciple of the old regime is better mannered, for it is only the vulgar democrat or aristocrat who flings his follies in your face.

—Theodore Parker

The Sage of Concord attracted like minds. Even now his way of thinking has not lost its power to generate enthusiasm, as in this gloss by Sherman Paul:

By scholar, he meant "intellectual." He meant the free spirits, the "genius" and the artist, whose stock-in-trade is in themselves and their perception of truth. The times call for apostles of Being, not defenders of Seeming; and against the manipulators of masses and matter, he put the man of ideas. He believed the truth—spiritual power—would prevail; not by itself, however, but through man, in his resolute heroism, in his daring to use ideas as weapons in the face of a deaf and hostile society.

Emerson occupied the individualist end of the spectrum of early Transcendentalism, the end that Americanist literary histories have treated as definitive of the whole. His "scholars" included Thoreau, Frederic Henry Hedge, Bronson Alcott, and Margaret Fuller. But Brownson, the vulgar democrat, the egalitarian firebrand at the head of the Church of the Future, had staked out a clear alternative at the other end of the spectrum. Among the reformers who clustered toward his position during the late 1830s were William Henry Channing, Elizabeth Palmer Peabody, and George Ripley. What drew people in one direction or another? It would be possible to make the mechanical claim that Emersonian individualism, with its emphasis on the self-authenticating Higher Reason, was the inevitable subject position of a newly dominant bourgeoisie. But both scholars and reformers were mostly members of ruling-class families. If we turn to the detail of biography, beyond static attributions of class origin, it quickly becomes clear that what distinguishes the two groups is political education. Brownson and the other reformers had concrete experience of the class fracture in society and of the hard fight to close it. The circumstances of urban evangelical posts led many to apply the new views to the problem Channing had raised, the elevation of the labouring portion of the community. And they did so in the crucible of deeply challenging lessons in working-class aspirations and habits of thought. The scholars, on the other hand, were rarely pushed beyond the brahminical pale. Why then did not they stick to the safe haven of empiricist Unitarianism? Emerson and Thoreau, for example, both lesser sons of ruling-class families that had fallen on hard financial times, found in Transcendentalist ideas a way to make a virtue of an often debilitating sense of isolation. Margaret Fuller was fairly driven into the movement by her father's tyrannical program for her home-education, and she found in her famous conversations a fulfilling ritual of release and inspiration. The scholars, in other words, were united in seeing individual insight as the key to breaking down a narrow utilitarianism that seemed to impinge on their personal lives, and that they felt must also have caused the social chaos around them.[1]

Schematic divisions, such as this one between reformers and scholars, should be taken as no more than crude aids to reflection. This is especially true of a movement as tightly knit as the Transcendentalists, in which divided loyalties and the uncertainties of prolonged argument about strategies for change left some seeming to speak from many positions at once. Most participants in the newness did not see the opposition between reformers and scholars as antagonistic, or as requiring the choosing of sides. A year before he read Locke and Emerson in college, Thoreau boarded for a time with Brownson, in Canton, Massachusetts, just when Brownson was working on his *New Views of Christianity, Society, and the Church*, which Thoreau probably bought when it was published in 1836. In 1837, he read *Nature* and came to admire the Sage of Concord. By 1840, his friendship with Emerson had been cemented, yet his admiration for Brownson was still strong enough to impel him to call their weeks of study together "the morning of a new Lebenstag" in his life, and to close a coyly inventive letter to Brownson with a postscript deriding himself for being "cold." Emerson himself was deeply respectful of Brownson's relentless argumentation, if never able to convince himself that it was quite gentlemanly.[2]

The scholars could not accept their colleagues' narrative of collective social change, and at the same time they were unwilling to simply abandon the field on the social question since this would amount to abdication of leadership. So they pieced together a strategy for addressing increasing class conflict that was based on the renewed conquest, not of political power, but of the cultural authority of their class. The key to understanding their ideas is recognizing the complexity of their political and rhetorical situation: they were defending the legitimacy of their class against the demands of the increasingly organized workers. At the same time, closer to home, they found it necessary to argue against both an entrenched tradition of aristocratic arrogance and the egalitarian ideas of their more radical colleagues, who seemed dangerously close to losing track of their first loyalties in their enthusiastic sympathy for the demands of the poor.[3]

In this context, Emerson and the scholars elevated Channing's doctrine of self-culture from a nostrum for the working class into a course of study for elite radicals. Self-reliance would produce representative men who could lead a fractured republic. That is, the scholars made a bid for cultural authority based on the idea that they could operate most powerfully on society by living well. For instance, in an early Journal entry, Thoreau responded to the pressure of the reformers' enthusiasm for political activism with a surprising admission:

> I must confess that I have felt mean enough when asked how I was to act on society—what errand I had to mankind—undoubtedly I did not feel mean without a reason—and yet my loitering was not without defense. . . .
> I would fain communicate the wealth of my life to men—would really give them what is most precious in my gift—I would secrete pearls with the shellfish—and lay up honey with the bees for them. I will sift the sunbeams for public good. . . .

Thoreau takes this anxiety on the offensive in his published writings, mounting a direct attack on the reformers at the end of *Walden*'s chapter, "Economy":

> Philanthropy is almost the only virtue which is sufficiently appreciated by mankind. Nay it is greatly overrated; and it is our selfishness which overrates it. I would not subtract anything from the praise that is due philanthropy, but merely demand justice for all who by their lives and works are a blessing to mankind. (W 76)

Lydia Maria Child, in an 1854 review, took this to be *Walden*'s main point. She writes that the book shows, more than anything else, that political engagement is misguided:

> As a thing by the way, aside from our proper work, we may seek to remove external obstacles from the path of our neighbors, but no man can help them who makes that his main business, instead of seeking evermore, with all his energies, to reach the loftiest point which his imagination sets before him, thus adding to the stock of true nobleness in the world.

Emerson, in "Self-Reliance," protests in similar terms: "Do not tell me, as a good man did today, of my obligation to put all poor men in good situations." He asks himself a pugnacious question and answers impatiently: "Are they *my poor*? I tell thee, thou foolish philanthropist, that I grudge the dollar, the dime, the cent I give such men as do not belong to me and to whom I do not belong" (CW 2.30–2.31). Finally, Frederick Henry Hedge, in his essay "The Art of Life," presents a clear choice between reforming zeal and scholarly ideas about how to change the world:

> In self-culture lies the ground and condition of all culture. Not those who seem most earnest in promoting the culture of Society, do most effectually promote it. We have reformers in abundance, but few who, in the end, will be found to have aided essentially the cause of human improvement. . . . The silent influence of example is the true reformer. The only efficient power, in the moral world, is attraction. Society are more benefited by one sincere life, by seeing how one man has helped himself, than by all the projects that human policy has devised for their salvation.

We may wish to read here no more than another example of a long-reliable justification for retreat from active political and social engagement. But again, this was felt to be a serious program for millennial transformation. The scholars were united behind the proposition that attempts to directly address social problems were a distraction from the more important work of making oneself a beacon to the times.[4]

Emerson's "The American Scholar" tells a fully developed version of this scholarly tale. Modernization has "divided Man into men" and in this "*divided* or social state" the scholar is "the delegated intellect" (CW 1.53). Of course, the "first in time and the first in importance of the influences upon the [scholar's] mind is that of nature. Every day, the sun; and after sunset, night and her stars" (CW 1.54). After his apprenticeship in nature, the "office of the scholar is to cheer, to raise, and to guide men by showing them facts amidst appearance." More than just deliver knowledge, he teaches how to feel about it: "He is the world's eye. He is the world's heart" (CW 1.62). And his "private life . . . shall be a more illustrious monarchy,—more formidable to its enemy, more sweet and serene in its influence to its friend, than any kingdom in history" (CW 1.65–1.66). This aristocratic man of genius, will naturally lead during an "age of Revolution; when the old and the new stand side by side and admit of being compared; when the energies of all men are searched by fear and hope; when the historic glories of the old can be compensated by the rich possibilities of the new era" (CW 1.67). Of course, the revolution Emerson envisions is of neither the jacobinical nor the republican sort. Rather, it is the kind that, in the lexicon of idealist historiography, differentiates the "genius of the Classic, of the Romantic, and now of the Reflective or Philosophical age" (CW 1.66). The defining characteristic of the incoming age was "the new importance given to the single person. Every thing that tends to insulate the individual,—to surround him with barriers of natural respect, so that each man shall feel the world is his, and man shall treat with man as a sovereign state with a sovereign state,—tends to true union as well as greatness" (CW 1.68). In "Self-Reliance," Emerson makes explicit the claim that is implied here: "a greater self-reliance,—a new respect for the divinity in man,—must work a revolution in all the offices and relations of men; in their religion; in their education . . . their association; in their property; in their speculative views" (CW 2.44).

William Charvat, generalizing about the scholars, argues that their ideas were shaped by the struggle "between their own homogenous patrician society and a rising materialistic middle class without education and tradition, who were winning cultural and economic power and changing the tone of American life. . . ." Charvat sees Emerson's "The American Scholar" as "a plea to his own class to recapture cultural power and leadership by reforming its education and vitalizing its ideals. . . ." Kenneth Sacks particularizes this claim by demonstrating that "in 1837 Emerson, hardly their leader, was still struggling for his place" in a Boston whose attention was more immediately focused on reformers like Ripley and Brownson. Sacks argues that the combative rhetoric of "The American Scholar" reflects "the hesitation and ultimate courage of an insecure intellectual trying to become simultaneously self-reliant and famous." In order to impress his Transcendentalist colleagues, Emerson spoke in a voice that was flagrantly vernacular, consciously insulting the sensibilities of his Whiggish Harvard audience, as he "proposed an extreme vision of the intellectual, who transcends all convention, including the institutions of one's own country, to speak the truth that emerges from within." The polemical address won him the admiration of many of his peers. And the ideal of the self-reliant scholar that he had provisionally articulated quickly solidified into a specific alternative to their more collective programs for change.[5]

Sam McGuire Worley has proposed a reading of scholarly Transcendentalism from the standpoint of "communitarian philosophy." He argues that the Emersonian scholar is an "immanent critic" of society "who observes and advises from the authority of a position within a culture rather than a position of superiority or detachment outside it." Worley concludes that this way of thinking about the role of the cultural critic "reconciles the demands of both leadership and democracy." This is an accurate representation of Emerson's own way of thinking about the scholar's role in society, but his individualism should definitely not be mistaken for egalitarianism, despite his talk of "the literature of the poor, the feelings of the child, [and] the philosophy of the street" (CW 1.67). For in "The American Scholar," he also writes that "The one thing in the world of value, is, the active soul [which] every man has within him, although in almost all men, obstructed, and as yet unborn" (CW 1.56). Thus, the scholar "is to resist the vulgar prosperity that retrogrades ever to barbarism" and "defer never to the popular cry." After all, "men in the world to-day are bugs, are spawn, and are called 'the mass and 'the herd'" (CW 1.62–1.63). Similarly, in his Journal for December 9, 1834, he observes that "there is imparted to every man the Divine light of reason sufficient not only to plant corn & grind wheat by, but also to illuminate all his life his social, political, religious actions. . . ." The universality of Divine light implies a question, though it is merely rhetorical: "does it mean . . . that whatever crude remarks a circle of people talking in a bar-room throw out, are entitled to equal weight with the sifted & chosen conclusions of experienced public men?" Emerson answers himself in general terms: "Democracy has its root in the Sacred truth that every man hath in him the divine Reason, or that, though few men since the creation of the world live according to the dictates of Reason, yet all men are created capable of so doing. That is the equality & the only equality of all men."[6] Emerson firmly believed that social hierarchies were, like everything else in nature, a direct reflection of divine law. Authority was as natural as rain and the people "behold in the hero or the poet their own green and crude being,—ripened; yes, and are content to be less, so that may attain to its full stature . . ." (CW 1.65) Thus, the importance of the new individualism was that, by organically embodying this ruling idea more thoroughly than anyone else, the age's representative men, its natural aristocracy, would attain eminence above the grubby squabbling of the marketplace and the campaign, and they would lead the world by their example.

Evidently, Thoreau was not present when Emerson delivered "The American Scholar," but he did read a transcript of the speech soon thereafter. And he checked *Nature* out of the Harvard library twice during the spring of 1837. His 1840 essay, "The Service," which Margaret Fuller rejected for publication in the *Dial* despite Emerson's urgings, shows just how closely he followed his new mentor's thinking. Little has been made of this piece, partially because of its tortuous publication history, and partly because it had been dismissed as juvenilia. However, it may be read as a kind of expository preface to *Walden*, a direct statement of the theory Thoreau dramatizes there. The essay's first section, entitled, "Qualities of the Recruit," begins:

> The brave man is the elder son of creation, who has stept boyantly into his inheritance. . . . He rides as wide of this earth's gravity as a star. . . . His bravery . . . is a staying at home and compelling alliance in all directions. So stands his life to heaven, as some fair sunlit tree against the western horizon, and by sunrise is planted on some eastern hill, to glisten in the first rays of the dawn.

This serenely autonomous figure, moves through the pages of the essay in "a stately march to an unheard music," deriving his power from unselfconscious unity with the laws of nature, with "the golden mean, [which] in ethics as in physics, is the center of the system." The essay is structured by a series of contrasts between this figure of masculine virtue and the coward, who contains all "the materials of manhood, only they are not rightly disposed. We say justly that the weak person is flat, for like all flat substances, he does not stand in the direction of his strength, that is, on his edge, but affords a convenient surface to put upon." Throughout, the tenor of Thoreau's layered imagery is that the brave man does not do, but simply is. He organically, necessarily, leads by living out the promptings of an "accordant universe." "The bravest deed, which for the most part is left out of history, which alone wants the staleness of a deed done, and the uncertainty of a deed doing, is the life of a great man." In sum, Thoreau was convinced that the problem in the New England was not that capitalist relations of production had deepened the class divisions in society, but that those who occupied the top rungs of the social order—whether they had held their position for generations or had just arrived—were not fulfilling the duties that accompanied their eminence. The social transformation the scholars envisioned was the appearance of great men who would lead the upper orders back to a just paternalism that would both defuse increasing class conflict and fulfill the young republic's potential for cultural achievement. "Why," Thoreau asks, "has man rooted himself thus firmly in the earth, but that he may thus rise in the same proportion into the heavens above?" (W 15). He specifies who should lead this flowering of New England: the "authors [of great books] are a natural and irresistible aristocracy in every society, and, more than kings or emperors, exert an influence on mankind" (W 103).[7]

Orestes Brownson was considerably more critical of Emerson's theory of organic individualism than Thoreau. Brownson reviewed Emerson's Dartmouth College address, "Literary Ethics," which was a reprise of "The American Scholar," and he delivered a sharp class-based critique of scholarly disdain for reform: "Instead of regarding the material improvements of society, efforts to perfect political institutions, and increase the physical comforts of the people, as low, sordid, mercenary, he should elevate them to the rank of liberal pursuits." After all, if the majority of Americans are utilitarian, it is because they are poor and see material success as the road to independent self-reliance. And if they do not engage in abstruse philosophy, this does not mean that they have no respect for intellect, but simply that they have applied their considerable powers to making newspapers, railroads, and mills. Brownson maintains that Emerson's ways of thinking about the role of the scholar in society imply the formation of "a literary caste, which when it is a caste, is no better than a sacerdotal caste or a military caste." Should this occur, the "scholars would have constituted a nobility," which "would have been at war with the mission of this country."[8]

Brownson mounts a similarly direct critique of the theory of self-culture in an article on Brook Farm in the *Democratic Review*: "We can never cultivate ourselves by direct efforts at self-culture; we cultivate one another,—ourselves only in seeking to cultivate others. This is what is implied in that fact that we are social beings; that we can live and grow only in the bosom of society." For Brownson, the scholars' theory is not only inadequate as an account of how individuals develop. He also remarks that the "advocates of *self-culture*, as the medium of social regeneration, proceed on the hypothesis that the evils mankind endure are merely an aggregate of individual evils. . . ." He then observes that "There are very few evils that spring from the depravity of isolated wills, or that mere private morality . . . can cure. What we complain of in the actual condition of mankind is the result of no one cause; has been produced by nobody in particular; but is the growth of ages." Just what he means by this vague last phrase becomes clear as he delivers concrete examples. A "single bad law, touching social and political economies" can make "the great mass of the people poor and wretched." He almost certainly has in mind the law of inheritance that he proposed repealing in "The Laboring Classes." Likewise, he asks, who "can estimate the amount of public and private wrong, individual vice, crime, poverty, and suffering, occasioned by the combined influence of our banking and so-called protective systems." Such legal and financial systems and the social relations they encode and enforce are beyond the reach of self-culture. And as a direct result of their influence, it "is impossible to practice, however enlightened or well disposed we may be, all the Christian virtues in society as it is now organized." After all, in this society, what "two men about to make a bargain" will endeavor "to do by each as each would be done by?" Brownson concludes that "Private virtues are no doubt the great matter, the one thing needful; but it is only when they are directed to the removal of the depravities of the social state that they become efficient agents in the amelioration of mankind."⁹

The "Church of the Future" was the means by which Brownson hoped to direct private virtues to the amelioration of mankind. If there was a tableau that emblematized his narrative of social reform, it was a congregation of all classes, gathered together in prayer, reading in their hearts the body of natural law that decreed their common rights. Nature plays a key role in this story, but it remains behind the scenes as an ontological order that is the invisible ground of political thought. Thus, *New Views* proceeds almost entirely on the basis of abstract theological reasoning in which nature does not appear significantly either as an immediate subject or even as the raw material of figurative language. There is one exception, one of the book's most suggestive passages, in which Brownson argues that a society in which class inequality has been erased will have a new kind of relationship with nature. After the "atonement," the synthesis of materialism and spiritualism, he writes, "Industry will be holy. The cultivation of the earth will be the worship of God. . . . The earth itself and the animals which inhabit it will be counted sacred. . . . Man's body will be deemed holy. It will be called the temple of the living God." A few years later, Brownson went on to make the physical earth the central example in his scandalous call for outlawing inheritance, which he believed necessarily concentrated estates and excluded the vast majority of the population from their rightful access to the land: "Man's right to the earth, to possess it, to cultivate it, to enjoy its fruits, is Divine, and rests on the will of the Creator. . . . God gave the earth to the children of men." For Brownson, nature was not a

Transcendental ideal, it was the material world in its entirety, half of the complete reality that he attempted to account for dialectically. And it was the necessary field of life. Brownson's way of thinking was quite influential in the broad movement. The New England Workingmen's Association resolved at its 1845 convention that "the shameful and scurrilous monopoly of the soil [should be] entirely abolished, and the public lands which are now held by the government . . . retained for actual settlement to the people." And Albert Brisbane argued before the delegates that "the two great fundamental rights of man [are] the right of labor, and the right to the soil."[10]

In contrast to Brownson's tableau, Emerson's scholars painted a new scene, that of a wandering autodidact, self-isolated from the degenerate society he is destined to redeem, and working to master a very different kind of law written in his natural surroundings. In place of an urban congregation, the hero was a young man, a "scholar" self-isolated from the degenerate society he is destined to redeem, a "schoolboy under the bending dome of the day" (CW 1.54). The most central keyword in this tale of apprenticeship is the title of its most central manifesto, *Nature*. Emerson defined Nature as "all that is separate from us, all which Philosophy distinguishes as the NOT ME, that is, both nature and art, all other men and my own body . . ." (CW 1.8). Nature is an inexhaustible source of correspondential images, where the scholar discovers the truths he will deliver to the future: "Embosomed for a season in nature, whose floods of life stream around and through us, and invite us by the powers they supply, to action proportioned to nature, why should we grope among the dry bones of the past . . ." (CW 1.7). More, Nature is "the present expositor of the divine mind" and its highest function is to discipline the developing scholar (CW 1.39). For "the world is emblematic. . . . The laws of moral nature answer to those of matter as face to face in a glass. . . . The axioms of physics translate the laws of ethics" (CW 1.21). And although we may doubt whether Nature "outwardly exists," Emerson insists that it "is a sufficient account of that Appearance we call the World, that God will teach a human mind, and so makes it the receiver of a certain number of congruent sensations, which we call sun and moon, man and woman, house and trade" (CW 1.29).

Donald Pease argues that Emerson's transpersonal nature is the ground of a "visionary compact" that he forms with the nation, since self-reliance "directs the individual as well as the culture to a vision of the innermost principles underlying both." For Pease, because Emerson's individualism is rooted in nature, it is in fact a politics of self-transcendence, so that when he "opposed the Fugitive Slave Law, his person became transparent so the principle of liberty could speak through it."[11] This is true, but it is a particular version of the language of liberty that nature speaks. Nature performs the "same good office" as does "Property and its filial systems of debt and credit." Emerson's language becomes quite terse and urgent as he contemplates the tough love delivered by both nature and poverty: "Debt, grinding debt, whose iron face the widow, the orphan, and the sons of genius fear and hate . . . is a preceptor whose lessons cannot be foregone, and is needed most by those who suffer from it most. . . . In like manner, what good heed, nature forms in us! She pardons no mistakes. Her yea is yea, and her nay, nay" (CW 1.24). It was just this kind of discipline that Boston, and perhaps Brownson's congregants in particular, seemed to need most.

A curious thing happens as *Nature* progresses in the direction of this insight about nature's stern preceptorship. The category becomes increasingly specific and concrete as Emerson focuses more and more closely on the discipline of nature in the woods around Concord. Emerson, the idealist, paradoxically, was deeply fascinated by the concrete physicality of nature. As Laura Dassow Walls has shown, "science permeated his thought and writing at every level, from its deepest structure to his most casual analogies." In opposition to the mechanical "world of trades and manufactures and commercial enterprises," for Emerson, "science and literature formed one single intellectual culture." Thus, "the true man of science and the American scholar were one and the same," both were intellectuals dedicated the cultivation of moral knowledge of nature. Despite his idealism, then, what Emerson had initially conceived as an ontological category, the "Not Me," becomes increasingly a geographical one. Nature becomes a concrete site of correspondential instruction that necessarily occurs away from town:

> In the woods, is perpetual youth. Within these plantations of God, a decorum and sanctity reign, a perennial festival is dressed, and the guest sees not how he should tire of them in a thousand years. In the woods, we return to reason and faith. . . . In the wilderness, I find something more dear and connate that in the streets or villages. (CW 1.10)

Where Brownson and the reformers thought about nature as a potentially sacred material world that incarnates natural law, Emerson and the scholars looked to the discipline of nature in the woods for emblems of the laws of human nature. Where the reformers read the inalienable rights of humankind as part of a collective program for changing the structure of society (and its relations to the physical natural world), the scholars scanned the operations of physical nature for confirmation of the inevitability of the current social order and the kinds of human relationships and experiences it produced.[12]

CHAPTER 11

BROOK FARM AND ASSOCIATION

> In order to live a religious and moral life worthy the name, they feel it is
> necessary to come out in some degree from the world. . . . They have
> bought a farm in order to make agriculture the basis of their life, it being
> the most direct and simple in relation to nature.
> A true life, although it aims beyond the highest star, is redolent of the
> healthy earth. The perfume of clover lingers about it. The lowing of cattle
> is the natural bass to the melody of human voices.
>
> —Elizabeth Palmer Peabody

By 1840, after three long years of economic stagnation, the sharpening
reformist critique of capitalism as a social system that had marked the
1830s reached a crescendo.[1] People of all kinds had come to understand
the ongoing depression as a refutation of the system's claim to legitimacy,
for it clearly could not keep its promises of prosperity and stability. The
Workingmen's Party had been undercut and absorbed by the Democrats
who limited themselves to antimonopoly legislation. The labor movement was in full retreat. And the now consolidated Whig Party shocked
all observers by beating the Democrats at their own game. They chan-
neled working-class desperation into the infamously cynical Log Cabin
and Hard Cider Campaign. The campaign was the apotheosis of a trend
Brownson had identified two years previously in the pages of the *Boston
Quarterly Review*: "The Whig party, which, whether right or wrong, we
have been in the habit of regarding as the legitimate heir of the old
Federal Party, [has] challenged success on the ground of being more
democratic than the democratic party itself." The Whigs ran William
Henry Harrison for president under specific orders not to speak about
policy or political ideas. Instead, they staged mass rallies, barbecues,
clambakes, and parades designed to do no more than proclaim the candidate's populist roots and military heroism. Emerson's essay "The Poet"
registered the disgust shared by all Transcendentalists at the electorate's

vulnerability to inauthentic symbols and language:

> In our political parties compute the power of badges and emblems. See the huge wooden ball rolled by successive ardent crowds from Baltimore to Bunker Hill! In the political processions, Lowell goes in a loom, and Lynn in a shoe, and Salem in a ship. Witness the cider-barrel, the log-cabin, the hickory-stick, the palmetto, and all the cognizances of party. See the power of national emblems. (CW 3.10)

During the Harrison Campaign, medals, charms, and prints were distributed by the thousands, carrying images of "Old Tippecanoe" in uniform astride a charger, or standing outside a log cabin posed as Cincinnatus at the plow. Full sized log cabins and barrels of cider were set up in town squares across the country. Local Whig clubs held marches in which they pushed huge wood, twine, or sheet-tin balls from town to town, shouting, "The ball is rolling for Old Tip."[2]

At the height of the electioneering, Brownson had published his review of Carlyle's *Chartism*, "The Laboring Classes," in his *Boston Quarterly Review*. He had been moving steadily in the direction of a synthesis of the piecemeal critique of capitalism he had been developing over the course of the previous four years. In this landmark essay, he delivered this synthesis, arguing: "What is purely individual in its nature, efforts of individuals to perfect themselves, may remove. But the evil we speak of is inherent in all our social arrangements, and cannot be cured without a radical change of those arrangements."[3] Having come this far toward a revolutionary position, he made a last appeal to the ruling class to pass ameliorative legislation, legislation that would have struck at the very basis of that class's power by outlawing inheritance of private property. Realist that he was, he had little hope that his audience would follow his advice. But hoping to startle the patient into some kind of activity, he concluded the article by declaiming that if they did not act in time the matter would be solved for them by a cataclysmic revolution. Brownson's article was immediately taken up by Whig hacks across the country, who triumphantly cried that he had revealed the hidden platform of the Democrats. Brownson was immediately precipitated from his position of de facto leader of reform Transcendentalism into a kind of internal exile. Boston's elite radicals detached themselves from him and began seeking a new lead.

At this moment, George Ripley, who had been a part of the committee that first called Brownson to Boston, galvanized the city by announcing that he planned to separate from his congregation and move his family to a small farm outside Roxbury. There he and a band of like-minded experimenters hoped to found a cooperative school and farm, the Brook Farm Institute of Agriculture and Education. In a letter inviting Emerson to join his community, Ripley summarizes his goals this way: "Our objects, as you know, are to insure a more natural union between intellectual and manual labor than now exists; to combine the thinker and the worker, as far as possible, in the same individual. . . ." All members of the community would be provided "with labor, adapted to their tastes and talents and securing to them the fruits of their industry. . . ." The material proceeds of labor would "guarantee the highest mental freedom." And ensuring that all members of the community participated in both head and handwork would "do away with the necessity of menial services, by opening the benefits of education and the profits of labor to all. . . ." This transformation of social relations would "prepare a society of liberal, intelligent, and cultivated persons, whose relations with each other would permit a more simple and wholesome life, than can be led amidst the pressures of our competitive institutions. . . ." In short, Brook Farm was established specifically as a collectivist alternative to capitalism. But if Brownson was denounced as an outrageous leveler, Ripley was welcomed as one whose aim was to level all upward. An article in the August 1841 issue of *The Monthly Miscellany of Religion and Letters* makes the connection explicit:

> It seems to me that here we see brought about, in the most peaceable manner in the world, that very rectification of things which Mr. Brownson in his Article on the Labouring Classes is understood to declare will require a bloody revolution, a war such as the world has not heard of; viz., that no child shall be born richer or poorer than another, except by an inward gift of God, but all shall inherit from society a good education and an independent place.

Brownson was on record, in his review of Wordsworth's poetical works, describing the French Revolution as "a great, though terrible effort of Humanity" that "had doubtless its excesses, but needs no apology." Brook Farm seemed far preferable to Boston's elite.[4]

When Brownson had predicted revolutionary violence in New England, he was extrapolating quite logically from a materialist analysis of the economic basis of class, and a clear-headed assessment of the probable behavior of those in power. And although Ripley shared Brownson's indignation at the misery he saw around him, he explained it in more uncertain terms. He did talk of "the pressures of our competitive institution," but most fundamentally he believed that the hardening hierarchy of classes resulted from invidious judgments of the relative moral and economic value of intellectual and manual labor. Therefore, the best possible response was to challenge these prejudices by engaging in manual labor himself in cooperation with others like himself. Ripley was far from alone in thinking this way about the power of prejudicial ideas of manual labor. Most of the trades union manifestoes and working-class newspapers of the period couched their demands in the language of respect, arguing that the economic positions of the classes followed from the relative degrees of dignity accorded to their callings. Moreover, this line of reasoning was accepted throughout the Transcendentalist movement. Theodore Parker stated the argument succinctly in, "Thoughts on Labor," in the *Dial*: "Now, as there is one mouth to each pair of hands, and each mouth must be filled, it follows quite naturally, that if a single pair of hands refuses to do its work then the mouth goes hungry, or, which is worse, the work is done by other hands." Parker's use of the image of food production is not merely metaphorical. Based in part on a revival of agrarian social theory, this way of thinking emphasized the fundamental role that agriculture played in the national economy and then extended a moral imperative to take part in it. In the same issue of the *Dial*, Emerson published his lecture "Man the Reformer," in which he describes what he calls "the doctrine of the Farm." He argues that "every man ought to stand in primary relations with the work of the world, ought to do it himself, and not to suffer the accident of having a purse in his pocket . . . to sever him from those duties. . . ." Emerson, of course, went further, attaching a spiritual significance to farm work: "labor is God's education" and "he only is a sincere learner, he only can become a master, who learns the secrets of labor, and who by real cunning extorts from nature its sceptre" (CW 1.152). Suiting deeds to words, he set about becoming a gardener, though he always felt clumsy and inadequate. He was also determined to recognize the true value of his menials by inviting them to dine at table with him. They refused.[5]

As with Emerson, efforts to engage in handwork preoccupied most of the members of the broader Transcendentalist movement during the first years of the 1840s. Thoreau's bean field is merely the most famous in what was wide range of experiments in self-sufficiency. Hopedale, one of the most successful, was organized in early 1841 by Adin Ballou. Located on a 600-acre farm near Milford, Massachusetts, about 30 miles from Concord and West Roxbury, Hopedale combined radical religious and political ideas into a fully developed Christian Socialism. Ballou wrote that the community "affords a most desirable opportunity for those who mean to be practical Christians in the use of property, talent, skill or productive industry, to invest them." Shared labor and property meant that "those goods and gifts may all be so employed as to benefit their possessors to the full extent of justice, while at the same time they afford aid to the less favoured. . . ." Hopedale's members expected that their project would not only succeed for them as a community, but also would "help build up a social state free from the evils of irreligion, ignorance, poverty, and vice." And they explicitly saw their work as continuous with the movements to spread temperance, abolish slavery, win women's rights, and prevent war and political violence. Hopedale thrived well into the 1850s, when it collapsed after two of its wealthiest investors succeeded in staging a hostile financial takeover.[6]

Two years after the founding of Hopedale, Emerson's close friend, Bronson Alcott, together with English reformer Charles Lane, set out to "initiate a Family in harmony with the primitive instincts of man" at a 90-acre farm in a "serene and sequestered dell" near Harvard, Massachusetts. Alcott and Lane made an "arrangement with the proprietor . . . which liberates this tract from human ownership." In a letter they sent to the *Dial*, they announced its future: "Consecrated to human freedom, the land awaits the sober culture of devout men." Their community, Fruitlands, was to be a more radical version of Brook Farm. Lane mounted a critique of the larger community, again in the *Dial*: "Its aims are moderate; too humble indeed to satisfy the extreme demands of the age. . . ." After all, a "residence at Brook Farm does not involve either community of money, or opinions, or of sympathy." Moreover, Brook Farm engaged in "intimate intercourse with the trading world" by bringing its crops to market, and it was clear that to "enter into the corrupting modes of the world, with the view of diminishing or destroying them, is a delusive hope."[7] Thus, the 11 adults at Fruitlands, along with several children, set out to raise the ingredients of a vegetarian diet solely by the work of their own hands. "Ordinary secular farming is not our object," they announced. "Fruit, grain, pulse, garden plants and herbs, flax and other vegetable products for food, raiment, and domestic uses, receiving assiduous attention, afford at once ample manual occupation, and chaste supplies for the bodily needs." Their goal was to grow only enough pure crops to feed themselves, so that they could focus their attention on higher things: "Pledged to the spirit alone, the founders can anticipate no hasty or numerous accession to their numbers. The kingdom of peace is entered only through the gates of self-denial and abandonment. . . ." The members carried no money, even when they traveled to town. No being, including insects, could be injured during the working of the fields, and the members forswore the use of appropriated labor, including the labor of draught animals. Manure was considered an unfairly requisitioned pollutant, and since wool could only be stolen, the members wore tunics and trousers sewn from brown linen and broad-brimmed straw hats. A library of Bronson Alcott's books guided daily philosophical discussions, which were conducted in place of religious services. Alcott and Lane lectured regularly in Boston and elsewhere on vegetarianism and the virtues of their spiritual life. In part because of their regular absences, it proved impossible to raise enough food to last the winter, and the community survived only seven months, from June 1843 to January 1844. Louisa May Alcott, who was a young girl during this adventure, concluded later that her father and "the brethren . . . were so busy discussing and defining great duties that they forgot to perform the small ones."[8]

By all accounts, the members of Brook Farm shared the sense of high purpose that informed the experiments of their neighbors. But at the same time, they built an inventive and playful communal culture. Hawthorne, who later satirized Brook Farm in *The Blithedale Romance*, joined early and wrote enthusiastic letters about his life with the group: "The whole fraternity eat together; and such a delectable way of life has never been seen on earth since the days of the early Christians." All the cooking and eating occurred in a large building known as "The Hive" and the members lived cooperatively in structures to which they gave names like "The Nest" and "The Eyrie." The women wore bloomers and large straw hats while the men wore trousers, belted blouses, and beards. Both men and women participated fully in democratic decision-making by council. And the members practiced a creative pantheism, blending elements of Christian and classical myths into impromptu masquerades, tableaux, and other playful ceremonies in the fields. The school, which drew students from as far away as Cuba and which was run according to the kind of progressive educational theories Alcott had pioneered, provided income while the members attempted to develop agricultural and manufacturing capacity.[9]

Although most of the Farmers came to feel passionate about the importance of manual labor, this did not necessarily translate into principled solidarity with the working class. Many were convinced by the success of the cynical Whig election strategy that the vast majority of people had been irretrievably debased by life under capitalism and thus could not to be trusted to make decisions. So, at the same time that Brook Farm seemed to offer a solution class antagonism, it also required an initial joint-stock investment of 500 dollars. This not only promised to place it on a firm financial footing, but also to set a high bar that would exclude the farmers and mechanics who had so ignominiously proven their unreliability and ignorance. A less frequently quoted passage from Ripley's letter to Emerson makes clear the extent to which Brook

Farm, in its inception at least, seemed to offer a way to come out of class conflict entirely, to join a peaceful society of one's equals:

> I believe in the divinity of labor; I wish to "harvest my flesh and blood from the land;" but to do this, I must either be insulated and work to disadvantage, or avail myself of the services of hirelings, who are not of my order, and whom I can scarce make friends; for I must have another to drive the plough, which I hold. I cannot empty a cask of lime upon my grass alone. I wish to see a society of educated friends, working, thinking, and living together, with no strife, except that of each to contribute the most to the benefit of all.

Ripley's feelings were far more complex than the seeming arrogance of this passage suggests. His hauteur has partly to do with the audience to which he is playing. If he seems here to hope that the unwashed will simply disappear if ignored, he raises the issue again in a delicate postscript, in which his manner suggests that he has forced himself to confront Emerson's well-known uneasiness around his inferiors:

> I recollect you said that if you were sure of compeers of the right stamp you might embark yourself on the adventure: as to this, let me suggest the inquiry, whether our Association should not be composed of various classes of men? If we have friends whom we love and who love us, I think we should be content to join with others, with whom our personal sympathy is not strong, but whose general ideas coincide with ours, and whose gifts and abilities would make their services important. For instance, I should like to have a good washerwoman in my parish admitted into the plot. She is certainly not a Minerva or a Venus; but we might educate her two children to wisdom and varied accomplishments, who otherwise will be doomed to drudge through life.

At the same time that Ripley saw an unclosable gap between him and those below him, he also passionately hoped that Brook Farm would be part of the process of transforming the society that had raised him.[10]

The idiosyncratic mixture of conservative and radical ideas at Brook Farm was to be hardened and sharpened by ensuing events. In the early months, Ripley and the small group who followed him there knew they wanted to build a microcosmic society based on cooperation, that it should be self-sustaining on a basis of agriculture and education, and that it should be a standing sermon to the world on right and wrong ways of getting a living. Beyond this their ideas were by no means clear or tested. The practical experience of building a community forced a systematic examination of their project. Uppermost among their problems was that of making the Farm pay in a depressed economy and in the face of the intense competition from Western imports that had already driven under many of the area farmers. Before long, they concluded that the experiment needed a far more hard-nosed plan and a firmer ideological footing, especially since the lax discipline of the early years had produced a de facto division of labor between most of the intellectuals and the few workers and farmers they convinced to join them. After much soul searching, the association selectively appropriated the doctrines of the French utopian socialist Charles Fourier.

Fourier's writings had been imported first by Albert Brisbane, who returned to the United States in 1834 after a period of apprenticeship to the master on his deathbed, and began to tirelessly propagate his ideas. Brisbane's *Social Destiny of Man: or, Association and Reorganization of Industry* achieved wide circulation after its publication in 1840. And it was soon followed by Parke Godwin's *Popular View of the Doctrines of Charles Fourier* (1844). In a lecture on Fourier, Ripley explains that "the sublime laws of Social Harmony" discovered by Fourier were analogous to Newton's "Laws of Material Harmony." Thus, "the affinity which binds the atom, the attractive power which governs the planets, the affections which bind human beings to each other in society, are only so many different modes of the one universal law of attraction and repulsion." Fourier developed three practical concepts from this single principle: (1) "association," or the principle of forming large communities, or "phalanxes" in which the economies of scale could be applied to domestic arrangements; (2) "attractive industry," or the idea of organizing labor around the propensities and abilities of the individual community members in order to make it pleasant; and (3) equality of compensation for capital and manual and intellectual labor.[11]

Carl Guarneri argues that "Fourierism won a widespread hearing on this side of the Atlantic because it clarified and expanded ideas and tendencies already present in many American minds." A particular historical conjuncture allowed for the broad popularity in the United States of this seemingly unlikely ideological import: "The traditions of American politics, Transcendentalism, millennial Christianity, and native reform all shared common presuppositions and ideals which, galvanized by the conditions of the 1840s, cleared the path to communitarian socialism." Moreover, because the leaders of the movement were quite conscious of the deep suspicion with which all things French were regarded, they set about aggressively naturalizing, or nationalizing, their rhetoric:

> They argued that far from repudiating American values, utopian socialism was merely a more effective way to realize the goals of republicanism,

democracy, Christianity, and missionary nationalism. They promised that the new order would bring an abundant, satisfying, and equal society without renouncing conventional ways or liberal beliefs. And their phalanxes incorporated familiar capitalist features such as private property, interest, and a modified wage system inside the communitarian frame. In this sense the Fourierists were proposing not just a cooperative substitute for competitive capitalism but an alternative, more community-minded version of the American Dream.

During the 1840s, when that dream had receded beyond the reach of all but those at the very top of U.S. society, it is not surprising that such ideas should take a strong hold.[12]

Brook Farm is commonly regarded as a kind of historical freak, a fit of whimsy on the part of an isolated group of intellectuals. Hawthorne did much to help this view along with *The Blithedale Romance*, which describes the farmers as "a knot of dreamers," partaking in an "exploded scheme for beginning the life of Paradise anew." Hawthorne blames the failure of the farm on the weather of human nature, for "with such materials as were at hand [in] our bleak little world of New England" not even "the most skilful architect [could] have constructed any better imitation of Eve's bower, than might have been seen in the snow-hut of an Esquimaux. But we made a summer of it, in spite of the wild drifts." The historical assessment that Hawthorne's mocking hindsight inspires ignores the available facts. Brook Farm was unavoidably visible. Brownson was a vocal supporter and sent his son to be educated at the school. Soon after it opened, a dedicated coach line was opened in order to carry visitors from Boston to the Farm, which was able to turn the care and feeding of the curious into a paying business. Thousands visited each year, including a majority of the elite radicals of the period. From the time of its conversion to Fourierism in January 1844, the Farm grew rapidly, changing in character from a kind of barely self-sustaining retreat for a like-minded elite into a burgeoning center of agricultural and industrial production. The old guard of intellectuals were soon mixed with a large influx of new working-class members. Increasingly, because of the prominence of a number of its members and of its proximity to Boston, the Farm came to be seen as the flagship of the national Associationist movement. Brisbane's magazine, *The Phalanx*, was relocated to the Farm and placed under Ripley's editorship, with the new name *The Harbinger*. A number of Brook Farm residents became able propagandists for the movement, traveling and lecturing throughout the Northeast and the West.[13]

Just as significantly, Brook Farm was rooted in a long-standing tradition of North American socialist communities that arguably extends as far back as William Bradford's Plymouth Plantation. In just the first two decades of the nineteenth century, there was a burst of communitarian experimentation—both sectarian and secular. The Shakers remained a prominent and controversial example of Christian socialism throughout the period, with their fervent mass meetings, as did numerous communities of Rappites, Zoarites, and other communities of European religious immigrants. Robert Southey and Samuel Taylor Coleridge had announced their plan for a Pantisocracy on the banks of the Susquehanna in Pennsylvania. The most widely known socialist experiment was Robert Owen's New Harmony, founded on May 1, 1825 on the site of a lapsed Rappite village in the Ohio Valley. Owen's "Declaration of Mental Independence" declared that "*Man, up to this hour, has been, in all parts of the earth, a slave to a TRINITY of the most monstrous evils that could be combined to inflict mental and physical evil upon his whole race.* I refer to PRIVATE, OR INDIVIDUAL PROPERTY—ABSURD AND IRRATIONAL SYSTEMS OF RELIGION—and MARRIAGE. . . ." Owen's son, Robert Dale Owen, together with Fanny Wright, founder of the free black commune, Nashoba, moved to New York City in 1828. There they published the radical newspaper, the *Free Enquirer*, and founded the New York Workingmen's Party, together with agrarian radical, George Henry Evans, publisher of the newspapers, *The Working Man's Advocate* and *Young America*. The first historian of the American socialism, John Humphrey Noyes, observes that the "same men, or at least the same sort of men that took part in the Owen movement were afterward carried away by the Fourier enthusiasm. The two movements may therefore be regarded as one; and in that view the period of the great American socialistic revival extends from 1824, through the final overwhelming excitement of 1843, to the collapse of Fourierism after 1846."[14] Thus, there was both substantial ideological continuity and transfer of personnel between the Association and the working-class radical movement. The periodicals of the 1840s are filled with impassioned debate about the doctrines of the Association movement. Horace Greeley's *New York Tribune* carried a front-page column by Albert Brisbane for a year and a half. Everyone who read was forced to take a position on Associationism. At least thirty phalanxes were founded in the United States, with memberships ranging from one to five hundred. And each attracted a large periphery of interested observers, many of whom would have joined had the price of shares not been so high. Estimates of the number of Associationists and their active supporters range as high as 100,000. And, it should be remembered that the movement was composed not only of dislocated farmers and mechanics, but also substantially of members of the new middle classes: lawyers, merchants, doctors, shopkeepers, ministers, and writers. The national movement into which Ripley led the more radical of Boston's Transcendentalist intellectuals was not a mere curiosity, but a sustained and highly visible ideological challenge—if not, finally, a material one—to the developing course of capitalism. Emerson put it this way: "the whole world is awaking to the idea of union" (CW 3.267).

CHAPTER 12

CAPITALISM AND THE MORAL
GEOGRAPHY OF *WALDEN*

A peripatetic philosopher, and out-of-doors for the best part of his days
and nights, [Thoreau] had manifold weather and seasons in him; the
manners of an animal of probity and virtue unstained. Of all our moralists, he seemed the wholesomest, the busiest, and the best republican
citizen in the world; always at home minding his own affairs. A little over-
confident by genius, and stiffly individual, dropping society clean out of
his theories . . . there was in him an integrity and love of justice that made
possible and actual the virtues of Sparta and the Stoics—all the more
welcome in this time of shuffling and pusillanimity.

—Bronson Alcott

Thoreau is extravagant, even self-consciously defiant, when he claims in
Walden to feel more at home at the Pond than in Concord:

Yet I experienced sometimes that the most sweet and tender, the most
innocent and encouraging society may be found in any natural object,
even for the poor misanthrope and most melancholy man. There can be
no very black melancholy to him who lives in the midst of nature and has
his senses still. There was never yet such a storm but it was Aeolian music
to a healthy and innocent ear. Nothing can rightly compel a simple and
brave man to a vulgar sadness. While I enjoy the friendship of the seasons
I trust that nothing can make life a burden to me. (W 131)

This is more than a simple claim to be comfortable in woods where his
neighbors felt uneasy. The invidiousness of the distinction between nature
and society becomes so strong that Thoreau transplants the few desiderata
remaining in Concord, cultivating them in the woods instead:

I have never felt lonesome, or in the least oppressed by a sense of solitude,
but once, and that was a few weeks after I came to the woods, when, for
an hour, I doubted if the near neighborhood of man was not essential to
a serene and healthy life. To be alone was something unpleasant. But I was

at the same time conscious of a slight insanity in my mood, and seemed to foresee my recovery. In the midst of a gentle rain while these thoughts prevailed, I was suddenly sensible of such sweet and beneficent society in Nature, in the very pattering of the drops, and in every sight and sound around my house, an infinite and unaccountable friendliness all at once like an atmosphere sustaining me, as made the fancied advantages of human neighborhood insignificant, and I have never thought of them since. Every little pine needle expanded and swelled with sympathy and befriended me. I was so distinctly made aware of the presence of something kindred to me, even in scenes which we are accustomed to call wild and dreary, and also that the nearest of blood to me and humanest was not a person nor a villager, that I thought no place could ever be strange to me again. (W 131–132)

Gentle, sweet, beneficent, friendly, sustaining, sympathetic, kindred, nearest of blood, humanest: this rising catalogue paints a community all the more tightly bound the larger it grows, with nature occupying the far end of every social bond. It is not just that Thoreau feels strongly about rural landscapes. The sharp negative remains firmly in place: such feelings are not possible in the company of other people.[1]

Reversals like this seemed perverse to many of Thoreau's early readers. For instance, Emerson records, in his Journal for August 1843, his feelings about the early excursion essay, "A Winter Walk," which rehearses many of the distinctive rhetorical strategies on which *Walden* depends:

H. D. T. sends me a paper with the old fault of unlimited contradiction. . . . He praises wild mountains & winter forests for their domestic air; villagers & wood choppers for their urbanity; and the wilderness for resembling Rome & Paris. With the constant inclination to dispraise cities & civilization, he can yet find no way to honour woods & woodmen except by paralleling them with towns and townsmen.

Emerson's frustration measures the degree to which his *protégé* was writing against the grain.[2] The most familiar contemporary idiom for description of forested hills such as those around Walden Pond focused exactly on their forbidding emptiness, on the awful sublimity of endless repetition. Such a landscape was read as a field of conquest, of struggle for the establishment of civilization within and against an encompassing, and potentially engulfing, nature. By describing a comfortable community in nature and opposing it to the alienated life of Concord, Thoreau was appropriating and modifying an alternative tradition. The pastoral valorized a middle or picturesque landscape in opposition to the deprivations of both the city and the wilderness. His strongest modification of the pastoral, then, is to erase the bonds between humans that had been its central focus and claim membership in a community of nature.[3]

Thoreau's sense of kinship with raindrops and pine needles has been central focus of the ecocritical reassessment of his work. His writing records, it is argued, the lived experience of ecocentric consciousness compelling an ethical stance toward nature. His sympathy with the nonhuman is said to mark him as ahead of his time, as recognizing the moral standing of beings now included, by the more environmentally advanced, in a concentrically expanding ecological republic. He is said to have practiced, a hundred years early, what Aldo Leopold later formalized when he argued that the social contract should include "soils, waters, plants, and animals" and that "a thing is right when it tends to preserve the integrity, stability, and beauty of the biotic community. It is wrong when it tends otherwise." This is a powerful reading of Thoreau's significance. But how do we respond to the cynical response to Thoreau's professed love of nature that has been common for so long? James Russell Lowell, for instance, makes this famous postmortem assessment:

> Thoreau's experiment actually presupposed all that complicated civilization which it theoretically abjured. He squatted on another man's land; he borrows an axe; his boards, his nails, his bricks, his mortar, his books, his lamp, his fish-hooks, his plough, his hoe, all turn state's evidence against him as an accomplice in the sin of that artificial civilization which rendered it possible that such a person as Henry D. Thoreau should exist at all.

Although we can simply dismiss this as cynical chatter and move on, we would do well to assess seriously Lowell's implied claim: that perfection of the kind Thoreau sought is only possible under tightly controlled conditions, that moral absolutism is based on an erasure of the social context within which alone such choices become meaningful. Michael Gilmore updates Lowell's claim, reading *Walden*'s density and opacity as a rhetorical strategy meant to render the book uncommodifiable by a developing literary market that Thoreau saw as impure. Thoreau voices a "profound hostility to the process of exchange" along with a "conviction that literature can change the world," but "the aesthetic strategies he adopts to accomplish political objectives involve him in a series of withdrawals from history; in each case the ahistorical maneuver disables the political. . . ." Chief among these maneuvers is the hypostatization of nature into an unchanging transcendental reality. Gilmore goes on to argue that *Walden* is a "defeated text" since Thoreau's retreat into the transcendental is the outcome of "a crisis of confidence in the likelihood of civic reform and the idea of writing as a means of instigating it."[4]

But when Thoreau declared independence from a degraded historical republic and allegiance to an alternative natural community, he hoped that his retreat would end in a decisive advance. The simple problem/ solution structure of *Walden* attests to Thoreau's immersion in the main currents of thought in New England: "Economy" delivers its harsh critique of Concord, where "the mass of men live lives of quiet desperation" (W 8), then the rest of the book builds gradually to the redemptive climax of "Spring" and "Conclusion." And since Emerson remarked in his eulogy that Thoreau was in himself "a practical answer to the theories of the socialists," it has been common to observe that in moving to Walden Pond, Thoreau established an experimental community of one, analogous in its impulse to the collective venture at Brook Farm. But the observation usually stopped there, largely because of Thoreau's proverbial hostility to reformers, recorded in the numerous jabs at urban philanthropists for their unctuousness and punctilio, and in one seemingly conclusive passage from his Journal for March 1841: "As for these communities—I think I had rather keep a batchelor's hall in hell than go to board in heaven.—Dost think thy virtue will be boarded with you? It will never live on the interest of your money, depend upon it."[5]

Thoreau's disagreements were more thoughtful than such an easy jab indicates. Sterling Delano recently discovered, at long last, documentary evidence that Thoreau visited Brook Farm. He went there on December 3, 1843 and not long afterward Farm resident George P. Bradford wrote at letter to Emerson, inquiring worriedly after Thoreau and expressing regret at having allowed a man with such delicate health to depart in an omnibus during a snowstorm. Bradford also remarks, tantalizingly, "We are quite indebted to Henry for his brave defense of his thought which gained him much favor in the eyes of some of the friends here who are of the like faith." Bradford's letter confirms what has long been suspected— that Thoreau was more than simply aware of the goings on at Brook Farm. He saw himself as engaged in a vitally important conversation with the utopian socialists there. In February 1847, Thoreau lectured at the Concord Lyceum on the Walden experiment. Emerson's account of that evening in a letter to Fuller makes clear not only the intended audience of Thoreau's performance, but also the quite genial tone of the relationship: "Mrs. Ripley & other members of the opposition came down the other night to hear Henry's Account of his housekeeping at Walden Pond . . . and were charmed with the witty wisdom which ran through it all." We often spend our best energies differentiating ourselves from those to whom we are closest. The fact is that Thoreau and the Brook Farmers were far closer in their thinking about society and the meaning of leaving it than it has been common to admit. And *Walden*, both the book and the retreat, was an attempt to answer the socialists by putting into practice Emersonian ideas about the pedagogy of nature, cultural leaders, and national revival.[6]

Walden follows the logic of Association by articulating a moral critique of capitalist social relations that is rooted in a tentatively materialist analysis of economic relationships. The book's first sentence frames its concerns: "When I wrote the following pages, or rather the bulk of them, I lived alone, in the woods, a mile from any neighbor, in a house which I had built myself, on the shore of Walden Pond, in Concord, Massachusetts, and earned my living by the labor of my hands only" (W 3). Rhetorically, the emphasis here is on the last phrase. The cabin is located in an intermediate space, just a short walk into the woods, and the pond is firmly contained in the township. Moreover, the string of miscellaneous descriptors that locate the cabin also foreground the definite assertion about who built it, an assertion that is repeated in the alliterative final phrase. *Walden* is not a book that is mainly about the woods. It is about earning a living there. And its accounts of aesthetic experience of nature mainly demonstrate what gets lost—along with reading, introspection, spirituality—when work dominates our lives. The book's introduction, the pages that precede its systematic discussion of the four basic necessities of life, "Food, Shelter, Clothing, and Fuel," mount an analysis of the process whereby these forms of ideal experience have been cheapened (W 12).[7]

"Economy" begins by announcing as its topic its audience's "outward condition or circumstances in this world, in this town, what it is, whether it is necessary that it be as bad as it is, whether it cannot be improved as well as not" (W 4). From this starting point, Thoreau describes the effects of capitalist property relations, labor relations, and competition on the lives of individual workers and farmers. One on hand, there are those small farmers "whose misfortune it is to have inherited farms, houses, barns, cattle, and farming tools; for these are more easily required than got rid of" (W 5). On the other, there are those who "are poor . . . and have come to this page to spend borrowed or stolen time, robbing your creditors of an hour" (W 6). Both face the trap of debt and to escape it must "persuade your neighbor to let you make his shoes, or his hat, or his coat, or his carriage, or import his groceries for him . . ." (W 7). Thoreau performs a delicate balancing act here, giving clear attention to the hard material reality of economic relationships between individuals, but then showing that these relationships have moral and social content that gets forgotten. The things that get done for money are the kinds of basic human tasks that carry individual lives forward and bind communities together, and they are demeaned, as human interactions, by their intrication in a cash economy. Thoreau generalizes from his observations on the "outward condition" of his readers to an overall assessment of the effect of capitalist social relations on the character of human aesthetic and spiritual experience. Not only do most people work so much that their inner lives are emptied out, but also the moral character of individual human lives is compromised specifically because they occur within a constraining web of competitive economic relationships, a market: "the laboring man has not leisure for a true integrity day by day; he cannot afford to sustain the manliest relations to men; his labor would depreciate in the market" (W 6).[8]

Much of the rest of "Economy," after this first framing section, sets out to document various forms of moral debility that are produced when basic human needs are transformed by competitive social relations. Thoreau deplores luxury as an accretion, a kind of plaque that comes with civilization, and focuses especially on the competitive acquisition and ostentatious display of luxury goods as a display of social and economic power: "It is an interesting question how far men would retain their relative rank if they were divested of their clothes. Could you, in such a case, tell surely of any company of civilized men, which belonged to the most respected class" (W 22)? Thoreau describes how this kind of competition for cultural power entraps people so that they become "slave-drivers" of themselves. And he observes that this process is set in motion by the ruling class: "It is the luxurious and dissipated who set the fashion which the herd so diligently follow" (W 36). Thus, it is specifically in the context of class societies that most "of the luxuries, and many of the so-called comforts of life [become] positive hinderances to the elevation of mankind" (W 14). Fine clothes, for instance, are hindrances not only because the hard labor required to get them prevents plucking life's finer fruits. But also, they require participation in an economic system based on exploitation, a "factory system" in which "the condition of the operatives is becoming every day more like that of the English" of Manchester and Birmingham (W 26). After all, in this degraded society, "the principal object is, not that mankind may be well and honestly clad, but, unquestionably that the corporations may be enriched" (W 27). In other words, material structures at the level of whole social orders entangle people in moral relationships that must be taken seriously.

Thoreau recognizes most clearly that moral experience is rooted in materiality when he states that people "are so occupied with the factitious cares and superfluously coarse labors of life that its finer fruits cannot be plucked by them." But this crucial sentence also reveals his conviction that "most men even in this comparatively free country" become entangled in capitalist economic relations "through mere ignorance and mistake" (W 6). After making such a clear assessment of the moral effects of material social relations, Thoreau adopts a cavalierly voluntarist position about how to respond. He is startling confident. He is astonished that people "honestly think there is no choice left" (W 8), after all, "what a man thinks of himself, that it is which determines, or rather indicates, his fate" (W 7). And he sets out to demonstrate just this possibility by renouncing all forms of luxury, choosing not to spend his time "in earning rich carpets or other fine furniture, or delicate cookery, or a house in the Grecian or the Gothic style" (W 70). Moreover, because he acknowledges that the basic necessities must be secured before it is possible "to entertain the true problems of life with freedom" (W 12), he determines to secure them by his own labor outside the nexus of material social relationships.

Thoreau carries this anticapitalist polemic through to the end, but he hints at a consciousness that his experiment has failed. Individual withdrawal from the market into the world of ideal beans turns out not to be as easy as it might seem, for "wherever a man goes, men will pursue and paw him with their dirty institutions" (W 170). Thoreau reveals this anxiety quite clearly at the end of "Economy": "When formerly I was looking about to see what I could do for a living . . . I thought often and seriously of picking huckleberries." Like hoeing beans, berry picking would have been an attempt to negotiate an individual solution to a social crisis, and Thoreau acknowledges as much: "But I have since learned that trade curses everything it handles; and though you trade in messages from heaven, the whole curse of trade attaches to the business" (W 70). An individual solution, in other words, is incommensurate with the problem as he has laid it out—unless his individual actions can be made to seem a necessary prelude to a broader social transformation.[9]

In these last pages of "Economy," Thoreau acknowledges that his experiment "is very selfish," but he defiantly, even petulantly, satirizes his socialist neighbors: "a large house is not proportionally more expensive than a small one, since one roof may cover, one cellar underlie, and one wall separate several apartments." Still he insists that he prefers to live alone since "it will commonly be cheaper to build the whole yourself than to convince another of the advantage of the common wall; and when you have done this, the common partition, to be much cheaper, must be a thin one, and that other may prove a bad neighbor, and also not keep his side in repair." He goes on to accuse the Farmers of hypocrisy, claiming that "what so saddens the reformer is not his sympathy with his fellows in distress, but, though he be the holiest son of God, is his private ail. Let this be righted, let the spring come to him, the morning rise over his couch, and he will forsake his generous companions without apology." And he concludes by offering this characteristic advice: "If, then, we would indeed restore mankind by truly Indian, botanic, magnetic, or natural means, let us first be as simple and well as Nature ourselves, dispel the clouds that hang over our own brows, and take up a little life into our pores. Do not stay to be an overseer of the poor, but endeavor to become one of the worthies of the world."

As if to demonstrate the power of his ideas, Thoreau enacts restoration by natural means in "The Ponds," *Walden's* central chapter, which dramatizes the scholarly narrative of natural instruction, with its new geography of nature versus society. But it also reveals the existence of a critical fault-line built into that geography. The chapter opens with a four-paragraph proem in which its controlling themes are established in two emblematic excursions. The first is a westward ramble, a release from "human society and gossip." This ramble delivers a compressed reminder of the full-blown analysis of Concord that Thoreau carries out in the book's first chapter, "Economy":

> [Huckleberries] do not yield their true flavor to the purchaser of them, nor to him who raises them for the market. . . . It is a vulgar error to suppose that you have tasted huckleberries who never plucked them. A huckleberry never reaches Boston; they have not been known there since they grew on her three hills. . . . The ambrosial and essential part of the fruit is lost with the bloom which is rubbed off in the market cart, and they become mere provender.

What is lost when natural objects are incorporated into commercial transactions is a cluster of desiderata: spontaneity, organicism, authenticity, individuality, "the tonic of wildness"—all these are "rubbed off" by commodification and what should be a meal for the spirit becomes "mere provender" (W 173).

If the right way to get hold of huckleberries is to gather them yourself, the same goes for fish, the object of the second excursion in Thoreau's proem. It turns out there is far more to harvesting food in the wild than the pleasure of outwitting the market. Doing so, one is returned, sometimes sharply, to transcendental truths:

> These [midnights spent fishing] were very memorable and valuable to me,—anchored in forty feet of water, and twenty or thirty rods from the shore, surrounded sometimes by thousands of small perch and shiners, dimpling the surface with their tails in the moonlight, and communicating by a long flaxen line with mysterious nocturnal fishes which had their

dwelling forty feet below. . . . At length you slowly raise, pulling hand over hand, some horned pout squeaking and squirming to the upper air. It was very queer, especially in dark nights, when your thoughts had wandered to vast and cosmogonal themes in other spheres, to feel this faint jerk which came to interrupt your dreams and link you to Nature again. It seemed as if I might next cast my line upward into the air, as well as downward into this element which was scarcely more dense. Thus I caught two fishes as it were with one hook. (W 175)

Thoreau, in this tableau, plays a representative scholarly seeker of (self-) knowledge. He floats alone above nature's glittering surface. He is initially distracted by thousands of bright, but insignificant phenomena of the kind immediately accessible to empirical observation, or "understanding." But he is quickly hailed by deeper noumena, which reveal themselves to him by direct intuition. The truths apprehended by intuition operating on nature are the higher laws that form the basis of Transcendentalist ontology. These laws explain the connections between apparently unrelated things. Water and air, for instance, a liquid and a gas, are both fluids and thus behave alike. Just so, and crucially, the natural and the supernatural worlds are structured by cognate laws. Thoreau's punch line—two fishes, one hook—is a distillation of the doctrine of correspondence. Sherman Paul remarks that for "those who see the creation as broken in half, correspondence is a way of joining the spiritual and natural halves" for natural phenomena, if properly apprehended, indicate the working of the divine laws according to which creation was and remains structured.[10]

Thoreau's proem, then, like *Walden* as a whole, takes the form of a problem and solution. There is Concord with its deadening commercial order. Then there is Walden Pond, offering restorative contact with the ideal. Having established this basic opposition, Thoreau moves on to an extended illustration of right and wrong ways of being in nature. The main body of the chapter opens with a straightforwardly factual description of the pond and the topography of the land around it. The tone is consistently flat:

The scenery of Walden is on a humble scale, and, though very beautiful, does not approach to grandeur, nor can it much concern one who has not long frequented it or lived by its shore; yet this pond is so remarkable for its depth and purity as to merit a particular description. It is a clear and deep green well, half a mile long and a mile and three quarters in circumference, and contains about sixty-one and a half acres. . . . (W 175)

Thoreau proceeds in this mode from topic to topic: the water's changing color in different lights, its peculiar clarity, its fluctuating level and temperature, the species of fish caught there, the curious circular nests on the bottom. His characteristic extravagance is held on short leash as he rehearses the narrow empiricism of an Enlightenment natural philosopher or a State Street utilitarian.

Then, several pages into the chapter, Thoreau quite abruptly shifts tack. He abandons facticity, declaring that a lake is "earth's eye, looking into which the beholder measures the depth of his own nature" (W 186). The long paragraph that follows begins with a description of the pond as it looked once when he bent over and stared at it through his legs from atop a nearby hill. In part this lampoons the conventions of picturesque travel, whose cartoonishly empiricist participants often used concave mirrors made of smoked glass to look over their shoulders at landscapes that they then evaluated according to accepted rules of painterly composition. But, as so often, Thoreau combines the ridiculous and the serious. He sees "a thread of finest gossamer stretched across the valley, and gleaming against the distant pine woods, separating one stratum of the atmosphere from another. You would think you could walk dry under it to the opposite hills, and that the swallows which skim over might perch on it" (W 186). By looking at the pond "upside-down," by deliberately tinkering with the act of perception, he sees its surface as a permeable membrane between the material and spiritual worlds. This emblem of nature as a window on divinity completes the foundation for the famous apostrophe:

> It is a soothing employment . . . to sit on a stump on such a height as this, overlooking the pond and study the dimpling circles which are incessantly inscribed on its otherwise invisible surface. . . . Not a fish can jump or an insect fall but it is thus reported in circling dimples, in lines of beauty, as it were the constant welling up of its fountain, the gentle pulsing of its life, the heaving of its breast. The thrills of joy and the thrills of pain are undistinguishable. How peaceful the phenomena of the lake! Again the works of man shine as in the spring. Ay, every leaf and twig and stone and cobweb sparkles now at mid-afternoon as when covered with dew in a spring morning. Every motion of an oar or an insect produces a flash of light; and if an oar falls, how sweet the echo!
>
> In such a day, in September or October, Walden is a perfect forest mirror, set round with stones as precious to my eyes as if fewer or rarer. Nothing so fair, so pure, and at the same time so large, as a lake, perchance, lies on the surface of the earth. Sky water. (W 187–188)

Rhetorically, Thoreau leaves his desk behind to enter, across several years, the present perfect of his former self, and then enacts, in the telling, a moment of further communion, a moment in which the scene so exactly mirrors his state of mind that he begins to disappear into it. He becomes visible only in reflection, in the expanding disturbance set off by a lackadaisically relinquished oar (and, of course, in the exclamation that disturbs the reportorial surface). Thoreau associated critical self-consciousness with "lower," learned forms of thought, with the dull predictability of premise and syllogism. Its absence indicates the operation of pure, spontaneous intuition— the direct inrush of unexpected truths. And yet, paradoxically, nothing could be more self-conscious, more cultivated, than his assuming the mantle of natural unreason, of true Reason.[11]

Thoreau's enactment of double communion marks the chapter's crescendo; its denouement, though, is none too peaceful. In its remaining pages, Society returns with a vengeance. His tale of natural pedagogy has relied, so far, on a carefully protected scene: the idyllic schoolroom of nature in which the student roams freely and alone. The vulnerability of this tableau is a measure of its artificiality. And the violence of Thoreau's reaction to an immanent threat to its stability indicates just how tense are the oppositions, the geographical segregations, established during its construction. "Nothing so fair, so pure, and at the same time so large, as a lake, perchance, lies on the surface of the earth. Sky water." Then, Thoreau adds, "It needs no fence" (W 188). This fence marks a crucial turning point in "The Ponds." Thoreau has patiently worked his way up to this apostrophe, and its dramatization of *Walden's* main point, that spontaneous intuitive apprehension of spiritual correspondences in Nature offers the key to individual generation, and, thus, to national regeneration. But, quite suddenly, he seems to lose control of his metaphors. Until now, he has managed to keep town and country cleanly segregated. "It needs no fence." Of course, Thoreau was all too aware of Concord's seemingly uncontrollable urge to build fences. And not needing a fence is quite different from being unfenceable. Nature's divinity, its dependability as a source of spontaneously apprehended truths, depends, paradoxically, on its being immutable, transhistorically stable. Walden Pond's plausibility as a vehicle for that burden depends on the absolute absence of fences, on its being sacrosanct, impenetrable by Concord's grasping farmers. This nature, Emerson's nature of "space, the air, the river, a leaf," proves considerably less dependable than natural law (CW 1.8). For fences are only the first in the series of changes by which a piece of land like that which contains Walden Pond can be transformed into a farm, which, although it may be a "mute gospel," is also a unit of degraded production (CW 1.26).[12]

The mere suggestion that nature, the schoolroom of genius, might be vulnerable to human transformation, that it might be an unreliable text, requires a sturdy response. In the next sentence, Thoreau reassures, firmly: "Nations come and go without defiling it." He turns here to one of the central arguments of Romantic historiography—the idea that the forward progress of humankind must be read on a world-scale, that the fates of individual nations are insignificant oscillations on a larger rising curve. This idea has done great service for the Transcendentalist movement as a whole, offering a way to reconcile political and religious optimism with the dispiriting record of European history. In this context, on the other hand, it allows Thoreau to level temporal, geographic, and ethnic distinctions between nations, and to range them under the homogenizing term, Society, as a collective enemy to nature and to his total immersion in its unspoiled peace.[13]

Negative assertion of the pond's unsulliedness proves insufficient though, so Thoreau returns to the reassuring image of its mirrored surface in which spiritual and material worlds, the self and nature, meet:

> Nations come and go without defiling it. It is a mirror which no stone can crack, whose quicksilver will never wear off, whose gilding Nature continually repairs; no storm, no dust, can dim its surface ever fresh;—a mirror in which all impurity presented to it sinks, swept and dusted by the sun's hazy brush,—this is the light dust-cloth,—which retains no breath that is breathed on it, but sends its own to float as clouds high above its surface and be reflected in its bosom still. (W 188)

Now that his concern is to shut down the border rather than to see his transcendent self, the pond as mirror proves quite unreliable. First, he tries several phrases that extrapolate from a common piece of coated glass—this one cannot be broken, it will not wear out, and so forth. All rather tenuous. So, he turns from disappointing materiality to miraculous resilience, fluid stability. The pond can, he thunders, absorb impurities without changing, can repel the noxious vapors of the world while remaining pure. The final result is semantic overload. Such zealous defense of the border makes its artificiality unmistakable. The chapter never recovers.

For the remainder of "The Ponds," Thoreau oscillates between these modes—idyllic description of Walden Pond and bitter condemnation of Concord. In the last paragraph, his assurance about the side to which the victory will finally go seems to have dissolved, replaced wholly by the rage that has been mounting since the first apparition of the fence. He closes the section down with a jarring blast:

> White Pond and Walden are great crystals on the surface of the earth, Lakes of Light. . . . They are too pure to have a market value; they contain no muck. We never learned meanness of them. . . . Nature has no

human inhabitant who appreciates her. The birds with their plumage and with their notes are in harmony with the flowers, but what youth or maiden conspires with the wild luxuriant beauty of Nature? She flourishes most alone, far from the towns where they reside. Talk of heaven! ye disgrace earth. (W 199–200)

Thoreau gestures at the heart of the matter, the market. But notice what happens: what begins as an assertion of the superiority of Walden to Concord—an assertion meant to call Concord to its senses—collapses into an abstract and demoralized denunciation of towns in general.

The moral geography of the scholars' tale, then, lays the foundation for an invidious and disabling distinction. As Emerson puts it, nature's "serene order is inviolable by us" (CW 1.39). Its ideal truths, especially about organic, peaceful change, will ground the scholars when they step forth to lead the nation out of crisis:

> The poet, the orator, bred in the woods, whose senses have been nourished by their fair and appeasing changes, year after year, without design and without heed,—shall not lose their lesson altogether, in the roar of cities or the broil of politics. Long hereafter, amidst agitation and terror in national councils,—in the hour of revolution,—these solemn images shall reappear in their morning luster. . . . (CW 1.21)

Nature materialized as a rural landscape has become a sacred pedagogical space, in which the young genius is exposed to none of the corrupting influences of the city he is destined to redeem. But the energy required to maintain its purity absolutizes both it and the society to which it is opposed. Nature becomes "a fixed point whereby we may measure our departure. As we degenerate, the contrast between us and our house is more evident" (CW 1.39). What began in the reformer's vocabulary as a liberatory distinction between a specific social order and a regime of transcendent laws has now become a Manichean moral opposition between a permanently vicious society and a transhistorically innocent but threatened nature. Nature has been materialized as a metaphysical ideal. Finally, reading nature has become definitively important, but it is no longer legible for all: "There is a property in the horizon which no man has but he whose eye can integrate all the parts. . . . To speak truly, few adult persons can see nature. Most persons do not see the sun. At least they have a very superficial seeing" (CW 1.9). Nature is now a reproach to that mass of townish misreaders who, in their irredeemable ignorance insist on defacing the text.

CHAPTER 13

WALDEN, ASSOCIATION, AND ORGANIC IDEALISM

> When my hoe tinkled against the stones, that music echoed to the woods and sky, and was an accompaniment to my labor which yielded an instant and immeasurable crop. It was no longer beans that I hoed, nor I that hoed beans; and I remembered with as much pity as pride, if I remembered at all, my acquaintances who had gone to the city to attend the oratorios.
>
> —Henry David Thoreau (W 159)

It would have been impossible, even in Concord and Roxbury, certainly in Boston, to avoid daily confrontation with the brutal, often fatal, immiseration of thousands in the years following the Panic of 1837. Yet, both Thoreau and the Associationists are mostly quiet on the issue. Occasional passages indicate awareness. Charles Anderson Dana, for instance, in a lecture delivered before the New England Fourier Society in Boston, gestures briefly at the people his auditors have walked by on the way into the hall:

> No one who has had any experience in our cities, where, within the sound of music and gay company, with half frantic eyes lighted only by gleams from luxurious halls, hunger and pain lie gasping . . . could fail of regarding with peculiar gratitude a method of escape from such fearful evils, which, in offering abundance to all, invades the established rights of none. . . .

Dana aesthetizes Boston's paupers almost to the point of invisibility in front of an elite crowd of potential recruits. Association was not a program of or for the lower orders, whose hunger and pain Dana decorously personifies. Rather, as he makes clear, it was a plan aimed quite specifically at outflanking the threat of working-class radicalism:

> It is an essential characteristic of the new Social Science, that it is pacific and not destructive. It does not so much seek to overturn the old order of things, as to supplant it; it does not tear down our rotten and creaking

shelter, until its own beautiful mansion invites us to a more secure abode. It aims first of all at a reconciliation of interests: it appears in the world with only words of peace in its mouth, and only implements of peace in its hands. It calls on individuals, on parties, and on nations, to lay aside their differences, and to find, in a just union of material forces, the only sure means of private success, and of public well-being.

The narrative of withdrawal here makes clear that Dana has pointed to the spectacle of misery alongside opulence, not to harness his audience's energies to the defense of the poor, but to force them to reflect on their own participation in such immoral tableaux. The invocation urges their quick departure from society into a community of like-minded utopians. The poor occupy the same place rhetorically in Association as they do politically, that of soft-focused markers of a dying order.[1]

Similarly, in *Walden*, Thoreau's interest in involuntary poverty is limited to its potential rhetorical uses. He, too, is concerned above all to borrow the reflection that the irretrievably poor cast on society:

> It is a mistake to suppose that, in a country where the usual evidences of civilization exist, the condition of a very large body of the inhabitants may not be as degraded as that of savages. . . . To know this I should not need to look farther than to the shanties which everywhere border our railroads, that last improvement in civilization. . . . Their condition only proves what squalidness may consist with civilization. (W 34–35)

This passage is part of the discussion of shelter in "Economy," throughout which Thoreau assails his audience for its ignorance of the true necessaries of life, for its descent into the greedy scramble after merely financial wealth. Occasionally, he raises the issue of unequal access to social resources as part of this argument, but his point is not to encourage redistribution. His paramount concern about capitalism is that it breeds not material, but spiritual and intellectual poverty.

Similarly, Ripley, writing in *The Harbinger*, argues that life in society soon teaches people "to calculate on selfishness, more or less disguised, on falsehood, however glossed over with the appearance of truth, on fraud, which though in fear of public opinion, is always ready to entrap the heedless." He offers a thumbnail sketch of the problem's cause: "the man who is so devoted to gaining wealth, that he appears on 'Change like a walking money-bag, with no ideas beyond his ledger and cash-book, with no hope but that of becoming a millionaire. . . ."[2] Thoreau, likewise, directs his critique at what he sees as the degenerative influence of greed among "that seemingly wealthy, but most terribly impoverished class of all, who have accumulated dross, but know not how to use it, or get rid of it, and thus have forged their own golden or silver fetters" (W 16). Here is the true enemy of both Thoreau and the Associationists: amoral capitalists who single-mindedly pursue material wealth and disregard the noblesse oblige—the duty to the poor incident on such a position in society. The central problem was how to effect the ethical regeneration of the ruling class.

An immediate problem, though, for themselves as would-be reformers, and by implication for those they hoped to reform, was to steal enough time away from work to pursue programs of improvement. Elizabeth Palmer Peabody zeroed in on what was therefore a main attraction of Brook Farm:

> The hours redeemed from labor by community, will not be reapplied to the acquisition of wealth, but to the production of intellectual goods. This community aims to be rich, not in the metallic representative of wealth, but in the wealth itself, which money should represent; namely, THE LEISURE TO LIVE IN ALL THE FACULTIES OF THE SOUL.

Acquisitive labor, manual or otherwise, impinges on higher pursuits, not only by corrupting the laborer, but also by the more mundane mechanism of requiring too much time. Thus, the Brook Farmers redirected the call for the ten-hour day so that the object of concern is not the working class, but the potentially salvageable burgher, the slave-driver of himself. It is a symptomatic formulation. The pursuit of intellectual goods is limited to a special kind of time—leisure time—that is directly opposed to labor time. For many of those concerned, this was, to be sure, a commonsensical idea. Thoreau and most of the early Brook Farmers were, after all, producers of intellectual goods—writers, editors, artists, ministers who had come out of their churches to devote themselves to reform. For many of them, getting a living, while also getting to the activities on which they had staked their identities, had been a problem that occupied a great deal of hard thought.[3]

The problem, so conceived, admits of two solutions. One is to reduce the amount of time necessary to get a living by labor. The Brook Farmers were confident that cooperation would produce vast economies of scale. Thoreau, of course, decided to reduce his wants to a bare minimum. The second solution is to spiritualize labor, thus transforming it into an activity that develops integrity and character in its own right. The young Hawthorne caricatures the latter tactic in one of his first letters from Brook Farm:

> At the first glimpse of fair weather, Mr. Ripley summoned us into the cow-yard, and introduced me to an instrument with four prongs, commonly called a dung-fork. With this tool, I have already assisted to load twenty or thirty carts of manure, and shall take part in loading nearly three hundred more. Besides, I have planted potatoes and pease, cut straw and hay for the cattle, and done various other mighty works. . . . I have gained strength wonderfully—grown quite a giant, in fact, and can do a day's work without the slightest inconvenience. In short, I am transformed into a complete farmer.

He signs himself "Nath Hawthorne, Ploughman." The spiritualization here of manual labor is partly a matter of applying old ideas to a new situation—a revival of agrarian republicanism, with its opposition between, on one hand, an independent yeomanry who produce for their own use and, on the other, parasitical merchants who profit from the needs of others.[4]

But were it only necessary to distinguish oneself from brokers and merchants, it would be enough to display one's scholarly credentials, or to join the thousands still engaged in the home manufacture of shoes and palm-leaf hats. Farmwork was a means to a far richer distinction. Ripley writes:

> We cannot believe that the selfishness, the cold-heartedness, the indifference to truth, the insane devotion to wealth, the fierce antagonisms, the painted hypocrisies, the inward weariness, discontent, apathy, which are everywhere a characteristic of the present order of society, have any permanent basis in the nature of man; they are the poisonous weeds that a false system of culture has produced; change the system and you will see riches of the soil; a golden fruitage will rejoice your eye; but persist in the mode, which the experience of a thousand years has proved defective, and you can anticipate no better results.

The use here of an extended agricultural metaphor to frame the relation between human nature and nurture is no accident. Ripley understood the litany of moral failings, with which he begins the passage, as the consequence of poor human culture:

> It is an easy inference, that these monstrous evils are the true growth of human nature, that they belong to man as man, that they will never cease while his passions and propensities remain unchanged. A more profound view, however, shows us that the fault is not in the intrinsic elements of human nature, but in the imperfect institutions under which that nature is trained and developed.

A prior, fundamentally benign, human nature has been deformed by the imposition of the unnatural institutions of civilization. The solution to the problem of such institutions was to rediscover the lineaments of human nature, which were located in a pre-civil state of nature. Through a familiar reduction, nature (in the sense of prior laws and realities) was located in rural settings. Finally, labor on the farm was isolated as the ideal means of discovery, for it put one in direct contact with nature, the better to apprehend its laws. "I came to love my rows, my beans, though so many more than I wanted. They attached me to the earth, and so I got strength like Antaeus" (W 155). For Thoreau, the laws of human nature were the laws of his own nature, of his potential spiritual perfectibility. For the Brook Farmers, these same laws were the bedrock on which they hoped to build new, natural social institutions.[5]

Despite their desire to get their hands into the soil, Thoreau and the Associationists were by no means after a merger with the agricultural yeomanry. There is a clear element of self-conscious picturesqueness in both experiments. In "The Bean-Field," Thoreau writes:

> But labor of the hands, even when pursued to the verge of drudgery, is perhaps never the worst form of idleness. It has a constant and imperishable moral, and to the scholar it yields a classic result. A very *agricola laboriosus* was I to travelers bound westward through Lincoln and Wayland to nobody knows where; they sitting at their ease in gigs, with elbows on knees, and reins loosely hanging in festoons; I the home-staying, laborious native of the soil. (W 157)

Thoreau is anxious to point out that the travelers, of whose gaze he is so aware, ride in gigs, not wagons. They are wealthy urbanites, headed perhaps to country homes where they will dawdle on lawns maintained by hired hands. He tells us twice that he belongs here because he is laborious. Nina Baym argues that, in response to "rural economic decline, depopulation of the countryside, Yankee out-migration, non-Anglo (specifically Irish) immigration, urbanization, railroads, mills, and generalized agricultural malaise," *Walden* "is about preserving the New England way." For Baym, "Thoreau's Yankee nature is a farmer's nature, not a nature of gentry poseurs, scientific or gentlemen agriculturalists, sportsmen, landscapers, tourists, weekend gardeners, or retired millionaires." In other words, Thoreau's self-consciousness in his bean field, his concern to be observed, is not a matter of mere pride; rather, it is a sign of his close attention to the central process by which his splendid self-reliance, his spiritual progress, will inspire those who live off the labor of others to follow his lead. What Thoreau hoped to accomplish in his field was not only to make the earth say beans, but also to teach his neighbors a lesson on the spiritual value of manual labor.[6]

In his invitation to Emerson, Ripley writes of the Farm: "If wisely executed, it will be a light over this country and this age. If not the sunrise, it will be the morning star." Similarly, a letter from Brisbane to Ripley, in which he brushes off requests for a campaign to raise further capital, shows the extent to which the Farmers, like Thoreau, were concerned to be observed so that they might inspire others to emulate them:

> We have a great work to accomplish, that of organizing an Association, and to do it we must have means adequate to the task, and to get these means we must make the most persevering and Herculean efforts. . . . Fifteen thousand dollars might do a great deal at Brook Farm, but would it do the thing effectually—would it make a trial that would impress the public? And for anything short of that, none of us, I suppose, would labor.

It was far more important that one of the U.S. phalanxes succeed unequivocally and, most important, publicly, than that any one of them survive. The Farmers believed in a kind of epidemiological theory of revolution, whereby the clear advantages of life under socialism in a well-publicized experiment would convince increasing numbers of people to come out of their lives of individual toil. Socialism would exist alongside capitalism, growing ever stronger, until it finally supplanted its former rival. In an announcement of the May 1846 formation of the American Union of Associationists, the movement's national body, William Henry Channing puts it this way:

> From [the] horrible destiny which awaits the Working-Man, in his hope-less contrast with Machinery moved by Capital, we say there is no escape except by peaceful revolution. Destructive radicalism will but ensure a wider wo; and passive submission will but hasten the fast coming era of the reign of Money over Men.

Observed farmwork, then, for Thoreau and the Associationists, was a way of hastening the replacement of the spirit of commerce with new and more organic human relations.[7]

The theory of peaceful revolution was shared widely by the broad Transcendentalist movement. Frederick Henry Hedge, in "The Art of Life," gives it a succinct statement: "What the age requires is not books, but example, high, heroic example; not words but deeds; not societies but men,—men who shall have their root in themselves, and attract and convert the world by the beauty of their fruits." In "The Great Lawsuit," Margaret Fuller condemns the "French revolution, that strangely disguised angel," during which "the Goddess of Liberty was impure." However, she predicts that "a new manifestation is at hand, a new hour in the day of man" in which changed ideas about "inward and outward freedom for woman" will produce wholesale change. For Fuller, if sexist ideas can be overcome, a flowering of feminine influence will follow, and it will result in a complete organic transformation of society. Similarly, in "The American Scholar," Emerson defines the problem in society in characteristic terms as a matter of habits of thought: "Men such as they are, very naturally seek money or power; and power because it is as good as money,—the 'spoils,' so called, 'of office.' And why not? for they aspire to the highest, and this, in their sleep-walking, they dream is highest" (CW 1.65). The obvious solution to such philistinism then is to "Wake them, and they shall quit the false good, and leap to the true, and leave governments to clerks and desks. This revolution is to be wrought by the gradual domestication of the idea of Culture." Finally, it is the job of the individual scholar to domesticate this idea, not so much through the cultural products he makes, as through the cultivation of an exemplary life, a life of peaceful and benign influence: "The private life of one man shall be a more illustrious monarchy,—more formidable to its enemy, more sweet and serene in its influence to its friend, than any kingdom in history."[8]

Thoreau's eventual rejection of Association has usually been explained as an outcome of his doctrinal commitment to this kind of individualism, and there is a good deal truth to this assessment. However, it is also true that the Associationists were explicitly committed to the free development of the self, and argued that this was impossible under the limiting conditions of the broader society. Here, for instance, is how John Sullivan Dwight argues the matter in "Individuality in Association" in the first number of *The Harbinger*:

> We are prepared to take the ground that there is not and never can be Individuality, so long as there is not Association. Without true union no part can be true. The members were made for the body; if the whole body be incoherent, every member of it will be developed falsely, will become shrunken or overgrown, distorted and weakened, since it will have either more or less than its share, both of duty and sustenance.

Thoreau would have been willing to go some distance with this argument. For his most central objection to the institutionalized culture of regenerated souls at Brook Farm was not so much that it was a collective process, as that it relied on organized artifice. Emerson agreed, and in his *Dial* article, "Fourierism and the Socialists," makes this objection explicit. After describing the major points of Associationist doctrine in an odd tone that mixes appreciation with cool sarcasm, Emerson writes:

> Our feeling was, that Fourier has skipped no fact but one, namely, Life. He treats man as a plastic thing, something that may be put up or down, ripened or retarded, moulded, polished, made into solid, or fluid, or gas, at the will of the leader. . . . The faculty of life . . . spawns and scorns systems and system-makers [and] makes or supplants a thousand phalanxes and New-Harmonies with each pulsation.

Emerson uses Brook Farm as a metaphor in "Self-Reliance": "Society is a joint-stock company in which the members agree for the better securing of his bread to each shareholder, to surrender the liberty and culture of the eater" (CW 2.29). Although Emerson and Thoreau admired certain of the ends that Associationist plans were meant to achieve, they felt that the only reliable means to those ends was the spontaneous operation of broad trends in the history of ideas of which intellectuals like themselves were the organic expression. In a tantalizing aside in *Walden*, Thoreau remarks that "to act collectively is according to the spirit of our institutions" (W 110). The institution he has in mind is the Concord Lyceum, a collective mechanism whereby the village actively pursued its own culture. However, in a jab at the Brook Farmers, he also insists: "The only coöperation which is commonly possible is exceedingly partial and superficial. . . . If a man has faith, he will coöperate with equal faith everywhere; if he has not faith, he will continue to live like the rest of the world, whatever company he is joined to" (W 72). Emerson, in his letter to Ripley, refusing to join Brook Farm, portrayed Concord as his individual Utopia: "Here I have friends & kindred. Here I have builded & planted: & here I have greater facilities to prosecute such enterprises as I may cherish, than I could probably find by any removal." Association seemed to be a complicated and mechanical contrivance for solving a simple problem: "I cannot accuse my townsmen or my social position of my domestic grievances:—only my own sloth and conformity. It seems to me a circuitous & operous way of relieving myself of any irksome circumstances, to put on your community the task of my emancipation which I ought to take on myself." In his Journal, Emerson was more direct: "To join this body would be to traverse all my long trumpeted theory . . . that one man is a counterpoise to a city, that his solitude is more prevalent and beneficent than the concert of crowds." For both Emerson and Thoreau, then, one community was the appropriate target of their efforts to provoke organic change through self-culture, and it was the one in which they lived there and then, Concord.[9]

Farmwork may be honest, but it can also be, as Thoreau discovers, numbing drudgery. Hawthorne too came to feel that his mind could as easily be buried under a pile of manure as a pile of money. After all, the point was to grow into a giant, not just of the body, but of the mind and spirit. There were other ways too in which farmwork proved to be less than ideal. Alcott took Brook Farm to task for the enslavement of draught animals, polluting their fields with manure, and for the decision to carry crops to the market in Boston. Likewise, Thoreau was acutely aware of the ways in which the market had invaded the countryside:

> Ancient poetry and mythology suggest, at least, that husbandry was once a sacred art; but it is pursued with irreverent haste and heedlessness by us, our object being to have large farms and large crops merely. . . . By avarice and selfishness, and a grovelling habit, from which none of us is free, of regarding the soil as property, or the means of acquiring property chiefly, the landscape is deformed, husbandry is degraded with us, and the farmer leads the meanest of lives. (W 165)

Farmwork lost its charm when pursued for more than symbolic value; it threatened to become a business and to require capitulation to the low rationalism of the market. After that first season of producing for market, Thoreau scaled back to planting a few rows for personal consumption, limiting himself to keeping his fields in a "half-cultivated" state, saying to himself, grandly, "I will not plant beans and corn with so much industry another summer, but such seeds . . . as sincerity, truth, simplicity, faith, innocence, and the like . . ." (W 163–164). And finally, he concluded his experiment in farmwork by reformulating the question of where to go to contact nature:

> We are wont to forget that the sun looks on our cultivated fields and on the prairies and forests without distinction. They all reflect and absorb his rays alike, and the former make but a small part of the glorious picture which he beholds in his daily course. . . . This broad field which I have looked at so long looks not to me as the principle cultivator, but away from me to influences more genial to it, which water and make it green. These beans have results which are not harvested by me. Do they not grow for woodchucks partly? (W 166)

This is the root of the image of community in the wild to which Thoreau returns so often:

> The indescribable innocence and beneficence of Nature,—of sun and wind and rain, of summer and winter,—such health, such cheer, they afford forever! and such sympathy have they ever with our race, that all Nature would be affected and the sun's brightness fade, and the winds would sigh humanely, and the clouds rain tears, and the woods shed their leaves and put on mourning, if any man should ever for a just cause grieve. Shall I not have intelligence with the earth? Am I not partly leaves and vegetable mould myself? (W 138)

Intelligence with the earth offered Thoreau a spontaneous, organic means of connection with the redemptive laws of nature. This is the heart of his disagreement with Association, the heart of the change from *agricola laboriosus* to surveyor of the community of the woodlots. This is the logic of the final investiture of his utopian desire for a new moral order in the society of nature.

The two concluding chapters of *Walden* are structured by a vision of social regeneration driven by organic community with nature. There is, perhaps, no more extravagantly affirmative piece of oratorio in Thoreau's writing. These chapters have, of course, formed the subject of a huge body of scholarly interpretation, much of which sets out to explain just this quality of rhetorical extravagance. Most conclude that the chapters register the confidence and exhilaration of one who has discovered a reliable means of self-transformation, but miss or de-emphasize the point that, for Thoreau, this is the means to broader changes. Charles Anderson makes the most extreme version of this argument, arguing that "Spring" and "Conclusion" are flawed by occasional passages of sententious moralism that confuse its record of escape from time and space through self-transformation achieved by the practice of artistic craft. Sherman Paul, on the other hand, one of Thoreau's most sympathetic readers, shows how the principle of renewal in the deep cut passage holds out the promise of individual and therefore social redemption. He remarks that Thoreau "went to the woods, therefore, to try this experiment, with no intention of abandoning society or going primitive. Instead, by beginning from scratch, he would relive all human life and history and test the achievement of civilization by what he found, hoping, of course, to demonstrate that choice was still possible and to reorient society by showing what had been lost on the way." For Paul, the real center of dramatic interest is Thoreau's self-transformation, rather than its performative nature. But it is just this aspect of *Walden* that explains the fervor with which it announces the familiar idea that one must start at home to change the world. It is just this that explains why Thoreau reaches for such prodigious rhetorical heights at the end of a book that is by turns so unremittingly critical of the contemporary social order, so laconically derisive of projectors of a better collective future.[10]

"Spring" begins in the scientistic mode with which Thoreau so often sets up correspondential revelations. He notes differences in water temperature at different points in the pond on March 6, 1847, the effects of several variables on the rate at which pond-ice melts. As usual he builds irregularly from the strictly factual to the marvelous, moving next to the pond's booming, "Who would have suspected so large and cold and thick-skinned a thing to be so sensitive? Yet it has laws to which it thunders obedience when it should as surely as the buds expand with spring" (W 302). Before long, he comes to the sandbank, working his way into it slowly:

> Few phenomena gave me more delight than to observe the forms which thawing sand and clay assume in flowing down the sides of a deep cut on the railroad through which I passed on my way to the village, a phenomenon not very common on so large a scale, though the number of freshly exposed banks of the right material must have been greatly multiplied since railroads were invented. (W 304)

This passage is followed by the remarkable paragraph in which he traces the movements of, and the shapes assumed by, fingers of sediment as they emerge from the bank, intertwine, and eventually merge at the base of the slope into an irregular playa:

> What makes this sand foliage remarkable is its springing into existence thus suddenly. When I see on one side the inert bank,—for the sun acts on one side first,—and on the other this luxuriant foliage, the creation of an hour, I am affected as if in a peculiar sense I stood in the laboratory of the Artist who made the world and me,—had come to where he was still at work, sporting on this bank, and with excess of energy strewing his fresh designs about. (W 306)

Thoreau has discovered what he takes to be a fundamental law of nature, a law of organic regeneration, in the cutbank's transformation. Emerson too was fascinated by the idea of universal physical laws operating on different physical scales or in different media. In the essay, "Nature," he declares that the "whole code of her laws may be written on the thumbnail, or the signet of a ring. The whirling bubble on the surface of a brook, admits us to the secret mechanics of the sky. . . . A little water made to rotate in a cup explains the formation of the simpler shells . . ." (CW 3.103). The Associationists similarly conceived of laws of nature as applying across a startlingly broad range of phenomena, as in this passage from Albert Brisbane's biography in which he elaborates the idea of "unity of law and variety of manifestation":

> The same law, for instance, which governs the distribution, co-ordination, and arrangement of the notes of music governs the distribution, co-ordination, and arrangement of the planets and the solar system. As sounds are notes in musical harmony, so the planets are notes in a sidereal harmony. Continuing the analogy: the species in the animal or vegetable kingdom are the notes of a vast organic harmony; the bones in the human body are the notes of an osseous harmony, and these with the muscles and other parts of the human organism, are the notes of a physical harmony.

Further extension, people are the notes in a social composition that has fallen out of tune with the laws of its potential harmony.[11]

Thoreau agreed, and his language in "Spring" reaches a pinnacle of extravagance as he shows how his new law governs human physiology:

> What is man but a mass of thawing clay? The ball of the human finger is but a drop congealed. The fingers and toes flow out to their extent from the thawing mass of the body. Who knows what the human body would expand and flow out to under a more genial heaven? (W 307)

Just as the individual body is organically structured, so too is human social organization: rivers are vast "leaves whose pulp is the intervening earth, and towns and cities are the ova of insects in their axils" (307). Thoreau's law explains not only the geography of the human society around him and his place in it, but also the principles by which that society's institutions might change:

> Thus it seemed that this one hillside illustrated the principle of all the operations of Nature. The Maker of this Earth but patented a leaf. What Champollion will decipher this hieroglyphic for us, that we may turn over a new leaf at last? . . . The earth is not a mere fragment of dead history . . . but living poetry like the leaves of a tree, which precede flowers and fruit,—not a fossil earth, but a living earth. . . . And not only it, but the institutions upon it are plastic like clay in the hands of the potter. (308)

Given the historical context of the Walden project, given Thoreau's deep intrication in the ideological currents of anticapitalist reform, it is clear why he insists on bringing this theme of vernal regeneration to bear on the social order he so eloquently denounces in "Economy." The sand-bank passage implies that frozen, lifeless masses—such as corpse-cold souls and oppressive social institutions—have the potential to come spontaneously and beautifully to life under the right genial influences.[12]

Having flown to this height, Thoreau immediately descends, returning to the solid ground of observations on the first shoots of wild grasses. There is a kind of caesura in the chapter here, a point of rest before it begins a second irregular ascent, to a second rhetorical pinnacle in the penultimate full paragraph. This time Thoreau arrives at a rather different assessment of principle of regeneration:

> I love to see that Nature is so rife with life that myriads can be afforded to be sacrificed and suffered to prey on one another; that tender organizations can be so serenely squashed out of existence like pulp,—tadpoles which herons gobble up, and tortoises and toads run over in the road; and that sometimes it has rained flesh and blood! . . . The impression made on a wise man is that of universal innocence. Poison is not poisonous after all, nor are any wounds fatal. Compassion is a very untenable ground. (W 318)

Whereas spring had been a promise of redemption, grounds for hope that a degenerate civilization will be rejuvenated in the natural course of time, here it is an image of the transcendental fecundity in relation to which civilization's daily fatalities of body and soul stand as nothing—an idea that authorizes detachment, organized retreat from utopian desire.

The chapter "Spring" opposes, without reconciling, this pair of inter-pretations. The next and final chapter of *Walden*, however, offers a pro-visional resolution, a determined attempt to build a vision of redemption on ground cleared by the principle of fecundity. This chapter begins with the ringing passages of exhortation to self-knowledge and awakening, encouraging all "to explore the private sea, the Atlantic and Pacific Ocean of one's being alone" (W 321). Then there is the parable of the artist of Kouroo in which, by focusing wholly on his craft, the artist makes "a new system in making a staff, a world with full and fair proportions; in which, though the old cities and dynasties had passed away, fairer and more glorious ones had taken their places" (W 327). We begin to see where he is headed:

> However mean your life is, meet it and live it; do not shun it and call it hard names. It is not so bad as you are. It looks poorest when you are richest. The faultfinder will find faults even in paradise. Love your life, poor as it is. You may perhaps have some pleasant, thrilling, glorious hours, even in a poorhouse. The setting sun is reflected from the windows of the

almshouse as brightly as from the rich man's abode; the snow melts before its door as early in the spring. (W 328)

This answers the question first posed in "Economy," during the discussion of shelter: "But how do the poor minority fare? . . . The luxury of one class is counterbalanced by the indigence of another. On the one side is the palace, on the other are the almshouse and the 'silent poor' " (W 34). Spring, the principle of fecundity, pays no heed to riches. The idea is as old as class society: equal access to a transcendental democracy redeems the brutal inequality of this life.

But Thoreau is not vending analgesics. He is issuing an antimaterialist manifesto: "If you are restricted in your range by poverty . . . you are but confined to the most significant and vital experiences. . . . It is life near the bone where it is sweetest. You are defended from being a trifler. . . . Superfluous wealth can buy superfluities only. Money is not required to buy one necessary of the soul" (W 329). He is making a public virtue out of private necessity, to be sure, nevertheless, this passage sets up *Walden's* final call to intellectual arms in the battle against the spirit of commerce. Having unburdened himself of compassion on one hand, and worldly ambition on the other, Thoreau returns, metaphorically, to his craft:

> I would not be one of those who will foolishly drive a nail into mere lath and plastering; such a deed would keep me awake nights. Give me a hammer, and let me feel for the furring. Do not depend on the putty. Drive a nail home and clinch it so faithfully that you can wake up in the night and think of your work with satisfaction,—a work at which you would not be ashamed to invoke the Muse. So will help you God, and so only. Every nail driven should be as another rivet in the machine of the universe, you carrying on the work. (330)

Here at last is the method of Thoreau's social experiment, the means by which his community of one shall lead to the renovation of Concord: he will pursue his craft with such determination and focus that the result, *Walden*, shall be as a well-hit nail binding the beams of a new moral order.

CHAPTER 14

NATURE, POLITICS, AND THOREAU'S
MATERIALISM

> Had his genius been only contemplative, he had been fitted to his life, but
> with his energy and practical ability he seemed born for great enterprise
> and for command; and I so much regret the loss of his rare powers of
> action, that I cannot help counting it a fault in him that he had no ambition.
> Instead of engineering for all America, he was the captain of a huckleberry-
> party. Pounding beans is good to the end of empires one of these days; but
> if, at the end of years, it is still only beans?
>
> —Ralph Waldo Emerson

When Thoreau and the Brook Farmers planted and pounded their
beans, they *were* engineering for all America, but they were confronted
with hard limits to the independence of their projects for reform.[1] In the
end, they could not come out of society, for it came after them. Thoreau's
experiment, his model citizenship in the utopian community of nature,
could only have its desired effect with the publication of his report. But
this meant devoting himself to the hard labor of taking the manuscript
of *Walden* through seven substantive revisions over as many years, which
itself meant returning to the labor of making pencils and surveying town
lots. What his report finally produced was not a new dawn, but luke-
warm reviews emphasizing the peculiarity of a Yankee woodsman who
inexplicably felt he should do everything himself. The Brook Farmers
watched their nearly completed, but uninsured, phalanstery burn to the
ground. This was a fatal blow to the finances of the phalanx and, after a
short flurry of desperate activity, the members dispersed. George Ripley
moved to New York, where he worked for decades in various editorial
capacities in order to pay off the farm's debt. Most members, though,
were so disheartened as to abandon their dreams of socialism entirely. In
later years, they produced a number of sentimental (or cynical) memoirs
of what they now regarded as an episode of youthful enthusiasm. Thoreau
and the Farmers were forced, in other words, to abandon their utopian

projects by quite amoral, material exigencies. Despite their wishes, the present world intransigently demanded to be included in their plans for a brighter future.

Perhaps the most famous moment at which Thoreau fails in an encounter with an oblivious world occurs near the summit of Mount Ktaadn. Here, Nature's refusal to submit to his desires provokes a famously ecstatic disintegration of the self:

> Think of our life in nature,—daily to be shown matter, to come in contact with it,—rocks, trees, wind on our cheeks! the *solid* earth! the *actual* world! the *common sense! Contact! Contact! Who* are we? *where* are we?

Thoreau's retrospective outburst about climbing Ktaadn is so extravagantly fractured that its argument can get lost. It begins with relaxed contemplation of the central Romantic idea, "our life in nature," and then descends rhythmically from the abstract to the concrete until it grounds that idea in the irreducible facticity, the thingness, of the planet. Having found hard ground, it rises again, the rhythm more insistent and confident now, opening outward from the actuality of the nonhuman "earth," to the materiality of the complete ecosocial "world," and finally to the patterns of human understanding that bind its communities. The climactic ejaculation—"*Contact! Contact!*"—occurs only now, with the thought that we live together not only with nature but also with each other, that we, people and the earth, are in material fact a "we."[2]

The movement of this soliloquy mirrors Thoreau's intellectual growth over the course of his adult life. He fledged in the thin atmosphere of Emersonian idealism, with its sharp distinctions between spirit and matter, "man" and nature, and its central axiom: "The Times, as we say—or the present aspects of our social state, the Laws, Divinity, Natural Science, Agriculture, Art, Trade, Letters, have their root in an invisible spiritual reality" (CW 1.167). But Thoreau changed over time, coming to see the natural and social worlds as inseparably integrated and concrete. His thinking about natural and human history developed in parallel until, in his final years, he connected issues of environmental and social justice into a synthetic critique of the priorities of capitalism. Moreover, rather than remain satisfied with attempting to perform alternative ideas, he began to experiment with strategies for intervening materially to change the society around him. In other words, he moved away from Transcendental individualism and organic idealism, becoming not only the scientific ecologist we see in the late natural history manuscripts but also a political radical as well—one who stressed the need to make ideas into tools for collectively transforming the existing ecosocial order.

Part of what makes Thoreau's writing so compelling is that we encounter there, as James McIntosh argues, "opposed attitudes vibrating against each other in the crucible of an essay, a poem, or a day's journal." Thoreau's texts are structured by a "programmed inconsistency" that reflects his constantly "shifting stance toward nature."[3] It has usually been thought that the axis along which this shifting occurs had Mind and Nature as its poles, so that the metaphysical question Thoreau faced was this: which of these two forces dominates as they interact to create human experience of the world. *Walden* suggests that he placed his final faith in the power of the imagination to make a new day dawn. However, recent readers describe Thoreau's dilemma as a complex choice between idealist and materialist accounts of the world and between intuitive and empiricist modes of knowing it. Thoreau died just as his later ways of thinking about mind and matter, about people and nature, had begun to reach maturity, and just as he was beginning to articulate a new way of thinking. He continued to deplore the alienation from both labor and nature produced by life under capitalism, but in his late natural history essays, and especially in the guidebook he left in manuscript, *Wild Fruits*, he had begun to envision a utopian alternative, an organic community living in daily communion with the physical body of the land.

Robert Sattelmeyer observes that "the central debate over Thoreau's career" centers on "whether his late years form a record of declining power and a straying from the vision that led to *Walden*, or whether they furnish evidence of significant new directions and works which he did not live to complete." Thoreau himself occasionally expressed anxiety along these lines: "I fear that the character of my knowledge is from year to year becoming more distinct & scientific—That in exchange for views as wide as heaven's cope I am being narrowed down to the field of the microscope. . . ." It is common to read the trajectory of his life as a descent from high idealism and seriousness to a crabbed and narrow materialism, from truth to mere fact. Thoreau read both John Locke's *Essay Concerning Human Understanding* and Emerson's *Nature* during his senior year at Harvard. And according to this way of thinking about him, *Nature* convinced him to reject Locke's empiricism and to see nature as God's thought for America, rightly apprehended through intuition and sympathy. If this was so, then the unrelenting facticity of the Journal in the 1850s may be read as evidence of a failure of Thoreau's imagination.[4]

On the other hand, readers who truly appreciate the richly detailed passages of nature description in the Journal often see the same trajectory but make the reverse evaluation. For instance, William Howarth reads Thoreau's career as "a continuous ascent, sustained by the Journal, and rising from youthful confusion into a triumphant maturity." Howarth argues that in his apprentice years as a writer, Thoreau operated according to a "Platonic bias" he had learned from Emerson, transforming "the particulars of nineteenth-century New England into universal symbols." But later Thoreau came to believe that "the mind must absorb facts and adjust to their complexity," so he used his Journal "as a place to test his powers of seeing and hearing." Gradually, his "entries on birds and plants became more precise and detailed" and he became "less fanciful in his reading of their metaphysical significance" and "gravitated in his writing from the ideal of mystery to that of truth."[5]

Perhaps the most important achievement of Howarth's transformative reading will be that it demonstrates the power of reinterpreting Thoreau from the perspective of texts other than *Walden*. This shift in emphasis has made possible, over the last two decades, a series of increasingly sensitive and accurate readings of Thoreau's relationship to the science of his day. These studies, all of which begin from the late natural history manuscripts, have shown that at the same time that he was strongly attracted the idea of nature as a subject of systematic study, Thoreau rejected narrow forms of empiricism that emphasized objective observation of tightly limited phenomena. Instead, as Laura Dassow Walls has demonstrated, he participated in a proto-ecological "empirical holism" based on "relational knowing," a form of scientific practice typified especially by the work of Alexander von Humboldt, who saw mind or knowledge, not as supervening the world of particulars, but as an emergent property of their interrelationships. Thoreau saw his "task to be the joining of poetry, philosophy, and science into a harmonized whole that emerged from the interconnected details of natural facts." In order to come to understand such complex systems, Thoreau attempted to perfect what Donald Worster calls "a new, more intense empiricism" rooted in "day-to-day physical intimacy with nature." In other words, for much of his adult life he was actively mediating between idealist and materialist accounts of the world, as well as between intuitional and empiricist modes of investigating it.[6]

Thoreau's interest in science and the philosophy of science is recognizable as early as his first piece of environmental writing, "The Natural History of Massachusetts," which he ends by observing, "we do not learn by inference and deduction and the application of mathematics to philosophy, but by direct intercourse and sympathy." Thoreau is not rejecting empiricism here, but calling for a more wholly engaged mode of observation: "The true man of science will know nature better by his finer organization; he will smell, taste, see, hear, feel, better than other men. His will be a deeper and finer experience" (CE 41). Despite this early manifestation, Thoreau's interest in natural history and science would remain largely undeveloped during the 1840s. After graduating from Harvard, he moved home to Concord where he struggled to shape his writing to Transcendentalist conventions, composing poems along with essays on literary and philosophical topics that would suit the needs of the *Dial*.

In 1849, Thoreau's relationship with Emerson cooled, and he turned wholeheartedly to interests and proclivities that he may formerly have suppressed in deference to his mentor. His reading shifted sharply, from the classics, philosophy, comparative religion, and poetry on one hand, to natural history, American history, ethnography, and travel writing on the other. By this time, daily walks had become a routine and the Journal had shifted in the direction of systematic observation of natural phenomena. The 1850s, then, was a decade of renewed and intensified mediation between idealism and materialism for Thoreau during which, as Alfred Tauber argues, he "regarded epistemology as a fundamentally moral problem of situating objective knowledge within a humane context." This philosophical conflict was concretized by the fierce competition between two models of the study of natural history. On one hand, there was the residual idealist notion of creation, principally defended in the United States by Harvard's Louis Agassiz, who posited multiple episodes of divine intervention. On the other, there was the emergent materialist theory of evolution, which would triumph with the publication of Charles Darwin's *On The Origin of Species* in 1859, which Thoreau read eagerly as soon as it arrived in Concord. Over the course of the 1850s, Thoreau was clearly moving in Darwin's direction, as evidenced by his two essays in scientific ecology, "The Dispersion of Seeds" and "The Succession of Forest Trees." At the same time, he continued to think of nature as "an externalization of spirit" and of divine creation as an ongoing process in a continuous material present. In other words, he remained committed to the idealist notion of an active supernatural force driving natural processes, while his study of those processes, and the language he used to describe them, became increasingly materialist and empiricist.[7]

It has been common to assume that Thoreau's increasing interest in science in his last decade constituted a retreat from the social world of politics and history. Joan Burbick, for instance, claims that Thoreau "placed history within the natural world, where he found records of a story more capable of redemption than those of civilization." But, to complicate this picture, Robert Sattelmeyer observes that Thoreau's overall "development . . . was clearly in the direction of increasing interest in the study of and writing about nature on the one hand, and on the other the expression of increasingly sharp and outspoken views on sensitive social and political issues of his day." But after mapping Thoreau's reading in the sciences and the complexity of his ways of thinking about natural history, Sattelmeyer observes that Thoreau's "political writing . . . is less susceptible to analysis in terms of specific intellectual debts than most other areas of his thought. . . ." His political thought, rather than responding directly to the political economists and philosophers of his day, "developed in a sort of organic way out of certain political pressure points of his age—the extension of slavery and the question of individual rights versus civil law in particular—coming into conflict with some of his most fundamental and strongly held convictions about the purposes and conduct of life." His increasing radicalism, that is, was partly a consequence of participating in the abolitionist movement's increasing willingness to go beyond moral suasion to various forms of direct political action. As Leo Stoller puts it, Thoreau made a series of conjunctural compromises between perfectionism and direct action as theories of political action, "with the drift of the nation gradually modifying the proportions in favor of the direct assault." Although the pressure of events and of the abolitionist movement's evolution was surely decisive, it is also true that Thoreau's increasing radicalism found a theoretical warrant in his increasingly materialist understanding of ecosocial history.[8]

William Howarth observes that through the 1850s, Thoreau increasingly "moves away from problems of self-definition toward broader issues of history and culture" and that as this process goes on, Thoreau does not differentiate clearly between human and natural history. "By early 1857 Thoreau's studies in Concord had turned from detailed natural facts to the broader subject of community," so that his Journal became "an open history of his people and the land." More and more, he saw natural and human history as parts of an integrated ecosocial process, and he attempted, as Laura Dassow Walls puts it, "to read and tell a history of man and nature together, as and in one single, interconnected act." Howarth maintains that Thoreau draws quite conservative final political conclusions as a result of reasoning by analogy from his studies of natural cycles. Thoreau, he argues, arrived in his Journal at "a new vision of America's destiny: the country was not immortal, moving always onward and upward, but was caught in cycles of birth and death, the law of natural succession." But this conclusion cuts against the evidence of the reform essays, which become increasingly radical over time.[9]

Thoreau's first published political essay is "Paradise (To Be) Regained," a review of J.A. Etzler's technological utopian manifesto, *The Paradise within the Reach of all Men, without Labor, by Powers of Nature and Machinery* (1842). The young Thoreau ridicules what he sees as the mechanical thinking behind Etzler's scheme, making an explicit contrast with Emersonian ways of thinking: "there is a transcendentalism in mechanics as well as in ethics. . . . While one [reformer] scours the heavens, the other sweeps the earth. One says he will reform himself, and then nature and circumstances will be right. . . . The other will reform nature and circumstances, and then man will be right" (CE 116). Thoreau reserves his sharpest sarcasm for Etzler's vision of a rapid transformation of human social relations by machines that will harness the power of the sun, wind, tides, and waves: "We will not be imposed upon by this vast application of forces. We believe that most things will have to be accomplished still by the application call Industry" (CE 132). And in reply to Etzler's claim that large-scale projects of the kind he envisions will require planned collective action, Thoreau endorses self-reliance: "Alas! this is the crying sin of the age, this want of faith in the prevalence of a man. Nothing can be affected but by one man. . . . In this matter of reforming the world, we have little faith in corporations; not thus was it first formed" (CE 133). In the end, he maintains that "a moral reform must take place first" and he denounces Etzler's mechanical approach to social change, declaring somewhat lamely that "Love is the wind, the tide, the waves, the sunshine. Its power is incalculable; it is many horsepower. . . . True, it is the motive power of all successful social machinery . . ." (CE 136–137).

"Life Without Principle," another essay in which Thoreau engages directly with the question of economic reform, appeared twenty years after "Paradise (To Be) Regained" and was in development as a lecture through much of the 1850s. Thoreau begins by acknowledging that a profit-driven social order stands between him and a fulfilled life of the mind: "This world is a place of business. What an infinite bustle. I am awaked almost every night by the panting of the locomotive. It interrupts my dreams. . . . I think that there is nothing, not even crime, more opposed to poetry, to philosophy, ay, to life itself, than this incessant business" (CE 348–349). In such a utilitarian world, if "a man walk in the woods for love of them half of each day, he is in danger of being regarded as a loafer; but if he spends his whole day as a speculator, shearing off those woods and making earth bald before her time, he is esteemed an industrious and enterprising citizen" (CE 349). This is a society that is obsessed with money, but the "ways by which you may get money almost without exception lead downward" (CE 350). Wage labor cheapens human experience, but the average worker "consumes the greater part of his life getting his living" (CE 352). In "Life Without Principle," not only does Thoreau shift his emphasis from individual morality to the aggregate moral effects of social and economic relationships, but the target of his anger has changed as well: "The highest advice I have heard on these subjects was groveling. The burden of it was,—It is not worth your while to undertake to reform the world in this particular. Do not ask how your bread is buttered; it will make you sick if you do . . ." (CE 357). As a result of this abjectness before an imaginary necessity, the republican experiment has failed, for even "if we grant that the American has freed himself from a political tyrant, he is still the slave of an economical and moral tyrant" (CE 363). "Life Without Principle" is one of Thoreau's most unrelentingly pessimistic essays. He makes no attempt to gesture in the direction of a solution to the problem he has identified. Perhaps self-culture had at last come to seem wholly inadequate to interrupt the trajectory along which America was traveling with so much momentum. Pessimism aside, Thoreau's has recognized clearly that the conformity and dullness he despises in Concord have their roots in solidly material relationships and needs.

A similar movement from orthodox scholarly moralism toward more radical politics can be seen in the abolition essays. His earliest published documents that demonstrate antislavery sentiment are two commendations of prominent abolitionists. In the first, Thoreau praises Nathaniel Rogers, publisher of the abolitionist newspaper, *Herald of Freedom*, in clearly Garrisonian terms: "Such timely, pure, and unpremeditated expressions of a public sentiment, such publicity of genuine indignation and humanity, as abound every where in this journal, are the most generous gifts which a man can make" (CE 160). Similarly, in "Wendell Phillips Before Concord Lyceum," Thoreau extols Phillips in terms that belie his own acceptance of the logic of moral suasion: "He stands so distinctly, so firmly, and so effectively alone, and one honest man is so much more than a host, that we cannot but feel that he does himself an injustice when he reminds us of 'the American Society, which he represents' " (CE 162). Phillips demonstrates a "freedom and steady wisdom, so rare in the reformer" when he declares "that he was not born to abolish slavery, but to do right" (CE 163). Rather than enjoin his audience to take action, Phillips simply speaks his convictions with such clarity that "the audience might detect a sort of moral principle and integrity, which was more stable than their firmness . . ." (CE 164).

In the later abolitionist essays, written during the 1850s, Thoreau makes a very different kind of argument, in a very different voice:

> [When] a sixth of the population of a nation which has undertaken to be the refuge of liberty are slaves, and a whole country is unjustly overrun and conquered by a foreign army, and subjected to military law, I think it is not to soon for honest men to rebel and revolutionize. What makes this duty the more urgent is the fact, that the country so overrun is not our own, but ours is the invading army. (CE 206)

In "Resistance to Civil Government," Thoreau no longer places his faith so wholly in the power of ideas to spontaneously reform individuals and through them, to organically transform whole societies. He advocates action. After all, even "voting *for the right* is *doing* nothing for it" (CE 208). He is inconsistent, to be sure, retreating a few pages later to the more comfortable idea that it "is not a man's duty . . . to devote himself to the eradication of any, even the most enormous wrong . . . but it is his duty, at least, to wash his hands of it . . ." (CE 209). And the action he emphasizes is the somewhat negative one of withdrawing support "both in person and property" from the state (CE 212). Nonetheless, in response to fugitive slave laws that demanded active compliance, this kind of refusal amounts to an immediate and direct response to wrong: "Unjust laws exist: shall we be content to obey them, or shall we endeavor to amend them, and obey them until we have succeeded, or shall we transgress them at once?" (CE 210). The outcome of such a transgression was likely to be a prison sentence, but Thoreau calls on his neighbors: "Cast your whole vote, not a strip of paper merely, but your whole influence" and he concludes that if enough people participate in this kind of active disobedience, the result will be a "peaceable revolution" since if "the alternative is to keep all just men in prison, or give up war and slavery, the State will not hesitate which to choose" (CE 213). What "Resistance to Civil Government" shows most clearly is that Thoreau has recognized that ideas about reform become a force for material change in the world only when they inspire people to take direct action, to intervene in the course of history: "Action from principle, the perception and performance of right, changes things and relations; it is essentially revolutionary, and does not consist wholly with anything which was. It not only divides states and churches, it divides families; ay, it divides the *individual*, separating the diabolical in him from the divine" (CE 210, emphasis in original). It was no long step from here to defending John Brown's raid on Harper's Ferry as "a brave and humane deed" (CE 405) carried out by a "man of rare common sense and directness of speech, as of action; a transcendentalist above all, a man of ideas and principles . . ." (CE 399). That is to say, as Thoreau moved increasingly toward a materialist understanding of nature, he applied this same mode of analysis to the capitalist social order, and was therefore was driven more and more toward radical political conclusions.[10]

CHAPTER 15

WILD FRUITS, CAPITALISM, AND COMMUNITY

> I respect not his labors, his farm where everything has its price, who would carry the landscape, who would carry his God, to market, if he could get any thing for him; who goes to market for his god as it is; on whose farm nothing grows free, whose fields bear no crops, whose meadows no flowers, whose trees no fruits, but dollars; who loves not the beauty of his fruits, whose fruits are not ripe for him till they are turned to dollars. Give me the poverty that enjoys true wealth.
>
> —Henry David Thoreau (W 196)

Thoreau spent his final winter putting his literary affairs in order. At the beginning of April 1862, a month before he died, he sent his last essay, "Wild Apples," to the *Atlantic Monthly*. He had excerpted the essay from a longer book-length manuscript, which he left wrapped in a large sheet of paper. On this wrapper, he had written a title, *Wild Fruits*. This manuscript passed through several collections for the next century and a half and has only recently been published.[1] On its surface, the book is a botanical guide to the wild plants of New England. But it moves far beyond the work of cataloguing and identifying. "Most of us are still related to our native fields as the navigator to undiscovered islands in the sea. We can any afternoon discover a new fruit there which will surprise us by its beauty and sweetness" (WF 3). These are the book's first sentences. Most of us, it turns out, are related to Thoreau's writings in the same way. To read *Wild Fruits* is to be surprised by a beauty and sweetness we do not at all associate with the antagonistic hermit of *Walden*. The manuscript is incomplete, fragmentary, and sometimes self-contradictory, so any reading of it necessarily amounts to a speculative construction of a possible book. Even so, *Wild Fruits* clearly confirms the trajectory of Thoreau's traverse from idealism and individualism to materialism and communalism. It is a guidebook, yes, but it is also a visionary portrait of a devotional life on the land. It not only envisions an organic community as an alternative to capitalism, it works to convoke such a community by modeling rituals of natural communion.[2]

Wild Fruits consists of more than a hundred entries, widely variable in length and completeness, each describing a variety of plant that produces recognizable fruits. The product of a decade of systematic natural history observation, the book is rich in botanical information. Some of the less finished entries consist of little more than the dates on which, from year to year, a particular species first produces fruit. Others work up this and other information into treatments of proto-ecological hypotheses. For instance, the entry for "Black Huckleberry," reflecting Thoreau's 1860 reading of Darwin, describes how speciation allows plants, "slightly modified by soil and climate," to exploit a variety of niches. "Corn, and potatoes, apples and pears, have comparatively a narrow range, but we can fill our basket with whortleberries on the summit of Mount Washington" (WF 45). The various species of huckleberry have evolved for different elevations, so that at least one species occurs in every available New England habitat.

Unlike most guidebooks, though, Thoreau organizes his entries chronologically by date of fruit production, so that *Wild Fruits* is in effect a botanical almanac. Like all almanacs, it does not contain undifferentiated scientific information, but information relevant to the ongoing relationships between humans, plants, and the seasons. However, Thoreau focuses not on agriculture, but the human significance of *un*cultivated plants. The book's first entry is for "Elm," quoted here in its entirety:

> Before the tenth of May (from the seventh to the ninth), the winged seeds or samaræ of the elms give them a leafy appearance, or as if covered with little hops, before the leaf buds are opened. This must be the earliest of our trees and shrubs to go to seed. It is so early that most mistake the fruit before it falls for leaves, and we owe to it the first deepening of the shadows in our streets. (WF 6)

The opening sentence here deals in recognizably empirical botanical information, with matters of fact interrupted only briefly by a simile employed only to allow for accurate visualization. The second sentence, though, quietly introduces a plural subject of this knowledge. And the third flowers into truth, but not the kind of transcendental truth we might expect from Thoreau. Instead, he explains a truth about the experiential meaning of elms for the plural subject of which he is a part—his community. Elms are responsible for the sudden and mysterious transition from the hard white daylight of the New England winter to the warm green shade of summer. Similarly, the next entry, for "Dandelion," notes that at the same time that elms fruit, "we begin to see a dandelion gone to seed here and there in the greener grass of some more sheltered and moist bank, perhaps before we had detected its rich yellow disk—that little seedy spherical system which boys are wont to blow to see if their mothers want them" (WF 6). This sentence, like the entry as a whole, is structured around the relationship between an implied community and natural phenomena.

This emphasis on collective aesthetic and ritual experience of nature holds true throughout *Wild Fruits*, and it allows Thoreau to introduce a wide range of kinds of material including quotations from old herbariums and narratives by explorers and settlers, as well as anecdotes about both Native American and folk uses of plants. Of the "Black Cherry," for instance, he writes:

> Some, I hear, make a spiritous drink with them, which they disguise under such names as "cherry-bounce." The common way of gathering them is to shake them down upon sheets spread beneath the tree. I remember once shaking a tree in this wise, and when I came to gather up the edges of the cloth, I found an old cent of the last century among the cherries. (WF 98–99)

Individual and collective experiences of this kind, collected across time and cultures, cohere to make up the longest entries. And it soon becomes clear that what determines the fullness of an entry is not the amount of botanical information Thoreau wishes to set down, but the relative cultural importance of the plant described. Thus, the names he chooses for many of the plants, especially those that produce edible berries, are not scientific, but common. Thoreau satirizes the irrationality of naming Black Huckleberry, "*Gaylussacia resinosa*, after the celebrated French chemist":

> If he had been the first to distill its juices and put them in this globular bag, he would deserve this honor; or if he had been a celebrated picker of huckleberries, perchance paid for his schooling so, or only notoriously a lover of them, we should not so much object. But it does not appear that he ever saw one. What if a committee of Parisian naturalists had been appointed to break this important news to an Indian maiden who had just filled her basket on the shore of Lake Huron! (WF 37)

Thoreau's alternative to Linnean binomials is to differentiate between kinds of berry according to where and when they can be found by pickers: "Early Low Blueberry," "High Blueberry," "Late Low Blueberry," and so on. This pragmatic method of naming emphasizes the relevance of the book's information to those who wish not just to know abstractly about plants, but also to live interactively with them.[3]

Interestingly, this interactivity is not only transcultural, but also transspecific. For instance, the entry for "Sweet Flag" describes the growth of that species in the spring, notes that it is a favorite food of muskrats, and then relates that the "Indians of British America" use it as a remedy for colic. Thoreau continues: "Who has not when a child had this same remedy administered to him for that complaint—though the medicine came recommended by a lump of sugar, which the Cree boys did not get. . . . Thus we begin our summer like the musquash. We take our first course at the same table with him. . . . He is so much like us; we are so much like him" (WF 8). The basic likeness across cultures and species that Thoreau emphasizes here is one of materiality, of a necessary rootedness in physical nature. This is a common motif throughout the text. Writing of the "Early Low Blueberry," he describes how two species, endemic to different areas, "pass into one another" in one location "by insensible degrees, so that it appears as if the seeds of the downy Canada blueberry carried far enough south would at length produce the smooth Pennsylvania one, and vice versa—just as men wear furs in the north, but linen in the south" (WF 26). Similarly, in the entry for "Thistle," Thoreau observes that "What is called the Canada thistle is the earliest, and the goldfinch or thistlebird . . . knows when it is ripe sooner than I. So soon as the heads begin to be dry, I see him pulling them to pieces and scattering the down, for he sets it a-flying regularly every year all over the country, just as I do once in a long while" (WF 100). For Thoreau, plants, animals, settlers, natives, all beings with physical bodies, share parallel experiences of accommodation to and interaction with nature, the ground of existence, the material world.

Thoreau consistently represents the collective experience of the material world in devotional terms. In his introduction to *Wild Fruits*, Bradley Dean rightly observes that Thoreau "would have been most interested in our reading the work as a uniquely American scripture," noting that he refers to it in the Journal as "*my* New Testament" (WF xiii). Thus, the long entry for "Strawberry" describes picking and eating this fruit as an exercise in awareness. The first ripe berries of the season appear in spots well exposed to sunlight and they "are at first hard to detect in such places amid the red lower leaves, as if Nature meant thus to conceal the fruit, especially if your mind is unprepared for it" (WF 11–12). Because they present such a challenge to our powers of concentration, wild strawberries can be found only by the initiated:

> Only one in a hundred know where to look for these early strawberries. It is, as it were, a sort of Indian knowledge acquired by secret tradition. I know well what has called that apprentice, who has just crossed my path, to the hillsides this Sunday morning. In whatever factory or chamber he has his dwelling-place, he is . . . sure to be by the side of the first strawberry when it reddens. . . . It is an instinct with him. (WF 13)

Once found, strawberries are a pantheist "manna," (WF 12). "They are the first blush of a country, its morning red, a sort of ambrosial food which grows only on Olympian soil" (WF 15–16). Similarly, in the entry for "Early Low Blueberry," Thoreau writes, "These berries have a very innocent ambrosial taste, as if made of the ether itself, as they plainly are colored with it" (WF 22). New England is "a land flowing with milk and huckleberries" (WF 54) and although only a few may now seek wild berries, they remain available to all as a sign of the Earth's covenant with the communities it supports: "They seem offered to us not so much for food as for sociality, inviting us to a picnic with Nature. We pluck and eat in remembrance of her. It is a sort of sacrament, a communion—the *not* forbidden fruits, which no serpent tempts us to eat. Slight and innocent savors which relate us to nature, make us her guests, and entitle us to her regard and protection" (WF 52). The theological language here is no accident; it marks Thoreau's quite serious sense of the millennial importance of the rituals he describes: "It would imply the regeneration of mankind if they were to become elevated enough to truly worship sticks and stones" (WF 168). The sacramental consumption of wild fruits, should it be taken up by the hundred instead of just the one, might well redeem a New England society that has modernized itself into an almost total ignorance of nature.

New England's debilitating ignorance brings with it a whole host of other ills. Berries grow "wild all over the country—wholesome, bountiful, and free, a real ambrosia. And yet men, the foolish demons that they are, devote themselves to the culture of tobacco, inventing slavery and a thousand other curses for that purpose . . ." (WF 51). In *Wild Fruits*, Thoreau develops and makes even more explicit the materialist analysis that he begins to articulate in *Walden* of the way that capitalist social and economic relations have destroyed humankind's immediate collective relationship with nature. He describes much more particularly than in *Walden* the concrete ways in which the specific institutions of private property and competitive commerce prevent the citizens of a no longer classless republic from experiencing wild land either aesthetically or devotionally. First and foremost, there is the simple problem of decreasing access as more and more wild land is brought under private ownership: "But, ah, we have fallen on evil days! I hear of pickers ordered out of the huckleberry fields, and I see stakes set up with written notices forbidding any to pick there" (WF 57). Thoreau emphatically deplores the motive behind this ongoing process of enclosure:

> What sort of a country is that where huckleberry fields are private property? When I pass such fields on the highway, my heart sinks within me. I see a blight on the land. Nature is under a veil there. I make haste away from the desecrated spot. Nothing could deform her fair face more. I cannot think of it ever after but as the place where fair and palatable berries are converted into money, where the huckleberry is desecrated. . . . (WF 58)

Importantly, Thoreau does not single out the farmer who has fenced his fields, but immediately places the profit motive in a broader social context: "I do not mean to blame any, but all—to bewail our fates generally," for privatization shows "to what result our civilization and division of labor naturally tend" (WF 57, 58). This is a significant departure from the voluntarism of *Walden*, with its insistence that we each freely choose our own way of life. In *Wild Fruits*, Thoreau consistently places himself inside the community damaged by modernization, rather than haranguing it from afar: "It is my own way of living that I complain of as well as yours, and therefore I trust that my remarks will come home to you" (WF 235). The logic of this rhetorical shift is clear. For Thoreau, the "division of labor" is not a static fact, but an ongoing process whereby the relatively uniform population of the postrevolutionary agrarian republic has been divided into far more rigid economic classes. This process has produced a society that exerts a constant pressure on its members to make decisions according to the bottom line of profit. The aggregate result of these innumerable decisions is a privatized rural landscape where huckleberries are guarded by fences. Thoreau looks to postenclosure England and sees a dismal prognosis: "I suspect that the inhabitants of England and the continent of Europe have thus lost in a measure their natural rights with the increase of population and monopolies" (WF 57). Thoreau was, in fact as well as in rhetoric, one of those whose access to the land was increasingly being limited by modernization under capitalism.

What is most important about these changes, for Thoreau, is not merely that people have lost access to natural resources formerly held in common. It is true that "in laying claim for the first time to the spontaneous fruit of our pastures, we are inevitably aware of a little meanness, and the merry berry party which we turn away naturally looks down on and despises us" (WF 59). But again, Thoreau is not making a moralistic attack on individual humans for participating in the low business of trade. In fact, he reports wryly on sending two and a half bushels of cranberries to Boston, where he got four dollars for them. This success led him to consider taking up the business on a larger scale, by shipping larger quantities to New York, but he was dissuaded by the discovery that they sold cheaper there than at Boston. Thoreau tells this story to illustrate not his own moral lassitude, but the vitiated taste of urbanites by contrast with "country people" (WF 104–105). The problem with privatization of the land is that when "we exclude mankind from gathering berries in our field, we exclude them from gathering health and happiness and inspiration. . . . We thus strike only one more blow at a simple and wholesome relation to nature . . . (WF 58). In other words, the majority of people have been forcibly excluded not just from gathering up some supplementary nutrition, but from entering into rich ideal relationships with the wild: "It is a grand fact that you cannot make the fairer fruits or parts of fruits matter of commerce; that is, you cannot buy the highest use and enjoyment of them" (WF 5). Human relations to nature under capitalism, for those now fenced off the land, have been stripped of their most fulfilling content. The growing numbers of landless workers and the poor in the cities have been, to be precise, alienated from nature: they confront nature only in the marketplace as an alien object: "You cannot buy that pleasure which [a huckleberry] yields to him who truly plucks it. You cannot buy a good appetite, even. In short, you may buy a servant or a slave, but you cannot buy a friend" (WF 5). The comparison to slavery here is not accidental. Thoreau turns to this metaphor repeatedly. Of farmers who fence off their berry fields, he writes, "They have no other interest in berries but a pecuniary one. Such is the constitution of our society that we make a compromise and permit the berries to be degraded—to be enslaved, as it were" (WF 58–59). In other words, what is true of social relationships is true of human relations with nature as well: the moral content of such relationships is rooted in, flowers from, the material structure of a whole ecosocial order.

Wild Fruits envisions a potential alternative to capitalist ecosocial relations. It recounts a body of natural knowledge and experience of which the implied subject is an organic community living "a simple and wholesome" life on the land, "gathering health and happiness and inspiration" in the woods of New England. And more than envisioning such a utopian community, the text attempts as well to convoke it, to call it into existence by encouraging the ritual harvest and consumption of wild fruits. For Thoreau, gathering berries is an activity for a sacramental party, a collective aesthetic experience. In the entry for "Viburnum Nudum," he writes, "September 3. Now is the season for these comparatively rare but beautiful wild berries which are not food for man. . . . Now is the time for *Beautiful* Berrying, for which children have no vacation. They should have a vacation for their imaginations as much as for their bodies" (WF 121). Like gathering beautiful berries, eating wild apples demands a communal subject: "You cannot read at the same time, as when you are eating an apple. It is a social employment" (WF 219). Moreover, Thoreau's community of fruit pickers and eaters takes its identity and character from its particular environment: "The tropical fruits are for those who dwell in the tropics. . . . It is not the orange of Cuba but rather the checkerberry of the neighboring pasture that most delights the eye and the palate of the New England child" (WF 3). Not only is this community rooted in a specific place, its annual experience is tuned to the cycle of the year: "Our diet, like that of the birds, must answer to the season" (WF 107).

As utopian and apparently whimsical as this vision is, Thoreau recognizes that wild fruits can only take on the meaning he ascribes to them within an entirely new kind of society. Investing wild fruits with such rich meanings is a matter of artifice, of deliberately envisioning an alternative to the course of historical development he has described. This way of thinking is implied, for instance, in his description of the wild apple as "wild only like myself, perchance, who belong not to the aboriginal race here, but have strayed into the woods from the cultivated stock" (WF 79). Convoking such a community is a matter, then, of deliberately straying into the woods, of rewilding society, of collectively reviving lapsed ways of living on the land that were characteristic of native and agrarian cultures:

> It would be well if we accepted these gifts [of wild apples] with more joy and gratitude, and did not think it enough simply to put a fresh load of compost about the tree. Some old English customs are suggestive at least. I find them described chiefly in Brand's *Popular Antiquities*. It appears that "on Christmas eve the farmers and their men in Devonshire take a large bowl of cider, with a toast in it, and carrying it in state to the orchard, they salute the apple trees with much ceremony, in order to make them bear well the next season." (WF 76)

Consciously reinhabiting such lost lifeways can, for Thoreau, transform human relations with the land. Thus, after describing the experience of preparing and eating acorns for the first time, Thoreau concludes, "now that

I have discovered the palatableness of this neglected nut, life has acquired a new sweetness for me, and I am related to the first men. . . . Nature seems the more friendly to me" (WF 182). Likewise, Thoreau reports with obvious pleasure on the new urban ritual of eating roasted chestnuts: "I have seen more chestnuts on the streets of New York than anywhere else this year—large and plump ones roasting in the street, and popping on the steps of banks and exchanges. Was surprised to see that the citizens made as much of the nuts of the wild wood as the squirrels. Not only the country boys—all New York goes a-nutting" (WF 213). Throughout the text, the suffix, "a-," designates the ritual activities that bind together Thoreau's imagined community: a-strawberrying, a-huckleberrying, a-nutting. Thoreau did more than write about berrying as a ritual of communion; his Journal, along with the journals and correspondence of such friends as Louisa May Alcott and Ellen Emerson, are full of accounts of berrying and nutting excursions to the Concord woods. These group excursions, these huckleberry parties, "took place every year" and Thoreau "was the acknowledged town leader," organizing in material reality what he envisions in *Wild Fruits*.[4]

Given the social forces that Thoreau saw as responsible for alienation from nature, it is not perhaps surprising that he saw eating wild fruits as a democratic activity. He not only celebrates the way that "all New York goes a-nutting" so that there are "chestnuts for cabmen and newsboys" (WF 213), but he also ridicules, in antielitist terms, what he represents as overly cultivated fruits. Pears, for instance, "are a more aristocratic fruit than apples." He describes the extraordinary care that is taken to bring them to market, wrapped in tissue for wealthy customers. "Yet they have neither the beauty nor the fragrance of apples. Their excellence is in their flavor, which speaks to a grosser sense. They are *glout-morceaux*. Hence, while children dream of apples, ex-judges realize pears." Hyper-cultivated fruits are for hyper-cultivated members of the ruling classes: "They are named after emperors, kings, queens, dukes, and duchesses. I fear I shall have to wait till we get to pears with American names, which a republican can swallow. The next French Revolution will correct all that" (WF 127). By contrast, with the overrefined pear that vitiates tastes and appetites, wild fruits invigorate the democratic consumer: "It takes a savage or a wild taste to appreciate a wild fruit. What a healthy out-of-door appetite it takes to relish the apple of life, the apple of the world then!" (WF 87). Now, renewed vigor is not just a matter of individual well-being, though health was of course a matter of grave concern for Thoreau; renewal is also a communal, even a political concern. It is no rhetorical accident that he defiantly celebrates the eating of chestnuts "on the steps of banks and exchanges." These institutions operate as synec-doches for the profit-driven social order that produces the debilitating alienation from nature he hopes wild fruits will cure. More generally, the democratic community of wild fruit eaters will be fortified to bear the general malaise of modernity: "We require just so much acid as the cranberries afford in the spring. . . . They cut the winter's phlegm, and now you can swallow another year of this world without other sauce" (WF 106).[5]

In one entry, for the "European Cranberry," Thoreau does seem to suggest that going a-berrying is a form of political escapism, an "absorbing employment" that "drives Kansas out of your head, and actually and permanently occupies the only desirable and free Kansas against all border ruffians" (WF 165). This last sentence implies the possibility that Thoreau's community is a compensatory fantasy and introduces this remark: "The attitude of resistance is one of weakness, inasmuch as it only faces an enemy; it has its back to all that is truly attractive" (WF 165). Thoreau seems here to ventriloquize quite directly the ideal-ist politics of nonresistant moral suasion that characterized *Walden* and the 1840s. He even goes so far in this entry as to satirize political reformers and utopian socialists, including himself: "Our employment generally is tinkering, mending the old worn-out teapot of society. Our stock in trade is solder. Better for me, says my genius, to go cranberrying this afternoon for the *Vaccinium oxycoccus* in Gowing's Swamp . . . than go consul to Liverpool. . . ." (WF 166). It is tempting to conclude on the basis of this passage that gathering wild fruits is no more than another form of come-outerism, the isolato's way of abandoning modernity in hopes that it will collapse. But this is precisely the position Thoreau explicitly rejects not only in the contemporaneous John Brown essays, but also in much of the rest of the *Wild Fruits* manuscript, especially in its final pages. In effect, this anachronistic voicing of Thoreau's former individualism and idealism, localized as it is within a fragmentary man-uscript, serves only to reinforce the text's overall communalism and materialism.

For some readers, the sweetest discovery in *Wild Fruits* will come in an untitled section that makes up the last the six pages of the book. Leo Stoller combined this passage with material from several entries into an essay that was published in 1970 as a small book titled *Huckleberries*.[6] But it is in *Wild Fruits* that this material has been restored to its original textual environment, where it comes as a culminating peroration. The passage, which appears to be a draft of material for a lecture, is an explicit argument in support of collective action to preserve large tracts of land as wilderness. Its first paragraph contains a precise abstract of its overall argument. Thoreau begins with a lament: "How little we insist on truly grand and beautiful natural features. There may be the most beautiful landscapes in the world within a dozen miles of us, for aught we know—for their inhabitants do not value nor perceive them, and so have not made them known to others. . . ." The problem is identified as one of recognizing the importance of wilderness, but more than that, Thoreau implies that people have been blinded by something quite specific: "if a grain of gold were picked up there or a pearl found in a fresh-water clam, the whole state would resound with the news." So far, this is a consolidating restatement of themes that have been developing throughout *Wild Fruits*.

But now Thoreau introduces a new thought: "Thousands annually seek the White Mountains to be refreshed by their wild and primitive beauty, but when the country was discovered a similar kind of beauty prevailed all over it—and much of this might have been preserved for our present refreshment if a little foresight and taste had been used" (WF 233). He is proposing explicitly here, what he has elsewhere in his work only hinted at: conscious decision-making by the community to preserve wild land. Next Thoreau describes a "noble oak wood" at the town of Boxboro: "Let it stand fifty years longer and men will make pilgrimages to it from all parts of the country" (WF 233). Nevertheless, "it is likely to be cut off within a few years for ship-timber . . ." (WF 235). Arguing that the "rising generation" should have an opportunity to learn what an oak or a pine is by observing the "best specimens," he argues that "it would be wise for the state to purchase and preserve a few such forests. If the people of Massachusetts are ready to found a professorship of Natural History, do they not see the importance of preserving some portions of Nature herself unimpaired?" (WF 235).

Thoreau immediately comes to the necessary point that such a goal conflicts with the ongoing trend of privatization of wild lands and turns to Native American ecosocial relations for an alternative model of land ownership: "Among the Indians the earth and its productions generally were common and free to all the tribe, like the air and water, but among us who have supplanted the Indians, the public retain only a small yard or common in the middle of the village, with perhaps a graveyard beside it" (WF 235). He next turns to English common law for a second precedent: "In some countries precious metals belong to the crown; so here more precious objects of great natural beauty should belong to the public" (WF 236). On this basis, Thoreau argues that rivers, upon which "the town, as a corporation, has never turned any but the most utilitarian eyes" should be held too as a "common possession forever" (WF 236). Not just rivers, but "central and commanding hilltop[s]" should likewise be preserved, for each is a "sacred place," a "temple" that should not be "private property" (WF 237). Thoreau concludes that "each town should have a park, or rather a primitive forest, of five hundred or a thousand acres, either in one body or several, where a stick should never be cut for fuel, not for the navy, nor to make wagons, but stand and decay for higher uses" (WF 238). Repeating what is clearly a key phrase for him, he maintains that each such tract of land should be held as "a common possession forever" (WF 238). The navy and wagons here stand in for the modern state and the market it protects. And it is in opposition to these institutions that the land must be protected. Crucially, Thoreau recognizes that preservation will require concerted conscious action: "It is for the very reason that some do not care for these things that we need to combine to protect all from the vandalism of the few" (WF 237). By implication, the rituals Thoreau represents in *Wild Fruits* will produce devotional experience on the land, which will in turn motivate the community to combine and take action in defense of what they will now see as the basis of their collective identity.

Wild Fruits, then, offers a second answer to the question framed by the "Economy" chapter of *Walden*. Where *Walden* offers an idealist and organic individualist solution to that problem, *Wild Fruits* offers a process—utopian to be sure, but significant nevertheless—for transforming ideas into motivating collective experiences and therefore into material forces for change. There is a moment in which *Walden* hints at this future: Thoreau describes a transformative epiphany in which he merges his "intelligence with the earth" (W 138). This is a significant departure from the disembodied consciousness, the "transparent eyeball" of Emersonian orthodoxy (CW 1.10). More and more, Thoreau saw understanding as a moment of active integration with the world, rather than one of contemplative separation or abstraction. And more and more, Nature was the material world of Concord *and* the Walden woods, rather than an ideal category—the Emersonian "Not Me" (CW 1.8).

On January 24, 1856, Thoreau meditated in his Journal on elms, the species that is the subject of the first entry in *Wild Fruits*. "I find that into my idea of the village has entered more of the elm than of the human being" for most people do not have "a tithe of the dignity, the true nobleness and comprehensiveness of view" that the elms do. This pessimistic assessment may seem to cut against his hopes for collective transformation of ecosocial relations, but it soon becomes clear that he has only certain human beings in mind. Elms "are free-soilers" for they "send their roots into many a conservative's Kansas and Carolina, who does not suspect such underground railroads." Not only are Thoreau's elms antislavery activists, but like the ecosocial historian of *Wild Fruits* and the community he hoped to call together, they took "a firmer hold on the earth that they may rise higher into the heavens." Perhaps, Thoreau remembered this vision of the abolitionist elms of Concord on the day he drafted several pages *Wild Fruits* on the reverse sides of broadsheets he had printed to announce a memorial service for John Brown. And perhaps it was with a sense of the social and political importance of serious play that Thoreau that inhabited the office of "captain of a huckleberry party."[7]

CHAPTER 16

ECOCRITICISM AND THE USES OF NATURE WRITING

On the 29th of April, as I was fishing from the bank of the river near Nine-Acre-Corner bridge, standing on the quaking grass and willow roots, where the muskrats lurk, I heard a singular rattling sound. . . . Looking up, I observed a very slight and graceful hawk, like a night-hawk, alternately soaring like a ripple and tumbling a rod or two over and over, showing the underside of its wings, which gleamed like a satin ribbon in the sun, or like the pearly inside of a shell. . . . It was the most ethereal flight I had ever witnessed. . . . It sported with proud reliance in the fields of air; mounting again and again with its strange chuckle, it repeated its free and beautiful fall, turning over and over like a kite, and then recovering from its lofty tumbling, as if it had never set its foot on terra firma. It appeared to have no companion in the universe,—sporting there alone,—and to need none but the morning and the ether with which it played. It was not lonely, but made all the earth lonely beneath it.

—Henry David Thoreau (W 316–317)

Just as Thoreau projected his ambitions onto an idealized nature, so do we see ourselves in him. His extravagant descriptions of the natural world have produced remarkably divergent readings. The first verdict, passed by Ralph Waldo Emerson and James Russell Lowell, was that he had failed to live up to his potential greatness, managing no more than to become a describer of pretty scenes. This judgment was influential enough that early attempts to revive his reputation, such as by Vernon Louis Parrington and Van Wyck Brooks, were carried out by ignoring the nature writing and emphasizing the democratic political implications of his radical individualism. Then, in the mid-century climate of political reaction, scholars limited themselves to reading *Walden* as a well-wrought urn. In Perry Miller's words, it was "a highly schematized pattern of words . . . designed not so much to make a sociological point, as to become a thing of beauty" in and of itself. Similarly, R.W.B. Lewis gave us a Thoreau who was the paradigmatic "American Adam," the self-creating artist, sporting there alone in the universe. *Walden* was a portrait of a self-reliant consciousness soaring above a utilitarian society. On this reading, Thoreau's nature was seen as little more than a rhetorical strategy: Walden Pond and figures like the hawk in this passage were vehicles of self-reflexive metaphor, the raw material of the literary craft that was his true concern.[1]

In *The Machine in the Garden*, a book that decisively refuted the apolitical readings of its predecessors, Leo Marx mounts a sympathetic and incisive accounts of how *Walden* uses pastoralism to critique the rise of capitalism. But he concludes that "in the end Thoreau restores the pastoral hope to its traditional location. He removes it from history, where it is manifestly unrealizable, and relocates it in literature, which is to say, in his own consciousness, in his craft, in *Walden*." In a later essay, Marx remarks that "in spite of the radical anticapitalist implications of the beginning of *Walden* . . . it is not the material or social conditions of life, it is not capitalism, that in his view accounts for the quiet desperation felt by the mass of men: it is their own spiritual inertia. So far from causing him to identify his interests with theirs, this awareness leads him to set himself apart from them. . . ." Thoreau's organic individualism amounts to a complete disengagement. For Marx, "politically minded admirers of *Walden* tend to ignore . . . the effect of the book's action as a whole in dissipating the radical social awareness it generates at the outset." Revisionist scholars working after Marx have often deployed poststructuralist models of linguistic construction to mount similar critiques of mid-century conservatism, and have tended to explain Thoreau's nature in similar terms. The Emersonian individualism to which Thoreau gives such a succinct iconographic summary in the passage on the hawk has been represented as, in Sacvan Bercovitch's phrase, "a form of utopian consciousness developed within the premises of liberal culture" that contains within safe channels the radicalism of its adherents. Thus, the hawk's flight is pure metaphor, and Thoreau's posture of self-reliance in nature is one more enactment of an all too familiar American ideology of unfettered individual freedom that has functioned to naturalize a sharply hierarchical social order.[2]

Ecocritics, on the other hand, argue that Thoreau's nature writing really is about what it depicts—namely, the wilder landscapes of New England. Ecocriticism claims, in fact, that the irreducibly material environment of the Concord woods transformed Thoreau's writing and even his consciousness. This emphasis on nature's reality, its materiality, and on the interactivity of text and environment, has allowed for a productive redescription of the individual psychology of Thoreau's growing love of nature, his growing commitment to the idea that the nonhuman world must be treated ethically. For instance, Lawrence Buell argues that during the ten-year process of composing *Walden*, Thoreau perfected "a strategy of substantialization." As he revised, he moved away from orthodox Transcendentalism, with its focus on spiritual and emotional correspondence between the individual and nature. He increasingly felt a self-abnegating "respect for the realm of physical nature whose substantial reality must be honored in the face of any desire to appropriate it for didactic or aesthetic uses." This new outlook led him to seek a high level of "representational density" in his writing. Over time, he achieved a rare facility at seeing minutely and accurately, and then at producing passages of dense, precise description. Finally, Thoreau's habit of close observation produced in him a proto-environmentalist commitment to the protection of the places and creatures he had come to know so intimately.[3]

William Howarth sees the pattern that Buell locates in *Walden* as the key to Thoreau's complete body of work. When read in sequence, Thoreau's writings depict in compelling detail the very process of re-education by the land that ecocritics hope to encourage in the present. His life was a journey from the orthodox extravagance of idealist speculation toward an increasingly open and careful engagement with the reality of nature in its own right. He began, when writing the early essays and *Walden*, as a hunter of symbols and correspondences in the sky. But he gradually became disenchanted with such transcendental ways, as the irreducible particularity of the woods around Concord sparked a determination to learn to see nature directly, for its own sake. Similarly, Sharon Cameron argues that whereas in *Walden*, Thoreau cultivates nature for use by civilized readers, in the Journal, he achieves an immediacy of perception that allows him to record nature without objectifying it. For John Hildebidle, the late natural history manuscripts show Thoreau grappling creatively with problems raised by examples of human activity operating as an important determinant of organic orders. In these essays, Thoreau adopts a strategy of accumulating precise facts until, in textual moments of transcendence, they "flower in a truth."[4]

Thus, ecocriticism argues that rather than experiencing a decline from the imaginative vitality of Transcendentalism, we should see Thoreau as finally achieving an empirically based ecocentrism. Robert Kuhn McGregor gives a synthesizing statement of this narrative that neatly embodies the paradoxes involved: Thoreau begins his adulthood entrapped in Emersonian idealism with its crudely anthropocentric doctrine of correspondence; he then rejects this for the morally superior procedures of scientific investigation in which valuation is subordinated to pure observation; finally, this discipline leads him to a revelation:

> Discovering that every aspect of nature had a value completely independent of human notions of worth, he had determined to deny humanity its traditional place as the pinnacle of creation. Thoreau . . . firmly understood that people were nothing more than component parts, equals of all the other parts in a large and complex natural community. Almost by himself, Henry Thoreau was inventing what we now call the principle of biocentrism and the science of ecology.

Lawrence Buell, similarly, sees Thoreau's biocentric desire to represent nature accurately as the most potentially redemptive aspect of his life-project, for "the practice of basing art on disciplined extrospection is in the first instance an affirmation of environment over self, over appropriative homocentric desire." Thoreauvian nature writing, with its insistence on measuring itself against what is out there, is not escapist or analgesic, but is an antidote to an urban, technological culture in which humans and their discourses are the measure of all things. Buell asks us to understand "nature-responsiveness as a kind of culture, or rather counterculture, that one must pursue in resistance to the intractable homocentrism in terms of which one's psychological and social worlds are always to some degree mapped." This is the heart of the ecocritical valorization of nature writing. The "environmental crisis involves a crisis of the imagination the amelioration of which depends on finding better ways of imaging nature and humanity's relation to it." And Thoreauvian nature writing has the potential to inspire its readers to assume an attitude of humility before the natural world.[5]

Now it is true that Thoreau's nature was far more than a field for speculation about the forms of his own awareness. The ecocritical account of complex interaction between Thoreau, his texts, and the land reveals the true seriousness of material that has all too often been regarded as merely loco-descriptive or evasively pastoralizing. The process of learning to see the land did change Thoreau into an environmentalist, and that kind of change is indeed urgently relevant in the present. Moreover, our attempt to practice a kind of disciplined critical extrospection, to examine and describe the dialectical interaction between texts and the extratextual physical environment—this is a welcome impulse, so far as it has gone. It points out the door through which literary analysis might escape from its self-imposed incarceration in the imaginary prison house of language, wherein we regard texts as narrowly self-referential phenomena.

However, the ecocritical discipline of extrospection has stopped short of incorporating the truth that the social world from within which

Thoreau wrote was as real and influential as the natural world he wrote about. One clear indicator of just how ahistorical ecocritics can be in their engagement with Thoreau is that way that his failure to more consistently advocate wilderness preservation induces a kind of anachronistic culture shock. For instance, Daniel Payne remarks that "given Thoreau's adoption of a worldview that clearly placed humankind in nature and not above it . . . his relative lack of activity in changing public policies toward the environment is somewhat puzzling."[6] Payne's surprise reflects the way that, for most ecocritics, the narrative of environmentalist conversion through contact with nature moves teleologically to presentist conclusions. In the end, we can only truly understand what Thoreau was saying about the hawk's grace when we see that in choosing to write about it at all he was responding to the turbulent social history of Jacksonian America. His decision to live alone in nature was part of a broad flowering of ideological experimentation. Where Ripley and Brownson preached cooperative strategies for peaceful revolution, in which natural law operated as the glue of cooperative utopias, Thoreau initially opted for a sharply individualized vision of social redemption; he imagined a redemptive relationship between people and nature according to the figure of an individual alone in the woods. And he did so because of a complex web of ideological and material determinants. The capitalist ecosocial revolution in New England produced a dynamic and increasingly urban and industrial society characterized by class conflict. The region's ruling class was deeply divided on how to respond to these developments. And this disagreement produced, among many other responses, the Transcendentalist movement, which itself quickly split into radical reformers and retrenching scholars. The scholars developed a theory of the organic cultural leadership of representative men, an organic aristocracy prepared for their role in society by the pedagogy of nature. The Walden experiment was an attempt to put this theory into action. The literary record of his "proud reliance in the fields of air" (W 316) would, Thoreau hoped, present such a thrilling spectacle as did the hawk he saw at Nine-Acre Corner. And thus he would exert such an influence on Concord as the sun did on the frozen banks of the deep cut, where, in the spreading fingers of sand, he found his individualist version of the millenarian optimism that he shared with his neighbors. Thoreau had followed the geographic logic of the scholarly tale of natural instruction away from society and further and further into the ideal woods. Once there, though, he found he was not alone. Concord had followed him to his schoolroom with a plan to mill beams out of his books.

Recognizing the full ecosocial environment that shaped *Walden* matters most because when we claim that Thoreau's habits of environmental thought remain viable in the present we imply that there is a fundamental continuity between the early nineteenth century and the early twenty-first. We imply that our relations with the land are still substantially the same. Thus, it matters a great deal whether we tell an idealist tale about the threat to Nature posed by the American Mind, or Society, or Humans, rather than an empirical narrative about the historical development of capitalism and its interactions with the environment. As part of that narrative, Thoreau does have a great deal to tell us, because he was reacting to a social and economic landscape that is *materially* contiguous with our own. His valorization of wild land was a direct reaction to the rapid expansion of market capitalism to the position of dominance within the whole social process that it still occupies. A clear understanding of his participation in the main current of anticapitalist thought in the 1830s and 1840s can only improve his relevance to our present struggle to keep State Street from destroying what is left of Walden Pond.

Thoreau's relevance will be even greater if we also recognize that the changes we admire in his thinking about nature paralleled developments in his thinking about how to change the world. Granville Hicks, writing as a socialist in the 1930s, objected to Thoreau's individualism and concluded that "nothing in American literature is more admirable than Henry Thoreau's devotion to his principles, but the principles are, unfortunately, less significant than the devotion." To put this in more positive terms, Thoreau's organic individualism was not a retreat from active commitment; it was an alternative strategy for change. *Walden*'s "Conclusion" is a limit case of moral suasion, as it was then called. This strategy, developed by Garrisonian abolitionists and conceived as an ethical form of political action appropriate to a republic, centers on the performance of convictions on the public stage of history. Once such moralists act to enforce their convictions, though, they have moved beyond ethics, beyond an ideal democracy of equal citizens, into the material mire of political struggle, where absolutes all too often conflict, and the desire for change must engage the realities of entrenched social and economic power. In the 1850s, Thoreau was forced to confront this truth and he responded by speaking out virtually alone in defense of John Brown's decision to abandon moral purity and to fight the slavocracy by any means necessary. Brown had decided to subordinate one ethical ideal, peaceful republican citizenship, to another, a more truly egalitarian republic. His strategy of small-scale guerilla violence failed, as it must, but he never repudiated the decision to meet the systematic violence of slavery with violence of his own. Thoreau agreed, and a more total conversion from the purist, come-outer politics of the *Walden* years can scarcely be imagined. This conversion drove him to perform some truly radical acts, such as his steady service as a conductor on the Underground Railroad. Although this kind of individual heroism could win local victories and inspire others to fight, it could not finally challenge the structure and priorities of society as a whole. It was with collective solutions to that problem that Thoreau was experimenting at the end of his life.[7]

What is at stake here is how our readings of Thoreau's writings and life combine in the cultural text, "Thoreau," that we use to inspire and inform our own practice. Lawrence Buell rightly points out the staggering variety in the iconography of Thoreau:

> During one ten-year span from the mid-sixties through the mid-seventies . . . Thoreau was acclaimed as the first hippie by a nudist magazine, recommended as a model for disturbed teenagers, cited by the Viet Cong in broadcasts urging American GI's to desert, celebrated by environmental activists as "one of our first preservationists," and embraced by a contributor to the John Birch Society magazine as "our greatest reactionary."

His legend has also been appropriated by a breathtaking variety of radical movements worldwide, from English "ethical socialists" in the 1890s (local branches of the Labor Party were called Walden Clubs) and American communists in the 1930s (Emma Goldman, Upton Sinclair, and Norman Thompson were jailed for publicly reading "Resistance to Civil Government"), to the struggles against imperialism and racial oppression led by Mahatma Gandhi and Martin Luther King, Jr.[8]

If Thoreau is to be truly valuable now to ecocriticism as a precursor, if he is to be a "source of inspiration and guidance for the subversive activism of the recent ecology movement," we shall need to continue down the road he was clearly on, but which he was not given time to pursue to its end. We shall need to follow through on the implications of his later thinking not only about the interrelatedness of nature and society, but also about political practice as collective "action from principle," as a process of testing theories against a material reality that is not just the nature of woods and ponds, but the nature of human social organization (CE 210). Thoreau's initial failure to make that connection led him to misread the threat to his green retreat. Despite the clarity of the social analysis he performs in "Economy," he rises in "The Ponds" from the ecosocial fact of capitalism's insatiable appetite to a vague, and therefore paralytic, vision of the inevitability of Society's destruction of Nature. By forfeiting the insights into the specific nature of Concord that he had briefly won, Thoreau set a sharp limit to his ability to defend Walden against its incursions. Likewise, when we continue to speak—all too often in the jeremiadic accents that Thoreau assumes at the end of "The Ponds"—of nature and society as enemies, when we continue to think of the changes necessary to achieve peace as a matter of the simple replacement of certain sets of ideas with new ones, we seriously compromise our own "rare powers of action." Examining Thoreau's contradictions and growth in context should help us see analogous contradictions in much green political and cultural theory. It should also help us rethink our ecocritical practice in solidarity with the materialist critique of capitalism that, as Thoreau eventually came to see, demanded a wholly other response than the idealist political strategy of organic individualism.[9]

The same is true of the period's other nature writers. For instance, the Wordsworth whom Emerson admired as a teacher and Brownson rejected as a hypocrite is the starting point of the ecocritical narrative in which a countercultural tradition of nature-love crosses the Atlantic to sink its firmest roots in America, transforming the howling wilderness into the site of restorative spiritual communion with a pre-civil state of nature.[10] On the other hand, he is also a primary exhibit in the New Historical argument that Romantic nature poetry is a mask of apostasy, founded on displacement of both the politics of revolutionary republicanism and the glaring brutality of the developing capitalist social order. One response to this disagreement is to maintain that nature writing is, as Lawrence Buell puts it, "ideologically multivalent," simultaneously complicit with *and* resistant to dominant ideologies. Buell's suggestion fits well with the way that Wordsworth's poems of rural poverty were simultaneously used by conservative reform movements intent on inculcating workers with the values of thrift, industriousness, and deference, and by radical working-class organizations who read them as primers in dignity, self-respect, and genuine independence.[11]

When we set out to recuperate texts that are so richly multivalent, Buell argues, we should see ourselves as engaged in critically selecting those elements that can most help us in the present. We must not only "imagine how the voices of environmentalist dissent within western culture might help reinvision it," but also "how they themselves must be critically reinvisioned in order to enlist them to this end." On these grounds, we can argue that Romantic poetry's turn to nature is by no means a turn away from political responsibility, since our highest responsibility in the present is to a threatened environment. Jonathon Bate, for instance, hopes to recuperate Wordsworth's politics of rural virtue. Wordsworth saw in the border country what Coleridge called "a particular mode of pastoral life, under forms of property, that permit and beget manners truly republican." And the pastoral poetry inspired by this mountain republicanism "begets both reverence for nature and political emancipation." As proof of the poetry's effectiveness, Bate points to the story of John Stuart Mill's return from the brink of insanity with the help of Wordsworth's poems, stressing that "Mill did not propose the reading of Wordsworth as an 'alternative' to the desire for social reform. He claimed that Wordsworth taught him to commune with nature 'not only without turning away from, but with greatly increased interest in the common feelings and common destiny of human beings.' " In further support of this interpretation, Bate reads *The Prelude*'s crucial sections, books seven through nine, as political allegory, as "a progression from alienation in the city through love of nature to the recognition of individual human love and tenderness in the city to the general love of humanity in the revolutionary spirit of book nine." Finally, he makes a case for the contemporary relevance, even radicalism, of such ways of thinking: "To go back to nature is not to retreat from politics but to take politics into a new domain, the relationship between Love of Nature and Love of Man and, conversely, between the Rights of Man and the Rights of Nature."[12]

The suggestion that there are intimate connections to be made between the politics and poetics of human social progress and those of ecological preservation is welcome. After all, what we admire in Wordsworth's nature poems, and in the mountain republic they evoke, is not merely a self-aggrandizing image of peaceful social hierarchy. It is the vision of an altogether more inclusive stability. The emphasis falls on the discipline of nature, on how learning to live well on the land can help us learn how to live well together. But, if we are to take seriously the claim that nature poetry engenders both "Love of Man" and "Love of Nature," then we must once again face this question: is Wordsworth's "visionary mountain republic" merely an evasion of political reality? Is it utopian in the negative sense Marx used of the many socialisms of the early nineteenth century? Or can it usefully inspire and inform activism in our phase of the long revolution? Bate argues that Wordsworthian nature writing records an alternative to the politics of right and left, that it points out a third way leading beyond the thicket of capitalist and communist versions of an epochal anthropocentric industrialism. He goes on the say that the dominant modern ideologies are rooted in a tale of the sublimity of humankind's rational transformation of nature to the end of social progress, and unless we achieve the harmonious relations with nature envisioned by Wordsworth, the question of improving relations between humans will become moot.[13]

In fact the reverse is true. Unless we succeed in changing the current structure of human social relations, the question of improving human relations with nature will become moot, for the current system of production not only encourages, but also requires, that the necessary process of getting a living from the land be conducted irrationally and destructively. The truth about the rational conquest of nature is this: what we need is more rationality, not less. Capitalism's wholesale transformation of ecosystems worldwide has been everything but reasonable. It has been a process of irrational destruction driven by a social order in which decisions are made on the basis of profit rather than the health of humans and the ecosystems on which we depend. Moreover, although it is true that nature writing like Wordsworth's can help us envision a different way of living on the land, we need to be skeptical about the claim that such texts render obsolete the long struggle for human emancipation from the despotism of capital. In truth, texts like Wordsworth's neither evaded nor transcended this struggle; instead they were urgently and contradictorily engaged. What has been represented as either the retreat or the leap to nature was in fact the clearing of a simultaneously utopian and reactionary position in the period's complex political spectrum. The final evasiveness of the politics of natural virtue rested, then as now, not on an ignorance of, or irrelevance to, the bitter social conflicts to which they passionately responded, but on the insufficiency of the response to the circumstances. What was missing was not passionate idealism, but an accurate appraisal of the power of the historical forces militating against revolutions of the spirit.[14]

In the end, we must make a similarly two-sided assessment of the historical progressiveness of the elite radicals who imported Wordsworth to New England. At the same time that they were responding inadequately to the historic intensification of the exploitation of the northern working class, they were also successfully developing the revolutionary convictions and energies that would overthrow the slave-owning South. Their appropriation of the poetry of humble country life was, thus, quite politically complex. The poems were used as manuals for self-instruction in democracy, in natural feelings of brotherhood with the common people. Yet, the final goal of such training was to reclaim the social authority necessary to address the double threat of, on one hand, the pro-slavery Jacksonian Democrats and, on the other, the emergent working class, as each adapted the rhetoric of republican virtue and democracy to their own equally complex ends. Of course, the conjunctural uses to which a historical social formation puts a text or an idea can by no means be said to exhaust its potential utility. However, clearly understanding such cultural histories can help us achieve a more thorough self-consciousness about our own acts of appropriation. The ecocritical claim that nature writing points to a world beyond matters of merely human relations is analogous in its utopianism, in its evasion of the realities of the historical process, to the New England elite's turn to nature for the reinvigoration of their authority as leaders of the embattled republic. Although it is true that their vision of intimate relations between people and the nature may now flower into meaningful activism, it will only do so if we disengage it from the politics of nostalgia within which it initially struck root and replant it in the democratic radicalism to which it so compellingly responded.

There is a final scene, in the last chapter of *Summer on the Lakes*, in which Fuller pursues a specific perceptual effect in search of a natural alternative to the spirit of commerce. She is making her way home to Boston, traveling by steamship between Lake Michigan and Lake Huron. During a stop to take on wood for the boilers, she "ordered a canoe to take me down the rapids" at Sault St. Marie. The boat is handled by "two Indian canoe-men in pink calico shirts, moving it about with their long poles, with a grace and dexterity worthy fairy land. Now and then they cast the scoop-net; all looked just as I had fancied, only far prettier" (150). These representatives of a noncommercial culture, performing the unalienated labor of fishing for subsistence, seat her on a mat in the middle of their canoe. "In less than four minutes we had descended the rapids, a distance of more than three quarters of a mile." Fuller is crestfallen.

> I was somewhat disappointed in this being no more of an exploit than I found it. Having heard such expressions used as of "darting," or, "shooting down," these rapids, I had fancied there was a wall of rock somewhere, where descent would somehow be accomplished, and that there would come some one gasp of terror and delight, some sensation entirely new to me; but I found myself in smooth water, before I had time to feel anything but the buoyant pleasure of being carried so lightly through this surf amid the breakers. (150)

Fuller complains that even though it is "an act of wonderful dexterity to steer amid these jagged rocks, when one rude touch would tear a hole in the birch canoe," the boatmen are so practiced that "the silliest person could not feel afraid." Nevertheless, she insists on desiring that fear: "I should like to have come down twenty times, that I might have had leisure to realize the pleasure" (150). This canoeing scene is one of the earliest accounts, perhaps the earliest account, of recreational white-water boating in American literature. In recounting this exploit as one for which the sole purpose was "pleasure," Fuller transforms what had been a difficult and risky mode of travel for natives, trappers, and explorers, into a touristic experience, a deliberately nonproductive exploit in which she engages as means of achieving self-transcendence and reconnecting with nature. In doing so, she gives us a harbinger of the nature-obsessed future we now inhabit, with its innumerable strategies for producing utopian experiences in the wilderness. The passage also indexes the extent to which wilderness recreation, like the older art of landscape appreciation, is so frequently, an act of forgetting. Both, like the Thoreauvian tradition of nature writing, depend on a conventional geography in which a degraded and oppressive society is opposed to a pure and free wilderness. Witnessing the way in which Fuller and other nature writers so actively map that border in order to cross it can help us to remember that societies are rooted in the land, and wilderness is not a place outside town, but a monument we have built to desires that capitalism cannot fulfill. At the same time, that monument may inspire us to engage in the kinds of activism that may replace capitalism and its alien geography with a society in which we can heal the planet into a home.

CHAPTER 17

MARXISM, NATURE, AND THE DISCIPLINE OF HISTORY

> Let us settle ourselves, and work and wedge our feet downward through the mud and slush of opinion, and prejudice, and tradition, and delusion, and appearance, that alluvion which covers the globe, through Paris and London, through New York and Boston and Concord, through church and state, through poetry and philosophy and religion, till we come to a hard bottom and rocks in place, which we can call *reality*, and say, This is, and no mistake; and then begin, having a point d'appui, below freshet and frost and fire, a place where you might found a wall or a state, or set a lamp-post safely. . . .
>
> —Henry David Thoreau (W 97–98)

Most ecocritics indulge in quite scholarly beliefs about what is wrong with society and how to change it. Most believe that such things as deforestation and pollution are symptoms of a society in which our ethical priorities have been disordered by a culture of utilitarianism, a tradition of humanism, or the pressure of another ideological misalignment. And most hope that the force of example, especially the example of rightly interpreted nature writing, will inspire an epochal realignment. A revolution in our relations with the environment will be accomplished above all by rethinking nature. We call upon ourselves and our readers to engage in an Emersonian exercise:

> Build, therefore, your own world. As fast as you can conform your life to the pure idea in your mind, that will unfold its great proportions. A correspondent revolution in things will attend the influx of the spirit. So fast will disagreeable appearances, swine, spiders, snakes, pests, mad-houses, prisons, enemies, vanish . . . (CW 1.45)

The trouble with this way of thinking about the ongoing history of environmental devastation, and about the potential for our work to redirect it, is not that it is too optimistic, but that it is not ecological enough.

When we, as ecocritics, talk of ideological revolutions, we make a connection between thought and the material world, but it is unidirectional. We imagine that people first think of nature as an inexhaustible fund of resources and then set about destroying its delicate equations of productivity. We conceive of ideas as discrete objects, and of thought, whether at the level of the individual or the entire society, as a simple matter of "holding" these ideas rather than those.

Thus, when describing the process of environmental awakening either in literary texts or in present lives, most ecocritics prefer to tell the tale of a solitary visionary walking in the woods. James McKusick, for instance, affirms that ecocriticism hopes to accomplish "the elucidation of the *total material context* of literary production." By way of example he points to the "environmental context that surrounds the production of any literary work, providing 'raw materials' that range from sensory inputs for the writer's cognitive production of imagery to the physical paper, ink, cloth, and leather that make up the finished book." We might expect these manufactured objects to stand metonymically for the complex ecosocial process of production that makes writing possible. Instead, McKusick tells us that these "materials come from *somewhere* out there—a place beyond the purely social realm that we may designate 'Nature' without stipulating a definition of the latter term." This reluctance to confront the materiality of the social process reveals the incompleteness of the discipline's departure from the historiographical idealism of orthodox literary studies and cultural analysis. In the early 1970s, Leo Marx criticized this idealist structure of feeling as "New Left pastoralism" that he called, borrowing a phrase from Lenin, an "infantile disorder." As incisive as his comments were, he finally set aside his own analysis, claiming that in an era when bread-and-butter issues had been largely resolved, the pastoral aesthetic ideals of beauty, simplicity, and harmony could motivate new forms of collective political commitment. This may have been true, and may still be true, but the last 30 years of increasing economic disparity, with falling living standards for the vast majority of Americans, have decisively put bread-and-butter issues back on the table. And over the course of the same period, issues like environmental racism, nuclear proliferation, privatization of land and water, and industrial pollution have deepened immeasurably. They have also inspired new and promising forms of commitment. The challenge now is to reintegrate movements and perspectives driven by capitalism's accelerating destruction of the earth with those responding to its intensifying destruction of working people's lives. As categories of analysis, "nature" and "society" are inadequate to this task.[1]

It is therefore not enough to describe anthropocentric habits of thought and offer an alternative in ecocentrism. We need to explain why the habits of thought that we deplore became and remain dominant within this specific ecosocial order. What specification of that order should we make? One influential claim is that Christianity is the driving force of the scientific and technological revolutions and thus of environmental crisis. Then there is the ecofeminist position that environmental damage is another effect of androcentricism. More recently, it has become common to blame the replacement of animism by Renaissance and Enlightenment humanism. Judeo-Christian, Androcentric, humanist, rationalist—each of these adjectives offers to explain modern society's apparent failure to foresee, or even much care about, the environmental damage it does. But each explains the dominance of that habit of thought by reference to another. Ideas, like forests, are not static things; they are dynamic processes responsive to a wide range of determinants. A fully ecological analysis of ideas requires us to recognize that, like anything we temporarily isolate for examination, they are ultimately recognizable only when returned to transitive interrelations with their environments. If it is to follow through on the implications of its position on nature's reality, ecocriticism must truly recover the full materiality of the capitalist social order—not only in its account of nature writing, but also in its account of itself as a force for social change.

There is another law of ecology that ecocriticism would do well to consider: the most fundamental relationships structuring the operation of natural (and social) systems are those that regulate the production and exchange of energy. Thus, particular ideas are connected to other ideas, but all ideas are rooted in the ecosocial order within which they develop, or in Marxist terms, in the mode of production. To argue that we should rethink our response to the environmental crisis in these terms is to ask for reconsideration of a number of deeply held convictions. The current ecocritical rejection of Marxist cultural theory is partly a reaction against the imbalances of New Historicism, which has often placed a totalizing emphasis on ideology as false consciousness in its polemic against the idealism of prior critical orthodoxies. The impulse to transcend the pessimism of a critical practice that appears to be blind to the potential for human creativity to be a positive force in this world—that impulse is sound. But it has driven many to reject, in an equally totalizing way, any notion of the conditions that limit and shape such creativity. Marxism, like ecocriticism, is, or should be, thinking in service to a politics of world emancipation. And when it focuses on the limits of human creativity, it does so, or should, in order to imagine more realistically how people can take control of their own history, of their relations with each other and nature. So, while ecocritics are right to reject the hard determinism of much academic Marxism, they are wrong to dispense altogether with what must be regarded as the most sustained, diverse, and serious tradition of thought about how to get from this world to one where people can decide to live well together on the land.[2]

John Bellamy Foster refutes the common ecocritical claim that Marxism is oblivious to the delicate complexity of the natural systems on which we all depend. It was the process of making a systematic study of the soil science of his day, which had developed out of changes in agricultural modes of production, which were themselves driven by population growth made possible by capitalist industrialization that motivated Marx to apply fundamentally ecological modes of analysis to the ways that human societies have organized themselves within nature. According to Marx, capitalism was built by two acts of theft: the alienation of people from the land through enclosure and displacement, and the alienation of the resulting workers from the produce of their labor. Thus, the rising bourgeoisie reduced most of humanity to a shadow life in cities where "darkness, polluted air, and raw, untreated sewage constituted their material environment. Not only creative work but the essential elements of life itself were forfeited as a result of this alienation of humanity and nature." But through the collective ownership of the land, Marx argued, "earth ceases to be an object of barter" and there can be a final "resolution of the conflict between man and nature, and between man and man." Marx spent his career thinking in terms of complex coevolutionary relationships between particular societies and specific places, and he therefore based his historiographical practice in *Capital* on the idea that no history is adequate if it abstracts any one analytical category—economy, technology, ideology, or environment—from what is a combined, uneven, and, above all, a specific process of human subsistence in the material world. His "worldview was deeply, and indeed systematically, ecological [and] this ecological perspective derived from his materialism . . . for it allowed him to develop the central metaphor of 'metabolism' to capture the complex, interdependent process, linking human beings to nature through labor." Foster's most relevant emphasis, finally, is on the activist character of Marx's ecology, on the way that Marxism makes materialism into the most fundamental tool for achieving "nothing less than the transcendence of alienation in all of its aspects: a world of rational ecology and human freedom with an earthly basis—the society of associated producers." That is, at their best both Marxism and ecology, which was founded by German socialist, Ernst Haeckel, harness materialist analysis of the whole ecosocial process to a creative political commitment to change.[3]

Marx's collaborator, Frederick Engels consistently and explicitly connected the social and environmental costs of capitalism. For instance, in *Dialectics of Nature*, he describes the destruction of forests by mono-cultural production of coffee in the Caribbean: "What did the Spanish planters in Cuba, who burned down forests on the slopes of the mountains and obtained from the ashes sufficient fertiliser for *one* generation of very highly profitable coffee trees, care that the tropical rainfall afterwards washed away the now unprotected upper stratum of the soil, leaving behind only bare rock?" Engels located the motivation for this evidently irrational and destructive behavior, not in theology or philosophy, but in the logic of the commodity: "When individual capitalists are engaged in production and exchange for the sake of the immediate profit, only the nearest, most immediate results can be taken into account in the first place." As a result, the "individual manufacturer or merchant . . . is not concerned as to what becomes of the commodity afterwards or who are its purchasers. The same thing applies to the natural effects of the same actions." For Engels, capitalism was an increasingly destructive force "in relation to nature, as to society," since it is "predominantly concerned only about the first, tangible success; and then surprise is expressed that the more remote effects of actions directed to this end turn out to be of quite a different character." In the end, Engels was convinced that "we by no means rule over nature like a conqueror over a foreign people, like someone standing outside nature—but that we, with flesh, blood, and brain, belong to nature, and exist in its midst. . . ."[4]

In line with their interest in agriculture and ecology, Marx and Engels formulated a particular way of thinking about the historical process, which they summarized famously in *The German Ideology*:

> The first premise of all human history is, of course, the existence of living human individuals. Thus the first fact to be established is the physical organization of these individuals and their consequent relations to the rest of nature, [to] the natural conditions in which man finds himself— geological, orohydrographical, climactic, and so on. The writing of history must always set out from these natural bases and their modification in the course of history through the action of man.

Environmental historian, William Cronon, extends this Marxist method of analysis, offering an integrated and ecological formula for under-standing the complex process of ecosocial history:

> An ecological history begins by assuming a dynamic and changing relationship between environment and culture, one as apt to produce

contradictions as continuities. Moreover, it assumes that the interactions of the two are dialectical. Environment may initially shape the range of choices available to people at a given moment, but then culture reshapes environment in responding to those choices. The reshaped environment presents a new set of possibilities for cultural reproduction, thus setting up a new cycle of mutual determination. Changes in the way people create and re-create their livelihood must be analyzed in terms of changes not only in their *social* relations but in their *ecological* ones as well.

However, within that combined and indissoluble historical process, certain relationships disproportionately shape social orders and their relations with nature. The most definitive of these relationships are those that confer effective control of the means of producing the material needs of human life through the collective application of labor to nature. In our modern society, the society whose behavior Marx set out to understand and change, that control remains in the hands of a tiny minority who own the vast material apparatus of agriculture and industry on which we all depend. To use the specification "capitalist" when talking about our society, as opposed to the term "anthropocentric" in all its varieties, is a finally matter of materialist description. The word "capitalism" describes not an ideology of growth, or a culture of greed, or a technological era of industrialization, although all of these also characterize our period, but a historically specific, and quite recent, regime of laws of property, methods of finance, distributions of power and wealth, and modes of exploitation of labor and land. It is that regime, that set of relations of production, that most fundamentally determines how we collectively treat the earth.[5]

We can, of course, point to apparently anthropocentric ideas in pre-capitalist societies, even in ones that were quite destructive of the ecosystems on which they depended. But it is a drastic oversimplification to argue that those ideas have remained in any way constant, or that they determined the historical process that has finally produced this particular social order. Such ideas have evolved beyond recognition, both in form and function, along with the social and natural systems to which they refer. In their current forms, they operate flexibly both to naturalize and to critique ecosocial conditions established by capitalist relations of production. To see this we need only examine, on one hand, how dominant representations of nature have changed over time along with the changing needs of capital, and on the other, how capital, over the last four decades of sustained attention to its environmental record, has managed to change its way of talking without changing its basic priorities and practices. Perhaps the clearest recent example of the way that environmentalist convictions can underwrite an equally strong commitment to extending capitalist patterns of ecosocial exploitation is Al Gore's best-selling *Earth in the Balance: Ecology and the Human Spirit*, which has mostly to do with convincing environmentalists to take up the spirit of commerce by endorsing pollution-credit trading schemes.[6]

To say, then, that people act as though they were more important than nature because they are anthropocentric is like saying that people use skin color and sex as indicators of intellectual potential because they are racist and sexist. Such ideas remain active, despite efforts to prove them inaccurate or to replace them through retraining, *because* they function as part of systems of differential exploitation. The sexual division of labor attempts to limit women to the unpaid work of caring for and training children and the racial division of labor creates a poorly paid reserve of easily identifiable deskilled workers who take up the slack in the business cycle. Racist and sexist ideas justify these hierarchies as natural. Likewise, anthropocentric ideas about the subordination of nature to human progress justify the oppressive patterns of resource exploitation on which capital depends. But the fact is that these patterns oppress not merely nature, but also most people. Access, not only to the produce of modern industry, but also to such things as clean air, water, and food, is sharply stratified by class and, within class, by race and gender. Thus, anthropocentric narratives of the triumph of human reason over nature serve above all to obscure that we live in a specifically capitalist society and that, therefore, the current mode of human interaction with nature is organized for profit, not for human needs (such as complex and productive ecosystems). When ecocritics speak of an innocent nature threatened by a society maddened by bad ideas, we tell that same old tale of human triumph, doing no more than to reverse the moral. And thus we perpetuate that other idea on which those who have presided over the destruction of our lives and world rely so heavily: that they do not, as a class, as a ruling class, exist.[7]

A good way to start the work of demonstrating the relevance of Marxism to the ecocritical project is to briefly revisit the cultural work of English socialist, Raymond Williams. Williams is at least familiar to most American readers of cultural theory, but usually in an attenuated form, since he has either been overshadowed by influential postmodernists, or incorporated into a bowdlerized American version of New Left Marxism that is substantially identical with postmodernism. For instance, cultural theorist Scott Wilson appropriates Williams into a postmodernist pluralism that sees itself as " 'postmarxist' to the extent that it no longer privileges class in its politics of difference." Wilson retreats far enough from materialism that Marx has become no more than a "spirit" of righteous anger inspiring the work of "the cultural materialist pedagogue, the last intellectual action hero." The best cure for this kind of silliness is to return to Williams himself.[8]

In addition to the practical ecocriticism of his history of English pastoralism, *The Country and the City*, Williams also produced a number of pioneering essays on the challenge presented to socialism by evidence, mounting through the 1960s and 1970s, which pointed to ecological damage on a global scale. In these essays, Williams was able to recover one of Marxism's most powerful historiographical emphases in its account of the ecosocial process: "If we talk only of singular Man and singular Nature we can compose a general history, but at the cost excluding the real and altering social relations [within which] the conquest of nature . . . will always include the conquest, the domination or the exploitation of some men by others." It was necessary to grasp the connection between these two forms of material conquest in order to go on to understand how the cultures they produced represented themselves. The narratives according to which capitalism understood itself, "the conquest of nature, the domination of nature, the exploitation of nature—are derived from the real human practices: relations between men and men."[9]

Beyond identifying this central ideological pattern, further study of which will remain central to the ecocritical project, Williams also elaborates a set of theoretical terms and procedures that have the potential to resolve ecocriticism's long-standing desire for a new mode of critical practice. In *Keywords* and *Marxism and Literature*, as well as in several retrospective collections of essays, he outlines what he calls "cultural materialism," which is "the analysis of all forms of signification, including quite centrally writing, within the actual means and conditions of their production." Because Williams never loses his focus on "the extraordinary process of human creativity and self-creation in all its modes and means," his approach to the question of historical determination provides a solution to the central contradiction in ecocritical thought—the contradiction between its idealist theory of social change and its proto-materialist approach to nature.[10]

For Williams, Marx's focus on the material history of human labor in nature, his emphasis on "man making himself" through "producing his own means of life . . . offered the possibility of overcoming the dichotomy between 'society' and 'nature,' and of discovering new constitutive relationships between 'society' and 'economy.'" He goes on, though, to critique the shallowness of much pseudo-Marxist work that makes that emphasis into the ground for new kinds of abstraction. "Instead of making cultural history material . . . it was made dependent, secondary, 'superstructural': a realm of 'mere' ideas, beliefs, arts, customs, determined by the basic material history." Williams opposes both this reduction of culture to an epiphenomenon, and the opposite (and now more common) one of making language or ideology into a determining structure in its own right. Instead, he emphasizes the totality of an integrated process. For Stuart Hall, one of Williams's close colleagues, the distinctive emphasis was on the way that "every mode of production is also a culture, and every struggle between classes is always also a struggle between cultural modalities. . . ." Thus, the material processes of human life and historical development include not only production and reproduction, but also language, thought, ideas, the full range of signifying practices we study under the rubric of culture. Culture is neither a mere reflection of an economic base, nor a determining ideological structure, but is inextricably part of—both constituted by and constituting—the whole material social process.[11]

It is important to keep in mind the polemical situation within which Williams wrote much of his explicitly theoretical work. Just as Marx emphasized the importance of the mode of production in shaping cultural life in his arguments against Hegelian idealism, Williams focuses on the spaces for resistance and creativity within the process of determination in his argument against the mechanical determinism of most Marxist theory of the mid-twentieth century. Richard Johnson recalls that the "recovery of 'values' against Stalinism was a leading impulse of the first new left, but the critique of economism has been a continuous thread through the whole 'crisis of marxism' which has followed." In other words, Williams was far from alone in his attempt to work out an alternative to "vulgar materialist" accounts not only of social evolution, but also of the place of literature and culture in society. Leon Trotsky, writing as early as 1923 in the heat of revolution, found time to articulate a clear agenda for cultural materialism:

> Keeping on the plane of scientific investigation, Marxism seeks . . . the social roots of the "pure" as well as of the tendentious art. It does not at all "incriminate" a poet with the thoughts and feelings which he expresses, but raises questions of a much more profound significance, namely, to which order of feelings does a given artistic work correspond in all its peculiarities? What are the social conditions of these thoughts and feelings? What place do they occupy in the historic development of a society and of a class? And, further, what literary heritage has entered into the elaboration of the new form?

On the basis of such an empirical approach to culture, Trotsky rejected crude equations of progressiveness with the class position of the author and the ideological content of the work of art. When such equations were made orthodox on the international left by cultural organs of the Stalin's Third International, the reaction of which Williams is a part began immediately.[12]

Crucially, though, "a Marxism without some concept of determination is in effect worthless." Williams argues that we must see determination as "a complex and interrelated process of limits and pressures . . . in the whole social process itself and nowhere else: not in an abstracted 'mode of production' nor in an abstracted 'psychology.' " Perhaps the most effective analogy for this process comes from ecology: ideas are determined, shaped, by the material social process in much the same way that the forms of life in an ecosystem are determined by its inorganic base. There is vast potential for variation, but always within specific limits, always in response to definite pressures. The fantastically creative processes of mutation and speciation are contained by the need to negotiate those limits and pressures. But crucially, there is always the potential for those processes to feed back into the inorganic base, changing it and thus the conditions under which further development occurs. The difference, of course, is that in the development of human ideas there is the further potential for this kind of feedback to become the self-consciously set goal of thought.[13]

All too frequently, that revolutionary potential remains unrealized. Williams turns to Italian socialist, Antonio Gramsci's decisive concept of "hegemony" for help with explaining how "relations of domination and subordination" are maintained. Hegemony is "a whole body of practices and expectations, over the whole of living: our senses and assignments of energy, our shaping perceptions of ourselves and our world." As the ground of daily life, hegemony "constitutes a sense of reality for most people in the society, a sense of absolute because experienced reality beyond which it is very difficult for most members of the society to move, in most areas of their lives." The power of this concept for Williams was in large part relative to the narrow bread-and-butter politics of both the Labor Party and the Stalinist Left in the 1960s. Hall makes this point especially clearly:

> Gramsci always insisted that hegemony is not exclusively an ideological phenomenon. There can be no hegemony without "the decisive nucleus of the economic." On the other hand, do not fall into the trap of the old mechanical economism and believe that if you can only get hold of the

economy, you can move the rest of life. The nature of power in the modern world is that it is also constructed in relation to political, moral, intellectual, cultural, ideological, and sexual questions. The question of hegemony is always the question of a new cultural order.

Too often, especially in the United States, Williams, Hall, and through them Gramsci, have been mistaken for postmodernist theorists of a narrow practice of intellectual resistance, when in fact their goal was to integrate cultural work into a comprehensive and revolutionary socialist politics.[14]

So, despite the sharp focus in the idea of hegemony on the way that dominant ideas can saturate experience, the point is to emphasize that the process whereby it is established is not a matter of abstract "subject-formation" or static subordination within false consciousness. Rather, it is an ongoing struggle, a battle of ideas. The hegemonic "does not just passively exist as a form of dominance. It has continually to be renewed, recreated, defended, and modified. It is also continually resisted, limited, altered, challenged by pressures not at all its own." This insight grounds Williams's commitment to the importance of cultural texts and their study. He maintains that cultural work can be an important form of activity not only within, but also against the hegemonic. Although he acknowledges that "the dominant culture at once produces and limits its own forms of counter-culture," he also insists that "authentic breaks within and beyond it, in specific situations which can vary from extreme isolation to pre-revolutionary breakdown and actual revolutionary activity, have often in fact occurred." Given the potential instability of the hegemonic, Williams argues for the importance of "creative practice."

> Creative practice . . . can be the long and difficult remaking of an inherited (determined) practical consciousness . . . not casting off an ideology, or learning phrases about it, but confronting a hegemony in the fibres of the self and in the hard practical substance of effective and continuing relationships. It can [also] be more evident practice: the reproduction and illustration of hitherto excluded and subordinated models; the embodiment and performance of known but excluded and subordinated experiences and relationships; the articulation and formation of latent, momentary, and newly possible consciousness.

Williams's strong sense of the importance of creative practice brings us, at last, to the question of cultural analysis, its purpose and methods: "It is the special function of theory, in exploring and defining the nature and the variation of practice, to develop a general consciousness within what is repeatedly experienced as a special and often relatively isolated consciousness." In Hall's words, the job of cultural producers is "to connect with the ordinary feelings and experiences which people have in their everyday lives, and yet to articulate them progressively to a more advanced, modern form of consciousness." Within that broader project, the job of cultural historians is to make available, as a living tradition from which we can learn in the present, the history of revolutionary consciousness in creative, cultural practice.[15]

What this brief summary should make clear is that a genuinely Marxist theory of culture simultaneously confirms the importance of the ecocritical project and suggests how it can more self-consciously and more realistically work toward its avowed goal of changing this society's way of living on the land. First, we should recognize that environmental writing is not a stable form of reaction to a stable problem (the ideologically driven human domination of nature). It is a dynamic tradition of response to the rise and development of the capitalist ecosocial order. The conventions of nature writing have been appropriated in a variety of ways to a variety of ends: it meant one thing for Thoreau to look for a solution to the economic and political crisis of the early 1840s at Walden Pond, and something quite other for Gretel Ehrlich to find solace in the open spaces of Wyoming, or for Eddy Harris to go solo down the Mississippi in the 1980s. In other words, environmental writing records a huge variety of structures of feeling about nature, and each is irreducibly specific, endemic even, to the conditions that produced it.

It follows that we cannot hope to understand the differences between environmental texts without examining the differences between the environments within which they grew. It has been productively suggested that we examine the actual places that nature writers visited and described. We should go further and investigate the historical social environments within those encounters occurred. For when nature writers write about and publish their feelings about nature, they are engaging, more or less self-consciously, in a form of cultural debate. They are, first and uncontroversially, testing the limits of inherited habits of thought about nature, and they are experimenting with new ones. At the same time though—and this is what remains largely unexamined—they are engaged in critiquing the specific ecosocial order within which those inherited habits have become dominant and adaptive. This critique may be more or less open. It may remain no more than a rejection implied by absence, by the transfer of affect and attention to nonhuman objects. It may operate solely at the level of representation, as in the retelling of old themes, the redrawing of old images, and the invention of new ones. Or it may become a full-blown argument about how a given society relates to nature in its day-to-day functioning, how its dominant representations of nature operate as part those relations, even about how its relations with nature are shaped by its mode of social organization. In this last case, it may be more or less empirical and specific in its description and analysis of that society and its relations with nature. And it may be more or less radical in its evaluation, more or less imaginative in the degrees and kinds of change it envisions, and more or less astute in its thinking about how to achieve such changes.

This engagement in political debate, at whatever level of development and self-consciousness, cannot be regarded as secondary or peripheral. For how nature writers see and understand nature has everything to do with how they see and understand the society whose relations with it they hope to change. The first premise of most nature writing—that human and nonhuman places belong to sharply separate categories of being—reveals the genre's immediate engagement with one of the most fundamental inheritances of capitalist geography. It is an indicator of the genre's potential critical strength that it so often returns from its observations in the field to bring that premise under sharp scrutiny. We should read the green canon, then, not only for its embodiment of idyllic individual relations with nature, but also centrally for its active participation in the ongoing cultural debates that arise about and as part of a whole developing ecosocial order. Our interpretive practice should, in other words, attend to the full range of the genre's reference and engagement, should map the fields of historical cultural argument within which it has taken its stands.

It should be clear that the success of this first extension of our critical practice would require a second,—namely, incorporation of a far broader range of evidence into the histories we tell. Not only must we incorporate dominant traditions of the representation of nature—such as the vast archive within which nature figures as a field of individual and national masculine conquest—and examine the ways in which green texts at once participate in and critique those traditions. We must also investigate texts representing both dominant and alternative positions within locally relevant cultural and political debates. Moreover, the debates within which we replace any text should be analyzed not merely internally as discursive fields, but as ranges of response to specific conjunctures in the development of the capitalist ecosocial order. Given this full range of evidence, we can begin to constitute ecocriticism as the flexible and encompassing interdiscipline it should be, as a community of emphasis within the broader field of materialist historiography. In other words, while connecting our work to that rich tradition, we can maintain our definitive focus on the culture of nature.

By extending our scholarly practice in this way, we will also come far closer to the goal of making the tradition of nature writing truly useful in present. Jonathon Arac makes a commendably measured assessment of the work many ecocritics do as educational professionals: "We will not transform American life today, or tomorrow, but what we do to change our academic habits and disciplines, the questions we dare to ask or allow our students to pursue, these are political and make a difference." The material institutions within which we operate are, of course, cultivating a new generation of (potential) environmentalists. Thus, William Rueckert urges us to "charge the classroom with ecological purpose." And ecocriticism has heeded his call with its distinctive emphasis on pedagogical practice, advocating various forms of reinstruction, from reading environmental texts, to more direct experiences such as fieldtrips in parks and wilderness areas and experiments with tracking personal waste production, to courses that blend the humanities and sciences into an holistic understanding of the beauty and complexity of healthy ecosystems. The goal of such instruction is to foster a new sort of ethical consciousness at the core of which is the conviction that people should treat all things in nature as equals, as beings with ethical standing. If such a consciousness can be reproduced widely enough, it is argued, there will follow a paradigm shift that will go far toward reversing a continuing history of destruction.[16]

This pedagogical program derives quite directly from ecocriticism's organic idealism. We regard destructive levels and forms of production, waste, and pollution as caused by greed and callous disregard of what is right and good. We tell our students that since values are the motor of history, if you change your values, history will change too. But this advice blinds them to fundamental political realities. For the corporations that make the decisions about how much of what to make and discharge, ethical considerations must remain secondary to profit. And profit depends on growth, on predictable obsolescence, and the constant creation of new needs. The economic laws of capitalism do certainly produce behavior that outrages our ideals of fairness and the wise stewardship of natural systems. But such laws are subject to final repeal, not by passive disagreement alone, but by large-scale social movements that set out consciously to overturn them. The cultural histories of those movements and of the debates within them should be the tools of our trade. And we should use them to teach the truth that we *are* connected to nature, that this connection is inescapably social, and that it is a material connection through the collective process of labor. If we wish to change our relationship with nature, we must change the way we work within it. To do that we will have to change the most basic relationships that structure our society. It should be clear then that the individualism we too often teach contains within it the seeds of future demoralization for those who take its dicta to heart. Encouraging people, in Aldo Leopold's famous phrase, to think like a mountain, is finally, if we leave it at that, a dead end. Those who make the decisions about building nuclear power plants, toxic waste incinerators, private automobiles, and gated subdivisions, not only will, but also must go on thinking, not like mountains, but like capitalists. Environmentalist commitment is finally a matter of consciously attempting to change the most basic structures of social power. This will be a long and difficult collective process to say the least, and one in which neither we nor our students can afford vulnerability to the dejection that follows when our passion meets silence.

This is not to say that it is unimportant to value nature. The long history of struggle for human emancipation would make a very short story had it not been for the dedication of millions to the positive values of fairness and equality. But the ethical commitments that inspired them were neither absolute nor universal; they were conjunctural expressions of desire arising in ongoing conflicts driven by the ecosocial dynamics of capitalism. Values are not standards to be lived up to, but goals to be fought for. They are potentially realizable, not when passively elevated as statements of belief, but when avowed as declarations of commitment. If, then, we are going to teach ecocentric consciousness, along with the vast extension of those values it entails, an indispensable part of it must be historical consciousness, must be detailed consciousness of the coevolution of material social and natural systems that has produced the present crisis, and of the long history of creative collective struggle to overturn an ecosocial order founded on the oppression and exploitation of people and nature. The tradition of Thoreauvian nature writing makes a fine *point d'appui* for such a project. Environmental texts provide a rich record of critical, and sometimes radical, response to the development of capitalism. By reading and teaching that tradition against the history that produced it, we not only will have vastly strengthened ecocriticism, but we will also have begun to return Marxism to its most productive focus—a focus on the process of conscious human self-determination, the hard and rewarding process of making revolutionary ideas a material force in this world.

NOTES

Foreword

1. "Destroying the world in order to save it," *CNN*, May 31, 2004, <http://www.cnn.com/2004/SHOWBIZ/Movies/05/31/film.day.after.tomorrow.ap/> (Accessed June 25, 2004). Sources for the epigraphs are as follows: William Rueckert, "Literature and Ecology: An Experiment in Ecocriticism," *Iowa Review*, 9 no. 1 (Winter 1978): 121; and Raymond Williams, *What I Came to Say* (London: Radius, 1989), 76, 81.

2. "Global warming is real and underway," Union of Concerned Scientists, n. d., <http://www.ucsusa.org/global_environment/global_warming/index.cfm> (Accessed June 25, 2004). "Larsen B Ice Shelf Collapses in Antarctica," National Snow and Ice Data Center, n. d., <http://nsidc.org/iceshelves/larsenb2002/> (Accessed June 25, 2004). Vandana Shiva, *Water Wars* (Cambridge, MA: South End Press, 2002), 98–99.

3. UN Intergovernmental Panel on Climate Change, "Projections of Future Climate Change," in *Climate Change 2001: The Scientific Basis*, <http://www.grida.no/climate/ipcc_tar/wg1/339.htm> (Accessed June 25, 2004). Shiva, *Water Wars*, 1.

4. Greg Palast, "Bush Energy Plan: Policy or Payback?" BBC News, May 18, 2001, <http://news.bbc.co.uk/1/hi/world/americas/1336960.stm> (Accessed June 25, 2004). Mark Townsend and Paul Harris, "Now the Pentagon tells Bush: Climate Change will Destroy Us," *The Observer*, February 22, 2004, <http://observer.guardian.co.uk/international/story/0,6903,1153513,00.html> (Accessed June 25, 2004).

5. Paul Brown, "Uranium Hazard Prompts Cancer Check on Troops," *The Guardian*, April 25, 2003, <http://www.guardian.co.uk/uranium/story/0,7369,943340,00.html> (Accessed June 25, 2004). Alexander Cockburn and Jeffrey St. Clair, "Radioactive War," *Counterpunch*, February 5, 2001, <http://www.counterpunch.org/ du.html> (Accessed June 25, 2004).

6. Tom Athanasiou, *Divided Planet: The Ecology of Rich and Poor* (Athens: University of Georgia Press, 1998), 304.

Chapter 1   The Commitments of Ecocriticism

1. Donald Worster, *Nature's Economy: A History of Ecological Ideas* (New York: Cambridge University Press, 1985), 68, 49. Three valuable histories of the American environmental movement are Anna Bramwell, *Ecology in the*

Twentieth Century: A History (New Haven: Yale University Press, 1989), Kirkpatrick Sale, *The Green Revolution: The American Environmental Movement, 1962–1992* (New York: Hill and Wang, 1993), and Philip Shabecoff, *A Fierce Green Fire: The American Environmental Movement* (Washington, DC: Island Press, 2003).

2. Cheryll Glotfelty, "Introduction," in Cheryll Glotfelty and Harold Fromm, eds., *The Ecocriticism Reader: Landmarks in Literary Ecology* (Athens: University of Georgia Press, 1986), xxi. William Rueckert, "Literature and Ecology: An Experiment in Ecocriticism," *Iowa Review*, 9, no. 1 (Winter 1978): 72–73.

3. Rueckert, "Literature and Ecology," 72–73, 86. Although the term "ecocriticism" came into common use in the 1990s, there is a large body of older work, from a number of disciplines, that has been adopted as a kind of canon of scholarship. Perhaps the earliest attempt to demonstrate the redemptive potential of nature writing is the long introduction to Joseph Wood Krutch, *Great American Nature Writing* (New York: William Sloane, 1950). Joseph Meeker, *The Comedy of Survival: Studies in Literary Ecology* (New York: Scribner, 1974) anticipates almost the whole of the ecocritical project, but because he focuses on what he sees as the ecologism of the tradition of dramatic comedy rather than on nonfiction nature writing, he has received very little attention. For a handy collection of major statements and precursor texts, see David Mazel, ed., *A Century of Early Ecocriticism* (Athens: University of Georgia Press, 2001).

4. William Howarth, "Some Principles of Ecocriticism," in *Ecocriticism Reader*, 69. Lawrence Buell, *The Environmental Imagination: Thoreau, Nature Writing, and the Formation of American Culture* (Cambridge: Harvard University Press, 1994), 430n. Lawrence Buell, "The Ecocritical Insurgency," *New Literary History*, 30, no. 3 (Summer 1999): 699–700.

5. Michael Branch, "Ecocriticism: Surviving Institutionalization in the Academic Environment," *Interdisciplinary Studies in Literature and the Environment*, 2, no. 1 (Spring 1994): 98. Jonathon Bate quoted in Jennifer Wallace, "Swampy's Smart Set," *Times Higher Education Supplement*, July 4, 1997, 4.

6. Glotfelty, "Introduction," in *Ecocriticism Reader*, xxi. Lawrence Buell, *Writing for an Endangered World: Literature, Culture, and Environment in the US and Beyond* (Cambridge: Belknap Press of Harvard University Press, 2001), 1. Buell, *Environmental Imagination*, 2–3. Glen A. Love, "Revaluing Nature: Towards an Ecological Criticism," *Western American Literature*, 25, no. 3 (November 1990): 213. Scott Slovic, *Seeking Awareness in American Nature Writing* (Salt Lake City: University of Utah Press, 1992), 169.

7. Buell, *Environmental Imagination*, 2, 4. Lynn White, Jr., "The Historical Roots of Our Ecological Crisis," *Science*, 155, no. 3767 (March 10, 1967): 1204–1205. Love, "Revaluing Nature," 203. For another influential early version of the ecocritical argument about the power of ideas, see William Leiss, *The Domination of Nature* (New York: George Brazillier, 1972). For ecocritical histories of the idea of nature in Euro-American culture, see Max Oelschlaeger, *The Idea of Wilderness* (New Haven: Yale University Press,

1991), and Neil Evernden, *The Social Creation of Nature* (Baltimore: Johns Hopkins University Press, 1992).

8. Jonathon Bate, *The Song of the Earth* (Cambridge: Harvard University Press, 2000), 245–247. James McKusick, *Green Writing: Romanticism and Ecology* (New York: St. Martin's, 2000), 11, 228. Daniel J. Philippon, *Conserving Words: How American Nature Writers Shaped the Environmental Movement* (Athens: University of Georgia Press, 2004). A history that parallels Philippon's, though with an earlier starting point, is Daniel G. Payne, *Voices in the Wilderness: American Nature Writing and Environmental Politics* (Hanover: University Press of New England, 1996).

9. Bill Devall and George Sessions, *Deep Ecology: Living as If Nature Mattered* (Salt Lake City: Peregrine Smith, 1985), 8. Charles S. Brown, "Anthropocentrism and Ecocentrism: The Quest for a New World View," *Midwest Quarterly*, 36, no. 2 (January 1995): 191–202. Robyn Eckersley, *Environmentalism and Political Theory: Toward an Ecocentric Approach* (Albany: State University of New York Press, 1992), 28.

10. John Elder, *Imagining the Earth: Poetry and the Vision of Nature* (Chicago: University of Illinois Press, 1986), 1. Peter Fritzell, *Nature Writing and America: Essays upon a Cultural Type* (Ames: Iowa State University Press, 1990), 73. Thomas J. Lyon, ed., *This Incomperable Lande: A Book of American Nature Writing* (Boston: Houghton Mifflin, 1989), 7.

11. Buell, *Environmental Imagination*, 77–82. Slovic, *Seeking Awareness*, 18. For systematic expositions of deep ecological ideas, see David Oates, *Earth Rising: Ecological Belief in an Age of Science* (Corvallis: Oregon State University Press, 1989), and Andrew McLaughlin, *Regarding Nature: Industrialism and Deep Ecology* (Albany: State University of New York Press, 1993).

12. Perry Miller, *Consciousness in Concord: The Text of Thoreau's Hitherto "Lost Journal" (1840–1841) Together with Notes and a Commentary* (Cambridge: Harvard University Press, 1959), 181–182n. See Russell Reising, *The Unusable Past: Theory and the Study of American Literature* (New York: Methuen, 1986) and Gerald Graff, *Professing Literature: An Institutional History* (Chicago: University of Chicago Press, 1987) for general accounts of the nationalistic impulses behind the formation of the canon of American Literature. Wendell Glick, *The Recognition of Henry David Thoreau* (Ann Arbor: University of Michigan Press, 1969) and Gary Scharnhorst, *Henry David Thoreau: A Case Study in Canonization* (Columbia: University of South Carolina Press, 1993) trace the history of Thoreau's political and literary reputation inside the academy.

13. Roderick Nash, *Wilderness and the American Mind* (New Haven: Yale University Press, 1967), 84–95. R.W.B. Lewis, *Virgin Land: The American West as Symbol and Myth* (Cambridge: Harvard University Press, 1950), 1. Nash's reading of Thoreau developed a thesis first proposed in Krutch, *Great American Nature Writing*, 3–4. Perhaps the most direct narrative of the development of nonfiction nature writing from Thoreau to Edward Abbey and Annie Dillard is Don Scheese, *Nature Writing: The Pastoral Impulse in America* (New York: Routledge, 1995). Michael P. Branch,

Reading the Roots: American Nature Writing Before Walden (Athens: University of Georgia Press, 2004) documents the rich prehistory of environmental literature.

14. Rueckert, "Literature and Ecology," 82. Don Scheese, "Thoreau's Journal: The Creation of a Sacred Space," in Wayne Franklin and Michael Steiner, eds., *Mapping American Culture* (Iowa City: University of Iowa Press, 1992), 140, 147. Slovic, *Seeking Awareness*, 15. Buell, *Environmental Imagination*, 23, 139. For an additional examples of the ecocritical argument about Thoreau's ecocentricity, see Roderick Nash, *The Rights of Nature: A History of Environmental Ethics* (Madison: University of Wisconsin Press, 1989), 36–38. Robert Kuhn McGregor, *Henry Thoreau's Study of Nature: A Wider View of the Universe* (Urbana: University of Illinois Press, 1997) is dedicated in its entirety to the demonstration of this claim.

15. Jay Parini "Greening of the Humanities," *New York Times Magazine*, October 29, 1995, 52. Glotfelty, "Introduction," in *Ecocriticism Reader*, xix. Karl Kroeber, "Ecology and American Literature: Thoreau and Un-Thoreau," *American Literary History*, 9, no. 2 (Summer 1997): 310. For a sharp critique of ecocriticism's attempts to import ecological concepts into literary analysis, see Dana Phillips, "Ecocriticism, Literary Theory, and the Truth of Ecology," *New Literary History*, 30, no. 3 (Summer 1999): 577–602. Also useful in this regard is Alan Marshal, *The Unity of Nature: Wholeness and Disintegration in Ecology and Science* (London: Imperial College Press, 2002).

16. Rueckert, "Literature and Ecology," 73. Barry Commoner, *The Closing Circle: Nature, Man, and Technology* (New York: Knopf, 1971), 29. Glen A. Love, "Ecocriticism and Science: Toward Consilience?" *New Literary History*, 30, no. 3 (Summer 1999): 561–576. See also Ursula K. Heise, "Science and Ecocriticism," *American Book Review*, 18, no. 5 (July–August 1997): 4 ff. For a valuable survey of the major sources and axioms of ecocritical theory, see William Howarth, "Some Principles of Ecocriticism," in *Ecocriticism Reader*, 69–91.

17. Kevin DeLuca and Anne Demo, "Imagining Nature and Erasing Class and Race: Carleton Watkins, John Muir, and the Construction of Wilderness," *Environmental History*, 4, no. 6 (October 2001): 541–560. Michael Bennett, "Anti-Pastoralism, Frederick Douglass, and the Nature of Slavery," in Karla Armbruster and Kathleen R. Wallace, eds., *Beyond Nature Writing: Expanding the Boundaries of Ecocriticism* (Charlottesville: University Press of Virginia, 2001), 195–210. Vera Norwood, *Made from this Earth: American Women and Nature* (Chapel Hill: University of North Carolina Press, 1993), 284. For a more materialist history of women and ecology, see Carolyn Merchant, *The Death of Nature: Women, Ecology, and the Scientific Revolution* (New York: Harper & Row, 1980). Joni Adamson Clarke, "Toward and Ecology of Justice: Transformative Ecological Theory and Practice," in *Reading the Earth: New Directions in the Study of Literature and the Environment* (Moscow: University of Idaho Press, 1998), 9–18, issues a call for ecocriticism to engage the concerns of the environmental justice movement, which she answers in Joni Adamson, *American Indian Literature, Environmental Justice, and Ecocriticism* (Tucson: University of

Arizona Press, 2001). Michael Bennett and David W. Teague, *The Nature of Cities: Ecocriticism and Urban Environments* (Tucson: University of Arizona Press, 1999) focuses on environmental issues and experiences in the literature of the multicultural metropolis. Two of the most influential texts of feminist ecocritical theory are Greta Gaard, *Ecofeminism: Women, Animals, Nature* (Philadelphia: Temple University Press, 1993) and Patrick Murphy, *Literature, Nature, and Other: Ecofeminist Critiques* (Albany: State University of New York Press, 1995). For tremendously influential study of how gendered representations of the frontier underwrote imperial expansion, see Annette Kolodny, *The Land Before Her: Fantasy and Experience of the American Frontiers, 1630–1860* (Chapel Hill: University of North Carolina Press, 1984). See also Louise Westling, *The Green Breast of the New World: Landscape, Gender, and American Fiction* (Athens: University of Georgia Press, 1996).

18. Vera Norwood, *Made from this Earth*, 284. Donelle N. Dreese, *Ecocriticism: Creating Self and Place in Environmental and American Indian Literature* (New York: Peter Lang, 2002), 113–114. Buell, *Writing for an Endangered World*, 7. For a collection of essays that expand ecocriticism's reach in similar ways, see John Tallmadge and Henry Harrington, eds., *Reading Under the Sign of Nature: New Essays in Ecocriticism* (Salt Lake City: University of Utah Press, 2000).

19. Jhan Hochman, "Green Cultural Studies: An Introductory Critique of an Emerging Discipline," in Lawrence Coupe, ed., *The Green Studies Reader* (London: Routledge, 2000), 187.

Chapter 2   The Nature of Cultural History

1. D.H. Lawrence, *Studies in Classic American Literature* (New York: T. Seltzer, 1923), 1–8. Norman Foerster, *Nature in American Literature* (New York: Macmillan, 1923), xii–xiii. Lucy Lockwood Hazard, *The Frontier in American Literature* (New York: Thomas Y. Crowell, 1927), 147–177. Lawrence Buell, "American Pastoral Ideology Reappraised," *American Literary History*, 1, no. 1 (Spring 1989): 6–29, maps the genealogy of the claim that American literature is diagnostically pastoral.

2. Perry Miller, *Errand into the Wilderness* (Cambridge: Harvard University Press, 1956), 205, emphasis in original. For accounts of how mid-century literary studies, especially as practiced by such figures as Perry Miller, R.W.B. Lewis, and Henry Nash Smith, responded to the politics of the Cold War, see Graff, *Professing Literature*, 183–243, and David R. Shumway, *Creating American Civilization: A Genealogy of American Literature as a Discipline* (Minneapolis: University of Minnesota Press, 1994), 299–344.

3. Sherry B. Ortner, "If Female to Male as Nature is to Culture?" (1974), in Jessica Munns and Gita Rajan, eds., *A Cultural Studies Reader: History, Theory, Practice* (New York: Longman, 1995), 496.

4. Alan Liu, "The Power of Formalism: The New Historicism," *English Literary History*, 56, no. 4 (Winter 1989): 747. For a historical analysis of the paradoxical pessimism that shapes much recent cultural studies scholarship,

see Alex Callinicos, *Against Post-Modernism: A Marxist Critique* (Cambridge: Polity, 1989), which argues that European postmodernism represents a retrenchment in response to the failure of the revolutionary movements of 1968. See also Gerald Graff, *Literature Against Itself: Literary Ideas in Modern Society* (Chicago: University of Chicago Press, 1979), 63–102, and Dick Hebdige, "After the Masses," in Nicholas Dirks et al., eds., *Culture/Power/History: A Reader in Contemporary Social Theory* (Princeton: Princeton University Press, 1994), 222–235.

5. James McKusick, *Green Writing*, 17. Jonathan Bate, *Romantic Ecology: Wordsworth and the Environmental Tradition* (London: Routledge, 1991), 1–11, 36–61. Buell, *Writing for an Endangered World*, 24.

6. Karl Kroeber, *Ecological Literary Criticism: Romantic Imagining and the Biology of Mind* (New York: Columbia University Press, 1994), 17. Kroeber, "Ecology and American Literature," 310. Joseph Carroll, *Evolution and Literary Theory* (Columbia: Missouri, 1995) appeared not long after Kroeber's call for an ecocriticism based on a recognition of the materiality of the brain. But Carroll materializes ecocriticism in precisely the wrong way, constructing a neoconservative cultural politics on the ground of sociobiology. This is not the place for an elaborate refutation, especially since this impressive tome, complete with gilt binding, has so far produced only a pleasing silence. If ecocriticism wishes to build a interdisciplinary project on the ground of the science of mind, it should start with Stephen J. Gould, *The Mismeasure of Man* (New York: Norton, 1981), the definitive refutation of sociobiology's repackaging of Social Darwinism.

7. Terry Gifford, "The Social Construction of Nature," *ISLE* 3, no. 2 (Fall 1996): 32–33. Verena Andermatt Conley, *Ecopolitics: The Environment in Post-Structuralist Thought* (London: Routledge, 1997), 47, 140, 94, 3, emphasis in original. Homi Bhabha, *The Location of Culture* (London: Routledge, 1994), 19–20. Chantal Mouffe, "Hegemony and New Political Subjects: Toward a New Concept of Democracy," Stanley Gray, trans., in Cary Nelson and Lawrence Grossberg, eds., *Marxism and the Interpretation of Culture* (Chicago: University of Illinois Press, 1988), 95–96. Another early culturalist rejoinder is Paul L. Tidwell, "Academic Campfire Stories: Thoreau, Ecocriticism, and Fetishism of Nature," *ISLE* 2, no. 1 (Spring 1994): 53–64. For additional examples of green postmodernism, see Andrew Ross, *Strange Weather: Culture, Science, and Technology in the Age of Limits* (London: Routledge, 1991), 169–249; Jane Bennett and William Chaloupka, eds., *In the Nature of Things: Language, Politics, and the Environment* (Minneapolis: University of Minnesota Press, 1993); Max Oelschlaeger, ed., *Postmodern Environmental Ethics* (Albany: State University of New York Press, 1995); and Jhan Hochman, *Green Cultural Studies: Nature in Film, Novel, and Theory* (Moscow: University of Idaho Press, 1998).

8. David Mazel, *American Literary Environmentalism* (Athens: University of Georgia Press, 2000), xii, xv, 4.

9. Ibid., xxi, 18, xiii.

10. Ibid., xvii–xviii, xvi. Terry Eagleton, *The Idea of Culture* (Oxford: Blackwell, 2000), 111.

11. Kate Soper, *What is Nature?* (London: Basil Blackwell, 1995). William Cronon, ed., *Uncommon Ground: Toward Reinventing Nature* (New York: Norton, 1995). Michael Soule and Gary Lease, eds., *Reinventing Nature? Responses to Postmodern Deconstruction* (Washington, DC: Island Press, 1995).

12. Glen Love, *Practical Ecocriticism: Literature, Biology, and the Environment* (Charlottesville: University of Virginia Press, 2003), 8, 3.

13. Dana Phillips, *The Truth of Ecology: Nature, Culture, and Literature in America* (Oxford; New York : Oxford University Press, 2003), "philosophize" xii, xi.

14. Buell, *Environmental Imagination*, 54. Phillips, *Truth of Ecology*, 6, 7.

15. I.G. Simmons, *Interpreting Nature: Cultural Constructions of the Environment* (London: Routledge, 1993), 159–160. Christopher Manes, "Nature and Silence," *Environmental Ethics*, 14 (Winter 1992): 339–350. Harold Fromm, "From Transcendence to Obsolescence: A Route Map," in *Ecocriticism Reader*, 39.

16. SueEllen Campbell, "The Land and Language of Desire: Where Deep-Ecology and Poststructuralism Meet," in *Ecocriticism Reader*, 127. Andrew McMurry, *Environmental Renaissance : Emerson, Thoreau, & the Systems of Nature* (Athens : University of Georgia Press, 2003), viii, 15, 227, 228. Michael Zimmerman, *Contesting Earth's Future: Radical Ecology and Postmodernity* (Berkeley: University of California Press, 1994). Timothy Luke, *Ecocritique: Contesting the Politics of Nature, Economy, and Culture* (Minneapolis: University of Minnesota Press, 1997).

17. Buell, "The Ecocritical Insurgency," 701–702. Buell, *Writing for an Endangered Planet*, 6. For a more extended meditation on Buell's contention about myth making, see Randall Roorda, *Dramas of Solitude: Narratives of Retreat in American Nature Writing* (Albany: State University of New York Press, 1998), 205–225. John R. Knott, *Imagining Wild America: Wilderness and Wildness in the Writings of John James Audubon, Henry David Thoreau, John Muir, Edward Abbey, Wendell Berry, and Mary Oliver* (Ann Arbor: University of Michigan Press, 2002) argues that these six writers engaged in conscious myth-making.

18. I am indebted to William Keach for drawing my attention to Lenin's epigram, which was a response to Hegel's *Lectures on the History of Philosophy* and is quoted in Frederic Jameson, *Marxism and Form* (Princeton: Princeton University Press, 1971). Howarth, "Some Principles of Ecocriticism," 69. Glotfelty, "Introduction," xix. Buell, "The Ecocritical Insurgency," 704.

19. Fredric Jameson, *Marxism and Form: Twentieth Century Dialectical Theories of Literature* (Princeton: Princeton University Press, 1971), 362.

20. Kate Soper, "Greening Prometheus: Marxism and Ecology," in Ted Benton, ed., *The Greening of Marxism* (New York: Guilford, 1996), 81–102. See Bate, *Romantic Ecology*, 1–4 and Kroeber, *Ecological Literary Criticism*, 31–32, for typical ecocritical denunciations of Marxism based on guilt by association.

21. Jameson, *Marxism and Form*, 306.

Chapter 3 Class Struggle in New England

1. Edward Waldo Emerson, ed., *The Complete Works of Ralph Waldo Emerson*, vol. 10 (New York: Houghton Mifflin, 1903), 328. Charles Sellers, *The Market Revolution: Jacksonian America, 1815–1846* (New York: Oxford University Press, 1991) provides an economic history of the antebellum period. William Cronon's path-breaking *Changes in the Land: Indians, Colonists, and the Ecology of New England* (New York: Hill and Wang, 1983) integrates social and economic changes into an analysis of how European and Native modes of production interacted differently with the land over time to produce the rural landscape of the region. Carolyn Merchant, *Ecological Revolutions: Nature, Gender, and Science in New England* (Chapel Hill: University of North Carolina Press, 1989) covers similar ground with a sharper emphasis on the internal dynamics of the rise of capitalism out of the colonial ecosocial order. For an analysis of the role Concord, Massachusetts played as an organizing center in the rise of capitalist agriculture, see Robert A. Gross, "Culture and Cultivation: Agriculture and Society in Thoreau's Concord," *Journal of American History*, 69, no. 1 (June 1982): 42–61.

2. Bruce Laurie, *Artisan into Workers: Labor in Nineteenth-Century America* (Urbana: University of Illinois Press, 1997), 15–46.

3. Robinson quoted in Philip S. Foner and Brewster Chamberlin, eds., *Freidrich A. Sorge's Labor Movement in the United States* (Westport, CT: Greenwood Press, 1977), 62. For focused histories of industrialization and class conflict in the Massachusetts shoemaking town, Lynn, see Alan Dawley, *Class and Community: The Industrial Revolution in Lynn* (Cambridge: Harvard University Press, 1976) and Paul G. Faler, *Mechanics and Manufacturers in the Early Industrial Revolution: Lynn, Massachusetts, 1780–1860* (Albany: State University of New York Press, 1981).

4. Milton Cantor, "Cultural Aspects of the Industrial Revolution: Lynn, Massachusetts, Shoemakers and Industrial Morality, 1826–1860," in Milton Cantor, ed., *American Working Class Culture: Explorations in Labor and Social History* (Westport, CT: Greenwood, 1979), 121.

5. Frederick Robinson, "An Oration delivered before the Trades' Union of Boston and Vicinity, July 4, 1834," in Joseph Blau, ed., *Social Theories of Jacksonian Democracy: Representative Writings of the Period 1825–1850* (New York: Liberal Arts Press, 1954), 321. Bruce Laurie, *Artisan into Workers*, 47–123.

6. Stephen Simpson, *The Working Man's Manual: A New Theory of Political Economy, on the Principle of Production the Source of Wealth* (Philadelphia: T.L. Bonsal, 1831) quoted in Blau, *Social Theories*, 148. Theophilus Fisk, "Capital against Labor, An Address delivered at Julien Hall before the mechanics of Boston on Wednesday evening, May 20, 1835," in Blau, *Social Theories*, 199, 201. Edward Pessen, *Most Uncommon Jacksonians* (Albany: State University of New York Press, 1967), 103–203 provides a summary analysis of the ideology of the movement. For a sketch of Paine's republicanism with an emphasis on the operations of the keyword "nature," see Jack Fruchtman, Jr., *Thomas Paine and the Religion of Nature* (Baltimore: Johns Hopkins University Press, 1993), 19–73.

7. Fisk, "Capital against Labor," 199, 201.

8. Seth Luther, *An Address to the Working Men of New England*, 2nd ed. (New York: Office of the Working Man's Advocate, 1833), i, 2, 6–7, 8, 16–17, 19, 29, 26, 32, all emphasis in original.

9. Seth Luther et al., "Ten-Hour Circular," in John R. Commons, ed., *A Documentary History of American Industrial Society*, vol. 6 (New York: Russell and Russell, 1958), 94–99.

10. For histories of the Working Men, see Alden Whitman, *Labor Parties, 1827–1834* (New York: International Publishers, 1943); Franklin Rosemont, "Workingmen's Parties," in Paul Buhle and Alan Dawley, eds., *Working for Democracy: American Workers from the Revolution to the Present* (Urbana: University of Illinois Press, 1985), 11–20; and Edward Pessen, "The Working Men's Party Revisited," in Edward Pessen, ed., *New Perspectives on Jacksonian Parties and Politics* (Boston: Allyn and Bacon, 1969), 191–215. There are several general histories of the working class during the antebellum period. The best is Philip S. Foner, *History of the Labor Movement in the United States*, vol. 1 (New York: International, 1947), 65–248. The first volume of John Commons et al., *History of Labor in the United States* (New York: Macmillan, 1935) remains indispensable. Important supplements include Samuel P. Orth, *The Armies of Labor: A Chronicle of the Organized Wage Earners* (New Haven: Yale University Press, 1919), 19–39; Anthony Bimba, *The History of the American Working Class* (New York: International Publishers, 1927), 66–114; Foster Rhea Dulles, *Labor in America: A History* (New York: Thomas Y. Crowell, 1949), 20–95; Joseph G. Rayback, *A History of American Labor* (New York: Macmillan, 1964), 75–103; and Pessen, *Most Uncommon Jacksonians*, 3–99.

11. "Statement of the Journeymen," *Independent Chronicle and Boston Patriot*, May 23, 1832, in Commons, *Documentary History*, vol. 6, 84.

12. Female Society of Lynn quoted in Mary Blewett, *Men, Women, and Work: Class, Gender, and Protest in the New England Shoe Industry, 1780–1910* (Urbana: University of Illinois Press, 1988), 35–36, emphasis in original. New York General Trades Union quoted in Philip S. Foner and Brewster Chamberlin, eds., *Freidrich A. Sorge's Labor Movement in the United States* (Westport, CT: Greenwood Press, 1977), 57.

13. Reginald McGrane, *The Panic of 1837* (Chicago: University of Chicago Press, 1924), 91–144, remains valuable though it is limited by a narrow focus on Andrew Jackson's battle with the United States Bank. See also Samuel Rezneck, "The Social History of an American Depression, 1837–1843," *American Historical Review*, 40 (1935), 73–100, and Peter Temin, *The Jacksonian Economy* (New York: Norton, 1969), 109–152.

14. "Convention of Mechanics," *Working Man's Advocate*, June 29, 1844, in Commons, *Documentary History*, vol. 8, 88–89.

15. Proceedings, *Working Man's Advocate*, October 19, 1844, in Commons, *Documentary History*, vol. 8, 92, 97. Lowell convention resolution quoted in Norman Ware, *The Industrial Worker, 1840–1860*. Boston, 1924 (Chicago: Quadrangle Books, 1964), 208.

Chapter 4   Transcendentalism as a Social Movement

1. Leon Trotsky, *Literature and Revolution* (Ann Arbor: University of Michigan Press, 1960), 178. Lewis, *The American Adam*, 5. There is an inexhaustible flow of new material on the Transcendentalists, both individually and as a group. I will indicate those sources that shape my thought the most strongly. The best synthetic history of the movement is Barbara Packer, "The Transcendentalists," in Sacvan Bercovitch, ed., *The Cambridge History of American Literature*, vol. 2 (New York: Cambridge University Press, 1995), 331–604.

2. Octavius Brooks Frothingham, *George Ripley* (Boston: Houghton, Mifflin, 1882), 156.

3. F.O. Matthiessen, *American Renaissance: Art and Expression in the Age of Emerson and Whitman* (New York: Oxford University Press, 1941), viii, xi. Perry Miller, *Nature's Nation* (Cambridge: Belknap Press of Harvard University Press, 1967), 13. Perry Miller, *The American Transcendentalists: Their Prose and Poetry* (Garden City, NY: Anchor Books, 1957), ix–x. For additional examples of the tendency to dismiss the radical Transcendentalists, see Lawrence Buell, *Literary Transcendentalism: Style and Vision in the American Renaissance* (Ithaca: Cornell University Press, 1973), 21 and David Reynolds, *Beneath the American Renaissance: The Subversive Imagination in the Age of Emerson and Melville* (Cambridge: Harvard University Press, 1988), 92.

4. Frank Lentricchia, *Criticism and Social Change* (Chicago: University of Chicago Press, 1983), 6. Myra Jehlen, *American Incarnation: The Individual, the Nation, and the Continent* (Cambridge: Harvard University Press, 1986), 9. Sacvan Bercovitch, *The Rites of Assent: Transformations in the Symbolic Construction of America* (London: Routledge, 1993), 170.

5. Carol Colatrella, "Bercovitch's Paradox: Critical Dissent, Marginality, and the Example of Melville," in Carol Colatrella and Joseph Alkana, eds., *Cohesion and Dissent in America* (Albany: State University of New York Press, 1994), 229. Bercovitch, *Rites of Assent*, 342–343. For a compelling critique of Bercovitch's theory of dissensus with specific reference to the self-conscious deployment of nationalist ideas by the utopian socialists of New England, see Carl J. Guarneri, "Brook Farm, Fourierism, and the Nationalist Dilemma in American Utopianism," in Charles Capper and Conrad Edick Wright, eds., *Transient and Permanent: The Transcendentalist Movement and its Contexts* (Boston: Massachusetts Historical Society, 1999), 447–470. The notion of a "national symbolic" operates quite similarly in Lauren Berlant, *The Anatomy of National Fantasy: Hawthorne, Utopia, and Everyday Life* (Chicago, University of Chicago Press, 1991).

6. Jeffrey N. Cox, "Communal Romanticism," *European Romantic Review*, 15, no. 2 (June 2004): 330. Elizabeth Palmer Peabody, ed., *Aesthetic Papers* (Boston: The Editor, 1849). Clarence L.F. Gohdes, *The Periodicals of American Transcendentalism* (Durham: Duke University Press, 1931) documents the vibrant journal culture of the Transcendentalist movement.

7. E. Malcolm Carroll, *Origins of the Whig Party* (Durham: Duke University Press, 1925), 221. Frederick Robinson, "An Oration delivered before the Trades' Union of Boston and Vicinity, July 4, 1834," in Blau, *Social Theories*, 323. Arthur M. Schlesinger, Jr., *The Age of Jackson* (Boston: Little, Brown, 1945), 273.

For histories of the two major antebellum parties, see Marvin Meyers, *The Jacksonian Persuasion: Politics and Belief* (Stanford: Stanford University Press, 1960); and Daniel Walker Howe, *The Political Culture of the American Whigs* (Chicago: University of Chicago Press, 1979), 11–42. Ronald P. Formisano, *The Transformation of Political Culture: Massachusetts Parties, 1790s–1840s* (New York: Oxford University Press, 1983), 57–83 and 268–320, shows that electoral politics in the half century following the Revolution were dominated, not by clearly defined party organizations, but by relatively flexible groupings within a small elite electorate who maneuvered to capture the "revolutionary center." Philip Gould, *Covenant and Republic: Historical Romance and the Politics of Persuasion* (New York: Cambridge University Press, 1996), 176–183, demonstrates the flexibility of republican ideology and how it was appropriated during the early national period by different and often conflicting social formations.

8. Tamara Plakins Thornton, *Cultivating Gentlemen: The Meaning of Country Life among the Boston Elite, 1785–1860* (New Haven: Yale University Press, 1989). Leo Marx, *The Machine in the Garden: Technology and the Pastoral Ideal in America* (New York: Oxford University Press, 1964), 73–144 provides what is still one of the best surveys of the ideology of agrarian republicanism.

9. Ralph Waldo Emerson, "Thoughts on Modern Literature," *Dial*, 1, no. 2 (October 1840): 148. Orestes Brownson, "The Laboring Classes," *Boston Quarterly Review*, 3, no. 4 (October 1840): 472. Orestes Brownson, "Review of *Chartism* by Thomas Carlyle," *Boston Quarterly Review*, 3, no. 3 (July 1840): 366. The best social history of the elite radical milieu is Anne Rose, *Transcendentalism as a Social Movement, 1830–1850* (New Haven: Yale University Press, 1981). Paul F. Boller, Jr., *American Transcendentalism, 1830–1860: An Intellectual Inquiry* (New York: Putnam, 1974) explores the connections between the Transcendentalists' "intuitional philosophy, idealism, and religious radicalism" and their commitment to social reform. For discussions of the rise of the literary marketplace that made the movement possible, see Lawrence Buell, *New England Literary Culture: From Revolution to Renaissance* (Cambridge: Harvard University Press, 1986), 56–83; William Charvat, *The Profession of Authorship in America, 1800–1870* (Columbus: Ohio State University Press, 1968), 3–67; and Helmut Lehmann-Haupt et al., *The Book in America: A History of the Making and Selling of Books in the United States*, 2nd ed. (New York: Bowker, 1951).

10. Orestes Brownson, "Brook Farm," *The United States Democratic Review*, 11, no. 53 (November 1842): 481. Margaret Fuller, "The Great Lawsuit. Man versus Men. Woman versus Women," *Dial*, 4, no. 1 (July 1843): 14.

Chapter 5   Nathaniel Hawthorne, Democracy, and the Mob

1. Thomas Jefferson, "Letter to John Adams, October 28, 1813," in Lester J. Cappon, ed., *The Adams-Jefferson Letters*, vol. 2 (Chapel Hill: University of North Carolina Press, 1959), 388.

2. Douglas Anderson, "Jefferson, Hawthorne, and 'The Custom House,'" *Nineteenth Century Literature*, 46, no. 3 (December 1991): 309–326. The dominant interpretive strategy has been to ignore Hawthorne's irony. See, for instance, Q.D. Leavis, "Hawthorne as Poet," *Sewanee Review*, 59 (1951): 179–205; Robert Grayson, "The New England Sources of 'My Kinsman, Major Molineux,'" *American Literature*, 54, no. 4 (December 1982): 545–559; Roy Harvey Pearce, "Hawthorne and the Sense of the Past or, the Immortality of Major Molineux," *English Literary History*, 21, no. 4 (December 1954): 327–349; and James Duban "Robins and Robinarchs in 'My Kinsman, Major Molineux,'" *Nineteenth-Century Fiction*, 38, no. 3 (December 1983): 271–288.

3. Margaret Bayard Smith, *The First Forty Years of Washington Society in the Family Letters of Margaret Bayard Smith*, Gaillard Hunt, ed. (New York: Charles Scribner's Sons, 1906), 290–298.

4. Henry Nash Smith, *Virgin Land: The American West as Symbol and Myth* (New York: Vintage Books, 1950), 126. See David Shi, *The Simple Life: Plain Living and High Thinking in American Culture* (New York: Oxford University Press, 1985) for a cultural history of the related idea of the simple life. Shi documents its appropriation for projects ranging from critiquing the narrative of social progress under capitalism to dampening the dissent of the poor.

5. Nathaniel Hawthorne, *Hawthorne's Lost Notebook, 1835–1841* (University Park: Pennsylvania State University Press, 1978), 46. Neal F. Doubleday, "Hawthorne's Estimate of His Early Work," *American Literature*, 37, no. 4 (January 1966): 403–409.

Chapter 6 Margaret Fuller, Rock River, and the Condition of America

1. Thomas Jefferson, *Notes on the State of Virginia*, William Peden, ed. (Chapel Hill: University of North Carolina Press, 1955), 164–165. Margaret Fuller, letter to Ralph Waldo Emerson, quoted in Thomas Wentworth Higginson, *Margaret Fuller Ossoli* (New York: Confucian Press, 1980), 193–194, 197.

2. Annette Kolodny, *The Lay of the Land: Metaphor as Experience and History in American Life and Letters* (Chapel Hill: University of North Carolina Press, 1975), 129, 111, 128–129.

3. Ibid., 120, 114–115, 119, 116, 120, emphasis in original.

4. Perry Miller, *Margaret Fuller: American Romantic* (Garden City, NY: Doubleday, 1963), 116. Orestes Brownson, "Review of Summer on the Lakes in 1843," *Brownson's Quarterly Review*, 1, no. 6 (November 1844): 546. See Nicole Tonkovich, "Traveling in the West, Writing in the Library: Margaret Fuller's *Summer on the Lakes*," *Legacy: A Journal of American Women Writers*, 10, no. 2 (1993): 79–83, for a reading of *Summer* from the perspective of the library where it was composed. For an account of the expurgation of Fuller's memoir, see Bell Gale Chevigny, "The Long Arm of Censorship: Myth-Making in Margaret Fuller's Time and Our Own," *Signs: Journal of Women in Culture and Society*, 2, no. 2 (1976): 450–460. For discussion of the aggressive editing of *Summer*, see Dorothy Baker,

"Excising the Text, Exorcising the Author: Margaret Fuller's *Summer on the Lakes in 1843*," in Sherry Lee Linkon, ed., *In Her Own Voice: Nineteenth-Century American Woman Essayists* (New York: Garland, 1997), 97–112.

5. James Freeman Clarke, "Review of *Summer on the Lakes in 1843*," *Christian World* (July 6, 1844): 2. Stephen Adams, " 'That Tidiness We Always Look for in Woman': Fuller's *Summer on the Lakes* and Romantic Aesthetics," *Studies in the American Renaissance* (1987): 250, 252, 259.

6. Kolodny, *Lay of the Land*, 115.

7. *Complete Works of Thomas Carlyle*, vol. 16 (New York: Collier, 1901), 36, 37, 95, 96.

8. *Complete Works of Thomas Carlyle*, vol. 12, 3.

9. Margaret Fuller, "Letter to Ralph Waldo Emerson, 1 June 1843," in *The Letters of Margaret Fuller*, Robert N. Hudspeth, ed., vol. 3 (Ithaca: Cornell University Press, 1983–1995), 128. Phyllis Blum Cole, "The American Writer and the Condition of England, 1815–1860," (Ph.D. Thesis. Harvard University, 1973), 520–521. Brownson, "Laboring Classes," 474.

10. Anne Baker, " 'A Commanding View': Vision and the Problem of Nationality in Fuller's Summer on the Lakes," *ESQ: A Journal of the American Renaissance*, 44, no. 1–2 (1998): 61–77. Manfred Putz, " 'Dissenting Voices of Consent': Margaret Fuller and Ralph Waldo Emerson on the Fourth of July," in Paul Goetsch and Gerd Hurm, eds., *The Fourth of July: Political Oratory and Literary Reactions, 1776–1876* (Tubingen: Gunter Narr, 1992), 167–184.

11. Margaret V. Allen, *The Achievement of Margaret Fuller* (University Park: Pennsylvania State University Press, 1979), 561. For accounts of Fuller's radicalization, see Margaret V. Allen, "The Political and Social Criticism of Margaret Fuller," *South Atlantic Quarterly*, 72 (1973): 560–573, and Bell Gale Chevigny, "The Edges of Ideology: Margaret Fuller's Centrifugal Evolution," *American Quarterly*, 38, no. 2 (1986): 185.

Chapter 7   William Wordsworth in New England and the Discipline of Nature

1. Karl Marx and Frederick Engels, *Selected Works* (Moscow: Progress Publishers, 1968), 53–54. F.W.P. Greenwood, "The Miscellaneous Poems of William Wordsworth," *North American Review*, 18 (April 1824): 356. Joel Pace, Letter to the Author, April 1, 2002. Karen Karbiener presented the results of her ongoing research on the American Lakers at the 2003 conference of the North American Society for the Study of Romanticism at Fordham University in New York City. See also Joel Pace, " 'Gems of a soft and permanent lustre': The Reception and Influence of the Lyrical Ballads in America," *Romanticism On the Net* 9 (February 1998): <http://users.ox.ac.uk/~scat0385/americanLB.html>; and Joel Pace, "Wordsworth, the Lyrical Ballads, and Literary and Social Reform in Nineteenth-Century America," in Marcy L. Tanter, ed., "*The Honourable Characteristic of Poetry*": *Two Hundred Years of Lyrical Ballads*, Romantic Circles Praxis Series (November 1999): <http://www.rc.umd.edu/praxis/lyrical/pace/wordsworth.html>. Pace's

forthcoming book promises to finally replace the only existing substantial study of Wordsworth's reception and influence in the United States: Annabel Newton, *Wordsworth in Early American Criticism* (Chicago: University of Chicago Press, 1928).

2. Charles Mayo Ellis, *Transcendentalism* (Boston, 1842; Gainesville, FL: Scholars' Facsimiles and Reprints, 1954), 65. James Freeman Clarke, *Autobiography* (Boston, 1891) quoted in Perry Miller, *The Transcendentalists: An Anthology* (Cambridge: Harvard University Press, 1950), 47. Elizabeth Palmer Peabody quoted in Mark Reed, "Contacts with America," in Nesta Clutterbuck, ed., *William Wordsworth, 1770–1970: Essays of General Interest on Wordsworth and His Time* (Westmorland: Trustees of Dove Cottage, 1970), 32–33. For a narrative of Thoreau's exposure to Anglo-European philosophy during his years at Harvard and after graduation, see Robert Sattelmeyer, *Thoreau's Reading: A Study in Intellectual History* (Princeton: Princeton University Press, 1988), 3–53. The best recent synthesis of New England Transcendentalism's importation of European ideas is Barbara Packer, "The Transcendentalists," in Bercovitch, *Cambridge History*, vol. 2, 331–375. See also Leon Chai, *The Romantic Foundations of the American Renaissance* (Ithaca: Cornell University Press, 1987).

3. *The Complete Poetical Works of William Wordsworth, together with a Description of the Country of the Lakes in the North of England*, Henry Reed, ed., (Philadelphia: James Kay, 1837). Henry Reed, Review of *The Complete Poetical Works of William Wordsworth*, *North American Review*, 4 (January 1839): 17. J. Walker, "The Complete Poetical Works of William Wordsworth," *Christian Examiner*, 22 (March 1837): 132.

4. Emerson, "Thoughts on Modern Literature," 150. Christopher Pearse Cranch, "Wordsworth," *Atlantic Monthly*, 45 (February 1880): 241–252.

5. *The Complete Poetical Works of Percy Bysshe Shelley*, Thomas Hutchinson, ed., vol. 2 (Oxford: Clarendon Press, 1972), 10.

6. Walter Harding, *Emerson's Library* (Charlottesville: University of Virginia Press, 1967), 305–306. *The Journals and Miscellaneous Notebooks of Ralph Waldo Emerson*, William Gilman et al., eds., vol. 5 (Cambridge: The Belknap Press of Harvard University Press, 1965), 60, 163, 370. For accounts of the influence on Emerson of Wordsworth's ideas of nature, see David Bromwich, "From Wordsworth to Emerson," in Kenneth Johnston et al., eds., *Romantic Revolutions: Criticism and Theory* (Bloomington: Indiana University Press, 1990), 202–218; and Linden Peach, *British Influence on the Birth of American Literature* (New York: St. Martin's, 1982), 29–57. For a thorough survey of the evidence that *Nature* was a direct response to Wordsworth, see Joel Pace, " 'Lifted to Genius'?: Wordsworth in Emerson's nurture and *Nature*," *Symbiosis: A Journal of Anglo-American Literary Relations*, 2, no. 2 (October 1998): 125–140.

7. Christopher Pearse Cranch, "Wordsworth," 251.

8. Nicholas Roe, *The Politics of Nature: Wordsworth and Some Contemporaries* (New York: St. Martin's Press, 1992), 9. Influential readings of Romantic nature as a displacement or evasion of politics and history occur in Jerome McGann, *The Romantic Ideology: A Critical Investigation* (Chicago: University of Chicago Press, 1983); Marjorie Levinson, *Wordsworth's Great*

Period Poems: Four Essays (Cambridge: Harvard University Press, 1986); and Alan Liu, *Wordsworth, the Sense of History* (Stanford: Stanford University Press, 1989).

9. Several scholars offer alternatives to the dominant New Historicist narrative of Wordsworth's descent into mere Tory reaction, each emphasizing different elements of his feudal utopianism. David Simpson, *Wordsworth's Historical Imagination: The Poetry of Displacement* (New York: Methuen, 1987) describes how the poetry is structured by an agrarian ideal of civic virtue. James K. Chandler, *Wordsworth's Second Nature: A Study of the Poetry and the Politics* (Chicago: University of Chicago Press, 1984) shows how Wordsworth's idea of feelings and tradition as reliable moral and political guides are based in the Burkean theory of second nature. Michael H. Friedman, *The Making of a Tory Humanist* (New York: Columbia University Press, 1979) argues that Wordsworth became committed to an ideal of affective community. John Rieder, *Wordsworth's Counterrevolutionary Turn* (Newark: University of Delaware Press, 1997) describes the continuity between Wordsworth's early radicalism and his later commitment to fantasies of agrarian community. Tim Fulford, *Landscape, Liberty, and Authority: Poetry, Criticism, and Politics from Thomson to Wordsworth* (New York: Cambridge University Press, 1996) traces the transformations in Wordsworth's lifelong commitment to Commonwealthsman and Country–Party ideas of liberty in a visionary mountain republic.

10. D.L., "Shelley and Pollok," *Western Messenger*, 3 (March 1837): 473–474, 478. See Elizabeth R. McKinsey, *The Western Messenger: New England Transcendentalists in the Ohio Valley* (Cambridge: Harvard University Press, 1973) for an account of the migration of a number of young Transcendentalists to the Ohio Valley. For discussions of nineteenth-century cultures of reading, see William Gilmore, *Reading Becomes a Necessity of Life: Material and Cultural Life in Rural New England, 1780–1830* (Knoxville: University of Tennessee Press, 1989), 34–50; Nina Baym, *Novels, Readers, and Reviewers: Responses to Fiction in Antebellum America* (Ithaca: Cornell University Press, 1984), 173–195; and Cathy Davidson, *Revolution and the Word: the Rise of the Novel in America* (New York: Oxford University Press, 1986), 15–79. For accounts of the Romantic author as public intellectual, see Baym, *Novels, Readers, and Reviewers*, 249–269, and William G. Rowland, Jr. *Literature and the Marketplace: Romantic Writers and their Audiences in Great Britain and the United States* (Lincoln: University of Nebraska Press, 1996), 171–193.

11. Henry Theodore Tuckerman, "Wordsworth," *Southern Literary Messenger*, 7 (February 1841): 105, 108.

12. Anonymous, "William Wordsworth," *Southern Literary Messenger*, 3, no. 12 (December 1837): 708, 705. For a fascinating reading of Wordsworth's own anti-Jacobinism focused on the opposition between the figures of Robespierre and the ideal poet, see Brooke Hopkins, "Representing Robespierre," in Stephen C. Behrendt, ed., *History and Myth: Essay on English Romantic Literature* (Detroit: Wayne State University Press, 1990), 116–129.

13. Anonymous, "William Wordsworth," 708, 709. Rowland, *Literature and the Marketplace*, 39–62, argues that Wordsworth formulates a rhetorical scene in which an inspired poet speaks to an audience united by an abstract human nature in order to create a spiritualized facsimile of the community he saw being materially destroyed by the rise of industrial capitalism. James K. Chandler, "Representative Men, Spirits of the Age, and Other Romantic Types," in Kenneth Johnston et al., eds., *Romantic Revolutions: Criticism and Theory* (Bloomington: Indiana University Press, 1990), 133–157, shows how Wordsworth studies are still shaped by the idea that he was the period's central representative poet and captured the spirit of the age. Willard Spiegelman, *Wordsworth's Heroes* (Berkeley: University of California Press, 1985), 1–23 compares the Wordsworthian poet-preceptor with other contemporary figures of the genius or hero.

14. N. Porter, "Wordsworth and His Poetry," *Quarterly Christian Spectator*, 8 (March 1836): 141, 129, 130–131.

15. Ibid., 131, 135, 137, 140.

Chapter 8　William Wordsworth, Henry David Thoreau, and the Poetry of Nature

1. *John Greenleaf Whittier, Complete Poetical Works* (Boston: Houghton Mifflin, 1881), 243. For ecocritical accounts of the relationship between Wordsworth and Thoreau, see James McCusick, *Green Writing: Romanticism and Ecology* (New York: St. Martin's Press, 2000), 27–33; Greg Garrard, "Wordsworth and Thoreau: Two Versions of Pastoral," in Richard J. Schneider, ed., *Thoreau's Sense of Place: Essays in American Environmental Writing* (Iowa City: University of Iowa Press, 2000). The best summaries of early scholarship on the relationship are Carl Dennis, "Correspondence in Thoreau's Nature Poetry," *ESQ: A Journal of the American Renaissance*, 58 (1970): 101–109, and Laraine Fergenson, "Wordsworth and Thoreau: The Relationship between Man and Nature," *Thoreau Journal Quarterly*, 11, no. 2 (1979): 3–10. For overviews of Thoreau's place in the international tradition of Romanticism, see Miller, *Nature's Nation*, 175–183; and Frederick Garber, "Thoreau and Anglo-European Romanticism," in Richard J. Schneider, ed., *Approaches to Teaching Thoreau's Walden and Other Works* (New York: Modern Language Association, 1996), 39–47.

2. Robert Weisbuch, *Atlantic Double-Cross: American Literature and British Influence in the Age of Emerson* (Chicago: University of Chicago Press, 1986), 133–150. Richard Gravil, *Romantic Dialogues: Anglo-American Continuities, 1776–1862* (New York: St. Martin's Press, 2000), 103–104.

3. Ralph Waldo Emerson and Thomas Carlyle. *The Correspondence of Emerson and Carlyle*. Joseph Slater, ed. (New York: Columbia University Press, 1964), 246. *Journals and Miscellaneous Notebooks of Ralph Waldo Emerson*, vol. 7, 230–231. Ralph Waldo Emerson, "Thoreau," *Atlantic Monthly*, 10 (August 1862): 24. The best discussions of Thoreau's poetic decade are Elizabeth Hall Witherell, "Thoreau as Poet," in Joel Myerson, ed.,

The Cambridge Companion to Henry David Thoreau (Cambridge: Cambridge University Press, 1995), 57–70, and Sattelmeyer, Thoreau's Reading, 3–24.

4. Sattelmeyer, Thoreau's Reading, 294. Henry David Thoreau, Early Essays and Miscellanies, Joseph J. Moldenhauer and Edwin Moser, eds. (Princeton: Princeton University Press, 1975), 122.

5. Henry David Thoreau, Journal, John C. Broderick, ed., vol. 2 (Princeton: Princeton University Press, 1981), 200–201. The Complete Works of Percy Bysshe Shelley, Roger Ingpen and Walter E. Peck, eds., vol. 7 (New York: Gordian Press, 1965), 140.

6. Thoreau, Journal, vol. 2, 223. Thoreau, Early Essays, 169, 165. William Wordsworth, Lyrical Ballads, Michael Mason, ed. (London: Longman, 1992), 59, 79.

7. Thoreau, Early Essays, 219, 222, 248. Cranch, "Wordsworth," 251.

8. Henry David Thoreau, A Week on the Concord and Merrimack Rivers, Carl F. Hovde et al., eds. (Princeton: Princeton University Press, 1980), 91–92. Thoreau, Journal, vol. 1, 338.

9. Thoreau, Journal, vol. 2, 44. Thoreau, Journal, vol. 1, 338. Of course, Thoreau shared many of his habits of thought about the poet and poetry with most of the Transcendentalist circle. For surveys of these ideas in the context of histories of the central Transcendentalist organ, The Dial, see Helen Hennesy, "The Dial: Its Poetry," New England Quarterly, 31 (1958): 66–87, and Joel Myerson, New England Transcendentalism and The Dial (Rutherford, NJ: Fairleigh Dickinson University Press, 1980).

10. Margaret Fuller, "The Great Lawsuit," 6.

11. There are substantial continuities between Emerson's notion of the poet's use of natural language and the ideas of rhetorical power dominant during the Revolutionary period as reconstructed in Jay Fliegelman, Declaring Independence: Jefferson, Natural Language, and the Culture of Performance (Stanford: Stanford University Press, 1993).

12. Thoreau, Journal, vol. 1, 69. Thoreau, A Week, 375. Scholarship on Thoreau's poetry is scarce. The best two essays are Elizabeth Hall Witherell, "Thoreau's Watershed Season as a Poet: The Hidden Fruits of the Summer and Fall of 1841," Studies in the American Renaissance (1990): 49–106, which reconstructs the composition of what she regards as Thoreau's crowning poetic achievement, a sequence of five related poems exploring the place of man in nature; and Arthur L. Ford, "The Poetry of Henry David Thoreau," ESQ: A Journal of the American Renaissance, 56 (1969): 40–52, which close reads much of the verse, focusing on Thoreau's desire to capture in poetry the experience of self-transcendence through total immersion in nature. Ford also provides an annotated bibliography of sources on Thoreau's poetry through 1970. Since then, critical work on the subject has been quite sparse and was mostly produced in a burst of activity during the early 1970s: Betsy Feagan Colquitt, "Thoreau's Poetics," ATQ, 11 (1971): 74–81; Robert O. Evans "Thoreau's Poetry and the Prose Works," ESQ: A Journal of the American Renaissance, 56 (1969): 40–52; Mary I. Kaiser, " 'Conversing with the Sky': The Imagery of Celestial Bodies in Thoreau's Poetry," Thoreau Journal Quarterly, 9, no. 3 (1977): 15–28;

Carla Mazzini, "Epiphany in Two Poems by Thoreau," *Thoreau Journal Quarterly*, 5, no. 2 (1973): 23–25; Kenneth Silverman, "The Sluggard Knight in Thoreau's Poetry," *Thoreau Journal Quarterly*, 5, no. 2 (1973): 6–9; Paul O. Williams, "Thoreau's Growth as a Transcendentalist Poet," *ESQ: A Journal of the American Renaissance*, 19 (1973): 189–198.

13. *Complete Works of Ralph Waldo Emerson*, vol. 10, 443. Ford, "Poetry of Henry David Thoreau," 21. Witherell, "Thoreau's Watershed Season," 62.

14. Thoreau, *A Week*, 343.

15. Laraine Fergenson, "Was Thoreau Re-Reading Wordsworth in 1851" *Thoreau Journal Quarterly*, 5, no. 3 (1973): 20–23. J. Lyndon Shanley, *The Making of Walden* (Chicago: University of Chicago Press, 1957), 18–33, 55–73. Karen Kalinevitch, "Apparelled in Celestial Light/Bathed in So Pure a Light: Verbal Echoes in Wordsworth's and Thoreau's Works," *Thoreau Journal Quarterly*, 12, no. 2 (1980): 27–30, documents *Walden's* many allusions to the great odes.

Chapter 9   Ralph Waldo Emerson, Orestes Brownson,
and Transcendentalism

1. John Quincy Adams, *Memoirs*, C.F. Adams, ed., vol. 10 (Philadelphia: J.B. Lippincott, 1874–1877), 345. Anonymous, Review of *Yarrow Revisited and Other Poems* by William Wordsworth, *American Quarterly Review*, 20 (September 1836): 79–80.

2. Orestes Brownson, Review of *The Poetical Works of William Wordsworth*, *Boston Quarterly Review*, 2, no. 2 (April 1839): 137, 139.

3. Ibid., 149–150, 151–152.

4. Ibid., 150, 164, 152.

5. Ibid., 152–153, 155, 160.

6. Ibid., 161, 162.

7. Ibid., 165, 160, 167.

8. William R. Hutchison, *The Transcendentalist Ministers* (New Haven: Yale University Press, 1959), 137–189, gives the best account of Brownson's Society for Christian Union and Progress. For a related radical congregation, see Dean Grodzins, "Theodore Parker and the 28th Congregational Society: The Reform Church and the Spirituality of Reformers in Boston, 1845–1859," in Capper and Wright, eds., *Transient and Permanent*, 73–117.

9. *The Works of William E. Channing, D. D.*, 12th edn. (Boston: Crosby, Nichols, 1853), 228, 230, 250. The best accounts of Unitarianism's detachment from Orthodox Congregationalism are Hutchison, *Transcendentalist Ministers* and Barbara Packer, "The Transcendentalists," in Bercovitch, ed., *Cambridge History*, vol. 2: 329–423. For an overview of elite reform movements, see Ronald G. Walters, *American Reformers, 1815–1860* (New York: Hill and Wang, 1978), 3–19.

10. William Ellery Channing, *Lectures on the Elevation of the Labouring Portion of the Community* (Boston: W.D. Ticknor, 1840), 10–11.

11. Channing, *Lectures*, 8–9. Also see William Ellery Channing, "Self-Culture—An Address Introductory to the Franklin Lectures, delivered at

Boston, Sept. 1938," in *Works* (Boston: American Unitarian Association, 1878), 12–36, for a culminating statement on the irrelevance of class differences.

12. Most of Brownson's biographers are attracted by one phase of his varied career and repelled by the rest. Arthur M. Schlesinger, Jr., *Orestes Brownson: A Pilgrim's Progress* (Boston: Little, Brown, 1939) sees a slow ascent to the vital years of Democratic partisanship and then a long decline into stale religiosity. On the other hand, Thomas R. Ryan, *Orestes A. Brownson: A Definitive Biography* (Huntington, IN: Our Sunday Visitor, 1976) narrates a pilgrim's progress to the palace of Catholic wisdom. Leonard Gilhooley, *In Contradiction and Dilemma: Orestes Brownson and the American Idea* (New York: Fordham University Press, 1972) focuses almost exclusively on Brownson's work at the *Boston Quarterly Review* and then *Brownson's Quarterly Review*. See also Henry F. Brownson, *Orestes A. Brownson's Life*, 3 vols. (Detroit: H.F. Brownson, 1898–1900).

13. Brownson, "Review of *Chartism*," 373–374. Orestes Brownson, "Conversation with a Radical," *Boston Quarterly Review*, 4, no. 1 (January 1841): 35–36.

14. Orestes Brownson, *New Views of Christianity, Society, and the Church* (Boston: James Munroe, 1836), 55–56. Orestes Brownson, "The Evidences of the Genuineness of the Four Gospels," *Boston Quarterly Review*, 2, no. 1 (January 1839): 102.

15. Orestes Brownson, Review of *Nature* by Ralph Waldo Emerson, quoted in Bercovitch, *Cambridge History*, vol. 2, 381.

16. Brownson, *New Views*, 5n, 16, 10, 17.

17. Lawrence Buell, *Emerson* (Cambridge: Belknap Press of Harvard University Press, 2003), 9, 5, 67, 63.

Chapter 10   Transcendentalist Reformers, Scholars, and Nature

1. Theodore Parker, "The Writings of Ralph Waldo Emerson," *Massachusetts Quarterly Review*, 3 (March 1850): 205–206. Sherman Paul, *Repossessing and Renewing: Essays in the Green American Tradition* (Baton Rouge: Louisiana State University Press, 1976), 1–2. See David Morse, *American Romanticism* (New York: Barnes & Noble, 1987), 119–168; and Merton M. Sealts, Jr., *Emerson on the Scholar* (Columbia: University of Missouri Press, 1992) for surveys of the Emersonian idea of the scholar. See Jay Grossman, *Reconstituting the American Renaissance: Emerson, Whitman, and the Politics of Representation* (Durham: Duke University Press, 2003), 116–160, for a searching account of Emerson's class-consciousness as it bears on his notion of the scholar. Taylor Stoehr, *Nay-Saying in Concord: Emerson, Alcott, and Thoreau* (Hamden: Archon Books, 1979) makes a spirited attempt to date to defend the radicalism of the scholarly position.

2. Walter Harding, *The Days of Henry Thoreau: A Biography* (New York: Knopf, 1965), 45–46; Sattelmeyer, *Thoreau's Reading*, 20n. Henry David

Thoreau, *The Correspondence of Henry David Thoreau*, Walter Harding and Carl Bode, eds. (New York: New York University Press, 1958), 19–20.

3. Cary Wolfe, *The Limits of American Literary Ideology in Pound and Emerson* (Cambridge: Cambridge University Press, 1993), 79–86, argues that Emerson developed his radical individualism in response to the spectacle of homogeneity presented by the Jacksonian masses. Bercovitch, *Rites of Assent*, 307–352, argues that this same ideological invention was a response to utopian socialism.

4. Thoreau, *Journal*, vol. 1, 393. Lydia Maria Child, Review of *A Week on the Concord and Merrimack Rivers* and *Walden* by Henry David Thoreau, *National Anti-Slavery Standard* (December 16, 1854): 3. Frederic Henry Hedge, "The Art of Life—The Scholar's Calling," *Dial*, 1, no. 2 (October 1840): 176, 180.

5. Charvat, *Profession of Authorship*, 64. Kenneth S. Sacks, *Understanding Emerson: The American Scholar and His Struggle for Self-Reliance* (Princeton: Princeton University Press, 2003), 2, 2, 4.

6. Sam McGuire Worley, *Emerson, Thoreau, and the Role of the Cultural Critic* (New York: State University of New York Press, 2001), 125. Emerson, *Journals and Miscellaneous Notebooks*, vol. 4, 356–357.

7. Thoreau, *Early Essays*, 3, 11, 5, 8, 16. Kevin P. Van Anglen, "True Pulpit Power: 'Natural History of Massachusetts' and the Problem of Cultural Authority," *Studies in the American Renaissance* (1990): 119–147, discusses Thoreau's adoption of a ministerial persona in "The Natural History of Massachusetts" and other natural history essays as examples of a "clerical" role of literary authority practiced by early national New England Whig-Unitarian writers.

8. Orestes Brownson, "Review of *An Oration Delivered before the Literary Societies of Dartmouth College, July 24, 1838* by Ralph Waldo Emerson," *Boston Quarterly Review*, 2, no. 1 (January 1839): 13, 9, 10.

9. Orestes Brownson, "Brook Farm," *The United States Democratic Review*, 11, no. 53 (November 1842): 482–483.

10. Brownson, *New Views*, 31. Brownson, "Laboring Classes," 484. "Proceedings," *Working Man's Advocate*, October 19, 1844 in Commons, *Documentary History*, vol. 8, 98. Brisbane quoted in Commons, *Documentary History*, vol. 8, 104.

11. Donald Pease, *Visionary Compacts: American Renaissance Writings in Cultural Context* (Madison: University of Wisconsin Press, 1987), 204.

12. Laura Dassow Walls, *Emerson's Life in Science: The Culture of Truth* (Ithaca: Cornell University Press, 2003), 4, 10, 4. For a valuable account of how the American Romantics "invoked nature as the ground of value (both economic and moral)," see Howard Horwitz, *By the Law of Nature: Form and Value in Nineteenth-Century America* (New York: Oxford University Press, 1991), 3–56.

Chapter 11   Brook Farm and Association

1. Elizabeth P. Peabody, "Plan of the West Roxbury Community," *Dial*, 2, no. 3 (January 1842): 361. Henry David Thoreau, *Journal*, vol. 1, 277.

2. Orestes Brownson, "Prospects of the Democracy," *Boston Quarterly Review*, 2, no. 1 (January 1838): 129. Schlesinger, *Age of Jackson*, 290–294.
3. Brownson, Review of *Chartism*, 375.
4. George Ripley, letter to Ralph Waldo Emerson, quoted in Frothingham, *George Ripley*, 307–308. Anonymous, "The Community at West Roxbury," *Monthly Miscellany of Religion and Letters*, 5, no. 2 (August 1841): 116. Orestes Brownson, Review of *The Poetical Works*, 167. For the best synthesis of the ideas that informed Ripley's experiment, see Richard Francis, *Transcendental Utopias: Brook Farm, Fruitlands, and Walden* (Ithaca: Cornell University Press, 1997), 35–139. The best biography of Ripley is Charles Crowe, *George Ripley: Transcendentalist and Utopian Socialist* (Athens: University of Georgia Press, 1967), which includes a substantial account of the farm. Also see Henry L. Golemba, *George Ripley* (Boston: Twayne, 1977).
5. Theodore Parker, "Thoughts on Labor," *Dial*, 1, no. 4 (April 1841): 497. For a comprehensive survey of the discourse of labor during the period, see Jonathon A. Glickstein, *Concepts of Free Labor in Antebellum America* (New Haven: Yale University Press, 1991). For more focused accounts of Transcendentalist anxieties about manual labor, see William Gleason, "Re-Creating *Walden*: Thoreau's Economy of Work and Play," *American Literature*, 65, no. 4 (December 1993): 673–701; Michael Newbury, "Healthful Employment: Hawthorne, Thoreau, and Middle Class Fitness," *American Quarterly*, 47 (December 1995): 681–714, and Rose, *Transcendentalism as a Social Movement*, 109–161.
6. Ballou quoted in Mark Holloway, *Utopian Communities in America, 1680–1880* (Mineola, NY: Dover, 1966), 122.
7. A. Bronson Alcott and Charles Lane, "Fruitlands," *Dial*, 4, no. 1 (July 1843): 135, 136. Charles Lane, "Brook Farm," *Dial*, 4, no. 3 (January 1844): 351, 354.
8. Alcott and Lane, "Fruitlands," 136. Louisa May Alcott, *Silver Pitchers: And Independence, a Centennial Love Story* (Boston: Roberts Brothers, 1876), 90–91. The fullest account of Fruitlands is Francis, *Transcendental Utopias*, 140–217. Clara Endicott Sears, ed., *Bronson Alcott's Fruitlands* (New York: Houghton Mifflin, 1915) collects a valuable documentary history of the episode.
9. Nathaniel Hawthorne, *The Letters, 1813–1843*, Thomas Woodson et al., eds. (Columbus: Ohio State University Press, 1984).
10. George Ripley, Letter to Ralph Waldo Emerson, quoted in Frothingham, *George Ripley*, 310, 312.
11. David A. Zonderman, "George Ripley's Unpublished Lecture on Charles Fourier," *Studies in the American Renaissance*, 5 (1982): 197–198. Jonathan Beecher, *Charles Fourier: The Visionary and His World* (Berkeley: University of California Press, 1987) surveys Fourier's massive body of writing and places it in the context of postrevolutionary French politics. The most effective popularizations of Fourier's doctrines were Parke Godwin, *Popular View of the Doctrines of Charles Fourier* (New York: J.S. Redfield, 1844) and Albert Brisbane, *Social Destiny of Man: or, Association and Reorganization of*

Industry (1840. New York: C.F. Stollmeyer, 1968). For an account of Brisbane's work, see Arthur E. Bestor Jr., "Albert Brisbane, Propagandist for Socialism in the 1840s," *New York History*, 28 (April 1947): 128–158.

12. Carl J. Guarneri, *The Utopian Alternative: Fourierism in Nineteenth-Century America* (Ithaca: Cornell University Press, 1991), 9.

13. Nathaniel Hawthorne, *The Blithedale Romance*, Bedford Critical Edition (Boston: Bedford, 1996), 47, 43. For an account of the central Associationist journal, see Sterling Delano, *The Harbinger and New England Transcendentalism: A Portrait of Associationism in America* (Rutherford, NJ: Fairleigh Dickinson University Press, 1983), 11–49.

14. Robert Owen, "Declaration of Mental Independence," *New-Harmony Gazette*, 1, no. 42 (July 12, 1826): 1, emphasis in original. John Humphrey Noyes, *History of American Socialisms* (Philadelphia : J.B. Lippincott, 1870), 24.

Chapter 12   Capitalism and the Moral Geography of *Walden*

1. Bronson Alcott, *Concord Days* (Boston: Roberts Brothers, 1872), 13. There are clear echoes in Thoreau's description of the community of nature of Scottish anti-Lockean theories of the socially stabilizing effects of the common sense of humankind. For an account of the social function of these ideas in the early-nineteenth-century United States, see Henry F. May, *The Enlightenment in America* (Oxford: Oxford University Press, 1976), 337–362. Sattelmeyer, *Thoreau's Reading*, 115, notes that James Munroe's 1833 edition of Dugald Stewart's *Elements of the Philosophy of Mind* (1792) was a required text at Harvard during Thoreau's years there.

2. Emerson, *Journal and Miscellaneous Notebooks*, vol. 9, 9–10. Compare the more collegial comments on "A Winter's Walk" in Ralph Waldo Emerson, Letter to Henry David Thoreau, September 18, 1843, in Walter Harding and Carl Bode, eds. *The Correspondence of Henry David Thoreau* (New York: New York University Press, 1958), 137.

3. Pamela Regis, *Describing Early America: Bartram, Jefferson, Crevecoeur, and the Rhetoric of Natural History* (DeKalb, IL: University of Pennsylvania Press, 1992), argues from texts by Bartram, Jefferson, and Crevecoeur that the terms sublime, beautiful, and picturesque were initially understood as scientifically precise markers of aesthetic response that implied a narrative of transformation. Cecilia Tichi, *New World, New Earth: Environmental Reform in American Literature from the Puritans through Whitman* (New Haven: Yale University Press, 1979) explores the period's urgent ideological commitment to changing the New World landscape. Additional valuable discussions of the cultural politics of transformative landscape aesthetics include Catherine L. Albanese, *Nature Religion in America: From the Algonkian Indians to the New Age* (Chicago: University of Chicago Press, 1990), 47–79; Edward Halsey Foster, *The Civilized Wilderness: Backgrounds to American Romantic Literature, 1817–1860* (New York: Free Press, 1975); Jehlen, *American Incarnation*; Angela L. Miller, *The Empire of the Eye: Landscape Representation and American Cultural Politics, 1825–1875*

(Ithaca: Cornell University Press, 1993); and Mary Louise Pratt, *Imperial Eyes: Travel Writing and Transculturation* (London: Routledge, 1992). The two best accounts of the cultural politics of the pastoral remain Marx, *Machine in the Garden* and Raymond Williams, *The Country and the City* (Oxford: Oxford University Press, 1973). Bernard Rosenthal, *City of Nature: Journeys to Nature in the Age of American Romanticism* (Newark: University of Delaware Press, 1980), 17–27, argues that the story of nature in early-nineteenth-century America, whether told in novels, travel narratives, or political orations, recounted the transformation of nature into its purest form, civilization. What distinguishes the American Romantics from their contemporaries is that they modify that story into the tale of an interior journey to a city of the self.

4. Aldo Leopold, *A Sand County Almanac* (New York: Oxford University Press, 1949), 224–225. James Russell Lowell, Review of *Letters to Various Persons* by Henry David Thoreau, *North American Review*, 101 (October 1865): 607. Michael T. Gilmore, *American Romanticism and the Marketplace* (Chicago: University of Chicago Press, 1985), 35, 49.

5. Emerson, "Thoreau," 248. Thoreau, *Journal*, vol. 1, 277.

6. Sterling Delano, "Thoreau's Visit to Brook Farm," *Thoreau Society Bulletin*, 220/221 (Fall 1997–Spring 1998): 1–2. Ralph Waldo Emerson, letter to Margaret Fuller, February 28, 1847, in *The Letters of Ralph Waldo Emerson*, eds., Ralph L. Rusk and Eleanor M. Tilton, vol. 3 (New York: Columbia University Press, 1939), 3: 377–378. Sherman Paul, *The Shores of America: Thoreau's Inward Exploration* (Urbana: University of Illinois Press, 1958), 301 shows that *Walden* follows the argumentative structure of *Nature* quite closely. Robert D. Richardson, *Henry Thoreau: A Life of the Mind* (Berkeley: University of California Press, 1986), 100–105, gives a brief account of Thoreau's relation to the Association movement. Also see John H. Matle, "Emerson and Brook Farm," *ESQ*, 58 (Spring 1970): 84–88. A section on *Walden*, emphasizing parallels with communitarian metaphysics and epistemology occurs in Francis, *Transcendental Utopias*, 218–240.

7. Leonard Neufeldt, *The Economist: Henry Thoreau and Enterprise* (New York: Oxford University Press, 1989) shows that *Walden* parodies the conventions structuring contemporary guidebooks for young men that propose to show them the path to material and social success. Bob Pepperman Taylor, *America's Bachelor Uncle: Thoreau and the American Polity* (Lawrence: University of Kansas Press, 1996), 75–97 provides a concise summary of Thoreau's economic argument in *Walden*.

8. The best summary analysis of *Walden's* critique of capitalist social relations is Gilmore, *American Romanticism*, 35–51.

9. Stanley Cavell, *The Senses of Walden* (New York: Viking Press, 1972), 7–8, notes that Thoreau emphasizes the date of his departure for the pond, July 4, as a broad hint that *Walden*, a heroic, scriptural book, recounts an attempt to individualize the ideals announced in the Declaration of Independence.

10. Sherman Paul, *Emerson's Angle of Vision* (Cambridge: Harvard University Press, 1952), 3–4. For an account of how this central idea structured the

whole of Transcendentalist millennialism, see Catherine L. Albanese, *Corresponding Motion: Transcendental Religion and the New America* (Philadelphia: Temple University Press, 1977).

11. For a narrative of Thoreau's initial admiration and final rejection of William Gilpin's theories of landscape appreciation, see Gordon V. Boudreau, "H.D. Thoreau, William Gilpin, and the Metaphysical Ground of the Picturesque," *American Literature*, 45, no. 3 (November 1973): 357–369. An additional source for the vocabulary of the picturesque was Wordsworth, for which see Neill Joy, "Two Possible Analogues for 'The Ponds' in *Walden*: Jonathon Carver and Wordsworth," *ESQ: A Journal of the American Renaissance*, 24 (1978): 197–205, which suggests that Wordsworth's *Guide to the District of the Lakes*, published as part of the 1837 *Complete Works*, shaped Thoreau's general ideas about landscape. Joseph Moldenhauer "*Walden* and Wordsworth's Guide to the English Lake District," *Studies in the American Renaissance* (1990): 261–292 documents the text's influence on *Walden*.

12. Walter Benn Michaels, "*Walden*'s False Bottoms," *Glyph*, 1 (1977): 132–149, performs a deconstructive analysis of *Walden*, focusing on the instability of oppositions between nature and culture, the finite and the infinite, and literal and figurative language.

13. For complementary reading of Thoreau's way of opposing history and nature, see Larry Reynolds's chapter "Kossuth Fever and the Serenity of Walden," in *European Revolutions and the American Literary Renaissance* (New Haven: Yale University Press, 1988), 153–170.

Chapter 13   *Walden*, Association, and Organic Idealism

1. Charles Anderson Dana, *Association in Its Connection with Education and Religion* (Boston: B.H. Greene, 1844), 25–26.

2. George Ripley, "Life in Association," *Harbinger*, 2 (December 1845–June 1846): 32.

3. Peabody, "Plan of the West Roxbury Community," 364, emphasis in original. See Michael Newbury, *Figuring Authorship in Antebellum America* (Stanford: Stanford University Press, 1997), 23–69, for an account of how the period's newly independent authors were driven by anxiety about their middle-class privilege and the loss of republican valorizations of manual labor. See also, Henry Nash Smith, "Emerson's Problem of a Vocation: A Note on the American Scholar," *New England Quarterly Review*, 12 (1939): 52–67; and Steven Fink, *Prophet in the Marketplace: Thoreau's Development as a Professional Writer* (Princeton: Princeton University Press, 1992). Neufeldt, *The Economist*, 23–69, reconstructs Thoreau's difficult, but eventually successful, project of imagining a literary career as both the pursuit of a vocation and as a process of self-culture, as a vocation of self-culture.

4. Nathaniel Hawthorne, letter to Sophia Peabody, April 13, 1841, *The Letters*, 539.

5. George Ripley quoted in Frothingham, *George Ripley*, 32. For a sensitive reading of Hawthorne's ambivalence toward Brook Farm and his eventual

transformation of pastoral landscapes from sites for work into bowers of imaginative play, see Kelly M. Flynn, "Nathaniel Hawthorne Had a Farm: Artists, Laborers, and Landscapes in *The Blithedale Romance*," in Michael P. Branch, ed., *Reading the Earth*, 145–164. For a well-built reconstruction of the cultural history of farm-work as a figure for the mixture of culture and nature, see Timothy Sweet, *American Georgics: Economy and Environment in Early American Literature* (Philadelphia: University of Pennsylvania Press, 2002).

6. Nina Baym, "English Nature, New York Nature, and *Walden*'s New England Nature," in Capper and Wright, *Transient and Permanent*, 171. For an insightful ecocritical analysis of Thoreau's bean field, see David M. Robinson, "'Unchronicled Nations': Agrarian Purpose and Thoreau's Ecological Knowing," *Nineteenth-Century Literature*, 48, no. 3 (December 1993): 326–340. Stanley Cavell, *The Senses of Walden* (New York: The Viking Press, 1972), 3–34, reads *Walden* as a "heroic book" that represents itself as a modern scripture and prophecy, a jeremiad directed at a fallen America.

7. Albert Brisbane, Letter to George Ripley, quoted in John Thomas Codman, *Brook Farm, Historic and Personal Memoirs* (Boston: Arena, 1894), 146. William Henry Channing, "To The Associationists of the United States," *Harbinger*, 3 (June–December 1846): 16. Leo Stoller, *After Walden: Thoreau's Changing Views on Economic Man* (Stanford: Stanford University Press, 1957), 306–315, shows that the doctrine of self-culture embodied in *Walden* was an alternative version of the period's strong current of social reform based on the idea that prominent self-transformation might spark broader change. Peter J. Bellis, *Writing Revolution: Aesthetics and Politics in Hawthorne, Whitman, and Thoreau* (Athens: University of Georgia Press, 2003), 121–152, reads *Walden* as an attempt to use representations of labor to clear a middle space between town and country wherein to build a future of unalienated labor and community.

8. Hedge, "The Art of Life," 181. Margaret Fuller, "The Great Lawsuit," 14.

9. John Sullivan Dwight, "Individuality in Association," *Harbinger*, 1 (June–December 1845): 264–265. Ralph Waldo Emerson, "Fourierism and the Socialists," *Dial*, 3, no. 1 (July 1842): 88. Ralph Waldo Emerson, letter to George Ripley, December 15, 1840, *The Letters of Ralph Waldo Emerson*, vol. 2, 369. Emerson, *Journals and Miscellaneous Notebooks*, vol. 7, 407–408. For treatments of Thoreau's commitment to the ideal of an organic community, see Philip Abbott, "Henry David Thoreau, the State of Nature, and the Redemption of Liberalism," *The Journal of Politics*, 47, no. 1 (February 1985): 182–208 and Mary Elkins Moller, *Thoreau in the Human Community* (Amherst: University of Massachusetts Press, 1980). Richard Grusin, *Transcendentalist Hermeneutics: Institutional Authority and the Higher Criticism* (Durham: Duke University Press, 1991), 9–54, uses Emerson's resignation from the ministry as a central example to argue that the Transcendentalists did not oppose institutions *per se*, but hoped to see them remade in the spirit of the age.

10. Charles Anderson, *The Magic Circle of Walden* (New York: Holt, Rinehart and Winston, 1968), 261–264. Paul, *Shores of America*, 306. See Joseph J. Moldenhauer, "The Extravagant Maneuver: Paradox in *Walden*," in *Critical*

Essays on Henry David Thoreau's Walden, Joel Myerson, ed. (Boston: G.K. Hall, 1988), 96–106 for a concise reading *Walden's* rhetorical strategies. Henry L. Golemba *Thoreau's Wild Rhetoric* (New York: New York University Press, 1990), 231, argues that Thoreau "hoped that a wild rhetoric had more linguistic power, that a language of gaps and indeterminacies, filled with smoky words, could more adequately suggest those higher truths."

11. Albert Brisbane quoted in Richard Francis, "The Ideology of Brook Farm," *Studies in the American Renaissance* (1977): 18. For a reading of the sand-bank passage as Romantic science focused on chaotic organic processes, see Eric Wilson, *Romantic Turbulence: Chaos, Ecology, and American Space* (New York: St. Martin's, 2000), 94–117. Richard Grusin, "Thoreau, Extravagance and the Economy of Nature," *American Literary History*, 5, no. 1 (Spring 1993): 30–50, focuses on the celebration of the extravagance in "Spring," arguing that Thoreau did not counterpose ethical simplicity to the chaos of the marketplace. Gordon Boudreau, *The Roots of Walden and the Tree of Life* (Nashville: University of Tennessee Press, 1990), 117–147 reads the deep cut passages as a myth of resurrection, seeing it as a "negative image" of the myth of the fall that structures Thoreau's response in *A Week* to the death of his brother John. See also, Robert E. Abrams, "Image, Object, and Perception in Thoreau's Landscapes: The Development of Anti-Geography," *Nineteenth-Century Literature*, 46, no. 2 (September 1991): 245–262, which reads the sandbank passage as a central example of the way that Thoreau destablizes the tightly framed landscapes that characterized the literature and art of national expansion.

12. Stephen Adams and Donald Ross, Jr., *Revising Mythologies: The Composition of Thoreau's Major Works* (Charlottesville: University of Virginia Press, 1988), 165–191, shows that the millennial exhortations of "Spring" and "Conclusion" were largely added in the final rounds of revision in 1851–1852. Also see Robert Sattelmeyer, "The Remaking of Walden," in James Barbour and Tom Quirk, eds., *Writing the American Classics* (Chapel Hill: University of North Carolina Press, 1990), 53–78. The timing of composition could be taken to refute my claim that these passages respond to the Associationist Movement, which had collapsed by then. However, the parallel ideological structures of the experiments remain conclusive for me as evidence that Thoreau set out for Walden Pond meaning to answer the socialists, despite the fact that he did not immediately bring his alternative theories to full fruition.

Chapter 14   Nature, Politics, and Thoreau's Materialism

1. Emerson, "Thoreau," 248.
2. Henry David Thoreau, *Essays,* Lewis Hyde, ed. (New York: North Point Press, 2002), 113.
3. James McIntosh, *Thoreau as Romantic Naturalist: His Shifting Stance Toward Nature* (Ithaca: Cornell University Press, 1974), 23, 17, 37.
4. Robert Sattelmeyer, "Introduction," in Henry David Thoreau, *The Natural History Essays* (Salt Lake City: Peregrine Smith, 1980), xxvi. Henry David

Thoreau, *Journal*, Elizabeth Hall Witherell, ed., vol. 3 (Princeton: Princeton University Press, 1990), 380. Sattelmeyer, *Thoreau's Reading*, 19, 22. Paul, *Shores of America*, 3–16, for a brisk statement of this position. See Laura Dassow Walls, *Seeing New Worlds: Henry David Thoreau and Nineteenth-Century Natural Science* (Madison: University of Wisconsin Press, 1995), 15–52, for the best account of Thoreau's negotiation in the 1830s with the inheritance of European empiricist and idealist theories of knowledge.

5. William Howarth, *The Book of Concord* (New York: Viking, 1982), ix, 10, 20, 64, 80, 118. Perhaps the most unequivocal statement of this position comes in Robert Kuhn McGregor, *A Wider View of the Universe*, 3–5, a hagiographical reading that sees Thoreau changing from "a classically and staidly trained transcendentalist into a radical naturalist" and makes him the inventor of "the principle of biocentrism and the science of ecology." Joel Porte, *Emerson and Thoreau: Transcendentalists in Conflict* (Middletown, CT: Wesleyan University Press, 1966) argues that Thoreau was in fact a Lockean empiricist. Victor Carl Friesen, *The Spirit of the Huckleberry: Sensuousness in Thoreau* (Edmonton: University of Alberta Press, 1984) maintains that the key to Thoreau's thought is his lifelong immersion in sensory experience. Oelschlaeger, *Idea of Wilderness*, 133–171, argues that Thoreau learns a holistic knowledge of nature by intuitively understanding the physical world through immersion in its particulars. Sharon Cameron, *Writing Nature: Henry Thoreau's Journal* (New York: Oxford University Press, 1985) reads the Journal as an extended meditation on how the mind apprehends nature, on the process of generalizing from a bewildering chaos of fragmentary information.

6. Walls, *Seeing New Worlds*, 4, 18, 76–93, 147. Worster, *Nature's Economy*, 75, 78. Sustained analysis of Thoreau's attitudes toward science begins with Nina Baym, "Thoreau's View of Science," *Journal of the History of Ideas*, 26 (1965): 221–234. William Rossi, "Thoreau's Transcendental Ecocriticism," in Richard Schneider, ed., *Thoreau's Sense of Place: Essays in American Environmental Writing* (Iowa City: University of Iowa Press, 2000), 32, argues that Thoreau maintains "twin commitment to the metaphysics of correspondence and to a densely empirical knowledge of nature." For accounts of Thoreau's engagement with the Agassiz–Darwin controversy, see Richardson, *Henry David Thoreau*, 362–384; and Laura Dassow Walls, "Believing in Nature: Wilderness and Wildness in Thoreauvian Science," in Richard Schneider, ed., *Thoreau's Sense of Place: Essays in American Environmental Writing* (Iowa City: University of Iowa Press, 2000), 15–27.

7. Sattelmeyer, *Thoreau's Reading*, 78–92. Alfred I. Tauber, *Henry David Thoreau and the Moral Agency of Knowing* (Berkeley: University of California Press, 2001), 140. Ronald Wesley Hoag, "Thoreau's Later Natural History Writings," in Joel Myerson, ed., *The Cambridge Companion to Henry David Thoreau* (Cambridge: Cambridge University Press, 1995), 152–170, describes the kind of natural history that Thoreau practiced during this decade as a form of humanistic science. Michael Benjamin Berger, *Thoreau's Late Career and "The Dispersion of Seeds": The Saunterer's Synoptic Vision* (Rochester: Camden House, 2000), 76–119, concludes that Thoreau reconciled

empiricism and idealism. H. Daniel Peck, *Thoreau's Morning Work: Memory and Perception in a Week on the Concord and Merrimack Rivers, The Journal, and Walden* (New Haven: Yale University Press, 1990), 39–114, argues that Thoreau thought of observation as "relational seeing."

8. Joan Burbick, *Thoreau's Alternative History: Changing Perspectives on Nature, Culture, and Language* (Philadelphia: University of Pennsylvania Press, 1987), 3. Sattelmeyer, *Thoreau's Reading*, 15, 50, 78. Stoller, *After Walden*, 36. John Hildebidle, *Thoreau: A Naturalist's Liberty* (Cambridge: Harvard University Press, 1983), 25, shows that Thoreau "applies the methods of natural history to the reading and writing of history generally."

9. Howarth, *Book of Concord*, 134, 136, 139. Walls, *Seeing New Worlds*, 4. Howarth, *Book of Concord*, 10.

10. Susan M. Lucas, "Counter Frictions: Writing and Activism in the Work of Abbey and Thoreau," in Richard Schneider, ed., *Thoreau's Sense of Place: Essays in American Environmental Writing* (Iowa City: University of Iowa Press, 2000), 266–279, argues from the evidence of the John Brown essays that Thoreau came to see writing as a way to inspire political action from principle.

Chapter 15   *Wild Fruits*, Capitalism, and Community

1. For an account of the provenance of the *Wild Fruits* manuscript, see 285–286, 287n. See William Howarth, *The Literary Manuscripts of Henry David Thoreau* (Columbus: Ohio State University Press, 1974), 322–326, for physical description of the manuscripts. Adams and Ross, *Revising Mythologies*, 240–252, gives a brief dismissive account of the late natural history projects.

2. The late natural history essays, "Autumnal Tints," "Wild Apples," and "Huckleberries," excerpted from the *Wild Fruits* manuscript have only begun receive serious critical attention in the past few decades. McIntosh, *Thoreau as Romantic Naturalist*, 280, claims that, in context of strong growth in the 1850s, Thoreau no longer appeals to nature as an alternative to economic crisis. On the other hand, Walls, *Seeing New Worlds*, 215–222, sees the essays as celebrating the collective identity of the village in contrast to the market; and Stephen Fink, "The Language of Prophecy: Thoreau's 'Wild Apples,' " *New England Quarterly*, 59 (September 1986): 212–230, maintains that the rhetorical understatement of "Wild Apples" is designed to undermine his readers' materialism. Madeleine Minson, "Seeds of Optimism: Thoreau's Late Field Studies," *The Concord Saunterer*, n.s. 7 (1999): 33–53, explores Thoreau's late use of seeds as symbols of potency and renewal. John Hildebidle, *Thoreau: A Naturalist's Liberty*, 69–96, provides a generic analysis of these as modified natural history essays.

3. See Peter Blakemore, "Thoreau, Literature, and the Phenomenon of Inhabitation," in Richard Schneider, ed., *Thoreau's Sense of Place: Essays in American Environmental Writing* (Iowa City: University of Iowa Press, 2000), 115–132, for a discussion of Thoreau's decision to ground his empirical observations of nature in the idea of home.

4. I am indebted to Sandy Petrulionis for pointing out the connection between Thoreau's imagined and actual berrying parties.

5. See Walls, *Seeing New Worlds*, 142–144, for a discussion of Thoreau's developing conception of knowledge production as a democratic and communal project.

6. Henry David Thoreau, *Huckleberries*, Leo Stoller, ed. (Iowa City: Windhover Press of the University of Iowa, 1970), 166–202. Stoller's version of "Huckleberries" has been reprinted in three Thoreau collections: Henry David Thoreau, *The Natural History Essays*, Robert Sattelmeyer, ed. (Salt Lake City: Peregrine Smith, 1980); Henry David Thoreau, *Collected Essays and Poems*, Elizabeth Witherell, ed. (New York: The Library of America, 2001); Henry David Thoreau, *Wild Apples and Other Natural History Essays*, William Rossi, ed. (Athens: University of Georgia Press, 2002). A small sample of the *Wild Fruits* manuscript is included in Henry David Thoreau, *Faith in a Seed: The Dispersion of Seeds and Other Late Natural History Writings*, Bradley Dean, ed. (Washington, DC: Island Press, 1993). See McGregor, *A Wider View of the Universe*, 181–184 for a brief discussion of Thoreau's calls for forest preservation in "Huckleberries." Burbick, *Thoreau's Alternative History*, 138–142, also discusses this essay.

7. Henry David Thoreau, *Thoreau's Writings*, Bradford Torrey, ed., vol. 14 (Boston: Houghton Mifflin, 1906), 139–140; Emerson, "Thoreau," 248; Howarth, *Book of Concord*, 181.

Chapter 16   Ecocriticism and the Uses of Nature Writing

1. Emerson, "Thoreau," 239–249. Lowell, Review. of *Letters*, 193–209. Perry Miller, *Consciousness in Concord: The Text of Thoreau's Hitherto "Lost Journal" (1840–1841) Together with Notes and a Commentary* (Boston: Houghton Mifflin, 1958), 27.

2. Marx, *Machine in the Garden*, 265. Leo Marx, *The Pilot and the Passenger: Essays on Literature, Culture, and Technology in the United States* (New York: Oxford University Press, 1988), 98. Bercovitch, *Rites of Assent*, 345. See Jehlen, *American Incarnation*, 1–21.

3. Buell, *Environmental Imagination*, 116, 125. Thoreau's rejection of Emersonian idealism has formed the subject of a number of important studies. Joel Porte, *Emerson and Thoreau: Transcendentalists in Conflict* (Middletown, CT: Wesleyan University Press, 1966) inaugurated this line of argument. H. Daniel Peck, *Thoreau's Morning Work* (New Haven: Yale University Press, 1990) provides the most sustained and sophisticated analysis of Thoreau's multiple modes of apprehending natural phenomena. For a fascinating related study, see Onno Oerlemans, *Romanticism and the Materiality of Nature* (Toronto: University of Toronto Press, 2002), which traces the development of the "material sublime," a sense of the absolute otherness and particularity of nature in works by the English Romantics.

4. Howarth, *Book of Concord*, 81–103. Sharon Cameron, *Writing Nature*, 3–26. John Hildebidle, *Thoreau: A Naturalist's Liberty* (Cambridge: Harvard University Press, 1983), 69–96. Robert F. Sayre, *Thoreau and the American Indians* (Princeton: Princeton University Press, 1977) explores an

intriguing parallel to the ecocritical account of Thoreau's increasing empiricism in the gradual process by which he overcame "savagist prejudice" in his
thinking about Native Americans.
5. McGregor, *Henry Thoreau's Study of Nature*, 3. Buell, *Environmental
Imagination*, 104, 114, 1–2.
6. Payne, *Voices in the Wilderness*, 49.
7. Granville Hicks, *The Great Tradition: An Interpretation of American
Literature Since the Civil War* (New York: Macmillan, 1933), 10. For a brief
account of Thoreau's work on the Underground Railroad, see Harding,
Days of Henry Thoreau, 205–206.
8. Buell, *Environmental Imagination*, 314. The most thorough survey of
Thoreau's modern political reputations is Michael Meyer, *Several More Lives
to Live: Thoreau's Political Reputation in America* (Westport, CT: Greenwood
Press, 1977). See also Edward Wagenknecht, *Henry David Thoreau: What
Manner of Man?* (Amherst: University of Massachusetts Press, 1981), 1–7;
Fritz Oehlschlaeger and George Hendricks, eds., *Toward the Making of
Thoreau's Modern Reputation* (Urbana: University of Illinois Press, 1979);
and Buell, *Environmental Imagination*, 339–369. Eugene F. Timpe, *Thoreau
Abroad: Twelve Bibliographical Essays* (Hamden: Archon Books, 1971)
collects essays demonstrating the variety of international response. John
Hicks, *Thoreau in Our Season* (Amherst: University of Massachusetts Press,
1966) richly demonstrates the passionate inspiration many in the Civil
Rights movement took from Thoreau.
9. Worster, *Nature's Economy*, 49. Emerson, "Thoreau," 248.
10. See, for instance, Oelschlaeger, *Idea of Wilderness*, 118–121.
11. Buell, *Environmental Imagination*, 22. Gary Lee Harrison, *Wordsworth's
Vagrant Muse: Poetry, Poverty, and Power* (Detroit: Wayne State University
Press, 1994), 173–193.
12. Buell, *Environmental Imagination*, 22. Bate, *Romantic Ecology*, 25, 26, 31,
32, 33.
13. See Kroeber, *Ecological Literary Criticism*, 1–21 for another version of Bate's
argument.
14. Leo Marx, in an address delivered on November 8, 2002 at the Center for
Western United States and Asia/Pacific Studies at the University of Paris IV—
Sorbonne, argued that during the initial marriage of the terms "nature" and
"progress" during the Enlightenment, the process of transforming nature into
progress was seen as a means to the end of a more just and egalitarian society,
but that in the aftermath of the rise of capitalism, the utopian political content
of the narrative had been erased. What had been "progress" toward the goal of
a better world, had simply become technological "progress" for its own sake.

Chapter 17   Marxism, Nature, and the
Discipline of History

1. McKusick, *Green Writing*, 15. Marx, *The Pilot and the Passenger*, 291–314. For
a forceful and mournful argument of the position that atmospheric pollution

has rendered the nature/society dichotomy irrelevant, see Bill McKibben's influential *The End of Nature* (New York: Random House, 1989). For a diagnostic example of the way that idealist theories of culture can mix with materialist science, see J.R. McNeill, *Something New Under the Sun: An Environmental History of the Twentieth-Century World* (New York: Norton, 2000), 325–356. McNeill's synthetic analysis of the available data about human-induced environmental change is a model of clarity, but his concluding survey of the historical process settles for the mysterious operations of scientific rationalism, nationalism, and the "growth fetish" in modern economics.

2. For a variety of approaches to the hybridization of red and green political theory, see Andre Gorz, *Ecology as Politics* (Boston: South End, 1980); Martin Ryle, *Ecology and Socialism* (London: Radius, 1988); David Pepper, *Eco-Socialism: From Deep Ecology to Social Justice* (London: Routledge, 1994); Paul Burkett, *Marx and Nature: A Red and Green Perspective* (New York: St. Martin's Press, 1999); John Bellamy Foster, *Ecology Against Capitalism* (New York: Monthly Review Press, 2002); and Joel Kovel, *The Enemy of Nature: The End of Capitalism or the End of the World* (London: Zed Books, 2002).

3. John Bellamy Foster, *Marx's Ecology: Materialism and Nature* (New York: Monthly Review Press, 2000), viii, 19–20, 75, 79, 159, 256. Useful supplements are Howard L. Parsons, *Marx and Engels on Ecology* (Westport, CT: Greenwood Press, 1977), 8–26, and Jonathon Hughes, *Ecology and Historical Materialism* (Cambridge: Cambridge University Press, 2000).

4. Frederick Engels, *Dialectics of Nature* (New York: International, 1940), 292, 295–296.

5. Karl Marx and Frederick Engels, *The German Ideology*, 7. William Cronon, *Changes in the Land*, 13. For a systematic exposition of the tendency of capitalist relations of production to produce environmental damage, see Benton, *Greening of Marxism*, 187–239. Steven Vogel, "Marx and Alienation from Nature," in Richard Schmitt and Thomas E. Moody, eds., *Alienation and Social Criticism* (Atlantic Highlands, NJ: Humanities Press, 1994), 207–222, diagnoses the idea of human alienation from nature as a symptom of alienation from the built environment, which is a product of social labor.

6. Al Gore, *Earth in the Balance: Ecology and the Human Spirit* (New York: Houghton Mifflin, 1992). See Craig W. Allin, *The Politics of Wilderness Preservation* (Westport, CT: Greenwood, 1982) for a historical analysis of the correlation between the accumulation of surplus capital and the rise of preservationist sentiment among the ruling class (24). Andrew Rowell, *Green Backlash: Global Subversion of the Environment Movement* (London: Routledge, 1996) documents capital's international ideological backlash against environmentalism. For an attempt to use postmodern culturalist theory to give a radical gloss to corporate green washing, see Andrew Jamison, *The Making of Green Knowledge: Environmental Politics and Cultural Transformation* (Cambridge: Cambridge University Press, 2001).

7. A commendable exception to the rule of ecocriticism's blindness to class is Stephen Rosendale, "In Search of Left Ecology's Usable Past: *The Jungle*, Social Change, and the Class Character of Environmental Impairment," in

Steven Rosendale, ed., *The Greening of Literary Scholarship: Literature, Theory, and the Environment* (Iowa City: University of Iowa Press, 2002), 59–76.

8. Scott Wilson, *Cultural Materialism: Theory and Practice* (London: Basil Blackwell, 1995), viii, 252. See also John Brannigan, *New Historicism and Cultural Materialism* (St. Martin's Press, 1998), which makes Williams nearly indistinguishable from Foucault. Andrew Milner, *Re-imagining Cultural Studies: The Promise of Cultural Materialism* (London: Sage, 2002) is the best of several volumes on Williams that have appeared in the last decade. An excellent critical survey of his work is John Higgins, *Raymond Williams: Literature, Marxism, and Cultural Materialism* (London: Routledge, 1999). See also Alan O'Connor, *Raymond Williams: Writing, Culture, Politics* (London: Basil Blackwell, 1989), and John Eldridge and Lizzie Eldridge, *Raymond Williams: Making Connections* (London: Routledge, 1994). A good biography is Fred Inglis, *Raymond Williams* (London: Routledge, 1995). Within a year of his death, a collection of commemorative essays appeared with contributions from Dai Smith, Stuart Hall, Terry Eagleton, and others: Terry Eagleton, ed., *Raymond Williams: Critical Perspectives* (London: Polity, 1989). Two additional collections are W. John Morgan and Peter Preston, eds., *Raymond Williams: Politics, Education, Letters* (New York: St. Martin's, 1993), and Jeff Wallace, Rod Jones, and Sophie Neal, eds., *Raymond Williams Now* (New York: St. Martin's, 1997).

9. Raymond Williams, *Problems in Materialism and Culture* (London: Verso, 1980), 84. Cultural materialism has of course continued to develop the positions and practice mapped by Williams. For a valuable survey of these developments, that compares materialist cultural studies with postmodernism on the ground of theories of determination, see Stuart Hall, "Cultural Studies: Two Paradigms," in Nicholas Dirks et al., eds., *Culture/Power/History: A Reader in Contemporary Social Theory* (Princeton: Princeton University Press, 1994), 521–538.

10. Raymond Williams, *Resources of Hope* (London: Verso, 1989), 187–244. Raymond Williams, *Problems in Materialism and Culture* (London: Verso, 1980), 84.

11. Raymond Williams, *Writing in Society* (London: Verso, 1983), 210. Raymond Williams, *Marxism and Literature* (Oxford: Oxford University Press, 1977), 211, 19. Stuart Hall, "Cultural Studies: Two Paradigms," in Nicholas Dirks, et al. eds., *Culture/Power/History: A Reader in Contemporary Social Theory* (Princeton: Princeton University Press, 1994), 528. Hall's article provides a valuable historical survey of cultural materialism, comparing it with postmodernism on the ground of theories of determination.

12. Richard Johnson, "What is Cultural Studies Anyway?" in Jessica Munns and Gita Rajan, *A Cultural Studies Reader: History, Theory, Practice* (New York: Longman, 1995), 575. Leon Trotsky, *Literature and Revolution* (Ann Arbor: University of Michigan, 1960), 169. One of the most trenchant early rejections of Stalinist cultural theory is James T. Farrell, *A Note on Literary Criticism* (New York: Vanguard Press, 1936).

13. Williams, *Marxism and Literature*, 83, 88.
14. Ibid., 110. Stuart Hall, *The Hard Road to Renewal: Thatcherism and the Crisis of the Left* (London: Verso, 1988), 170.
15. Williams, *Marxism and Literature*, 112, 114, 212. Hall, *The Hard Road to Renewal*, 171.
16. Jonathan Arac, *Critical Genealogies: Historical Situations for Postmodern Literary Studies* (New York: Columbia University Press, 1987), 315. William Rueckert, "Literature and Ecology," 84. For an influential statement on the importance of environmental education, see David W. Orr, *Ecological Literacy: Education and the Transition to a Postmodern World* (Albany: State University of New York Press, 1992).

INDEX

Abbey, Edward, 5
abolitionism, 30, 41, 43, 67, 92,
    108, 125, 166, 168–70, 183,
    190–1, 194
Adams, John Quincy, 39, 47–50,
    52, 97
Adams, Stephen, 58
Addams, Jane, 10
Aesthetic Papers, 38–9
Agassiz, Louis, 165
agrarianism, 40–1, 45, 50–2, 67,
    124, 130, 150
Al-Ali, Jawad, x
Alcott, Bronson, 87, 109, 125–6,
    133, 155
    "Orphic Sayings," 87
Alcott, Louise May, 126, 179
alienation, xiv, 56, 95, 134, 163, 167,
    175–80, 200
American First Class Book, 70
American South, 10, 92, 194
American Studies, 7
American Union of
    Associationists, 152
American West, xiv, 25, 32, 55–67,
    128, 129
Ammons, A. R. (Archie Randolph), 5
Anderson, Charles, 156
Anderson, Douglas, 46
androcentrism, 8, 10, 199
anthropocentrism, 4, 16, 21–2, 24,
    83, 187, 193, 199, 202–3
anticapitalism, 139, 158, 186, 190
anticommunism, 37

anti-Jacobinism, 40, 47–8, 100, 128
Arac, Jonathon, 210
Association for the Study of Literature
    and the Environment, 2
Associationism, 129–31, 137, 147–60
Athanasiou, Tom, xiii
Athenean Society, 52
Atlantic Monthly, 171
authority, 39, 41, 49, 60, 87–8, 111,
    114, 189, 194–5

Ballou, Adin, 124–5
Bank of the United States, 31
Bate, Jonathon, 3, 4, 16, 192–3
Baym, Nina, 151
Bee, The, 27
Bennett, Michael, 10
Bercovitch, Sacvan, 37–8, 186
Berkeley, Bishop George, 13
Bhabha, Homi, 17
Blair, Hugh, 70
Blake, William, 93
Boston Manufacturing Company, 26
Boston Quarterly Review, 104, 121–2
Boston Reformer, 106
Boston Trades Union, 31
Bowdoin College, 52
Bradford, George P., 136
Bradstreet, Anne, 7
Branch, Michael, 3
Brisbane, Albert, 118, 128, 130, 158
    *Social Destiny of Man: or,
    Association and Reorganization
    of Industry*, 128